THE WIDOWS' WINE CLUB

JULIA JARMAN

Boldwood

First published in Great Britain in 2023 by Boldwood Books Ltd.

Copyright © Julia Jarman, 2023

Cover Design by Lizzie Gardiner

Cover Illustration: Shutterstock

A CIP catalogue record for this book is available from the British Library.

Paperback ISBN 978-1-78513-007-6

Large Print ISBN 978-1-78513-006-9

Hardback ISBN 978-1-78513-005-2

Ebook ISBN 978-1-78513-008-3

Kindle ISBN 978-1-78513-009-0

Audio CD ISBN 978-1-78513-000-7

MP3 CD ISBN 978-1-78513-001-4

Digital audio download ISBN 978-1-78513-002-1

Boldwood Books Ltd
23 Bowerdean Street
London SW6 3TN
www.boldwoodbooks.com

1

11 SEPTEMBER 2008

Viv

How the hell do you choose?

Viv Halliday, assured of privacy for 'the delicate task' by the funeral director, was trying to match the coffins in front of her with the pictures in the catalogue. Coffins. Viv, a gardener, liked to call a spade a spade. She'd had enough of 'caskets' and 'precious contents' and 'resting places', and 'loved one' was beginning to grate. Jack wasn't a bloody jewel in a jewellery box and he wasn't having a kip. He hadn't passed away like a bad smell, he'd died, and she was trying to choose one of these *boxes* because that was what the What To Do When Someone Dies guide said she should. Downloaded from the Internet, it claimed to cover all aspects of the 'bereavement experience' but clearly didn't. Some of the funeral director's questions had taken her by surprise. 'Would you like your loved one embalmed a) fully, b) partially or c) not at all, Mrs Robson?' Embalmed – it was one of those words you thought you knew. Mummies came into it and royals and waxen Russian leaders. But she'd had to ask what he meant, reply 'not at all' to filling Jack with preservatives, and put him right about her name.

'My apologies.' Mr Crombie Junior, an elderly bald man, had corrected his notes. 'Now, what is Mr Robson going to wear, Ms Halliday?'

'Wear? But he's...' She'd caught on just in time. Did everyone else know these things? Jack didn't care what he wore when he was alive, for fuck's sake. Pass.

But shrugged shoulders wouldn't do. Mr Crombie had prompted gently, 'What he wore for a much-loved hobby, perhaps? A favourite suit? Or maybe...' he'd reached for another brochure '... one of our gowns?'

That was when she'd started giggling, picturing Jack in one of the *nighties* he was pointing to, 'available in pink, blue or oyster satin with or without a frill'. Well, Jack would have laughed. 'Bloody hell, do you want me to look like Widow Twankey?' She'd felt him by her side, heard him snort as he wiped his eyes.

'No worries, Ms Halliday.' Mr Crombie had retrieved the brochure. 'Grief takes the bereaved in different ways.'

The Bereaved, that was who she was now, ticking off items from a long list. Get medical certificate. Tick. Register death. Tick. Take birth certificate with you. Tick. Tick tick tick. Like a bloody clock. Or a bomb. The Bereaved must now choose a casket, but she couldn't because she hadn't got a clue, because she'd never done this before, because she didn't *feel* Bereaved. She felt like Viv Halliday wife, Viv Halliday mum, Viv Halliday gran, Viv Halliday, gardener, planting a beech hedge today in Mrs James's garden. That was what it said she was doing in her diary, and it was the right weather for it, a dull damp autumn day. She should be out there in the fresh air, not in this weird room staring at furniture she didn't want. She'd wandered into the wrong shop, and must say sorry, thank you, just looking, and leave. But who to? To *whom*? She'd been an English teacher once. Not to the glamorous black woman coming in now, dabbing her eyes. Clearly a mourner, she looked dressed for the part from stylish beret on well-groomed hair to shiny patent courts. Suddenly, Viv's own fleece, denims and trainers and dry eyes seemed not-right.

Get on with it.

The coffins all looked much the same, that was the main problem. On biers – was that the word for the metal stands? – with lids slightly raised, they spooked her a bit, though the layout was more IKEA than crypt. Did they come in flatpack? How did you choose between The Oak, The Mahogany, The Rosewood and The Maple, all available in light, dark, solid or veneer? Or the oddly named Last Supper, wood unspecified, or the Basic Funeral, also wood unspecified, or the Last Resting Place, material unspecified, but it looked like polystyrene and, oh – she glanced inside – was lined with pink taffeta, ruched. Well, not that one.

'Prices at the back, love.'

'Oh, thanks.' She turned towards the elegantly dressed black woman who'd spoken, and – 'Fuck!' – caught the lid of Last Supper with her elbow. 'Sorry.' But it bloody hurt.

The woman waved away Viv's apology as the lid snapped shut, loudly.

'My fault, shouldn't have butted in.' She dabbed at her eyes with a wad of sodden tissues and a man coming in harrumphed.

'Oh dear.' The frumpy older woman with him, his mother perhaps, looked embarrassed.

Viv found a packet of Kleenex in her pocket and gave them to her glamorous sympathiser. 'Have these, pet. Not your fault. Born clumsy, that's me, and I'm all over the place at the moment.' The woman, neat and petite, made her feel like a hollyhock at the front of the border. Too tall. Too floppy. Too *too*. 'No, keep the packet. I don't seem to need them.'

'Thanks.' The woman nodded. 'Still numb? Not done it before? Three times, me. Sorry, saying too much again, but the thing to remember—' she nodded at the coffins '—is there's not much to choose between them all except the prices. It's not as if you're buying it to last, is it?'

Viv laughed.

Oh. Was that another harrumph from the man now steering the tweed-clad frumpy woman towards the coffins as if she were a bit of unwieldy luggage? 'Let me sort it, Mum. That's what I've come all this way for.'

All this way? His accent was Antipodean, but, hurray, the luggage was fighting back, detaching herself from his grip. 'It's sorted, Grant, as I said. The coffin is ordered already. I did it when I came in yesterday. Now let's go and see your dad in the chapel of rest, shall we? That's what I thought we came for.' The luggage sounded a bit Scottish.

'But, Mum, Dad wouldn't like bamboo...'

'Grant, your father is dead.' She spoke firmly.

Intriguing. Viv liked bamboo but it was a surprise. The woman's tweed suit and permed grey hair said conservative, very.

'Oh, look, dear.' She took another step away from her son. 'The lights are coming on, Grant. I thought it was rather dark in here – and here's Mr Plunkett Senior. Has there been a power cut, Mr Plunkett?'

'Indeed there has, Mrs Carmichael and er...' The silver-haired portly Mr Plunkett, flanked by Mr Crombie Junior and a younger female, swivelled round to include them all. There had been a prolonged power cut, which had turned off, not only the lights and heating and sound system, but also the electronic device for alerting staff to the arrival of clients. That was why, sadly – he almost bent double – they were all here together in the casket room, without the privacy Plunkett and Crombie usually afforded The Bereaved.

As waves of Elgar began to lap around the room, and lights flickered into life, Mrs Carmichael asked the funeral director to take her son to the chapel of rest to see his father. 'No, no, thank you, Mr Plunkett, I won't go again. I paid my respects yesterday.'

Should I go and see Jack again?

When Viv had seen him last he was still in the hospital bed where he'd died, and his lips were warm when she kissed them. It had been hard to believe he wasn't asleep. Why, *why* had he done it like that, dying in the few minutes she'd taken to nip to the loo, so she couldn't say goodbye? Would seeing him now, chilled like a waxwork, cold to her touch, make her feel better, stop her feeling like an automaton? But before she had a chance to decide, here was Mr Crombie Junior again, clipboard at the ready, wanting to know what she'd chosen.

Ip dip sky blue, who's it, not you?

2

VIV

Decision made – oak, solid, because that was Jack – Viv got into her ancient Range Rover and drove to Elmsley, a village ten miles north of the town of Bedford, where she'd lived for over thirty years, first with Jack and the girls, then with just Jack, now... But it wasn't the time to reminisce, must concentrate. Reaching the village, she slowed down then stopped by the bridge on the high street, causing the Volvo that had been up her arse all the way from the bypass to screech to a halt, then roar past in a cloud of angry exhaust. Idiot male driver. What time was it? Should she go home to her empty house at the far end of the village or call on her bestie? That was what she'd stopped to decide. Would Angie be pleased to see her? She'd leaned on her heavily these last few days. Would she have a bottle open? If she hadn't it wouldn't take much to get her to open one. A crashing coffin lid would do it, embarrassment topping the Richter scale.

The church clock struck five as she reached Angie's picturesque thatch at the bottom of Church Lane. For Sale. Why, *why* did that sign still give her a jolt when it had been there for months? Because, recession or not, some rich bastard would snap it up before you could say off-shore account, and any day now her best friend would be gone. *Don't be selfish. Lily needs Angie more.* Angie's only daughter had just had triplets, and Angie was moving to be near her. Of course. Quite right too. Angie was kind and practical and sensible and supportive and wanted to know her grandchildren.

Too bloody sensible.

'Don't pull that face. I'm thinking of our livers.' Angie filled the teapot from the kettle. 'Tea first. Now, to answer your question – is burying Jack next door the right thing to do?' They could see the churchyard from the kitchen window. A few sunken gravestones were visible under the trees, their leaves tinged with autumn colour. 'What did the man say? Do what the hell you like, if I remember rightly. Whatever makes you feel better.'

'Nothing makes me feel better.' *Nothing ever will.* But she didn't say that, didn't want to sound pathetic, or *be* pathetic. Angie had done enough. She'd been by her side during the whole sodding business. She knew almost as much about Jack's horrible dying as Viv did. But she couldn't keep leaning on Angie.

'So, what would make you feel worse?' Angie filled mugs from a large red teapot.

'Sliding curtains?'

'Decision made. Tick. Where's your list? Viv Halliday, you've put hours of work into that churchyard, gratis, more than most of the faithful, so sod the holy snipers. You've got every right to plant Jack there. You've turned it into a nature reserve. I saw a couple of brimstone butterflies walking Buster this morning. Now, what's next?' Angie looked at the list, fingers pushing back her thick white hair. It had been black when they'd met at the school gate thirty years ago.

'But Jack didn't do God. And nor do I.'

'I said, decision made.' Angie's voice was firm. 'Now, what shall I open, red or white? You are staying, not a question. I've got pasta bake in the oven and I'll make a salad. Back in a mo.' She headed for the garden, Buster, an unattractive white bull terrier, plodding at her heels.

Get on with it. Viv gave herself a tick for choosing a coffin and a metaphorical smack for feeling sorry for herself. *Be grateful.* She'd had forty lovely years with Jack. He'd been a brill, supportive husband. She couldn't have given up teaching and started her gardening business without his support. And he hadn't buggered off when things got tough, like Angie's husband leaving her with a baby to bring up on her own. Now it was time to stand on her own two feet. See what she was made of. She was a feminist, FFS, though all three daughters laughed when she said so, Beth bordering on the contemptuous. 'Mum, you've never ever lived on your own, have you? Didn't you go straight from living at home with your mum to living in a hall of residence with other girls, to living with Dad?'

'Yes, I did. We did in those days.'

Sally had agreed with her sister. 'You do lean on Dad, Mum.'

'And he leans on me,' she'd snapped back. 'We lean on each other. When we need to. That's what a good marriage is about.'

Still-single Em had sighed. 'I wish.'

But Beth had rolled her eyes. Because if she leaned on Lionel he'd fall over?

'Where are your girls at the moment?' Angie and the dog were back with assorted green leaves. Could Angie read her mind?

'Gone home. I sent them. They managed to get on for a couple of days, doing looking-after-Mum rather competitively, but I didn't think it could last. And they have families to look after and jobs. They'll be here for the funeral.'

The funeral. They were back to that. 'Angie, the undertakers wanted to know what Jack would *wear*.'

* * *

Janet

A suit. What Malcolm would wear, dead or alive, wasn't a problem for Janet Carmichael. She'd been looking after his clothes for years, washing, mending and taking them to the cleaners; packing and unpacking his case for business trips and golfing holidays and occasional stays with relatives. She'd bought a lot of them herself. So she'd taken the pinstripe with her the previous day when she'd ordered the bamboo casket. It was one of two he had worn every day to go to the bank. Both had hung in the wardrobe since his retirement, except when he'd taken one out to wear for the all-too-frequent funerals of recent years. It was the obvious choice. Janet knew the form. She had buried her mother and father years before and a beloved maiden aunt more recently. She knew what to do and thought she knew how she would feel. She expected to feel low, to miss her husband of forty years, to weep even more perhaps than for Aunt Flo. She had, after all, been not only his wife but for the past thirty years his PA too.

Now, as Grant turned the Volvo into the close, she felt less sure about her feelings and a headache was pounding, not helped by his mounting tetchiness. Stuck behind a Range Rover for the last stretch along the village high street, driven by the woman at the undertakers, he'd said, the gawky one who'd crashed into the coffin and sworn, he'd accelerated aggressively past her when she'd stopped suddenly. Janet hadn't said, but thought it unlikely that it was the same woman. Even she would have heard if anyone else in the village had died. All she wanted to do now was get into the house without seeing any of the neighbours, tell Grant to get himself something for dinner, down a couple of paracetamol and go to bed.

But of course she didn't.

She found some potatoes and set about making a cottage pie, hoping no one else would knock on the door to express their condolences or push a card through the letter box. She'd been surprised at how many she'd received, many from people she didn't know, or didn't know she knew. Elmsley wasn't the sort of village where everyone knew everyone else, not with its mile-long high street and new developments full of young families. But it was becoming clear that more people knew her, or *of* her, than she'd realised. It was of course better than living in a town where you could die in a high-rise flat and not be found for weeks like some poor man she'd read about recently. You couldn't die in your bed unobserved in Elmsley.

Or do anything else.

Oh! The doorbell. Not again. Who was this? She waited for Grant to go and open it, hoping he wouldn't fetch her to talk to whoever it was.

'So sorry to hear about your poor dear father...' It was a woman's voice.

'Thank you, er, Mrs Thornton?'

'Yes!' The visitor sounded pleased.

Thornton. Barbara Thornton from over the road. She'd been the bursar at the school Grant went to, but it was odd that he remembered her. She'd had more to do with parents than pupils. Janet was straining to hear now, but didn't pick up anything else till Grant came into the kitchen holding a card.

'Mrs Thornton gave me this.' He held onto it.

'Is she still there?'

'No, she went home, said she lived over the road now?'

'Yes.' She'd moved in years ago but after Grant had left home.

Janet saw later that the card was addressed to him, which was interesting. It was because Grant was a former pupil, she supposed.

* * *

Zelda

Zelda Fielding got home before either Viv or Janet, despite leaving Plunkett and Crombie's after them. She lived on the outskirts of town, on an estate of houses built in the seventies. It was only about a mile away, so she could have walked to the funeral directors, and probably should have, but she'd taken the car. What was the point of keeping fit now?

Oh dear, there was William's car parked in the drive of her semi and Tracey was getting out, followed by Errol. That was why they weren't at the funeral parlour. She'd got it all wrong as usual. And there were Mack and Morag at the front-room window barking their little hearts out, so pleased to see her.

'Where have you *been*, Zelda?' Tracey flung her arms around her as soon as they met on the pavement. 'Didn't we say we'd pick you up and all go together?'

Errol and William hugged her as well. So-o-o like Harry, William was. Oh no, she was off again, but it didn't matter, Tracey was brimming over and so was Errol. Harry's kids were great. If she'd been their real mum they couldn't have treated her better. They went inside – the dogs were delighted – and Errol phoned to check what time Plunkett and Crombie closed. Then they all went back there and agreed quickly on Basic Funeral. Tracey said there would be so many flowers no one would see what was underneath. Then the three of them took her to The Swan in town for an early supper. 'You must eat, Zelda.'

Why? What was the point? But she didn't say that.

* * *

Twelve days later, on the same cold September day, the three women attended their husbands' funerals. Zelda said goodbye to Harry, wearing his best double-breasted suit, in a Full Gospel service at the crematorium. Viv saw Jack lowered into his grave in the churchyard of All Saints, wearing a pair of worn denims and a blue check shirt, a trowel in his hand. Janet dispatched Malcolm in a woodland cemetery in the next village, after a service at the Presbyterian church in town, the one they'd attended since leaving Scotland many years before. He wore his pinstriped suit complete with the contents of his back pocket. Let him explain those to his Maker. Jobs done, tick, tick, tick, with varying degrees of satisfaction, they all went home to begin their new lives alone.

* * *

NSNBW
Wallington Street
London SW1

4 March 2009

Dear Friend,

No one knows how I feel. Is that what you're thinking at this moment? Do you feel isolated and alone, as if no one understands? And as if this long winter will never end? Do you even feel that you might be going a little bit crazy? Let me offer my heartfelt sympathy on the recent loss of your life-partner and assure you that you are not alone. A widow myself and chair of a charity supporting women experiencing the loss of their life-partner, I'm inviting you to join us, the National Society for Newly Bereaved Widows, and meet others in the same situation. Our secular organisation exists to help the bereaved recover from their loss and develop a new sense of purpose as they face life alone, and provide opportunities to do so. Branches all over the country offer practical help, counselling if requested and most importantly, diverting social events. Your local branch meets at St Saviour's Church Hall, Linnet Drive MK44 1BD and meetings are held monthly Your next group meeting is on 25 March. Do come along to talk to women who have been through and come through what you are going through. You are guaranteed a warm welcome. Spring will come!

Yours sincerely,

Wilhemina (Allsop)

Viv binned the letter.

Zelda pinned it to her kitchen noticeboard.

Janet filed it under 'Malcolm Deceased'.

3

VIV

'What is your password, madam?'

As Viv clutched the phone, trying to be as civil as the man at the other end, a tile fell off the wall. 'My password is irrelevant.' She'd been trying to get into Jack's online bank account. 'I need my *husband's* password. Jack Robson's. My late husband's. Late as in dead,' she added for her own good as much as his, then, hanging on while he went to consult his line manager, she picked up bits of the jade-green tile, part of a border surrounding the kitchen window. They didn't make that colour any more or that size or that shape, so she must mend it, along with the corner-cupboard door and collapsing pergola in the garden, brought down by heavy snow in March. March. This winter was going on forever.

'Can you tell me your password, madam?'

Aaaagh! But she must persevere. She needed to know how much there was in Jack's bank account. And she couldn't get into his bank account without his password. And if she couldn't get into his bank account... Not that there was much in it. 'It's only money,' she used to say, till they hadn't got any. Till Northern Rock, the so-called ethical bank, disappeared with their savings.

'I am sorry for your loss, madam. Please tell me the maiden name of your late husband's father's mother?'

'I don't know.' Nor did she know the name of Jack's first pet, or his nickname at school or the first road he lived in. How many years had she known the man?

Concentrate.

'Madam—' the man was speaking again '—I need to consult my manager and ring you back.'

The phone rang again as she was congratulating herself on some excellent jigsaw work on the tile.

'Could I speak to the account holder please?'

Deep breath. 'Sorry, but I have explained that my husband is dead.'

'I am sorry for your loss, madam. Please can you tell me your late husband's full name?'

'John James Robson.'

'And your full name, madam?'

'Vivien Halliday.' Was her feminist gesture of years ago making things worse?

'And the maiden name of your late husband's father's mother?'

Aaaaaaaaaaaaaaaaaaagh!

The man tried to be helpful, and went off-script. Had her late husband possibly written this information down somewhere? No, because you were told not to and because Jack had a good memory, a very good brain, right to the end. He didn't need to write things down. He thought he was more likely to forget if he did write things down. *Stop! Stop rambling.* The man didn't need to know how clever and wonderful Jack was. Why, *why* hadn't she asked Jack about this stuff before he died? Because by the time she'd thought of it, it had been too late.

'Mrs Halliday.' The man broke into her thoughts, but only to suggest she make another search for the vital information. Fine, she said, but it wasn't. She couldn't think of anywhere else to look and she had a list as long as her arm to get through. Mrs O'Connor's greenhouse was waiting. There were seeds to set and bare-root roses to buy from George Beaumont Nurseries. And she must fit in a visit to Angie, who was moving today. But best not to think of that. Better perhaps to advertise for more work and ask George and Annie Beaumont to keep an ear open for people wanting help, preferably for garden design. A listed art deco house was expensive to run.

* * *

In the evening, optimism fuelled by a couple of glasses of wine, she decided to have one last search for Jack's passwords. He *must* have written them down. Didn't everyone? So, carefully, so the iron rungs of the spiral staircase didn't clang, she climbed up to his study, and even before she reached the landing she saw that the lamp in his study was on, the door framed with light. He was there! Must be. She tiptoed, then opened the door carefully, silently.

'Why are you avoiding me?' The light went out as she stepped inside.

Later, downstairs in her own study, she berated herself. For fuck's sake! Was she going mad? What would Jack think? What would he think of his rational, earthy, down-to-earth Viv, his touchstone, his voice of reality, going on like this? 'You are dead, six feet under,' she said aloud. 'Dead, dead, dead!' She all but banged her head on the desktop. Then she saw it, the letter she'd binned weeks ago, in the wastepaper bin, which she'd emptied umpteen times since. There it was stuck at the bottom, staring up at her. Was it a sign? A message saying she should go? She'd be reading tea leaves next, but she checked the date on her watch. Yes, that was tonight and if she didn't go she'd finish the bottle.

* * *

Zelda

Zelda was looking at the same letter, still pinned to her kitchen noticeboard.

'Shall I go?' She wiped her eyes.

You've been out all day. Mack stood by his empty dish.

Why not? Morag, more encouraging, looked up from her half-eaten dinner.

Tears dripped onto the ready-meal Zelda had just got out of the microwave. She'd managed all day in the salon without crying – no point in depressing the clients – but now her eyes were sore.

You've got us. The two little dogs followed her into the sitting room and got onto the settee beside her. White fur on blue fabric was not a good mix but they were worth the extra hoovering. What would she do without them? Such a comfort, but it was no good pretending, they weren't Harry. They missed him too. Harry was the one who'd been with them all day, after all. He'd got their meals – and hers. She put the bland whatever it was on the side table and pulled up the pouffe. 'No, Mack, leave it.' But it was too late, and he might as well finish it off as she wasn't going to. She put her throbbing legs up. 'I shouldn't be on my feet all day, not at my age.'

Retire, then? Morag nuzzled closer. *Stay at home with us.*

'And cry all day?' Retrieving the plate from Mack, she got up and took it to the kitchen. She couldn't afford to retire. The crash had hit her pension pot hard. Sophisticuts was surviving, but only just. No one would buy it, not at the moment, not with three more businesses up for sale in the high street. Before the crash she'd talked about handing over the day-to-day running to Carol as manager. She and Harry had made plans, lovely plans, his pension supplementing hers, moving to Spain or Barbados. She tore off more kitchen roll.

Don't cry. Morag had followed her into the kitchen.

But it was hard not to. Today was Wednesday, which was Harry's day for bringing his mum into the salon, so perhaps that was why she was having a bigger downer than usual.

Maybe you should go to that meeting? Was the clever little dog really looking up at the noticeboard? She read the letter again and checked the calendar. Yes, tonight at 8 p.m. *New sense of purpose. Practical help. Counselling.* Was that what she needed? It was only a short walk to St Saviour's church hall.

'Heads I stay, tails I go,' she said tossing a coin even as she stood by the front door. It was tails, so she left Mack with his tail between his legs.

4

ZELDA

When Zelda saw Viv standing under the porch light of St Saviour's church hall, she thought she'd met her before but couldn't quite place her. Was she one of her occasional clients? Did she come into the salon from time to time? If she could see her hair she would know, but, unlike Zelda, the woman was dressed for the weather in a hooded Barbour, which put her face in shadow.

'Come under here, pet.' The woman stepped to one side to make room for her. 'You look like a drowned rat.' The voice resonated too.

'Thanks. I feel like one.' Zelda felt the rain dripping down her face.

'Oh, didn't mean, sorry... big mouth...' She had a northern accent.

'No offence taken.' Zelda was sure she'd heard that voice before.

'You new here?' They both spoke at the same time, and then replied at the same time, 'Yes, are you?'

Then they laughed at the silliness of it and Zelda let her new acquaintance say, 'We're late, I think. Shall we go in?' But as they went to push open the swing doors a taxi drew up and a woman near tumbled out of the rear door. She would have fallen if they hadn't both rushed forward and grabbed an arm each.

'Th-thank you.' The woman sounded more cross than grateful. 'I can manage now. Are you both here for the widows' group?'

'Yes, well, I am. Zelda. Zelda Fielding. Pleased to meet you.' She offered her hand.

'Yes, I'm one of those too.' The Barboured woman offered hers. 'Viv Halliday. Shall we go in?'

Plunkett and Crombie. It clicked as soon as they got inside the hall, and uncovered their heads. Zelda could tell a lot from a head of hair. Coffin Lid Lady, that was who the woman in the Barbour was. Her auburn hair with a streak of white clinched it. And the Scottish lady – tight perm straggly now – was the one with the disapproving man. The scene was vivid in Zelda's mind, but the other two hadn't made the connection. Neither of them recognised her. Because all black faces looked the same?

Don't be chippy, Zeld.

Right, Harry, they obviously don't recognise each other either. And she had put on a few pounds in the last six months – custard creams – unlike the latest arrival.

'I'm J-Janet Carmichael, by the way.' Her tweed suit hung from her.

'Bloody hell, didn't know they were still going on.' Lid-lady – *Viv, Viv Halliday* – clearly not listening, was staring at the scene in front of them. Zelda, trying to fix the woman's name in her head, was back in a church hall in Hitchin, a teenager with her mum, at a – what did they call it? – a beetle drive! That was it. The green baize-covered card-strewn tables were exactly the same. So were the thick white cups on a table at the side, waiting to be filled with tea.

'Are we in the right place?' The Scottish lady, *Janet, Janet Carmichael*, had fished a letter from her handbag.

'Obviously not.' Zelda stepped back. The hostile stares of the beetle-drivers would have repelled invaders. But one of them was hauling herself to her feet.

'Can I help, ladies?' Stocky with grey cropped hair, she looked like the gym teacher who'd made Zelda's life a misery many years ago. *Of course you can run fast, Griselda.* Stereotyping wasn't the worst of it.

'I had this letter.' Janet Carmichael was handing it over. Did she *want* to join this crew? Well, she looked as if she'd fit in.

Gym teacher perused. 'Oh, yes... we *are* the NSNBW, and yes —' She turned towards the beetle-drivers. 'Ladies, chop-chop, another table, please.' She turned back to the three of them, smiling. 'We *do* welcome new members and offer support and diverting social activities. Tonight, it's a beetle drive, first prize a packet of Rolos, but no one goes home empty-handed.' She gave a little laugh. 'All participants get a sample of Dentufix. One of our members is lucky enough to have a daughter in the dental profession.'

'Barbara Thornton? What's she doing here?' Was that Janet who said that?

'Mardy Cow.' That was definitely Viv.

The other two had recognised one, possibly two, of the beetle-drivers, none of whom had moved to put up another table.

'I've had enough.' As Zelda turned, to her surprise so did the others. Their eyes met, brows raised in mutual disbelief. That was when they bonded, Zelda thought later, in that second of shared horror – *is this our destiny?* – before rushing for the door, gym teacher in hot pursuit.

'You've got to move on, ladies. You've got to move on!'

'Yes, but a lot further than this!' Viv was first out.

They paused under the porch light, watching the rain bouncing off the cars in the car park before Zelda said, 'We've met before, you know,' and they turned to look at her, recognition flickering first on Viv's face.

'Plunkett and Crombie.' She covered her mouth with her hand. 'Oh. My. God.'

'I'd never use them again.' Janet shuddered.

All three stared out at the rain, each with their own Plunkett and Crombie memories until Viv broke the silence. 'Stinking night, can I give anyone a lift?'

'Thanks,' Zelda accepted, telling them she only lived around the corner, and Janet said she would get a taxi as she lived out of town. Viv asked where and it turned out they lived in the same village, and they what-a-coincidenced about that and Janet accepted the lift. Then Viv made a dash to her car and brought it to the door.

Should I ask them in for a coffee?

Zelda, in the back seat, thought about it, decided against it, and found herself asking them anyway as Viv drew up by her gate. It was Fate, she'd decided in the short time it took to get to her house. Fate had brought them together twice now. They were obviously destined to get to know each other. 'Or a glass of wine,' she said as Viv and Janet consulted. 'I think I've got a bottle left over from Christmas.'

'You're kidding?' Viv laughed and turned off the engine. 'But why not, if that's all right with you, Janet? Just one for me though, sadly.'

What sort of houses did they live in? Zelda wondered as she led the way into her tiny hallway. Bigger than hers, she'd bet. People in the villages tended to be well-heeled. 'No, darlings.' The Westies hurtled out of the sitting-room, where they'd been looking out of the window, waiting for her. 'Back, Morag. It's all right, Mack.' He was making low warning growls. 'These are friends. Friends.' Though that might be presumptuous, she thought as she bundled the dogs into the kitchen. 'Viv, Janet, make yourselves at home in the sitting room. There's a button on the wall for the gas fire.'

When she joined them a few minutes later with a bottle of white and a bottle of red she'd found at the back of a cupboard, her little sitting room looked warm and welcoming. The curtains were closed and the gas fire was glowing and Viv and Janet were sitting either side of it discussing the neighbour they'd just seen. Seemed Mardy Cow and Barbara Thornton were the same person who lived in The Barns, the close where Janet lived.

'I'm told she came to Jack's funeral.' Viv accepted the bottle of red and the opener. 'Seems she goes to all the funerals, invited or not, not just the service but the wake afterwards.'

'A funeral scavenger is, I think, the term. She definitely came to Malcolm's—' Janet nodded a yes at the bottle of white '—wearing a hat with wavy black feathers.'

Zelda poured some white into Janet's glass to see if it was okay. Viv poured herself a glass of red, and it obviously was okay 'Don't worry, pet,' she addressed Morag, who was looking anxiously at her from the sofa, 'we're not staying all night.' But they had taken the precaution of booking a taxi, she revealed not much later.

How long are they staying? Zelda had to get up in the morning to open the salon.

Janet said the wine was pleasant, like a sweet sherry, Croft perhaps, and it seemed to loosen her tongue, almost instantly. The room went quiet as she started to speak, words jerking out of her like ketchup from a bottle unused for a very long time.

'I went. To that so-called bereavement group. To consult. A professional. To get help with something I can't get out of my mind.'

It was in its way a horror story, beginning at her late husband's funeral when she heard the church door opening and looked over her shoulder to see the *wrong casket* being carried in by the pall-bearers. *That's not Malcolm,* she thought, because she'd ordered bamboo and this was wood. *There has been a dreadful mistake. An awful mix-up.* Poor woman. She was reliving the moment as she told them, gripping the glass in her shaking hand. 'I said, "Grant," – that's my son who was sitting with me in the front pew – "there's been a terrible mistake, that's not your dad." But he muttered from the side of his mouth. "No worries, Mum. I changed the order to mahogany, that's all. Now don't make a fuss." And I d-didn't, I couldn't, I was speechless but—' She shuddered, her arm in spasm, and the glass flew from her hand.

'I'd have killed him right then.' Viv, on her feet, took hold of the sobbing Janet's hands as Zelda went to get the vacuum cleaner. When she returned Viv was reassuring Janet that the broken glass didn't matter but that her son – Grant, was that his name? – was a pillock. 'I hope you've told him what you think of him?' Janet shook her head and said that wasn't really her style.

Zelda tried to make the poor woman feel better too. 'That wasn't the first broken glass this room has seen, I assure you, Janet. I once hurled Harry from one end of the room to the other. His photograph, I mean.' It was on the side table, a lovely photo of him in his cricket whites, mended now. 'I was so *angry* with him for leaving me. But why,' she had to ask, 'did Plunkett and Crombie take your son's word over yours and not check with you, Janet?'

'Because Janet's a woman on her own.' Viv sounded certain. 'I've noticed a lot of people telling me what to do these days. As if I've lost my brain along with my husband. Trouble is, they may be right.'

She didn't expand on that and after Zelda had put the vacuum away she turned to her.

'Your turn now, Zelda. We know what Janet wanted and didn't get from the death-watch beetlers. What made you wend your way on a cold rainy night to the sodding useless NSNBW?'

Deep breath. Could she get through this? No! She was off again, demonstrating her problem. Was it normal, she wanted to know, to be racked with grief after six months, bursting into tears night and day? The dogs moved closer, resting their heads on her thighs as she wept.

'Normal? Is there a normal?' Viv put her glass down. 'If there is I'm sure it's closer to what you're feeling, Zelda. When I was sixteen and my dad died I was like you, still crying day and night months after he'd gone. I'd wake up with my pillow soaking, and I'd hide in the lavs at school so that others couldn't see, covering my red eyes with a curtain of hair when I came out. I'd think I was over it, then there'd be another wave. Wave was the word. Floods of tears. And even years later, it didn't take much to set me off, sad stories, films, the funerals of people I hardly knew. I expected that again, dreaded it, but also longed for the letting-go. But when I gave *myself permission to grieve* as all the fucking books tell you to do, there was nothing to permit. I haven't shed one tear.'

Janet moved back in her seat.

'Did you...?'

Viv anticipated Janet's question. 'Yes, Janet, I saw his body. Twice. I did everything the bloody how-to guide told me to do. Well —' she looked from one to the other '—do I need a shrink? That's what I wanted to find out from the group.' Viv drained the glass and refilled it. 'Or am I just a heartless bitch?'

'Perhaps,' Janet started to say something then shook her head, and Viv carried on as if thinking aloud.

'I don't *feel* as if Jack's dead, that's the trouble. I know he's dead but I don't feel it. I still talk to him.'

'I talk to Harry.' It was good admitting it. 'And I still think he might be here every time I come home from work.'

'Me too.' Viv nodded.

'I still hear Malcolm telling me what to do—' Janet accepted a refill '—and what not to do.' She took a gulp, frowned and raised her hand as if at a meeting, 'Excuse me, but I would like to say thank you to you both for this evening, especially you, Zelda, for inviting us into your home. It has been very helpful, much better than—' she hesitated '—the s-sodding useless NSNBW.'

'Well said.' Viv raised her glass with a smile. 'Thank you, Zelda, for your kindness and generosity.'

Crikey. All this praise. She didn't know where to put herself, or how to respond to Janet's next remark. Janet's hand was up again. 'Ladies, I would like to propose that we form our own widows' support group.'

Silence. You could hear the gas fire puttering. Viv obviously didn't know what to say, but her body language said *no*.

Janet Carmichael was *prickly*, for want of a better word, or *starchy. Unbending* might be better. *Prim. Proper.* You'd have to think twice before you opened your mouth.

'Sorry. I have spoken out of turn.' Janet struggled to her feet.

'No, no, you haven't. Sit down.' Viv looked at her watch, obviously playing for time, reluctant to hurt the other woman's feelings, but also reluctant to commit to seeing her again. 'Though we ought to be going soon. It is a good idea, Janet, giving each other support, I er... don't like the W word, that's all.'

W word?

'Widow,' Viv answered Zelda's unvoiced question. 'From the same root as void, as in *null and*? It comes with weeds and mites and other nasties. Sorry, I was a teacher, once.'

Janet nodded. 'I too care about words, Viv – I abhor cliché – but null and void accurately describes how I felt when my son ignored my wishes.'

'Because he treated you as a person of no account, but we mustn't let others define us.' Viv sounded defiant. 'Or define ourselves by how we feel at the moment. If I thought I *was* what I feel like now, like a bulb buried under several feet of heavy clay, unlikely to ever put up a green shoot, let alone burst into flower, I'd end it now.'

Zelda watched Mack and Morag get down from the sofa. It was time for their walk round the block. Mack fetched his lead and put it on her lap, but Viv and Janet had started brainstorming alternatives for the W word and a name for their group. The Newly Single? Janet didn't like that. She said it sounded like one of those dating agencies. Why did they need a name? As she wondered how to ask politely what time their taxi was booked for, Zelda's eyes fell on the empty bottle of white, a Muscat Blanc 2007. *Muscat. Muscateers.* She held up the bottle. 'How about The Three Muscateers?'

'Brilliant!' Viv raised her glass of red. 'To The Three Muscateers.'

Janet raised her glass too. 'All for one and one for all!'

But would they actually see each other again? As Zelda locked up for the night, she had her doubts. They'd exchanged mobile numbers, but when Janet had got out her diary and suggested some dates for a meeting, at her house next time, Viv had stalled, saying she would get in touch when she'd consulted her diary. And people often said things they didn't mean, especially after a few drinks.

5

JANET

As Janet recalled the previous evening, sunlight streamed through the gap in her bedroom curtains and a blackbird carolled away in the cherry tree outside, and she felt better than she had done for months. *Those ladies were a tonic. I can do what I want today, I can do exactly what I like.* The thought was thrilling. *I can stay in bed all day if I like and read.* But the book by her bed wasn't riveting. *I could go to London and see an exhibition. But I've got the Monet booked for next month. I needn't cook, I needn't clean. I can do anything I like.* As these unusual thoughts kept coming her eyes fell on the bedroom curtains. *I don't like them.* Regency stripes in beige and maroon had never appealed.

'Won't they do?' Malcolm had said when they'd been in the shop less than twenty minutes.

'Yes,' she'd said, 'yes, I suppose they will.' She'd known he'd be tetchy if she made him late for golf. And they had done. For years and years.

'But they won't do now.' She flung back the duvet.

Ridiculous extravagance. Malcolm was with her on the way to Cambridge in the taxi.

'I can't drive. You wouldn't let me learn.'

You didn't need to. I took you wherever you wanted to go.

'Wherever you allowed me to go.'

You don't need new curtains.

'But I want them.'

Waste is sinful. Whose voice was that? Malcolm's? Mother's? Father's? God's? There was a crowd in her head.

'I'll give the old ones to a charity.'

Fortunately, the partition was closed and the driver couldn't hear her talking, if she was talking aloud. She hoped she wasn't but didn't care too much. She would give away a lot of other stuff too. It would be the spring clean of all spring cleans. She would spend some of that amazingly large sum of money Malcolm had left her. As the taxi sped past the flat fenland fields, the sun on the surface water making them gleam, she planned the transformation of her house. Out would go the huge TV dominating the sitting room, along with the subscription to Sky Sports. In would come something more discreet. Out would go the never-comfortable black leather chesterfields more suitable for a men's club than a family sitting room. In would come something squashy and comfortable with a high back and foot supports. Out would go those gloomy dark wood units in the kitchen. In would come something lighter and brighter. But first she'd do their bedroom. *Her* bedroom.

Meeting Viv and Zelda last night was surely the catalyst for this readiness for change. Learning that Viv lived in that unusual art deco house on the high street was certainly a factor. Zelda's little house, too, was stylish, on the inside if not the out. The kitchen, which she'd caught a glimpse of, was blue and yellow like Monet's in Giverny. The sitting room was light and warm, colourful. *Not* beige and maroon. Janet was heading straight to John Lewis.

* * *

It was a delicious day.

She went from department to department, from curtains to carpets to lighting and then back to curtains after coffee. She had realised as soon as she stepped inside the store that the whole room needed a make-over. But where to begin? She started with ready-mades because it would be nice to go home and hang them that night. But none of them were exactly what she wanted. So, proceeding to fabrics, she spent the rest of the morning getting assistants to pull out the heavy rolls of linens and brocades and velvets so she could see and smell and hold the fabrics against her face, picturing how they would look in her room. Floor to ceiling, she soon decided, encouraged by an assistant specialising in interior design. Falling in rich folds, pooling on the floor, opulent, not short and skimpy barely meeting at the edges.

By one o'clock her head was a kaleidoscope of colours and she still hadn't decided on a colour scheme. She paused for thought over a proper lunch with a glass of wine, in the restaurant, and then decided to go home and mull it over. But then, on the way to the exit, walking through lighting, she saw them. Tiffany lamps in the classic dragonfly design that she'd always loved, in amethyst and emerald green and creamy white, suffragette colours.

Gorgeous.

It didn't take her long to choose curtain fabrics and carpets and cushions to tone in with the lovely lamps. Three, one for each side of the bed and an overhead. Then bed linen in the same creamy white, Egyptian cotton one thousand threads. Assistants helped her carry everything to the cash desk where Malcolm joined her again, muttering in her ear, *Do we really need all that?*

'Yes,' she snapped back, startling the girl on the till. Was that the magical thinking the American woman wrote about? There were so many books on bereavement these days, so many psychological theories. Five stages of grief, six, seven? Surely there were only two?

How do I live without him and how the bloody hell did I live *with* him?

'You all right with this?' said the girl cashier.

'Yes, I'm fine, thank you.' She wiped her eye. 'Perfectly fine.' She hadn't felt so good for years. *Why*, Malcolm, *why*? What were you saving it all *for*?

* * *

She was home by four. As the taxi drew up to her door Barbara crossed the road from her house on the corner, with her little hairless dog, which stopped at Janet's gatepost to pee.

'Hello, Barbara,' Janet said, suddenly full of goodwill and a twinge of guilt, remembering that she'd been at that dreadful widows' meeting last night. When had Barbara's husband died? It was remiss of her not to know. She'd always been Mrs Thornton at St Bede's prep, but when she'd moved into the close, she hadn't brought a husband with her. Janet resolved to try harder to be neighbourly. The taxi driver offered to carry her parcels to the door and by the time the taxi had gone, Barbara was back in her own front garden.

'Spending your inheritance, I see!'

What an odd thing to call out. What had Viv Halliday called her? Mardy Cow? She was more crow than cow with her scraped-back grey hair and garb of black trousers, not so very different from the business suit she used to wear all those years ago. *Move on, Barbara!* Rebuffed, and a bit hurt – she'd meant well – Janet closed her own front door, wondering if Viv would get in touch.

* * *

Viv

. . .

Viv was wondering if she should reach out too, as she tied in the long stems of a winter-flowering clematis flopping all over her pergola, aware that Janet Carmichael only lived round the corner, so now would be hard to avoid. What have I let myself in for? *Why did I say I'd get in touch with those two women, one a fountain of despair, the other an uptight disapproving old fuddy-duddy? They'll drag me down, make me feel worse.*

But she had said she would and she was a woman of her word. And she already felt she owed them, Zelda, for her hospitality. And they *had* both been supportive in their different ways. She had to admit she felt better because of the off-loading, lighter somehow. She did still need support, like this clematis, whose fragrant white flowers were almost hidden by the dark leathery leaves. Every year she wondered if she should replace it with something more attractive and trainable, till she got a whiff of its heavenly scent. What were these women's redeeming qualities?

What are yours? a voice muttered in her ear.

6

ZELDA

Zelda loved Viv's kitchen.

'Knickers?' Did Janet just say knickers? Surely not. *Concentrate.* Pen poised, Janet was taking notes, like the PA she'd once been, it seemed, though no one had asked her to. Or perhaps Viv had, while Zelda was studying her kitchen?

'Yes. *New* knickers.' Viv was pouring coffee from a blue enamel percolator into black and white china cups with triangular handles. 'Unless yours still have some zing in them? It's my morale-raising tip of the week, the result of a mind-blowing insight when I went to get clean pants on Thursday morning. Sloggis, I love them, but mine were slogged out.' She handed Janet a cup of coffee in one of the stylish cups. 'You don't have to write all this down, by the way. We don't need minutes, do we?'

It was Sunday morning, four days after they'd met at Zelda's own house. Viv's call on Friday night had come as one surprise, and her kitchen was another, old-fashioned in a way she couldn't date. They were back in the 1920s perhaps, sitting round a marble-topped table on bentwood chairs, more comfortable than they looked.

'Here.' Viv handed Zelda one of the black and white cups. 'Any-way, when I saw the dreary heap of grey cotton that constituted my lingerie collection, I knew I was doomed if I put a pair on. So I grabbed the M&S vouchers I got for Christmas and headed straight for town.'

'Without any knickers?' Janet was still pen poised.

Was that a dry sense of humour or a very literal mind? It was hard to tell. Viv's laugh came a moment later as if she'd been wondering too.

Viv's kitchen could not be described as dreary. It felt as if sunlight was streaming through the window, but it was the sunflower-yellow tiles on the walls that made it feel warm and sunny. Would Viv mind if she took a photo of it to show to Tracey? It was an unusual colour scheme. The window was bordered by sea-green tiles, like a proscenium arch, so the garden outside looked like the set for a play. The Importance of Being Viv? Would someone step out of that covered walkway and say, 'A handbag?' Now Viv was saying she'd ended up with seamless waist highs, cotton gusset, edged in black lace, 'Comfortable and stylish and a three for two. It's comfort first with me and I hope you?' She looked from one to the other and said she'd also bought a matching bra.

'For added uplift?' Janet's face gave nothing away.

'Yes,' said Viv, 'physically and mentally!'

'Good.' Janet put down her pen and said she'd been shopping too, in Cambridge, on the day after their first get-together when she'd woken up transformed. Shopping? She sounded as if she'd bought half of John Lewis!

'Excellent.' Viv was admiring. 'We must give ourselves these boosts as often as we can, though, speaking for myself, I'll need ways that don't involve cash.'

Me too, Zelda wanted to say but it was hard to get a word in. Viv was off again. 'I suggest we think of our meetings as Weight

Watchers in reverse. Instead of losing weight we aim to gain in confidence and self-esteem. So we start with a weigh-in, telling each other what we've each done to make ourselves feel better. Zelda, how has your week gone?'

Letter from someone who didn't know that Harry had died. Downer. Call from bank saying outgoings at Sophisticuts are exceeding income. Downer. Huge utility bills and Mack and Morag have got worms. Luckily, there was a distraction, in the form of a ginger cat clattering into the room through a cat-flap in the door.

'Meet Claudia,' said Viv as the animal headed for a dish under the table, 'a pushy independent female and role model for us all. Cats are always kind to themselves. But—' Zelda felt Viv's hand on hers '—we can share the shit stuff as well. Better out than in?'

So she told them about the downers, but also that Tracey, Harry's daughter, had asked her to go on holiday with her, which was an upper.

'Oh, lovely, where to?' Janet was pen-poised again.

'I didn't ask.'

'Why ever not?' Janet hadn't a clue how the non-rich lived.

So Zelda didn't say cash, lack of, because she didn't want to be embarrassing, and she could put a short holiday on the card. But it wasn't the only reason, so she said, truthfully, that it was Mack and Morag, who'd pined last time she'd put them in kennels.

'Would they pine with me?' Janet was persistent. 'I could have them. The walks would do me good. I'm trying to lose weight. Health reasons.' Janet started reminiscing. 'I used to be very fond of Rex, the Scottish terrier we had when I was a girl, and your little dogs – Westies aren't they? – reminded me of him. What if you brought them to my house one day to see how we get on?' It wasn't just words. Janet got her diary out. She was a bit like a terrier herself.

* * *

And that was how it began. They all got their diaries out and a date was agreed for Mack and Morag's visit to Janet, first with Zelda and then without. Other dates were put in for walks and visits to interesting places. Then the first Friday of each month was reserved for a pub lunch, taking it in turns to book if necessary. But the regular meetings weren't all they did. There were phone calls in between, and texts, sometimes in the early hours when life seemed bleakest. *Are you awake?* Usually one or the other was and they would talk till life felt better. There were also impromptu teas and coffees and glasses-of-something-chilled. They grew closer as they got to know each other better, revealing more of themselves.

Some more than others, of course.

Janet sometimes gave the impression she wasn't telling all, but the other women put it down to her more introverted personality. It wasn't that she was harbouring a dark secret. She was more private, that was all, not as open as they were. She didn't blab as they did about anything and everything. It took all sorts.

The anniversaries came round. Was it really a year since their husbands had died? A whole year since they'd formed their group? Janet, always generous, treated them to tickets for a London show to celebrate. Later they went to Amsterdam and Janet would have paid for that if they'd let her. The other two hung on financially and preferred to pay their way. Viv got more commissions when she won a silver medal at Harrogate Festival for small garden design. Business picked up a bit for Zelda, when other salons in the town sadly failed and she gained more clients, including Janet, whose hair she transformed.

The new, slimmer Janet bought new clothes, signed up for umpteen classes at the retirement centre, passed her driving test on the third attempt and bought a new car, a snazzy Fiat, white with a red and green stripe. She always had something positive to report, even when somebody scratched her lovely little car. Deliberately. There was no denying it, though Janet tried to. She was sometimes careless, she said. But Viv, the first to notice as she walked up Janet's drive, said the long line under the stripe was *gouged*, by someone very jealous of her good fortune. She looked across the road darkly, but Janet refused to believe it was Barbara. She got it repaired and forbade all mention of it.

Janet's frequent joyful, 'Who needs men?' irked the other two, who remembered happy times with theirs, but they made allowances for her miserable marriage to Malcolm and conceded the point. They didn't *need* men. They were thriving as single independent women with full and interesting lives. But then, on the first Friday in September, two years after their husbands had died, Zelda announced that she *did* want a new man in her life and she had one in mind.

Well, that put the cat among the pigeons and the fox in the henhouse – silver, as it turned out.

'Why, Zelda, *why*?' Janet wailed.

Viv wished she'd keep her voice down. Around them other diners were looking up, ears like radar dishes. They were in The Swan, one of their usual haunts, at their favourite table by the window overlooking the river. They'd begun the weigh-in. Viv had just said she'd finished clearing Jack's study so she could make it into a painting studio. Janet had regaled them with photographs of the new quilt she was making, branching out with her own design, and Zelda said she was branching out too, which was fine till she said in what direction. Towards a man who walked his dog past her house every morning.

Viv saw the horror on Janet's face, but Zelda didn't seem to notice.

'He's a widower who goes to your church, Janet, and I'd like to get to know him better.' The silence should have been a warning but she carried on. 'I wondered if you knew him well enough to invite him round for a coffee.'

'What's his name, Zelda?' Viv asked because Janet was still catatonic.

'Alan, Alan Loveday.'

Janet started, obviously recognising the name. Her well-shaped eyebrows shot up, but when, after a studied gulp of water, she leaned towards Zelda, it wasn't to answer her question. 'Look around you, my dear.' She lowered her voice, conspiratorially. 'Who's having fun? Who's having a conversation? The marrieds? I think not.'

It wasn't the most original of observations but, at a glance, it looked as if Janet was right. Viv scanned the room where several groups of women were talking to each other and laughing a lot. The men too, mostly business types, looked as if they were enjoying themselves, albeit more pompously swaying on their heels at the bar or lecturing each other at tables. But the married couples – if you could tell who was married – were mostly not talking to each other as they read menus or mobiles. Or filled in crosswords, separate crosswords from different newspapers in the case of the couple at the next table, but they looked companionable enough.

'Viv.' Janet tapped her hand. 'Back me up.'

Zelda was frosty. 'I wasn't asking you to arrange a wedding, Janet.'

'Point taken, but think about it.' Janet picked up a dessert menu. 'Who's not worrying if we've ironed someone's shirt before we came out, or if we need to cook another meal when we get back?'

Who was married to 1950s man? Viv spoke carefully. This had to be resolved. This was a test of 'all for one'. 'Janet, Zelda only asked you to help her get to know a man a bit better.'

'Only?' Janet sniffed and the temperature dropped several degrees.

* * *

Viv got into the back of Janet's Fiat, leaving the front passenger seat for Zelda. With luck the two in the front would start mending fences, but before the doors were closed Janet was digging more holes. 'Did you *see* the old men in there, Zelda? Did you see the beer bellies, the bent backs, the flaky heads? Is that what you want, to get lumbered with an old man for the rest of your life? Did you see the toothless man at the next table taking hours to get through that steak? Gels—' she sometimes did a Miss Brodie '—let us count our silver linings. We, the single, are looked at with envy by married women. They think we're the lucky ones.'

Viv felt herself stiffen.

Now a size fourteen, Janet had lost a lot of weight, but her mouth was sometimes still out-size. She meant well. She had Zelda's best interests at heart. She didn't want her friend to get lumbered with a needy old man and there were a lot of them out there. At the ticket barrier now, Janet was putting the token in. 'Look at it this way, Zelda. We three can *do* what we like, *go* where we like, *spend* what we like.'

If you're as well-heeled as you are, Janet.

'And, Zelda—' Janet waited for a Canada goose to cross the road '—men do not get abler or more attractive as they get older.'

'Janet,' said Zelda, turning to face her, 'women do not get abler or more attractive as they get older.'

Wow! That was something, coming from Zelda, who had never revealed her age and always looked stunning, with frequent changes of hairstyle and colour. Currently, it was short and relaxed with copper and caramel highlights.

'All the more reason not to hitch yourself to a geriatric, my dear.'

Stop now, Janet.

'For your information,' Zelda almost hissed, 'though you must know this, Alan Loveday is not a geriatric. He has a full head of hair and a straight back *and*, as I've already said, I wasn't talking about getting hitched, I simply said I'd like to get to know him better. *And*, because I believed in this *all for one* nonsense, I thought you would want to help, but clearly you don't. So, I'm sorry I asked. Stop the car and I will walk the rest of the way home!'

Janet didn't stop. She carried on driving, concentrating more now, which was just as well as they'd left the wide embankment, and she was having to negotiate narrow streets lined with terraced houses and parked cars.

Viv hated conflict. Ahead was the estate where Zelda lived and the church hall where they'd first bonded on that dreary rainy night. Now the modernist steeple of the church came into view, its stained-glass panels gleaming in the sunshine. Would the sight of it remind the other two of their friendship? No, not visibly. Janet zipped past, eyes straight ahead, and the two of them sat in sullen silence till they reached Zelda's house. 'There you go.' Janet's tone was clipped as she stopped and released the door-lock.

'No. Wait!' Viv grasped Zelda's shoulder. 'Engine off, Janet. We can't part like this. Zelda, correct me if I'm wrong but I think you were simply asking Janet to help you meet this man who you like the look of, to get to know him better, so you can decide if you would like to get to know him even better. Yes?'

'Yes.' Zelda opened the door and escaped Viv's grasp.

'Okay.' Viv managed to push the seat forward and get out before Zelda opened her garden gate. 'Janet and I will see what we can do. So get that wedding ring off your finger. I'm told it's a big turn-off!'

'*What* did you say that for?' Janet started the engine as soon as Viv got into the front passenger seat. '*Why* did you say *we* will see what we can do?'

'All for one? The Muscateers?' Viv searched for the seat belt.

'Not to help her walk into a minefield.' Janet pulled out without looking.

'That is a cliché and not worthy of you.'

'That is a metaphor and spot on. Men are incendiary devices. Most. I exclude the sainted Jack. Sorry again.' For the next few minutes she drove ostentatiously carefully, concentrating on the road, studying the rear-view mirror as if she were too absorbed by traffic to listen or talk. And to be fair there was a lot of traffic. Schools were out and there were cars and children all over the place. But words could be exchanged at red lights.

'Forming a support group was your idea,' Viv tried again.

'To help each other live independent lives.'

'It won't do any harm.'

'What won't do any harm?' Janet snapped.

'To help Zelda meet a man. We're her friends, FFS. Oh, go, Janet. Green.'

'Tell me, what have you in mind, Viv? You've obviously got it all worked out.'

Viv hadn't, but she had some ideas. 'This chap who goes to your church...'

'*How* does she know he goes to my church if she has only watched him walk past her house with his full head of hair and unbowed back?'

'Good question.'

'And how does she know his name?'

'Another, but never mind for the moment. How do you church-goers operate? Would inviting him for a coffee be *appropriate*, as they say?'

Janet was colouring up. Interesting.

'You've invited him already!' Viv couldn't help herself. '*You* want him!'

'I do not! You have intuited incorrectly, Viv Halliday.' But something was going on beneath that finely sculpted haircut. 'That load looks unsteady. I am not passing,' Janet said unnecessarily. They were behind a trailer full of hay, on the bypass now.

'I applaud your caution. Just hope that tractor isn't going all the way to Elmsley.'

They lapsed into small talk then with Janet oohing and ahing about the flooded fields to the left of them and the leaves in their autumn colours, and the poor blighted chestnut trees. What *had* happened to them? She hoped it wasn't Dutch elm disease all over again. And when would this cold, wet weather come to an end?

So, what is the real reason you don't want Zelda to meet this Alan Loveday? Viv kept her suspicions to herself as Janet burbled on about the weather, her face only slightly less red than it was earlier. Janet drove slowly, as if she were sitting her driving test, though the next village was a traffic-free dormitory with hardly anyone about. It wasn't till they got to Elmsley that she really did have to keep her wits about her because there was still a bit of after-school traffic, and mothers with pushchairs and young children rushing along the pavements.

'Drop me this end if you like, Janet...' Viv wanted to walk off dinner.

But Janet didn't hear or pretended not to. She carried on driving down the long high street, past thatched cottages and seventies semis, converted barns and nineteenth-century terraces, and The Wagon and Horses, and the village shop, now a Spar, and The Barns where she lived, till she came to Viv's house, where she pulled into the drive.

'An oasis, that's what it makes me think of. Or a small ocean liner.' She gazed at Viv's house as if seeing it for the first time. 'I love the whiteness and the curved corners and the porthole window by the door. And how come you have all those blazing colours in your borders in September? What are those flowers?'

'Dahlias, much maligned, but don't pretend you are fascinated by my planting, Janet Carmichael, or by art deco architecture. You have been deep in thought for most of the journey back. What are you hiding?'

Now colour blazed in Janet's cheeks. 'I will admit to having *contemplated* inviting Alan Loveday for a coffee before today.'

'Cuppa?' Viv opened the car door.

8

VIV

'Tell.' Viv put two cups of tea on the kitchen table. 'Why did you contemplate inviting this man for coffee?'

'He goes to my church, he's recently bereaved and he's lonely.'

'So, why haven't you?'

'He goes to my church, he's recently bereaved and he's lonely.'

Viv nodded. She got it. 'I told you about Cecil Byers, didn't I?'

They sipped thoughtfully from the striped cups. Cecil was an elderly man, a neighbour who Viv had invited in for a cup of tea a few weeks after his wife died, and she'd been taken aback by the strength and length of the hug he'd given her. He was in his eighties and very old-school – she'd expected a handshake. 'Poor man. I'm not being judgemental, but...'

Janet looked knowing and sniffed.

'Yes, he was, I think, up for it. It took a few moments to extract myself.'

Janet sniffed again.

'But this Alan, he's a churchgoer...'

'Viv, churchgoers aren't as different as you seem to think. We're not a different species. Alan Loveday misses his wife dreadfully, by all accounts, was very caring, uxorious is, I think, the word. He took early retirement to look after her when she was diagnosed with pancreatic cancer, but she died two weeks later and now he's got time on his hands.'

'And is needy?'

'Men are.'

'And women aren't?'

'Not in the same way. Men can't cope when they have to look after themselves.' Janet sipped her Earl Grey. 'But we can, and we're happy on our own, have been ever since we told ourselves that was okay.'

'Defying all the killjoys. How is Barbara, to name but one?'

'Still joy-killing but I don't let her get to me now. How's Mugwort?'

'Quiet recently, though I've been so busy I wouldn't have noticed if he bit me.'

They were both familiar with Viv's savage inner critic.

'Good for you. Why don't you wear a wedding ring, by the way?'

'Symbol of bondage.'

'Very advanced.'

'It was when I wed in the sixties, which weren't as revolutionary as people now seem to think. I was quite right-on then, my own woman and all that.'

'You still are.'

'Tell that to my daughters. They think I was a Stepford wife.'

They were quiet with their own thoughts then, in the comfortable way they'd grown used to. *My own woman.* Viv considered that. *I bloody well am now, but I loved being Jack's woman too.* She still missed him, like the much-quoted severed limb, there and not there, still hurting sometimes. Grief had given her a new respect for cliché. What was there new to say about dying?

'Viv, did you cry *before* Jack died? I mean, when he was ill?'

'Buckets. When I was sure I was alone. Except for once, disastrously, when he was having chemo, and I was escorted from the premises by a very disapproving nurse.'

'Pre-mourning, that's what it's called, but, as Harry's death was sudden, Zelda had all hers to do afterwards.' Janet was twisting her wedding ring round her finger. 'Can't get it past the first knuckle.'

Viv pressed for advantage. 'And Zelda hasn't got family like us.'

'Mine are in New Zealand.'

'Okay, but what about her request? Are we going to help?'

'As long as you realise that if she gets a man she'll start putting him first. Women always do. Did you know there were four musketeers, by the way?'

'Sorry?' Viv had lost track.

'Four musketeers. There were three to begin with, then D'Artagnan joined them. I watched *Les Trois Mousquetaires* last night, in French, to ward off dementia.'

Viv laughed. 'So, this Alan Loveday can join our merry throng, can he?'

'*Non! Certainement non.*'

Janet got up and left soon afterwards, and Viv refilled her cup and took it into the garden. Was Janet right to be so pessimistic? Would a man bring their friendship to an end?

Probably. Mugwort, king of the killjoys, was never far away.

'Sod off!' Her hand reached for her shoulder, where she pictured the creature, a crouching toad with teeth and claws, ready to spike any bubbles of happiness. He'd turned up one morning soon after Jack died when she was in the garden drinking coffee, the sun warm on her back. She was admiring a pool of autumn crocus under the birch tree, glowing like amethysts. *Enjoying that, are you? Can't have loved him that much, then.* The sun went in, but she'd fought back. Sadness was part of her life now, a thread but not the whole of it. She would find happiness where she could. They all must. If Zelda needed a new man to be happy, fine. They must help her. It could be interesting.

9
ZELDA

Sometimes you needed a good grizzle.

By the time Zelda had made herself a cup of tea she was wallowing in self-pity, which she knew was a slippery slope. 'I wish I'd never asked them.' Now she was reaching for the custard creams and confiding in the Westies, pathetic, but she didn't care.

The chunky little white dogs nuzzled closer on the blue sofa.

'They think I'm stupid.'

Mack's eyes were stern beneath his bushy brows.

'They're not going to help me.'

Morag put her head on her lap.

'All for one. How long did that last? There's only one person Janet Carmichael is all for and her initials are JC.'

Mack got down.

'Here.'

But Mack refused the custard cream. *Janet looked after us when you went on holiday, remember.*

'Traitor.' Now both dogs greeted Janet with adoring looks. They'd had a lovely time staying with her.

Janet wasn't self*ish,* but she was self-sufficient, that was it, not self-obsessed, but self-assured and self-contained. They both were, compared to her. Viv with her not crying. Ever. Janet positively glad her husband wasn't around. She didn't say so, of course, and she had burst into tears once, and rushed home – they'd been at Viv's – without saying why. Viv said it was her fault for going on too much about her own happy marriage to Jack. She thought Janet was grieving not so much for what she'd lost *but what she hadn't had*. One-to-ones were often more interesting than when there were three of them.

'And Viv and Janet must see lots more of each other, living so close.'

Cue, another custard cream.

Viv and Janet had more in common too, children and grandchildren to boast about. And parents. Viv was very proud of her coalminer father, and her mother was still alive, not that she seemed delighted by that. Janet's parents weren't alive but at least she knew who they were. And who her grandparents were.

'I know more about your pedigree than I do my own.' She fondled Morag's head and Mack clambered up again for his share. It was true. She had a certificate showing their heritage. All she knew about her own dad was that he'd been a black American GI. That was one big gap in her life, which she was trying to fill with research online, and when she retired she'd do even more, maybe join a family history club, something like that.

But since Harry died there was another gap. She *was* lonely. She couldn't deny it. She missed having a man around the place. She still longed to see Harry standing in the window when she walked up the garden path, literally looking out for her. Still yearned for him to open the door before she reached it. Still missed ordinary things like eating together and doing a jigsaw together and watching TV together and not having to worry about lights going out or pipes bursting or radiators needing bleeding. Now she spent hours looking for the right person to fix something, or hours looking for the right fuse or battery or light bulb. Oh no, not the fire alarm again!

Go and see if you've left something on the stove, Zeld.

'Okay, Harry.' She got to her feet. Sometimes it did feel as if he were still looking after her. But most of the time it didn't. Most of the time it felt as if she was struggling on her own. Janet said she should be grateful, for what she'd had and what she'd got. Being grateful was her golden rule. Count your blessings, in other words. Janet talked a lot about happiness psychology, but you didn't need to be a psychologist to know that. And she did it all the time anyway. She told herself lots of times that she had her own house and her own business and really nice grown-up stepchildren, especially Tracey, and Mack and Morag, but it only worked *up to a point*. You were still left with what you hadn't got.

Now guilt got a grip and led to two custard creams in a row, because she'd broken another of Janet's rules. Don't Feel Guilty. Viv's No Rules rule was better. 'We're all doing this in our own way, remember,' she'd said once when Janet had started laying down the law. Well, she wanted to do it her way, not Viv's, not Janet's or her neighbour-three-doors-up's way, with her condolence cards still up four years later. Viv didn't seem to mind alone; Janet loved it, but she was fed up with it. It was as simple as that. She wanted someone *there*. She wanted someone to do things with, to do things for, and to do things *for her* like fixing the bleeping fire alarm. Typical. It stopped bleeping as soon as she reached the kitchen. Needed batteries, then. Nothing burning, good, but nothing cooking either, so better get another tasteless meal-for-one out of the fridge. Michelle Obama smiled down from the cork noticeboard, an adoring Barack by her side. Go for it, she seemed to say, find yourself a lovely man, like I did. President of the USA! Fancy that! She could still hardly believe it. Things *were* getting better in some ways.

'I only asked Janet to invite him for coffee.' She addressed Morag, who'd followed her into the kitchen. 'It's not as if I'm going to meet someone like I met Harry.'

That had been perfect, getting to know him gradually when he'd brought his mum into the salon to get her hair done. Quite early on she'd started to look forward to Wednesday mornings when Doris had her shampoo and set, and had realised it wasn't just because she liked Doris, she liked Harry as well. She'd learned from Doris that Harry had come from Jamaica with her when she came over as a nurse to work for the NHS. Doris had told her ever such a lot about him, biased of course, but the facts had spoken for themselves. Harry had been kind and caring. He'd looked after his mum for years and years, ever since she'd been diagnosed with MS. That was after his first wife had died of cancer and he'd cared for her too. Harry had been a carer. He'd been an ambulance driver before they called them paramedics. When his mum had found it too hard to care for herself he'd moved into her house to be there for her night and day. He'd let Tracey have his house.

He'd had a lovely manner with his mum and when she'd died he'd been distraught. Zelda had gone with Carol to Doris's funeral and they couldn't get over how upset he was. And when he'd come into the salon on a Wednesday morning a few weeks later, to pick his mum up as usual, her heart had gone out to the poor man. She'd had to tell him gently that his mum wasn't there and assure him he wasn't barmy, and he'd said, 'You wouldn't come and have a drink with me, would you?'

She'd said, 'What, now?'

To which he'd said, 'Yes, please, if you like.' Carol had said she would hold the fort, so they'd gone to the pub around the corner and it had gone on from there. Third time lucky, she thought, as Gary and Igor had both been mistakes. Gary had left her, as her dad left her mum, when she was a pregnant teenager, though after a shotgun wedding that hadn't even given her a baby...

Why don't you give us our dinner? Mack had joined Morag.

The little dogs were right. Feeling sorry for herself wasn't doing her any good. *Count silver linings.* If she hadn't received some insurance money out of the blue after Gary died working on the North Sea oil rigs, she wouldn't have been able to buy the house and open her own salon. If Igor, the charmer, hadn't moved in and made a bit of a contribution, for a short time at least, she wouldn't have been able to keep up the mortgage payments when interest rates had gone sky-high. But she was right about third time lucky. She and Harry had been so happy and had started to think about moving somewhere sunny when she retired to make their pensions go further.

But then had come the cry in the night.

It had been in the early hours and she'd thought it was cramp as usual and started getting out of bed to go round to his side and give his leg a rub. But he'd cried out that the pain was in his chest, and then his arms. It had been awful standing there, hearing him in agony – till he'd gone quiet and that had been worse. She'd rung 999 and the paramedics had got to the house ever so quickly, in minutes though it had seemed like hours, and when they had, they'd done their best, thumping his chest, with all the electronic equipment on the go, but it had been too late. A heart attack. A massive heart attack. It was over. He'd gone.

So, no more sitting on the sofa watching TV together. No more doing crosswords together. No more companionable walks to the pub. No more pottering in the garden. No more eating his lovely dinners and washing up together afterwards, chatting about the day, or not chatting, just being comfortable saying nothing together.

No more together.

10

JANET

Bliss! Coming home to an empty house was bliss. Knowing you had the rest of the day to yourself was heaven. Having an afternoon zizz in your gorgeous bedroom was paradise. Easing off her shoes, Janet flexed her toes. Why would Zelda, why would *anyone* want a man to spoil it?

'Hello, Rocky. Hello, Woody.' Her spirits rose further at the sight of her grandchildren in the photo beside the bed. But then dropped. Oh dear. How quickly one's mood could change. That photo had come with the Christmas card nine months ago and she hadn't had as much as a Skype call lately. Hadn't seen them in real life since Grant and Belynda had carried them off to New Zealand as babies.

Go and see them.

Yes! She sat up straight, infused with positivity again, as she always was after seeing Viv and Zelda. *Be proactive.* Hoping for a 'Dear Mum, come and stay' was pointless. All her hints had been ignored, her suggestions rebuffed. One delaying tactic followed another. 'Yes, when we've moved into our new house.' Then, 'Yes, when the extension is finished.' 'Yes, when life is a little less hectic here.' Fine. *Don't ask. Tell. Tactfully, of course.*

It wasn't as if she had to stay with them. She got the message. She empathised with their feelings, especially Belynda's. It was a pain having your mother-in-law to stay. She used to dread Malcolm's mother's state visits. So, she would book into a hotel and hire a car so they didn't have to run her around. Driving over there shouldn't be too difficult. Wasn't it on the same side of the road? Elated now by her own positivity – she couldn't possibly sleep – she glanced at the clock. Five o'clock, so four in the morning in New Zealand and they would all be asleep. She'd ring this evening, at seven o'clock, catch Grant before he went to work and tell him her plan.

What could she do in the meantime? The *mean* time! Guilt squeezed her stomach. She'd been mean to Zelda. Insufferably negative and selfish.

She picked up the phone and dialled. Viv was right. They must help each other pursue happiness in their own way. That was what all for one meant. There was no answer so she left a message. 'Zelda, I'm so sorry for being a – a – a selfish, negative mardy cow. Of *course* I'll help you meet Alan Loveday. Will be in touch with dates soon!'

Very soon, because if she didn't Zelda might resort to one of those dating sites and meet a psychopath. Far better to have someone vetted by her friends. Now, what if she had a little supper party? She could call it a harvest supper and invite some friends from church, including Alan, of course, and Zelda. She owed a meal to Rona and Don, but must make the numbers odd, so it didn't look like matchmaking. Alan Loveday was a decent sort, everyone said so. He and Penny used to be very popular at church events. Malcolm thought he talked too much but that was a plus. Didn't

Zelda say she missed Harry's anecdotes? Buoyed up with generous feelings, she got out of bed to go down downstairs and get her diary. But what was this flashing red on her mobile?

Newsflash! Newsflash! Newsflash!

What came next made her sink back onto the bed.

Earthquake in New Zealand! Severe earthquake in South Island! Magnitude 7 on the Richter scale!

It was several minutes before she could move to switch on the TV in her room for as-it-was-happening reports. Devastating Earthquake *in Canterbury Area*! That was where Grant worked! Rigid with fear, she watched as buildings collapsed before her eyes. So far no one had been killed, someone said, and only two injured. It was a good thing, said another, that it was night and most people were sleeping. If it had happened when people were outside in the streets or working in the office blocks things would be a lot worse. Phew! Grant and family would be safe at home in Banks Peninsula. But wasn't that close to Canterbury? Another building crumbled as she watched. A state of emergency was declared.

Stunned, she could hardly breathe, but eventually remembered her mobile and dialled Grant's number. No answer. Nothing. The line was dead. Power lines were down, a commentator was saying. But no phone didn't mean no Grant. It didn't mean her family had been injured or worse. It didn't mean that Grant had died while she was still angry with him. *Do not let the sun go down on your anger.* But she had, she had let many suns rise and fall while her resentment festered. She had been cold and uncommunicative, right up to the moment he'd left for the airport. She hadn't kissed him or even patted his arm. It was her fault. She got out of bed and sank to her knees. 'Please God, let him be alive, let them all be alive, so I can make my peace.'

11

VIV

'Janet couldn't have planned an earthquake.' Viv was trying to build bridges.

'Are you sure?' Zelda handed her a mug of tea.

Viv was in Zelda's lovely blue and yellow kitchen, perched on a not-too-comfortable bar stool. 'It's a whole week since the earthquake and she still hasn't heard from Grant.'

'Sorry.' Zelda did look a bit shamefaced. A bit. 'She must be out of her mind. Poor Janet.'

'But? I can hear a "but" coming.'

'But I still don't think she wants me to meet him.' Zelda filled a mug for herself.

'Despite the message she left on your phone?' Janet had told her about that.

'Janet does what she thinks is right, Viv.'

'But isn't necessarily what she wants to do?'

Zelda nodded and Viv couldn't help thinking she was astute.

'But you still want to meet him?'

'Yes.' Zelda opened the door to let her dogs in. 'Attractive widowers are few and far between.'

'So...' Viv hesitated before her next question '... how did you find out this one's name?'

Zelda didn't take offence. 'I was proactive, like we all agreed we should be. Not wait for good things to happen. So when I was walking the dogs past his house one day and a delivery man was about to go up his drive – he seemed short of time – I offered to take the package to the door.'

'And his name was on it. Clever! But...' she hesitated again '... how did you know it was his house?'

Now Zelda looked wary, as if she might be under attack. 'Because I'd *seen* him go into it, Viv, before, when we were walking. People with dogs do walk them, you know.'

And did you just happen *to follow him to church one day too?* Viv didn't ask that. She'd said enough. Zelda's hackles were rising. She sounded as if she'd got a bit of a crush on this man and knew it. *Stop!* Viv felt bad for belittling Zelda's feelings. She shouldn't feel ashamed because she fancied someone. Good for her. But the sooner Zelda met this man for a reality check, the better. Sadly, that wouldn't happen any time soon, not if they were relying on Janet, who was still frantic with worry about Grant. She texted her.

Janet, any news from New Zealand?

* * *

Janet

Janet was reading something else.

IT'S GOD'S PUNISHMENT.
    YOU DIDN'T LOVE HIM LIKE I DID BUT WOULDNT LET HIM GO.

Who? What? What did it mean? It was written in spiky capitals, some of them ripping through the paper, blue Basildon Bond. Lined. Her next-door neighbour, Maggie, had just given it to her.

'Who, who did you say gave you this?' Janet couldn't stop her hand shaking. It was in its way another earthquake.

'Barbara, but she didn't exactly give it to me. Far from it. I arrived at your front door – you didn't answer the back – as she was putting it through your letter box. She didn't look too pleased when I offered to give it to you. May I?' Maggie took the note from her shaking hand and read it. 'Oh, OMG! Sorry, Janet, if I'd known... I thought she'd be complaining about parked cars or overhanging branches as usual.'

It still didn't make sense. 'You think Barbara Thornton wrote this?'

'Ye-es?' Maggie was looking at her, bewildered.

'But why?' Janet closed the still-open door.

'Because...' Maggie hesitated and shook her head.

'Because? I insist you tell me, Maggie.'

But Maggie was going red all the way from her neck to the roots of her curly blonde hair, clearly reluctant. 'Sorry, Janet.' She shook her head again. 'I thought you knew...'

'Knew what? Tell me.'

'About Malcom and Barbara? That they had an affair?'

Janet felt the blood draining from her face, her knees go weak, so she had to sit down, hard, on the stairs. Barbara? *Barbara?* Malcolm and *Barbara*? It was impossible.

Or maybe not?

'It was a long time ago.'

Did Maggie think that made it better?

When Maggie had gone, after making Janet a cup of tea and reminding her she was a solicitor, and offering to write an official letter warning Barbara against writing more anonymous letters, Janet went to the filing cabinet in her study. There, under Miscellaneous, she found another letter, hidden away long ago, in the last century, 1997 to be precise. The older one was typed and had come through the post, postmark indecipherable, with a lot of electioneering leaflets. Her name and address were typed on the envelope, but there was no sender's address in the corner of the note inside, and it wasn't signed.

YOU DON'T LOVE HIM LIKE I DO
    AND HE DON'T LOVE YOU!
    WHY WON'T YOU LET HIM GO?

She'd confronted him with it, well, she'd put it beside his plate that evening, and watched him carefully. She'd seen his sandy eyebrows jump into his bald head and a flicker of emotion in his eyes, maybe anger, then a bewildered slow headshake and a little smile as he pushed it aside. 'Some poor woman's fantasy.' Another little smile, not a preen, she remembered hoping. Surely he wasn't enjoying the thought of himself as the recipient of another woman's adoration? He'd picked up his knife and fork and changed the subject. 'Looks like that New Labour chap's going to get in.' He'd gone out to his bridge class as he did every Tuesday at seven, but returned later than usual.

Slowly, she pieced together what must have been happening under her nose. The bridge club. The golf club. The evening walks, once a week, to The Wagon and Horses to 'wet his whistle' by a man who begrudged the price of a glass of house wine. Barbara played bridge. Barbara played golf. Barbara obviously wetted his whistle.

So why didn't I see?

Did everyone know? Was the whole village talking about her,

sniggering behind her back, giving her pitiful glances? Was she that
cliché of all clichés, The Last To Know?

How will I ever show my face again?

Janet poured herself a glass of Pinot to steady her nerves. Did
Barbara go to the same bridge weekends in country hotels that
Malcolm went on, saying they would bore her? Did she go on
golfing holidays in Ireland and Portugal that Malcolm said were
'chaps only'? She poured herself another glass. Was Barbara the
beneficiary of the condoms 'ribbed and dotted for added pleasure'
in the back pocket of his best trousers? She poured herself another.
Did Malcolm end the affair that night? The night she showed him
the anonymous letter? Had Barbara been simmering away ever
since, nurturing her resentment? Malcolm had never asked for a
divorce or even a separation, but maybe he'd told Barbara he had.
Her mobile pinged.

How are you? Heard from Grant yet? Fancy a coffee? Need to talk about
Zelda. Viv

She texted back.

Need to talk about me before I drink myself under the table!

Viv came round straight away on her way from Zelda's. She said
she didn't know about Malcolm, she hadn't heard any gossip, and it
wouldn't make any difference if she had. 'Not your fault, Janet,' she
said, accepting a glass of Pinot. 'Hold your head high.' She was all
for letting Maggie write an official letter to Barbara warning her off,
but said she thought writing anonymous letters wasn't actually illegal, not unless they were defamatory.

Bottle empty, after Viv had gone home, Janet rang Maggie to say
go ahead, but then decided to write Barbara a kind note too, for

balance. She must be positive and find a way forward. Barbara was to be pitied. She had been used by Malcolm. They had both been used by Malcolm, but Barbara had let herself be eaten up with jealousy and bitterness and maybe grief. Definitely grief, if she had indeed loved Malcolm. It started to make sense, her OTT mourning outfit at Malcolm's funeral, that hat with black feathers and a veil. And at that bizarre widows' group. Poor woman. She must try to forgive. Her letter was short:

Dear Barbara,

There is no more need for deception. I now know what happened in the past and what you have been doing more recently – and I understand. But these letters and vindictive actions

She remembered the scratch on her Fiat.

must stop as no good will come of them. You will suffer far more than me if you continue.

Kind regards,

Janet Carmichael

PS Perhaps we should talk about this? If you would like to meet for coffee give me a ring.

It wasn't an empty offer. She added her phone number to her headed notepaper and hand-delivered it through Barbara's letter box. As she walked away she got her reward, or that was what it felt like, as her mobile pinged.

All well here. No injuries. No worries. Grant

That was all but it was enough. Joy and relief flooded through her. She almost skipped back to her house. Grant was alive and well. The family were alive and well. God wasn't punishing her! When she got in she found her diary and texted Viv and Zelda with the good news and suggested several dates for a supper party. She *would* help Zelda to get to know Alan Loveday. She sent her another text.

Alan Loveday has a sweet tooth if I remember rightly from harvest suppers at church. Suggest you make a dessert, but not with apples as I have decided on Normandy Pork for main course. Plum crumble with custard?

One for all and all for one!

12

VIV

Viv got to Janet's early to await the prey.

Fortunately, as it turned out, because Zelda wasn't as prepared as she ought to have been. Viv had time to decant her Tesco crumble into one of Janet's stylish ovenproof dishes, and was doing so when she heard the front doorbell go. Thinking it was Zelda, back with the 'home-made' custard and cream she'd forgotten to buy, she went to open the door, but Janet beat her to it. And it wasn't Zelda, it was the church set, all five of them, including Alan Love-day. Well, she assumed the tallest male, standing slightly apart from the couples, was he.

Yes, she found herself nodding with approval, though he wasn't her type. He was like that actor, tall, lean, silver-haired, hollow cheeked, from *Pretty Woman*, his name would come in a minute. Not quite as straight-backed as Zelda had described – *where* was she? – but that might have been because he was stooping to kiss Janet's cheek. And Janet looked terrific. She could have graced the cover of *Good Housekeeping*, very Judi Dench in black velvet pants and a tunic top in a rich ethnic brocade in shades of blue. *Get back here, Zelda!* Why hadn't she made an impressive pudding after the tip-off from Janet? Janet's talents were very visible, not just her appearance, but here in the kitchen. An array of home-made dishes, some in the oven, some yet to go in, and the wall festooned with Post-it notes specifying in and out of the oven times, all said, 'I am an accomplished woman.' She must have been slaving all day, all week even, and here she was returning from her welcoming act, looking a little flushed. From the heat of the kitchen or that kiss?

'I've left them to it, Viv, in the front room.' She sounded a bit breathless. 'They all know each other. Here—' she handed Viv a glass of fizz '—unless you want to go straight onto red?'

'This will do fine, thanks. Enough food for an army, by the way, except perhaps for pudding. How many are we all together?'

'Nine. Three men and six women, so it doesn't look contrived. We can make sure the right people sit together if we place ourselves strategically. I've put my neighbour Maggie in the picture so she doesn't hog a by-a-man space. We're eating in the conservatory, by the way.'

'I can see. The table looks lovely.'

The large conservatory opened out from the kitchen, and a navy cloth made a perfect foil for Janet's latest purchase, some beautiful white porcelain from Villeroy & Boch, sparkling in the glow of a copper lamp hanging low over the round table.

'All we need now is Zelda.' Janet frowned. 'Oh, here she is.'

'Sorry.' Zelda came in the back door. 'Thought I'd better get another pudding, as well as cream and custard, when I saw how many there were. Not home-made – sorry again, but I've had a busy week.'

'We're covering for you.' Janet reached for another dish as Maggie, her neighbour, came in from the other room, also wearing shirt and denims, Viv was relieved to see. Was Zelda more focussed than the lack of home-made puddings suggested? Always glamorous, she looked more formal tonight in a high-necked knee-length grey silk dress, which fitted perfectly, accentuating her voluptuous curves. Subtly. No décolletage. Had she dressed to appeal to the taste of a conservative, church-going man, perhaps? Her nail varnish was a paler pink than usual.

'Well, time for your entrance, Zelda.' Janet put a tray of canapés in her hands. 'Take that to the front room.'

But it was Janet who deserved an Oscar that night for acting and directing. Was this the same woman, in bits only recently, convinced everyone was sniggering behind her back because her husband had been playing away?

There was, Viv thought, a flicker of recognition on Alan Loveday's face when he met Zelda. He said he thought he'd seen her before and when Zelda said she thought she'd seen him walking past her house with a spaniel, they were soon into dog talk. His was called Kenny, he said, Kenny Dog Leash? Zelda got it – phew! – and laughed, but he left her side when Janet returned with another bottle of Prosecco. 'Man's job, eh?' He took it from her hand to open, and Viv was relieved to note the laughter in his attractive deep voice. He seemed comfortable in women's company, and familiar with the tastes of the two he'd arrived with, topping up their glasses, one with white the other red, after he'd refilled the fizz drinkers' glasses. But was he looking for a new partner after a mere six months on his own? That was the question. Viv looked for signs of grief and saw none. But that meant nothing as she well knew. Back by Zelda's side now, he was asking her what she did for a living. So far so good. He wasn't full of himself. Viv followed Janet into the kitchen to see if she needed help and got shooed out again. 'Project Zelda, that's your job, Viv. Watch Rona.'

'Which one's she?'

'Boobs.'

* * *

'You sit there, Alan.' Janet hadn't made name plates but obviously had a seating plan.

Placing herself at the end of the table nearest the kitchen, she directed the male lead to the seat opposite her. 'Don and Geoff, you space yourselves out so we can share you.'

Viv had already forgotten the newcomers' names, but tried to pick them up while wondering where to put herself. Geoff's wife – Edna? – sat down next to him but Don's – was that Rona-to-be-watched? – she had big boobs prominently displayed – went and sat on Alan's right. *Sit on his left, Zelda!* Oh, good, Alan was pulling the chair out for her. Keeping score now, Viv awarded him a point. Zelda gave him one of her lovely smiles, so a point for her too. So far so good. Gulping fizz – why was *she* nervous? – Viv sat on one side of Janet with Maggie on the other.

She relaxed a bit when they began to eat and there were murmurs of approval for Janet's excellent pork casserole, then a lull punctuated by the chink of glasses and cutlery. When they did start talking again Janet's friends stuck to safe topics like holidays and the weather and gardening. Safe enough here anyway, not like at some horticultural conferences Viv had been to, where rivals could come to blows over organic v non-organic.

The situation in New Zealand was another topic. Janet's friends were concerned about her. Was Grant really okay? Janet's voice faltered a little when she said he was, and Viv reminded herself that Grant was her beloved only son, even if he was a prat. One of the men ventured his opinion that the recently formed Conservative-Liberal Democrat coalition might be a good thing, but when his wife – Edna? – said, 'No politics, please, Geoffrey,' he shut up and Janet skilfully changed the subject. How was the vicar's sciatica?

There was a bit of church talk then back to gardening, where she suddenly found herself the unwelcome centre of attention. Zelda had just told everyone that Viv was a professional gardener, as she often did, which was fine. Usually. Neither Zelda nor Janet ever missed an opportunity to get her gardening work, for which she was often grateful, but this wasn't helping Project Zelda. Suddenly the whole table was bombarding *her* with questions. Should they be doing an end-of-season tidy-up? Ought they to cut back the dead perennials or leave the seed heads for the birds? Were they terrible to use the little blue pellets to keep down the slugs?

How can I change the subject?

Fortunately, someone said that Alan's wife's contributions to the harvest festival were sorely missed, which helped a bit. Helped her, that was, but not Alan Loveday, who looked uncomfortable and more so as Rona patted his hand. Penny Loveday had, it seemed, been a very keen gardener, the source of plants for plant stalls at fetes and fresh flowers for the church, the star of Open Gardens. With a sigh, he explained he had let the garden go a bit, quite a lot in fact.

'Then get Viv to help.' Zelda was at it again. 'She's brill, isn't she, Janet, a prize winner?'

'A silver medal at Harrogate last year and a highly commended at Sandringham,' said Janet, 'for small garden design.'

'Because you two helped me set up, saving me a fortune.' Viv enlarged on how her friends had helped her with the manual labour. 'Couldn't have done it without you.'

Alan topped up Zelda's glass. 'I love the way women pull together.'

Another point.

'Sandringham?' Rona was impressed. 'Don and I went last year when Charles presented the prizes. I love the royals. Did the Prince of Wales shake your hand, Viv?'

'No, but Camilla did, and you know where hers has been.'

Silence. *Too rude for the church crew clearly.*

'Does Camilla cut the royal toenails?' Alan Loveday, straight-faced, picked up the bottle of red and nodded at Rona's glass. 'Top-up?'

Three points? Four? Viv had lost count, but gave him another for helping her out, and another for having a sense of humour. And another for not ogling Rona's rather obvious décolletage. But his next remarks, addressed to Janet, were harder to assess. Was she into gardening? he asked, and when she replied, 'Not veg, I prefer mine washed from Waitrose,' he laughed. Then – sudden change of subject – he asked if her earrings were lapis lazuli. Nothing wrong with his eyesight to see them from the other side of the table – and Janet's hand rose to touch one of the dark blue drops, a blush rising up her cheeks. Yes, she said, they were, she'd bought them in Cairo on a cruise, the first holiday she'd taken alone after Malcolm died. 'My first holiday abroad, in fact, because Malcolm wouldn't go, well, not with me.'

There was a defiant note in her voice, and she looked round the table, as if to let her friends know that she now knew, what perhaps they'd known for years, that the man who had accompanied her to church every Sunday for umpteen years hadn't been what he had seemed to be. Everyone was listening, some looking at their plates, but none more intently than Alan, whose gaze said, 'Well done, you.'

You could feel his admiration for Janet. Well, Viv could, and maybe Zelda too. Janet said, 'S-seconds anyone?' picking up the ladle.

'Not for me. I think I've had enough.' Zelda was the first to answer.

It wasn't that Alan Loveday ignored Zelda. He didn't ignore any of the women. He talked to the women more than the men, Viv noted. Viv found herself wondering what sort of relationship he'd had with his wife, and at the end of the evening, when they were all in the hall saying their goodbyes, she noted that he held Zelda's hand for several seconds while thanking her for her advice on getting help in the garden. But then he held her own hand, saying he would be in touch, before he kissed Janet's cheek, holding both her hands. They were old friends, she reminded herself, as Janet closed the door on the last guest. Some of the other friends from church had given her a peck. Rona of the boobs had hugged her. 'You must miss him dreadfully, darling.'

Zelda was coming downstairs with her coat on. She'd texted for a taxi, she said.

'Oh, you could have stayed the night.' Janet suggested another coffee while she was waiting. 'There's some left in the pot.'

But Zelda declined, saying the taxi was due any minute. When had she decided she was wasting her time with Alan Loveday? She must get back to Mack and Morag, she said when she got a text to say the taxi was already outside. With a perfunctory thank you to Janet, she left. No hugs. No kisses.

Have I offended her? That was what Viv thought Janet was going to say as she closed the door, but she seemed oblivious to Zelda's slight. She led the way to the sitting room and flopped into a sofa. 'Well, did we fulfil Zelda's requirements? Did she get to know Alan Loveday better to see if she wanted to get to know him better?'

Viv sank into the chair opposite. 'She had the opportunity.'

'But did he rise to her expectations?'

'Dunno, couldn't see from where I was sitting. Sorry.'

But Janet didn't sigh as she usually did at a double entendre, when she got it. She looked thoughtful as she sipped a cup of what must be cold coffee. 'Viv, do you think I'd have been more *perceptive* if I had a filthy mind like yours?' Was this the beginning of a heart-to-heart about her husband? Viv waited, but Janet seemed more interested in Alan Loveday. 'How would you describe him, Viv?'

'Attractive. Affable. Charming?'

Janet sniffed and got up. 'Never trust a charming man, to which I'd add, or a charmless one.' She got up and started gathering glasses a bit too vigorously. 'He didn't bring a bottle, you know.'

'Tightwad. Freeloader. Bad sign.' Viv got up to help, wondering if it would be too late to ring Zelda when she got home.

13

JANET

Next morning Janet closed the door of the dishwasher, carefully. It was just a headache. A hangover.

No need to imagine a brain tumour. She'd had more to drink last night than she'd ever had before so it was only to be expected that she also had a headache like never before. Someone was knocking at the back door. *Please don't.* She opened it, expecting to see Maggie coming round to help clear up, which would have been nice, but it wasn't.

Oh dear.

Alan Loveday proffered a bottle of red. 'Sorry. Forgot last night.' His voice boomed. 'Wouldn't like you to think I'm a tightwad.'

'As if.' She managed a smile and took the bottle.

'Malbec. Very palatable. Thank you.' She put it on the work surface just inside the door.

'Came round the back because your front doorbell wasn't working.'

She noticed his weathered Barbour was getting spattered with rain.

'Thank you very much for last night, by the way.' He turned his collar up. 'Can't remember enjoying myself so much since... you know.'

'I know.' She wished she weren't wearing her old grey dressing gown.

'I know you know.'

'I know you know I know.' Was that appropriate?

He laughed – phew! – and she made a note that he had a sense of humour. Must tell Zelda, who sometimes needed jollying out of the doldrums. But it wasn't so good that he couldn't say 'since my wife died' or even 'passed away'. Poor man, he was still raw. Ought she to offer tea and sympathy? Or coffee? The kettle was coming noisily to the boil. He could see the cafetière. *And I might find out what he thought about Zelda.*

But half an hour later, he was still there, on the sofa in the front room, second coffee in hand, long legs stretched out, and he hadn't mentioned Zelda once. Janet now knew a lot about his daughters, two, his grandchildren, three, his parents, two, both still alive and looking as if they would go forever, and his dog, but not much else. Fortunately the paracetamol she'd taken when she went upstairs to get dressed was working. Was he nervous? Was that why he was talking so much? Or did she only think that because she wasn't used to a man who talked?

'Meal last night, excellent.' That was the second time he'd said.

'It was a joint effort and Zelda did the puddings.' Did. She didn't lie.

'You made it look so effortless. Nine of us, that's a lot.'

'As I said, Viv and Zelda helped.'

'Haven't had so many fresh veg since...' A nerve under his cheekbone twitched as he studied the bottom of his cup.

'So, what about Zelda's idea?' she said gently. 'Getting Viv to help with your garden?'

'I'm going to get in touch with her.'

But with whom? she wondered when he eventually left.

Alan Loveday was lonely, she thought as she walked back down the high street, having done her duty helping with lunches at The Beeches, but without the feel-good spring in her step she usually had after helping the old folk. The *old* old folk, she corrected herself. She wasn't there yet, sans teeth, sans sense, sans everything. *But I will be one day.*

Did Alan Loveday want a new partner? She tried to recall who he'd taken an interest in last night and concluded that it was most people. Zelda yes, but also Rona on his other side, who was married. And what about Viv? Like his wife, the late lamented Penny, she was a keen gardener. Not that Viv was a candidate. If you've had the best you can ignore the rest, she said frequently. But she had said Alan Loveday was attractive and Janet had to concede he was attractive for a man of his age. He had a good head of hair, as Zelda had noted, wasn't overweight, and that brushed cotton shirt looked properly washed and ironed. Did he do that himself? Above all he was kind. He'd been kind last night and he'd cared for Penny when she was dying, in an exemplary way, people said. Well, she had cared for Malcolm, thankful for her old nursing skills. And that had suited them both. When she wasn't professional it hadn't gone down well, like the time he found her weeping into the sink.

'What's the matter? Why are you crying?' He'd sounded cross.

'Because I'm sad that you're dying,' she'd replied, caught off guard.

'But I'm not,' he'd said, angrily. 'Don't be silly.' Though he'd been told he'd only got months left and all his medical documents had 'palliative care' stamped over them. So she'd had to pretend he was getting better when she could see he wasn't. Was her pretending a form of love? She'd thought they loved each other. They weren't ecstatically happy, but who was? They didn't have much sex but who did, after a certain time? It was by mutual agreement, or so she'd thought.

Oh, why, *why* was she having these dreary thoughts on such a beautiful autumn day? The trees along the high street were gorgeously golden and red. She must enjoy the moment, enjoy life while she could. Turning into The Barns, she saw a car parked behind her own in the drive. A swish car with a very presentable man getting out of it. And there was Barbara, garbed in black, looking like one of those daddy-long-legs spiders, letting her little dog pee against the gatepost. Did Malcolm really fancy *her*?

'Hello, Alan,' she said cheerily to dispel the vision of those two together. 'Did you forget something?'

'I've come to get your bell ringing, missus.' He laughed and so did she.

'How very kind!'

Put that in your goose and stuff it, Barbara Thornton. Poison your own life with your nasty vindictive actions, but you're not poisoning mine.

There had been no reply to her kind invitation to tea.

14

VIV

The phone rang on Saturday morning when she was in the kitchen surrounded by grandgirls. It was Alan Loveday, hoping this was a convenient time. Was she free to come around and give him some gardening advice? 'No,' she replied, aware she wasn't sounding 100 per cent professional. 'Not unless you'd like the advice of an opinionated twelve-year-old and two younger siblings.' Felicity, Faith and Fiona had been staying all weekend, while Sally and spouse were in Dubai, having what she hoped was a marriage-reviving holiday. Grandma Viv was supervising the creation of slime soup, blood and guts potatoes and witches' hair spaghetti, in a premature celebration of Halloween. But her lovely kitchen, unlike Nigella's, the originator of the recipes, looked as if it had been used for paintball practice. It was the beginning of half-term, and only two days, thank God – not that she didn't love the darlings – but she'd forgotten how exhausting having three of them together was.

'Granny, Fiona is sticking her finger in the slime.'

'It tastes yuk, Gran.' That was Fiona.

'It's supposed to taste yuk, I think.' Apologising to Alan, she managed to say she thought she could meet him the following

Tuesday afternoon, but would have to check her diary when she could. 'And if you'd like me to double-dig an acre of your garden and plant it with potatoes it will feel like a rest.' He laughed and said she must be fitter than he was and that he had grandchildren too and wouldn't she like his address?

* * *

It was a sparkling day when she set off at two, but when she drew up in front of The Poplars, 24 Lark Drive, the detached red-brick house facing east, was in shadow. Parking on the road outside so she could walk up the drive to the door and get a feel for the plot, she noted the short grass and weed-free drive. It looked as if Alan Loveday was a mower and murderer like most men, but didn't like to get his hands dirty. There were a lot of weeds in the attractive but overgrown raised border, mostly annuals but some mare's tail and ground elder that would take hold if it wasn't dealt with soon. The birds were appreciating the neglect though. She paused to watch a goldfinch clinging to a groundsel stem and a flock of long-tailed tits took off from the golden strands of a magnificent stipa gigantea. Further along a pair of bullfinches were bolder, undeterred by her presence as they crammed beaks with rowan berries as pink as their breasts. It was the lovely sorbus Pink Pagoda. Someone had planted imaginatively but the poor garden badly needed some TLC. The pots by the oak door were full of blackened geraniums.

Now where was the bell? She found it under a rampant wisteria, but it was still working at least. She heard it ringing inside the house as she identified the tangle of leaves beneath the window as a clump of iris reticulata, planted to delight the eye on a winter morning when you opened the door to get the milk in, and still delivered, she noted. As she crouched down to get a closer look she pictured the spiky blue and yellow heads of Katherine Hodgkin iris poking through the snow. She rang again, still not sure what she was going to say to him. Cash she needed, but not more back-breaking work.

'Hope you don't mind canines?' Alan hung onto the collar of a black and white spaniel, straining to greet her as he held open the door. 'Back, Kenny. Come in. Come in.'

Released, the dog bounded ahead to the kitchen and Alan offered tea or coffee, which she declined. Janet had warned he talked a lot.

'Thanks, but I need to get on. We can talk in the garden.'

It backed onto a golf course and the whole plot was about a third of an acre, she estimated, not too much for one fit and active man, which he seemed to be from the way he was hurling sticks for the dog to fetch. Bathed in afternoon sunlight, the back garden, like the front, looked attractive if overgrown. Most of it was set to lawn and shrubs and there was a smart Victorian-style greenhouse from Hartley Botanic, now unused as far as she could see. Would Zelda like to grow pot plants in there or tomatoes? Would this plot inspire a love of gardening? As the dog vanished into the bushes again, she asked about his mower and he said he had a ride-on. When she laughed he looked hurt.

'Sorry, but what do you do for exercise?'

'Golf,' he said. 'And walking the dog. They fill the time.' He turned away to blow his nose.

Oh. Had she been insensitive? Should she say, 'Early days,' or 'It's hard, I know,' because both were true? But before she could decide he turned back to her stuffing a handkerchief into his pocket. Instead of platitudes she went for brisk.

'Ideally, what would you like me to do?'

'Restore it to its former glory?'

'I'm afraid I won't be able to promise that. Not in a morning a week, which is the most I could manage.'

'I know. I know. And I can't turn back the clock. Must move on. Et cetera. Et cetera.'

Alan was clearly hurting.

'There's nothing like gardening for making time pass.'

'Okay.' He straightened his shoulders. 'Just tell me what to do. Prune or plant? Weed or water? The pots by the door, they need... catalogues keep coming, addressed to...' He didn't finish. 'But you're right, I could, *should* do more, and I will, with your help. Keeping busy, that's the key. And if you could give me a morning a week?'

'Give?'

'No, not *give*.' He caught on. 'I'm expecting to pay the rate required for a professional with your reputation.'

But would he? She might have a let-out there, if she wanted a let-out. It was amazing how even the well-heeled expected to pay a pittance for gardening. But when, back in the kitchen, she told him her hourly rate he didn't seem turned off and was perhaps turned on, she found herself thinking as she declined tea or coffee again. He nodded and carried on filling the kettle. There was nothing she could define, not the hint of a pass, but he was very *aware*, looking and listening in a very focussed way. Zelda shouldn't give up hope. There was a gap in the man's life. He didn't *need* a woman to look after him – his black and white Italian kitchen was clean and tidy – but, yes, he wanted one. Possibly to look after. That was an attractive quality in her opinion. She'd loved being looked after by Jack when he'd retired and she was still working.

When Alan went outside to see where his dog was she flicked through her diary. A Muscateers' lunch was coming up, first Friday in November, and it could be tricky, given how things went at the supper party. She got up, saying she would get back to him. Fighting her way out, through the wisteria round the front door, she suggested he make a start himself by cutting all the whippy stems back. 'Then you could open some of those catalogues on the hall table and choose bulbs for these lovely blue pots.'

'Yes. I will. Promise.' He held his hands up in front of him. 'Just get back to me, right?'

Would Jack have been like that? she wondered as she drove off. Looking for her replacement before she was six months gone? Funny how she used to think about that even though he was older and statistically unlikely to outlive her. She used to say to the girls, 'If I go first make sure your dad gets out and meets people.' She didn't like to think of him alone in his shed or study, becoming a complete anorak, which he might well have done. If only he were at home now cooking her something delicious. It was raining, and the wipers weren't working, something else to get fixed, and she did need a cuppa. Then Viv had a good idea, though she did say so herself. Zelda lived round the corner and a catch-up would be brill. They hadn't dissected the dinner party yet.

15

ZELDA

Zelda wasn't there when Viv called.

She was at the salon discussing handing over the everyday running to Carol, her manager, and found Viv's note when she got back. It was on the hall floor by the front door with a pile of travel brochures. She headed for the kitchen and the recycling bin, followed by Mack and Morag. An evening reading about two-for-one cruises in the Med was not what she needed right now. Looking at silver surfers holding hands as they climbed up ancient stairways, or gazed into each other's eyes over a candlelit dinner for two, wouldn't help at all.

The dogs were looking at her pleadingly, ready for their dinner.

'In a minute when I've checked the landline for messages.'

Zilch on the landline. Zilch on her mobile. Zilch on the PC in her mini-study under the stairs. Nothing. Absolutely nothing. Not that she expected him to get in touch. He hadn't asked for her number.

'He doesn't like me. He doesn't want to get to know me better.' She poured herself a consoling glass of Pinot, fed the dogs, then took it back to the sitting room where Mack, then Morag soon joined her.

They snuggled closer, which was good, because she was having a wobble. Alan Loveday was a no-go. It was obvious. He didn't even walk past her house any more. He fancied Janet. That was obvious too. He'd been round to hers with a bottle of wine. A thank you, she'd said in an email, to the three of them, so they must share it soon, but she hadn't said when.

The word wobble used to cheer her up. She'd got a merit mark for saying it once. Funny how she remembered that. The teacher, Miss Truss, had brought a yellow balloon into the classroom and let it rise to the ceiling, then asked the girls to say what it was doing.

'Oscillating,' said one of the clever girls.

'Vibrating,' said another.

Wobbling, thought the young Zelda but didn't dare say, till Miss Truss pointed at her and insisted she say something, and not saying anything became the riskier option. So she said what was in her head, and the teacher clapped her hands. 'Spot on, Griselda. Never use a long word where a short one will do, as George Orwell says.' She became a bit of a favourite after that until she said she was leaving after O levels to be a hairdresser. A *hairdresser*! 'But I thought you'd be a trailblazer, Griselda. I thought you'd do A level English with me.' *Grammar school girls don't become hairdressers. They go to college or university.*

As if. When her sisters' dad had just left her mum for another woman. Mum needed every penny she could scrape together to bring up Gina, aged eight, and Paulina, only six, even the earnings of a hairdresser's apprentice, so there was absolutely no talk of university. Zelda thought about the word trailblazer later. Miss Truss had meant well but obviously saw her, the only black girl in the school – half-caste, that was what they said then – as a representative of an oppressed minority, not as an individual with other pressures besides getting O levels and A levels and going to university.

That would have been great, but owning her own salon where people knew how to deal with hair like hers had been another dream. Her mother's hairdresser hadn't had a clue. Her mother hadn't had a clue. She could still feel her tugging at her hair with a fine-toothed comb, see the big bow she'd stuck on top when she'd given up trying to make it smooth. Mum had *so* wanted her to look good and had made sacrifices so Zelda had nice clothes. 'People will always stare at you, Zelda, so let's make sure you're worth staring at.'

No wonder she couldn't leave the house unless she looked her best. Not that it did any good. Not a word in thirteen days. Not one.

Morag licked her hand. *You shouldn't have walked past his house today.*

'I wondered if he'd gone on holiday.' He hadn't. He'd been busy hacking something back from round his front door. He hadn't looked up.

You can't rely on men.

But deep down she knew there were decent men out there. She just needed to be proactive to find one. It wasn't as if another Harry were going to walk into her life. So, should she try Saga Connections or go for Classic FM Romance or one of the other sites? Someone to go to concerts with would be lovely. She chose Saga first, where there were lots of men, lots of *tactile* men looking for attractive, vivacious females for Long Term Relationships, but not so many women wanting LTR with the tactile men. Why the mismatch? And how could you tell what Affable Romantic and Solvent and Sincere and Tall and Healthy were really like?

Tactile, she guessed, was code for wanting sex. But on closer inspection maybe she was wrong about tactile. Most men and women specified NS. They were looking for companionship. Like her.

That's a good idea. Morag nudged her hand with her cold nose.

Sometimes she thought the dogs had more sense than all the men she'd met put together.

* * *

As she'd decided Alan Loveday was a no-go, it was a surprise to find him on her front doorstep on Sunday morning. When she saw a hazy man-shape through the glass, she assumed it was a delivery man with some wine she'd ordered and shouted that she was coming in a minute. By the time she'd picked the dogs up and carried them into the back, and hurried back to open the door, she was out of breath.

'Oh!' Not a delivery man. Hope stupidly surged. Luckily, she was wearing her new kimono-style dressing gown, a sale bargain from M&S, and not her tired old towelling robe.

'Sorry!' They spoke together, trying to rise above the din of three dogs yapping and howling, the Westies in the kitchen, his spaniel tied up by the gate. 'Why...' they laughed, together '... do we have them?' But she heard him say he had tickets for a concert.

Oh! And that he was inviting her to go with him. Oh again! But she managed a 'Thank you, that would be nice.'

'Songs from the Shows,' he said, holding out a ticket. 'On Friday night. It's for a very good cause.'

'Yes.' She nodded, fearing she'd been too eager. 'Well, better get back to the dogs or they'll scratch the door down.'

But he didn't go, not straight away. 'Worth every penny, I'd say.'

'I'm sure it will be.'

But did he mean the concert? she thought when he'd gone, and she caught sight of the price ticket for her new dressing gown, dangling between her boobs. Did he mean her new dressing gown? And why had she agreed to so eagerly before looking at her diary? Now the date rang a bell and a glance at the kitchen calendar told her why. 'Concert at Corn Exchange' was pencilled in on the last Friday of October. Janet's concert. It was a three-line whip. Her choir was singing to raise money for the hospice, her favourite charity, and Zelda realised she might even have bought herself a ticket already.

Calm down, this might not be a date.

Alan had been vague. She didn't even know if he was calling for her or meeting her there. If she was paying for her own ticket or if he was treating her.

Ask Janet.

Why didn't she want to?

But next day she found herself behind Janet at the checkout in M&S and when she asked, Janet said yes, she'd sold him the tickets. 'We need to sell lots to fill the Corn Exchange. It's our biggest fundraiser for the hospice.'

'Did you ask him to take me?'

'Yes, I thought that's what you'd want me to do. Aren't you going to thank me?'

'Yes, yes, thank you. Trouble is he rushed off before we'd made proper arrangements. I don't even know if he's picking me up...'

'Ask him.' Everything was cut and dried for Janet.

'I haven't got his number.'

'I'll text it to you – see, done!' She put her mobile back in her pocket.

Why was Janet so snippy? So exasperated. So in-a-hurry. As she watched Janet walk to the door, head held high, Zelda wondered how much of Alan Loveday she was seeing.

16

JANET

Janet was seeing a lot of Alan Loveday.

Too much really. When she got home she was relieved his BMW wasn't in the drive. It was very convenient getting jobs done without going to the trouble of finding a tradesman or resorting to DIY, but it was becoming awkward. She paid for materials when she could, but more often than not he said he was sure he had something at home that would be 'just the ticket' or even right there in the boot of his car, a battery or a fuse or the perfect piece of wood or a nail. Or a *screw*. Alive now to double entendre, she was disconcerted. She was beginning to feel beholden.

She refrained from pointing things out, but he was very observant. When they had been having a cup of tea and a flapjack last Monday – he'd called in with a bulb for the outside light he'd noticed wasn't working on Friday – he'd noted wires hanging below the kitchen cupboards, a couple of drawers that didn't close properly and a leaking tap in the downstairs loo. On Wednesday afternoon – it had been pouring down – she'd opened the front door to see him on the other side of a waterfall. It was, he'd said when he'd dashed inside and taken off his coat, a blocked gutter causing the downpour, but he would go out and unblock it as soon as it stopped raining. But it had rained all afternoon so she'd had to stay in and miss her patchwork class. And here he was now, before she'd even opened the door, parking his car in the drive.

'You're blocking me in! I've got to go out later to French!'

'Won't be long! Come to fix the dripping tap!' He held his toolbox aloft.

Two hours later he was still there because she'd offered him mushroom soup. How could she not when he saw it bubbling on the stove and commented on the aroma? She should have asked him to come back later in the week, but it was too late now. Too late also to go to her French class, so she might as well stay at home and do the accounts for the choir's AGM. On the plus side she managed to ask him what he'd done for a living, because she had been wondering.

'A painter...'

How exciting!

'... and decorator.' He laughed. 'Don't worry, ma'am.' He tugged his forelock. 'I'll always use the tradesman's entrance.'

'Don't be silly.' Did he think she was a snob? To change the subject, she asked him how Viv was getting on with his garden. Brilliantly, he said, she had made a difference already, with a little help from himself following her detailed instructions. He listed the things Viv had told him to do, which he said he'd done of course, he didn't dare not! So, he thought Viv was bossy, but what was his opinion of Zelda? She mentioned seeing her in M&S and told him that Zelda wanted to know if he was picking her up or meeting her at the Corn Exchange.

'Oh. I'll pick her up, of course.' He said their dogs had made conversation difficult. 'I'll text her if you give me her number.' She

obliged and at last he reached for his toolbox to fix the tap before
going to meet his granddaughters from school at 3.15. 'Mustn't be
late.' One of his daughters lived in the next village.

As he went into the downstairs loo to fix the tap, she thought
about a job that really *did* need doing, the leaking shower in her en
suite. It was keeping her awake at night and wasting water. If only
she'd had it fixed pre-Alan, there wouldn't be a problem. The
Muscateers had their own very reliable plumber called Trevor, who
came promptly if asked.

So why haven't you asked? Because Alan's feelings would be hurt.
How would he know? He might drop in while Trevor was here.
He might not. Ring Trevor. But Trevor has a hefty call-out charge.
So why not ask Alan? Because. She slammed the dishwasher shut
to bring an end to this ridiculous inner dialogue.

But it continued.

Ask him now, while he's here. Can't! *Why not?* Because he would
have to go into my bedroom to look! her inner voice shrieked
hysterically. That was it. She didn't want a man in her bedroom.
Any man.

'Penny for them?' Penny! Had she missed a heartfelt revelation?
He looked amused, so maybe not. 'You were miles away.'

'No. I was...' *upstairs...* But the word didn't come out.

So he drove away to pick up his granddaughters, just as Barbara
emerged from behind the gatepost with her little dog.

'Your new friend?' Barbara actually smiled.

'Y-yes, Barbara.' *And I've been in bed with him all morning.* The
thought was almost as astonishing as Barbara's smart appearance
and smile. When had Barbara last *spoken*? But seize the day. 'Did
you get my letter?'

'Yes, yes, I did.'

Janet half expected her to add, 'Thank you, Mrs Carmichael.'

Wearing a white shirt and charcoal suit, she was the bursar again, addressing a parent whose signature she required. 'And I would like to accept your kind invitation.'

17

ZELDA

Zelda checked her face again in the mirror by the front door.

Alan Loveday had texted to say he would pick her up at a quarter to seven. It felt more like a date now, though that added as much pressure as it removed. She'd spent all afternoon trying on one thing and then another, before deciding on her old but still smart black velvet trousers, with a new black and white tunic top, and her favourite diamanté and jet drop earrings. By a quarter to seven she'd been ready for an hour, when the dogs, on watch at the sitting-room window, started barking before the doorbell rang. Slinging her long faux-Astrakhan coat round her shoulders, she opened the door.

'Your carriage awaits.' Alan looked very night-at-the-opera, in black DJ and long white scarf draped raffishly around his neck, and the look he gave her was approving. His black BMW was parked outside. Was her mournful neighbour watching? She felt waves of disapproval emanating from number twelve as Alan opened the passenger door and helped her inside, holding out his hand as she lowered herself into the seat. She just hoped that getting out wouldn't twist her back.

As he loped round to the driver's side and started the engine, it felt more and more like a proper date. But what was dating protocol these days? Should she offer to pay for her ticket? Would he be offended if she bought the interval drinks? There would be time at this rate for drinks before the show. There wasn't much traffic. At least she didn't have to worry about what to say. Janet and Zelda had both said he couldn't say his late wife's name, but he seemed to have got over that. Penny liked a good musical, he said twice, and light opera. Penny sang in *Oklahoma* and *South Pacific* and *The Desert Song*. Penny, she deduced, had belonged to the local amateur dramatics club. As he listed all the shows he and Penny had seen, she decided she would definitely suggest a drink before the concert. It would steady any remaining nerves and she'd say it was her treat.

When they arrived at the Corn Exchange, Alan pulled up quite suddenly outside the main doors, on double yellow lines. It was raining, he said, so if she'd like to get out and go inside, he'd go and park in the multistorey, and join her as soon as he could in the bar. Well, that was what she thought he said, as she levered herself out when he didn't come round to open the door, and she replied, 'Okay, I'll get the drinks in. What will you have?' But he drove off without answering. She went in and left her coat in the downstairs cloakroom, before going upstairs to the bar on the first floor, where there was already a long queue. Should she get in it? Yes, she decided. Service was notoriously slow at the Corn Exchange, so if she got in it now Alan would probably arrive before she had to order.

But he didn't.

Zelda bought a glass of Sauvignon for herself and a glass of Rioja for him, because that was what he'd drunk at Janet's, and soon after that the bell rang. So there she was, standing with a glass of white in one hand and a red in the other, wondering what to do. She kept looking round hoping to see him, especially as most people were leaving the bar. He shouldn't be hard to spot with his white hair above the other heads, but she couldn't see him anywhere. By the time the second bell went she'd finished her glass, so she put the empty on the bar and made her way to the circle carrying his, reasoning that if he'd said meet in the bar their seats were probably in the circle, so he might be waiting at that entrance.

But he wasn't.

As she peered into the auditorium hoping to see him looking for her, she saw that the choir was already on stage and most of the orchestra in front of it, some of whom were tuning up. 'Ticket?' said a lady usher and she was about to explain when Viv appeared, red-faced and breathless. She'd just galloped upstairs, she said. 'Sorry. Should have got in touch. Mad week. Explain later. Come on. We're in the stalls.'

We?

As she followed Viv downstairs, not fast because she was still holding the glass of red, she felt anxious. Had she got this completely wrong? 'We' was Viv and Alan, now clearly visible at the end of row E. Their three seats were together by the aisle. The only consolation was that she wouldn't have to squeeze past a whole row of people to get to hers.

Not a date, then.

Alan stood up to let them in as the lights went down, saying 'Sorry about the mix-up.' Viv went first and sat in the seat furthest from his and she followed, carefully, because of the glass in her hand. As the orchestra broke into 'There's No Business Like Show Business,' she said, 'Here, I got this for you,' and handed him the glass, or thought she did. But it ended up in his lap. The only slight relief was that he was wearing dark trousers and it didn't show up, not down there, not in the dark, but it did show on his long white scarf. He looked as if his throat had been cut.

'I'm so sorry.' She wanted to die.

He said, 'It doesn't matter.' But it did.

Viv, quick thinking, reached across with a handful of tissues and he did some dabbing. Tissue after tissue turned red as Zelda sat by his side rigid and helpless. But she couldn't very well dab for him. When she did manage to move and find more tissues in her bag, he waved them away. Then he sat looking straight ahead till the interval when he said sorry, but he had to go home and change. Would Viv be so kind as to take Zelda home? So, like another song they heard, it was over before it began.

18

JANET

I didn't pour wine over his private parts.

Janet was having a well-deserved lie-in on Monday morning, but her Earl Grey wasn't giving her the usual early-morning lift. She should be on a high, basking in the satisfaction of a job well-done. She should be relaxing after weeks of frenzied activity leading up to the concert. It was a triumph: two thousand pounds for the hospice, two new baritones for the choir if they passed their auditions and almost everyone in tune. The committee were delighted.

But Zelda wasn't.

Zelda was unhappy. Zelda was cross. Zelda blamed *her*. But had she not done her best? Had she not fixed her up not once but twice with an opportunity to attract Alan Loveday? She had sat them side by side on two occasions and it wasn't her fault if he was not attracted to Zelda. The phone rang and she saw it was Viv on the bedside landline. 'Zelda's in pieces, Janet. She hasn't heard from Alan since he vanished at the interval.'

'Lucky her.'

'She's upset.'

'I'm upset that she's upset – with me!' She got out of bed and drew back her beautiful curtains, half expecting to see the man in question walking up the drive looking for overhanging branches or slipping roof tiles or sliding fence panels, anything he could lop or stop or nail.

Viv went on. 'She wants to pay him for the ticket and the dry-cleaning but he's not replying to her texts. Janet, are you still there?'

'Of course. Tell Zelda to give me the cash next time she sees me and I will offer it to him when I see him next. If he declines it will swell the hospice funds.'

'When *are* you seeing him next, Janet?'

'I don't know, Viv. That's the problem. I never know when he's coming.'

Pause. For a snigger? No, a reproach. 'Janet, don't you think it's time to take control? Tell him to come only when invited.'

Take control! That would be her mantra for the rest of the day.

And it was – until Alan turned up just when she needed him.

* * *

Why are my toes cold?

Knife in hand, Janet was chopping mushrooms for a beef carbonnade when she saw water round her feet, and made a rapid deduction.

She switched off the washing machine, unplugged it and turned off the water by grasping the sadly named stopcock.

Water was still gushing out so her next plan was to ring Trevor, the plumber, but there was a hitch – Trevor was on holiday. For a fortnight. Trevor was sorry. But not as sorry as she was. She couldn't do without her washer for a fortnight. What now? She was thinking when there was a knock at the door, and there he was.

'What have we here?' Within seconds, Sir Alan of the Toolbox had diagnosed a leaking door seal, emptied the washer, stripped

out the perished seal and departed with it in his hand, saying he
might catch the suppliers before closing if he was very quick.

It was half past four.

After he'd gone Janet noticed the plastic Tesco bag on the
work surface and peered inside, recoiling at the smell of the
contents. And the sight. Why had he brought his trousers here?
His stained and smelly trousers. She could not wash them
because her washing machine was broken, not that he'd known
that when he'd bundled them into a bag and brought them to her
back door. Why here? Why her? Why hadn't he put the trousers
into his own washing machine or taken them to Zelda's or to a
dry-cleaner's? There was a Johnsons in Waitrose and maybe Tesco
too. Why had he waited nearly three whole days before doing
anything about the stain when the chances of removing it were
minimal?

But she had a go.

Because there was no such thing as a free washing machine
repair. Or a free porch-light repair, or a free unblocking of her
gutters. Because she owed him for all the jobs he'd done for her and
she didn't like owing him. As she reached for tongs and lowered the
relevant part of the garment into the washing up bowl, she remembered a handy tip she'd read about. It was the perfect use for a
bottle of unspectacular Chardonnay, and as she poured it over the
stain she hoped time would work its promised wonders.

Leaving the bowl in the sink with the trouser legs dangling over
the side, she thought about having a glass herself, but no, it was
only five o'clock and she had a bit of a headache. She always had a
bit of a headache these days. A broken washing machine was not a
crisis, she told herself, but she felt shaky enough to have to go and
sit down in the sitting room. She felt a bit dizzy. She should perhaps
consult the GP again, but last time he'd made her feel like a
hypochondriac. Brain tumours were not an inherited disease, he'd

said, when she'd told him about Aunt Flo's, and her headaches were tension headaches. He advised relaxation.

She was tense now because half an hour ago she knew exactly what she was doing for the rest of the day and now she didn't. She'd planned to cook the carbonnade and divide it into eight portions, eating one and freezing the rest. But now she didn't know when Alan Loveday would return or how long he would stay. Should she invite him to stay for a meal as a thank you? Had he seen her Le Creuset casserole bubbling away on the hob, and must she now cook carbs as well, potatoes or pasta or rice? She'd planned to have broccoli. Oh, where was that bottle of Sauvignon? It might relieve the tension.

Her knight in shining combos returned at six o'clock, triumphant. Not only had he reached the suppliers before closing time, he had also acquired the last door seal on the planet, and manoeuvred his trusty steed through horrendous traffic jams. And now – she saw him notice the bottles of Belgian beer on the side – he had a mouth, excuse the expression, like the bottom of a parrot's cage.

'Oh. Would you like one? I bought it for a carbonnade.'

'Smells great.' He drank from the bottle.

'You could stay if you like.'

'Love to. Oh, you found them!' He noticed his trousers in the sink.

'They're marinating.'

He laughed. 'Hope we're not eating them too? Sorry, there was no time to explain, but I knew you'd know what to do and you're always saying you'd like to do something for me.'

Am I?

While manoeuvring the new door seal into place, he apologised for not turning up after the show on Friday night and asked if she'd heard what happened. She had of course, but said she'd love to hear his perspective on it, while marvelling silently that he wasn't swearing. Fixing the seal was proving tricky and Malcolm, not a curser, would have uttered an expletive or two by now. But no. As to Friday night, it was all his fault – heave – he had been so stupid – heave – not telling Zelda where they were sitting – heave – so the poor lady had gone upstairs – heave – where she'd been kind enough to get him a drink from the bar. Big heave. He was mortified when he dropped the glass, plastic fortunately, and was so glad it had gone over him, not her. Janet marvelled again. A man who took the blame on himself! Was he a saint?

No.

Later, when they were eating, he asked if perhaps Zelda might have had a drink or two before the concert. She said Zelda would have had the glass she bought when she bought one for him. He said Zelda had seemed very vivacious when he picked her up, not that he was implying anything.

She said Zelda was very vivacious, a very lively person and very kind and very hard-working and generous. All for one. She didn't like his tone and regretted doing pan-fried potatoes and crispy dumplings. The man was presuming. He was too cocksure and his trousers too nonchalant, sloshing around in her mended washing machine. He was too close, the table too small, the room too hot. She should have added the table extension. Zelda probably did have a glass before he picked her up, understandably. She would be nervous going on a date for the first time in many years. Men made you nervous. Especially this one. Why was he looking at her like that, as if she'd said something amusing?

'Very good dumplings.' He waved his fork.

Take control.

Her sympathy for Zelda grew along with her shame. She had been hasty and judgemental, as she was prone to be. She should have told Zelda that Viv would be at the concert too, in the same row, that she'd sold him three tickets, but she'd been very busy, and she'd thought Viv would mention it. But Viv was busy too. They were all busy. They lived busy stressful lives. Well, if he disapproved of busy women who sometimes had a glass or two to help them unwind, she knew what to do. She stood up. 'I'd like a glass of red with this.'

She fetched the bottle of Malbec.

19

VIV

It was the first Friday again – November! – and she'd booked a table at The Ship. Would the others turn up though? That was the question. Neither of them had replied to her texts. Was Zelda still speaking to Janet? Was Janet speaking to Zelda? Was Zelda still speaking to *her*? Like the weather, things had been frosty since the concert.

Alan Loveday wasn't here this morning, thank heavens, inter-rupting her every five minutes to burble on. He'd rung while she was still eating breakfast to say he had to take his granddaughters to school, but should be back mid-morning. Just in case he wasn't, he'd put her cheque under one of the blue pots in the greenhouse. He had emptied the blue pots and washed them and filled them with fresh compost as per instructions so they were ready for her to plant up when she got the bulbs. He had delegated that task to her so she'd ordered a new variety from George Beaumont. If Alan wasn't back for coffee, and even if he was, she would skip the break and leave early for lunch. She sent another text to Janet and Zelda.

See you at The Ship 1 p.m. Yes? X

Well, if they weren't speaking to each other they could at least listen to her good news, an invitation to give a series of lectures at the retirement centre. Seemed a talk she'd given recently, Death in the Garden – it was about poisonous plants – had got good feedback and requests for more. The new course, which she thought she might call The Art of Gardening, would show how horticulture was depicted in the arts, and be more of a challenge. She'd have to do a lot of new research but that would be interesting, and lovely daughter Em had already said she'd help. She'd be paid, not a lot, but every little... A text pinged in.

Bulbs ready. Can drop them off if you like. George.

She texted back.

Perfect timing. Am at The Poplars, 24 Lark Drive till 12.30. Could you bring them here? Thanks. Viv.

As long as he didn't stay too long. George was another talker and a bit of a flirt.

* * *

'As sprightly as ever, Ms Halliday.' He kissed her cheek when she'd got to her feet and straightened up. She was tackling the narrow front border by the door.

'Quite spry yourself, Mr Beaumont.'

George searched her face as he always did. 'How are you?' He'd known Jack well. The two had drunk together sometimes as well as doing business.

'I'm okay, thank you.'

'Good to hear it, and glad to see you're rescuing Katharine Hodgkin from the dreaded equisetum arvense.'

'Is that who she is? I hoped so. The mare's tail's a pain.'

'Penny bought the bulbs from me some years back, an inspired choice.'

'You or the bulbs?' But she mustn't flirt with George, not that she was in danger of being taken seriously. He was long-time married to Annie, who was also his business partner. Lucky Annie Beaumont. George was good on the eye too for a sixty plus. 'Bred any new roses lately, George?' But she shouldn't have asked that, not if she wanted to get on. New hybrids were his obsession and he lingered to tell her about his latest creation, till she said she must get on and plant the bulbs he'd brought. They were the lovely new Green Star tulips, whose elegant white petals splashed with green would look great in the blue pots set off with dark green ivy round the base.

Later, she found Alan's cheque in the greenhouse under one of the blue pots as promised, stapled to a note telling her where she could find a hidden house-key, so she could go inside and make herself a coffee. Kind, but she'd brought a flask, and trusting, too trusting. She put the cheque in her pocket, still attached to the note he'd written. Daft to leave instructions for finding his key to a passing burglar.

* * *

Zelda's car wasn't in The Ship's car park when she arrived, only Janet's Fiat, so Viv was relieved to find them both inside, at a table by the window looking not-unfriendly. There was a bottle of Prosecco on the table.

'You're late,' they said in unison.

'I was working at Alan Loveday's,' she said tentatively.

'No worries, you may relax.' Janet nodded at the bottle. 'Just one? I have apologised to Zelda for my part in last Friday's debacle and we have moved on. We are celebrating our reconciliation.'

But were they as reconciled as Janet seemed to think? Zelda studied the menu intently when it came, and only opened up when Janet went to the bar to give their orders. She said Janet had rung that morning and insisted on picking her up and having a heart-to-heart.

'She did most of the talking, insisting that last Friday's debacle was her fault not Alan's, but they should both have made things clearer et cetera blah blah blah. Anyway—' Zelda drained her glass '—as I've decided to move on...'

'You have, really?' Viv cheered up.

'If Janet wants him...'

'You think she does?'

'I'm certain of it.'

'She *is* seeing a lot of him...'

Janet came back before they could compare perceptions, and they switched to a safer topic, Janet's imminent trip to see Grant in New Zealand. She was flying to Christchurch that night to reassure herself that the family hadn't been harmed by the earthquake in September, and because it was over two years since she'd seen Grant – when Malcolm died – and even longer since she'd seen her grandchildren. And of course, she planned to tell Grant what she thought about his intervention at his father's funeral.

'You haven't already?' Zelda spluttered Prosecco.

'I thought it best to do it in person.'

'Well—' Zelda wiped her mouth on a tissue '—I think I'd let it go now, Janet, and simply focus on being the perfect guest.'

Viv couldn't help agreeing. Janet had been persuaded to stay with her son, in his house, not in a hotel, so she needed to tread carefully.

'But I thought you both said I should speak my mind?' Janet, clearly perplexed, looked from one to the other.

Zelda nodded. 'At the time perhaps, but probably not now. How long are you staying, two weeks, nearly three? That's a long time to stay in someone's home. My advice is don't be critical. Ever. Praise, praise, praise.'

Again, Viv agreed.

'But you two have convinced me I should be more open and honest.' Janet looked more perplexed. 'I've been trying to change.'

Janet had changed a lot. Hair, figure, clothes, everything was different. The long cardigan she was wearing today, zingy stripes in heather shades, looked like a Kaffe Fassett, and she hadn't knitted it herself. But that wasn't all. Her personality was less buttoned-up. Unfortunately, sometimes when she did unbutton, she could burst out, like boobs from a tight bodice suddenly unlaced.

Viv, sipping water now, smiled at her own thought, and relaxed as Janet and Zelda moved to safer territory, what Janet was going to wear. She hadn't got a lot to say on that subject. Their food arrived as Zelda was saying she'd read that November was the perfect month to go to New Zealand, weather wise. 'It's the last bare shoulder month or maybe the first.' The two of them laughed about that. Bare shoulders they did not do, or arms, heaven forbid.

'Why not if it's warm?' Viv ventured an opinion. 'Fuck the fashion police.'

'Not fashion, my personal choice, Viv.' Janet picked at her risotto. 'What is concealed by these sleeves will remain concealed.'

'And mine!' Zelda tucked into her halibut.

Then suddenly Janet stood up. 'You haven't admired my denims, first pair ever, bought with backpacking in mind, the solo trips I'm going to take while I am there.' She sat down again. 'By the way, I shall not stay with the family more than four days at a time. Fish and guests stink after? You know that proverb? See, I'm still moving on.'

Janet certainly was, but what about Zelda? Viv observed, discreetly she hoped, as the two of them carried on discussing the various parts of their bodies they would never expose, arms, upper legs, the whole lot, it would seem, in Zelda's case. She would not be 'getting her kit off' for anyone.

'Nor me!' Janet laughed.

'But, Zelda...' *you're about to start dating again* – Viv tried to intervene, but couldn't get a word in edgeways.

Zelda agreed with Janet. Janet agreed with Zelda again. Viv needn't have worried about a bust-up. It was all for one and one for all big time, or maybe all for two, seeing as her friends seemed to have forgotten she was there. Now Zelda was asking Janet how she was getting to the airport and offering to take her. She was going to stay with an aunt in Croydon that weekend and could drop her off.

'Thank you, Zelda, I'll let you know,' Janet said, as if it were the end of a job interview.

Then she started fumbling about in her bag and Viv got an 'I told you' look from Zelda, who suddenly remembered she was there. It was interesting to say the least. Janet, red-faced, came out of her handbag, put cash on the table, and said sorry but she really must be going as she still had lots to do, including having Barbara Thornton round for a cup of tea.

'She accepted my invitation,' Janet went on as she stood up, 'didn't I say?'

'No, you didn't.' Viv found her voice. 'Still don't know why you invited her.'

'Well—' Janet buttoned her coat '—I like to think my gesture of forgiveness has brought about a reciprocal change of heart.' With that she was gone, before the others could say bon voyage, her risotto hardly touched.

'See!' said Zelda. '*He's* taking her to Heathrow.' There was no need to ask who. '*And* she's got the hots for him.'

'Proof?'

'Her face.'

'Fuchsia.' Viv had to agree. 'But why does she keep saying she's trying to discourage him?'

'Because she thinks she is, Viv.' Zelda sniffed. 'Janet may not be deceiving us, but she's certainly deceiving herself.'

* * *

Janet

Janet, driving home, was in turmoil.

Why didn't I tell them? Why did I *lie*? Not about Barbara. She was coming for a cup of tea, but Janet hadn't got lots to do; her bags were packed, ready in the hall by the front door. Now *she* was hastening the demise of The Muscateers as she herself had predicted, by deception and subterfuge. Good relationships were based on openness and mutual disclosure, not on secrets; she knew that now. *But if I told them Alan was taking me to Heathrow they would think things. They would discuss it and come to the wrong conclusions.*

What do you think they are doing now?

Oh dear! She nearly drove back to the pub to tell them exactly what had happened while they were sharing that bottle of Malbec. *He offered to take me to Heathrow. I declined. We had another glass. He offered again. I accepted. I changed my mind, that's all.* Getting to Heathrow by train was a drag. His offer was too good to miss. He had a lovely comfortable car with a heated passenger seat. There was no great mystery.

* * *

Viv

'And he's got the hots for her.' Zelda drained her glass. 'When she was on stage, he couldn't take his eyes off her. That's why he didn't see me giving him the wine.'

Viv ordered more coffee.

'The best I can say for her is that she didn't do it on purpose.' Zelda gathered steam. 'I'll give her the benefit of the doubt. She invited him to that dinner party on my account, but changed tack, driven by forces unknown, to Janet anyway.'

Viv agreed again. 'But what now? For you, I mean?'

'Get back on the horse?' Zelda raised two fingers in the direction of the departed Janet. 'Find other fish to fry? I've already signed up with an online dating site.'

Viv didn't voice her instant doubts. 'In which case you must tell me when you go on a date. In case you meet a psychopath.'

Zelda sighed. 'Now you're sounding like Janet.'

'You were sounding like her earlier.' Viv lowered her voice. 'What was all that not-getting-your-kit-off about?'

'What I said.'

'But why, Zelda? You've got a great figure. Okay.' She made inverted commas in the air. 'For. Your. Age. But I've been in a few changing rooms with you. You look good. What's the problem?'

'Testicles.' Zelda's voice was low, which was as well, as there were full tables close by. 'Not my body. Theirs. All that wrinkly reptilian skin in the nether regions. Till the tortoise pops out of its shell. I've had enough of it, Viv.'

'But—' Viv kept her voice down too '—don't you think most men on dating sites think sex is part of the package?'

'No. Have a look at this.' Zelda went into her bag and then handed her a magazine open at the dating page. 'See, most men, and women in fact, specify Good Sense Of Humour and No Sex.' She pointed at a preponderance of GSOH and NS among the small ads.

Oh dear. Should she tell her? Zelda would be mortified, but she had to know. Viv waited for the waiter delivering their coffees to leave. 'Zelda, sorry, but you're wrong, NS means Non-Smoker.'

She snatched the magazine back.

'No harm done.' Viv couldn't help smiling. 'But maybe study the key at the bottom of the page to see what all the other initials mean. Here, drink your coffee. At least you know now.' This woman needed a savvy friend.

'I'm worse than Janet, but...' Zelda uncovered her face and defended her view. There *were* men out there looking for companionship only, as she was. Men like Harry, who'd gone off sex when he got prostate trouble. 'He was devastated till I told him I was just as happy with cuddles and... well, I won't go into detail... And don't go thinking I've been traumatised or anything, Viv. It isn't PTSD. More a case of BTDT.'

Now Viv needed a translation.

'Been There Done That. I've been married three times, Viv, and I didn't live in a nunnery between times. Now I'm looking for someone I can talk to, or not talk to, who I can go out with or stay in with, watch TV with or play a game of Scrabble. Shared interests, that's what's important at this stage in our lives.'

To Viv's relief Zelda accepted her offer of help with online dating. They would draw up a shortlist of candidates together and she would be on standby if and when Zelda got a date. By the time they left the pub, they had a plan of action.

* * *

It was getting dark though it was only mid-afternoon, and a few fireworks lit up the sky as Viv dropped Zelda off, reminding them both it was 5 November. Viv put her foot down once she was on the bypass. She still had another forty miles once she got home. Sally, in Desborough, was expecting her for a bonfire supper, expecting her to cook the bangers and mash, that was. That was how it was these days, Sally permanently fraught. Was her marriage on the rocks? Steve was away a lot.

When Viv got home there were a couple of messages waiting for her, one long and rambling from Alan Loveday, thanking her for the work she'd done and asking if he could come round and see her pergola as he was thinking of getting one. Janet had said hers was lovely, blah. Okay, that would bring in some cash. And, oh yes, something else, he'd like to pick up the note the cheque was stapled to – if she'd happened to take it too? As there was something important, and private actually, on the back. He sounded nervous, but he'd filled the voice-box before he could finish. Oh dear. What could that be? She felt for the cheque in her Barbour pocket...

20

ZELDA

Determined to keep a clear head, Zelda resisted the booze. With a cup of tea instead she settled on the sofa with her laptop, reassuring the Westies who joined her, one on either side, as she logged in to Perfect Partners. 'I won't look at anyone who doesn't like you. Shared interests, that's the thing, and dogs are top of my Likes list.' She was getting to grips with the jargon now. Username? Password? Yes, she knew both of those. The screen was filling up with Short Profiles, dozens of passport-sized photographs of men looking for women.

Her tea was cold by the time she'd gone through them all. Only one appealed, the guy in the top right-hand corner with the short beard and white wavy hair. His eyes were kind and she liked his pseudonym. History Man. Everyone did pseudonyms. She was Vintage Champagne, which she hoped was honest. She was bubbly most of the time and she was definitely vintage, even more vintage than most people on this site, which was exclusively for over-fifties. She'd decided to be honest about her age and hoped others were too. History Man was a few years younger than she was, but his 'preferred age-range' included hers, so he was a realist, which made a change. Most men in their sixties or even seventies wanted women ten or twenty years younger. History Man was a widower who liked reading and visiting places of historical interest and, a big plus, he was local, lived in the same town, in fact. And they were 86.5 per cent compatible according to the agency's highly scientific psychological assessment!

So what do I do next? Rate him? Add him to my list of Possibles? If she Rated him, would he know? That was what she needed to know – and here was the answer. 'Your Rating of History Man is private and only visible to you.' Good, but first she needed to look at his Full Profile with his list of Likes and Dislikes and his description of his Ideal Mate. But should she Favourite him first, before doing that, so she didn't lose him among all the rest? Words didn't mean what they did in real life, that was the trouble. 'Favouriting' seemed to mean 'earmarking for later', which she'd like to do because more profiles were coming in. If she looked at them now, would she lose History Man? Was Favouriting 'private' and 'only visible' to her too like Rating? She assumed it was, because none of the others she had Favourited in the past had contacted her. And she hadn't contacted them, thinking better of it when she'd read their Full Profiles. Then she'd unfavourited them, hoping they wouldn't know as she didn't want to hurt anyone's feelings.

Here was History Man's Full Profile.

'Interesting, educated, active, creative and achieving male who enjoys feminine company.' Why did he say 'feminine' and not 'female'? 'Adventurous in earlier years, when leisure time was taken up with mountaineering in Europe and trekking in the Himalayas, but ready to settle down now.' Well, he had a good opinion of himself, but that was better than low self-esteem. That was Igor's problem despite being a very successful chef. But was she clever enough for History Man? His Ideal Mate was 'A person who has good self-awareness and who has travelled as a person if not geographically.' Well, she was more self-aware than some people she could think of.

She favourited History Man, to study later. But what was this? A message from him, a reply already?

Let's meet for coffee, Vintage Champagne. History Man.

But she hadn't sent him a message to reply to even though she had been *thinking* about sending him a message. Were his hands on the keys at the same time as hers? Was he Liking her at the same time as she was Liking him? How exciting! Fate was bringing them together!

She took a break to make fresh tea and then found his Full Profile again. 'I am a retired public-school history teacher who now gives classes in local and family history.' A history teacher! She loved history! 'I am a thoughtful, caring optimist who likes country walks and log fires and pub grub and I'm looking for a thoughtful and caring companion to share the travails of life's sometimes difficult journey.'

'Looking for a companion' was good, and so was 'sharing the travails' but liking log fires wasn't helpful. They all liked log fires but would they clean the grate if they had one? None of the profiles said, 'I'm a selfish sod with two previous wives to support and I'm looking for someone to look after me in my old age.' But at least he didn't say he was tactile.

So far, she'd had nothing for her fifteen pounds a month and that was the reduced rate for signing up for six months. It was a bit humiliating. No one had shown the slightest interest in meeting. There had been phone calls, some of them lengthy, but none had resulted in an offer to meet. She had nothing to lose, well, only another rebuff. But she'd survived one of those already and she could rebuff too if necessary. It wasn't as if she had to go far to meet History Man. So, with a deep breath, she messaged back.

Meeting for coffee would be convivial. Where do you suggest?

And he messaged straight back.

The Wheatsheaf at 11 a.m. tomorrow?

She paused.

Why The Wheatsheaf? It was out of town, only three or four miles, but she'd have to get in the car to get there. And why so soon? Was he desperate? But why not? She must be positive.

'I've got a date!'

Later, finding both dogs on her bed, she assured them she would be careful and texted Viv to let her know the details, as the guidelines instructed. Viv replied from her daughter's house.

Great, Zelda! That's the spirit! Coming home early tomorrow. Will be on standby. Know Wheatsheaf well, all low beams and settles, quite dark. Can come and observe discreetly if you like. Sitting in corner in dark glasses.

That would not be necessary.

Thanks, Viv. Good to know you'll be on the end of phone but that's enough.

Oh, here was Viv again.

You're well rid of Mr Love-Not, by the way. Have proof he's a total shite. Hope not too late to warn Janet.

Warn Janet? Why? She was on her way to New Zealand.

21

JANET

Turbulence. Why wasn't the sign on? Why wasn't the steward here? Janet was up in the air in every sense. She couldn't settle. Her expensive first-class seat wasn't as comfortable as promised and she should have had some fizz by now. It was very annoying. She ought to be luxuriating in her extravagance, not analysing a hug. Or trying not to analyse it. What, after all, was a hug these days when people, other people, jumped into bed with one other when they hardly knew each other's names? A hug, a friendly, encouraging, goodbye hug, that was all it was.

Alan had come into the terminal with her, after parking the car, and she was, she had to admit, grateful for his assistance. Free of her luggage, she should have been feeling less fraught, but she wasn't. She was tense. Nervous. Jittery. Tired. It was late evening and she didn't know which way to turn, literally. It was very confusing. There were so many people, so many *signs*. Why couldn't they use *words*?

She'd been to airports before of course, lots of times, post-Malcolm. She was a seasoned traveller, but in organised groups so she'd just had to follow the leader. But now she needed to think for herself. Should she go to Security next or Passport Control? The girl behind the check-in desk had just told her, but she'd already forgotten. She'd been dithering and, yes, almost tearful, when Alan had taken hold of her shoulders, looked her straight in the eye and said, 'Janet, you'll be all right. You're a very competent woman.' Then he'd pulled her towards him and held her close, so she could feel the heat of his body, and his heart beating against hers and, yes, his lips on the top of her head. Then he'd pulled back and pointed to Passport Control saying, 'That way. Off with you.' And when she'd hesitated he'd said, 'Go, woman,' and patted her bottom.

Although thinking about it now, he might not have. It could have been the woman behind her in the queue bumping her with her bag, which looked far too big for hand luggage. Yes, that was most likely it. She must have imagined it. Viv and Zelda were into hugging and kissing, she'd noticed early on, cheek-kissing or air-kissing, and she was a kisser now too, most of the time, with them. Everyone was. But did Alan Loveday want *more*? That was what was so worrying. Had he read *more* into her acceptance of a lift than she'd intended? Had she given the wrong signals?

She had tried to pre-empt any sense of obligation. When he'd offered a lift to Heathrow she'd said she wouldn't let him take her unless she paid for the petrol or diesel. *Take her.* Even as the words had come out of her mouth, she'd seen herself swooning in the arms of a periwigged suitor, bursting out of her bodice. She'd hardly dared look up in case he'd taken it the wrong way – they'd just finished the beef carbonnade – but when she had dared he'd seemed totally absorbed skewering a crispy dumpling on the end of his fork. And when he did look up, mouth full, he said eventually that she'd already paid him several times over with all the delicious meals she'd cooked for him. Up to the goodbye hug at Heathrow she'd managed to keep him at arm's length, literally. Managed wasn't the right word; there was no managing to do. They were friends. He'd shown no signs of wanting *more*. Till the goodbye hug.

'Zelda, listen to this.' Viv had the incriminating document beside the phone in her study, eager to share, but wasn't getting the reaction she expected.

'Not now, Viv. I'm getting ready for my date with History Man.'

'But—'

'Later, Viv. I don't want this date to be rubbish like the last one, and I've just realised I don't know if we're meeting in the pub or outside so need to message him.'

'Well, I just wanted to prove to you you're well rid of Alan Love Himself...'

'Okay, thanks, but I haven't decided what to wear yet.'

'You'll look lovely in a bin bag, Zelda, and—'

'Viv, sorry but I've just seen a *wire* on my chin! A white one!'

And then she was gone. Didn't she *care*?

Viv read the spreadsheet again, the *spreadsheet*, the survey, the sexist comparison of four different women's various charms or lack-of, as if they were washing machines! JANET LYNNE VIV ZELDA. There they were in alphabetical order, names across the top, desired criteria listed down the side. How methodical! How cold! GSOH was there. Janet 3 Lynne 1 Viv 4 Zelda 0. He'd change his mind if he heard Zelda's description of the male anatomy. So was NS. Janet 5. Lynne 0 Viv 5 Zelda 5. Lynne the only smoker, then. But what did SA stand for? Sex Appeal? Sexual Activity? Sex must come into this somewhere, though it could be Social Attributes, or something like that? He probably required the right sort of someone to take to dinner parties and golf-club soirées. Whatever, the bastard had obviously given this a lot of thought. It was customised, not just the usual initials and acronyms. Whatever SA was, she, Viv, scored 2, Janet 5, and Zelda 1. What about Lynne? She seemed to have dropped out of the running early on. WPFW, what was that? And WSD and WC, what were they? She could only guess.

The columns were filled in with pens and pencils of various types, which indicated that he'd been keeping score at random times, for quite a while, filling it in with whatever pen was to hand, when he came back from an encounter. Miss Marple looked more closely. The latest scores, all for Janet, were written with the same red biro as the note he'd written on the other side, so he'd probably been filling it in the morning he wrote the cheque. Only yesterday morning, though that was hard to believe.

Bastard!

She pictured him, red biro in hand, perusing the spreadsheet over breakfast, considering the attributes of the various candidates, suddenly interrupted by his daughter's Skype-call. Had he turned the page over quickly, covering it up, so his daughter wouldn't see what he was up to? And when he'd finished talking, had he rung gardener-Viv to say he wouldn't be there that morning? Later, before he'd left for the school run, had he realised he hadn't mentioned the cheque or the coffee, and so scribbled a note on the paper in front of him forgetting what was on the other side? Careless Bastard!

Janet, she noted again, was streets ahead, with especially high scores for WC, presumably not Water Closet, and ACC. Accommodation? Was owning a detached four-bedroom house a big attraction? Did he assume that Malcolm, a banker, had left Janet amply provided for? Calculating Careless Bastard! Well, let him sweat. If her friends weren't looking after their own interests, she must look after them instead. *Never fear, Viv is here!* She went to the kitchen, got a coffee and returned to sit by the phone. If Zelda texted, she was ready to zoom to the rescue.

23

ZELDA

Another rubbish date.

History Man was a joker. 'Closed till further notice.' The windows of The Wheatsheaf were boarded up, the potholed car park full of weeds. There was scaffolding. Reversing out, she braked suddenly, seeing something in the bushes behind. A deer? A dog? Had she hit it? Hoping not – she hadn't felt any impact – she heard a tap on the passenger-side window. OMG, an old man, very unkempt and hairy, wanting money perhaps. She lowered the window an inch. 'Are you okay?'

'Vintage Champagne?'

Did he say that? No! Couldn't have. But he said it again, then, 'History man,' in a la-di-da voice that didn't match the face. *Press door-lock. Start engine.* But the door was already open.

'Get out!' she screamed, but he was in the car reaching for the seat belt. 'Go back into town, shall we? Right out of the car park then left onto the main road.'

'I know the way.' She started driving. Why? *Why*, she'd ask herself a hundred times later, why didn't she insist he got out?

Because, because... As she reached the main road, stomach swirling, mouth dry, fingers gripping the steering wheel so hard they hurt, she told herself she was right to drive away, the sooner she got to where there were other people, the better. His hands were on his knees. No gun. No knife. That she could see. And his nails looked clean. But so what? Did serial killers all have dirt in their fingernails?

'The Swan suit you?' He sounded so respectable.

'Fine.' Keep him talking. Say something. Anything. 'You didn't check if The Wheatsheaf was open?'

'No.' No apology. No explanation. He was staring out of the passenger window.

Fine, it gave her a chance to plan. She'd drive into the car park at The Swan, let him get out, press door-lock, and drive straight out again. If she got to The Swan. There were woods coming up on the left. Would his hand now reach for knife or gun or blunt instrument? She decided not to give him a chance. Foot down, she zoomed past. Phew!

It was a nerve-wracking drive. She kept her eyes on him as best she could, on his hands, while watching the traffic and wondering how she could ring Viv.

Her phone was on the back seat in her bag. Had he seen it? Would he make a grab? Was he a thief? Ah, houses now and shops. Five minutes more and she'd be there with luck. But now the traffic slowed down almost to a standstill. She was in the town's best bit, the embankment, the river on the left. Drivers were looking for parking places at the side of the road. Not a chance. Chock-a-block. Hairy Man was looking out of the window at the view, at a swan swanning by. The sight usually calmed her but not today.

'Municipal beneficence.' His posh voice took her by surprise again. 'Suspension bridge. Commissioned by Joshua Hawkins 1888.'

The bridge was lovely, an elegant white trellised arch gleaming in the sunshine.

She edged the car forwards. Traffic was moving again but it was stop start stop and mostly stop. The jam, she could eventually see, was caused by cars waiting to turn right into The Swan's car park. Now she could see the car-park barrier rising and falling. Not long now, though it was one out, one in. But as she waited it dawned on her that you needed a token from Reception to get out of the car park. So if she went in she would have to go into the hotel to get a token to get out. Could she change her mind and park somewhere else? Too late. Her turn now. Here she was at the front of the queue so, no choice, she drove in as the barrier rose. It took a few minutes to find a spare space and park, and as they walked to the entrance at the back of the building she tried to plan her next moves.

But once they were inside he became the schoolmaster, or maybe the leader of a mountaineering expedition. 'Follow me.' He led her to a crowded coffee lounge. 'Right, what can I get you? You get that table over there. I'll get them in.' He was used to giving orders, obviously.

She texted Viv as soon as she was sitting at the table near the window.

Change of plan! Wheatsheaf closed! In Swan with eccentric old man.

Viv texted straight back.

On way. Stay where you are if people around. If not get out and hide in loos. I'll find you.

There were lots of people nearby, mostly women with bags at their feet or on their knees. The Swan was popular with Saturday morning shoppers. But no one she knew, she hoped. What would they think? She replied.

Swan crowded. No need to come. Think weird but not dangerous.

She watched him approaching as she finished texting. None too steady on his feet, he had a cappuccino in each hand.

'Well, Vintage Champagne, here we are at last.' He plonked the coffees on the table, half filling the saucers, and then plonked himself in the bucket chair opposite, knees wide apart. 'Cards on table, my dear, or should I say coffees? Ha ha! What exactly are you looking for? Okay. I'll kick off.' Was he completely unaware of his surroundings? Or her? Or anyone? She sensed ears pricking up all around the room as he started answering his own question. 'One, I'm looking for companionship. Two, long-term commitment. Three, but, no, fair's fair, your turn.' He picked up his cup.

'I like the sound of your history classes.'

'Enrol, then, if that's all you want.' He was plain bad-mannered, boorish.

She sipped at her coffee, planning to leave as soon as she'd finished, calling in at Reception for a car-park token on the way out, explaining the situation if she had to, as there was no sign of a bill. But then to fill the silence – never good at those – she said she especially liked the sound of his class on John Bunyan, who she'd been interested in ever since winning a copy of *The Pilgrim's Progress* as a Sunday school prize. She was burbling a bit, filling time, but what did it matter? She said she liked The Swan because of its association with the writer, who she imagined sitting by the window, watching the river flowing by just as they were maybe humming 'He Who Would Valiant Be'.

'Couldn't have. No tune to hum till Vaughan Williams. And John Bunyan wouldn't have hummed, because the Puritans disapproved of music along with the pleasures of the flesh. They were the Taliban of their day. Anyway, The Swan wasn't built till the eighteenth century, so that demolishes your little theory.'

It wasn't a theory – she'd been *imagining*, for heaven's sake – but she let that go. She was sure there had been *an* inn here back then, if not this one, so her imaginings weren't that far-fetched. But she couldn't let him get away with saying the Puritans were like the Taliban. They were fighting for democracy. The Taliban weren't. She said so and his bristly eyebrows jumped like a couple of athletic furry caterpillars. While he was recovering from the shock of a woman offering an opinion she offered another coffee and went to get them.

This was rather fun.

When she returned, parking token safely in pocket, he was a little more respectful. 'You'd have liked Elizabeth Bunyan, John's wife, second wife that is. Married her when his first wife died leaving him with four children. Not a suffragette exactly – but the Puritans were into parliamentary democracy, as you said – and she was an outspoken woman, especially when fighting her husband's case. She came here, well, to the Swan Inn, this building's predecessor, to try and persuade the judges to free John when he was in gaol.'

Zelda refrained from licking her finger and holding it in the air.

'There's a painting of the scene in the museum,' he said. 'Have you been?'

'No.' She shook her head.

'Sort of thing you'd like to do?'

'Yes. I want to do more history when I retire.'

'It's worth a look. Shows her on her knees, begging the three judges in their curly wigs and fancy lace collars, to meet her husband. Must have gone against the grain that, believing as she did that all men and women were equal before God.'

'Good for her! Did she think they were equal in the eyes of the law too?'

But she didn't get an answer to that question.

Another woman with a mission was crossing the room like an avenging Valkyrie, reddish hair flying behind her. 'Zelda, come on, we're late!'

24

VIV

Viv was on the phone to her mother, watching snowflakes spiralling past her study window.

'When are you coming up, Vivien?'

'Depends on the weather, Mum.' More snow was forecast.

'Well, come when you can fit me in, dear.'

Ignore. Ignore. Keep calm. She made a note to remind clients to wrap up their tender plants. 'Is the house nice and warm, Mum?'

'It is now Larry's bled my radiators, and Heather's brought me more dinners.'

Thank you, lovely brother and sister-in-law. 'You're lucky to have them so close, Mum.'

'They only pop in, Vivien.'

'But they do a lot when they're there, Mum.'

'Well, more than you, Vivien.'

No arguing with that. An email pinged onto her PC screen. From Janet. The first since her hasty departure last Friday. She scanned for mention of important details like who took her to Heathrow.

New Zealand is a beautiful country.

Well, yes.

It is summer here.

I know, Janet.

Grant took me to Christchurch to see the devastation caused by the earthquake.

Horrifying.

Aftershocks expected all the time.

Worrying.

'What are you doing, Vivien?' Mum's super-power was radar vision.

'Thinking, Mum, just thinking. When I do come up would you like to go and see the Pitmen Painters exhibition at the Woodhorn Gallery?'

'No, Vivien. I've told you before that I don't want to look at a lot of old pictures of pitmen hewing coal or sitting in tin baths. Now here's Mr Charlton to give me a lift to chapel.'

Thank you, Mr C. Her mum had excellent neighbours, always popping in.

Because they like her. Mugwort was back.

I like her when she isn't trying to run my life. Or run it down.

Lets you off the hook.

It did to some extent, but she tried to give it her all when she was there. 'Okay, Mum, think about what you would like to do when I come up. Go to a film or the theatre? And what shall I bring you, cakes, or a casserole?'

But Mother had put the phone down. Fine, if she didn't want to go to the Pitmen Painters Viv would go on her own. Going without Jack was going to be hard though. That was what made her sad these days, thinking of all the things he was missing, all the things she couldn't share with him, things he would love. They'd both longed to see the paintings, ever since they'd seen the inspiring play about the amazing artist-miners. It was where they'd first heard about them, though Woodhorn Colliery where the collection was housed was only a few miles from where they'd both grown up.

Thought you were going up there to give your mum a treat?

I'll give her lots of treats.

The least you can do is spend time with her.

I'll spend lots of time with her, most of the time, but I'll need a break too.

Now, where was her diary? She must go to Newcastle soon, to arrange getting Mother down here for Christmas, so Larry and Heather could have a break. Maybe Em would help with that? Yes, she could call at Em's in Yorkshire on the way, stay overnight even and pick her brains for her Art of Gardening course? That would be a bonus. A couple of days with her arty daughter would fortify her for her visit to Mother. She still needed more examples of art depicting ordinary home-grown veg and gardening tools, if she was going to do for gardening what the Pitmen Painters did for coalmining, in one session at least. Celebrate the ordinary, that was what she wanted to do, in all its extraordinariness. That, after all, was the key to happiness.

More snow flurried past the window, confirming the dire weather forecast. Lucky Janet, in the sunny Antipodes. Viv went back to her friend's email.

Have been to the local coast with family and will soon be off on solo trip to Marlborough, land of Sav, tra la la! Am being the perfect guest, never criticising, despite instant coffee, haphazard mealtimes, and a laid-back attitude to housework.

Crikey, she must be near to bursting.

Everyone is very hospitable. Grant is completely different here, a modern man, model husband, hands-on father.

That *was* interesting.

And the grandchildren are wonderful despite their nomenclature.

To Janet's horror her granddaughter was called Rocky and her grandson was called Woody. But they both read books and were sporty and polite. There was no mention of Janet's daughter-in-law, Viv noticed, not by name at least, or Alan Love-less.

Viv's phone pinged with a text from Zelda!

Yes to lunch today thanks if it isn't too late to say.

Phew! She must have imagined the hostility on Zelda's face when she'd turned up yesterday.

* * *

But she hadn't.

'You blurted out my name!' Zelda had just arrived. They'd hardly reached the kitchen.

'Sorry, it just slipped out.' Viv opened the fridge and held up a bottle.

'You told half the pub!' Zelda shook her head at the bottle.

'Only your Christian name.'

'Which is really common.' Sarky Zelda was furious. '*And* I told you not to come!'

'Sorry again.' Viv poured a glass for herself. 'I thought I was helping. And look, if he tries to see you again, just say, and I'll help you see him off.'

But Zelda was far from saying thank you. Or much else. She didn't want to talk about History Man or Scheming Bastard. She didn't want to see the email from Janet – 'I've had it too' – or the spreadsheet by her plate, printed out, when an optimistic Viv was anticipating a heart-to-heart discussion. 'I don't want to see his low opinion of me, Viv.' She pushed plate and spreadsheet aside.

Because she was hurt, of course! Viv realised she should have thought of that.

'You deserve better, Zelda. Alan Love-less is a total shit.'

'Not necessarily.' Zelda accepted a glass of apple juice. 'It's probably what you're supposed to do when you're looking for a partner. Decide what you want, then assess each date afterwards, rationally. I bet there's a spreadsheet you can download.'

'Sounds cold-blooded to me.'

'Or cool-headed?' Zelda smiled with a little shake of her head, indulgently, like a parent talking to a teenager. 'You're such a romantic, Viv. Hearts going boom ditty boom as eyes meet over a crowded room isn't a good basis for a relationship.'

'So you don't think we should warn Janet?'

'About what exactly?'

'That he's comparing us like kitchen appliances!'

Zelda shrugged. *Shrugged!*

Well, if Zelda thought spreadsheets were okay maybe she should have one? 'I could make you one on my PC this afternoon.'

Viv opened the oven door. 'Let's have dinner and discuss the age-old question: what do women really want?'

'What *do* women really want?'

'Our own way, of course. Don't you know the story of Sir Gawain and the Loathly Lady?'

Zelda didn't so Viv regaled her with the tale of the gallant knight, one of the knights of the round table, who transformed his mistress from loathly, meaning horrendously ugly, to absolutely gorgeous when he insisted she make an important decision affecting her own future. A revolutionary idea in the fourteenth century. Zelda raised her glass of apple juice to that, and the atmosphere lightened.

But not for long.

After lunch she wasn't much more forthcoming and they didn't get far with the spreadsheet. Zelda said she was looking for companionship based on common interests, like history and classical music, and that she thought the best you could hope for in a relationship was compromise. Very sensible. Then she said she had to get back to Mack and Morag and take them for a walk before the weather got worse. It was snowing hard now, building up on the study windowsill.

'Okay but hold on a sec.' Viv found the story of Sir Gawain and the Loathly Lady, a beautiful, illustrated edition, one of her most treasured possessions. 'Here, Zelda, read and digest when you get home. We don't let men tell us what to do!'

Zelda put it in her bag but hurried out to her car as if she couldn't get away fast enough, not like Zelda at all. She'd been cagey, like the old Janet, or even the new Janet. What was wrong with Viv's friends? She went back to her PC and perused the unrevealing email again. Well, if Janet was unaware of the danger she was in, and Zelda didn't care, she'd have to deal with Calculating Bastard herself.

25

VIV

When she heard the front doorbell go Viv observed Alan for several minutes from the side window, before opening the door. In a stylish Astrakhan hat, worn at an angle, he looked like an estate agent as he surveyed her house, no doubt assessing its value.

'Hello.' She made him jump when she opened the door.

'Oh, h-hello.' He sounded nervous or cold. She hoped both. There was an inch of snow outside. 'Lovely house.'

'Thank you.' She led the way to the kitchen, after taking his hat and putting it on the hallstand. 'Coffee?' She held up the pot.

'Only if you've got time. You said you had to leave by ten.' It was nine o'clock. He was prompt, obviously eager to get his hands on the document that incriminated him. But he'd said he wanted to see her pergola, and her pergola he would see.

'We can drink it outside.' She pointed out of the window. 'There's my pergola, leading to... but no, I won't tell you where it leads to. That's part of the point, to add interest, even an air of mystery to the garden, as well as giving shelter. I like my structures to have a purpose. It's made of teak, by the way, even though the inspiration came from Giverny.'

Was that a nerve jumping just below his cheekbone? Were his eyes glazing over already? Good. She would continue.

'I love the walkways in Monet's garden, with their arches and climbing plants, leading the eye upwards, but I'm not as fond of metal as he was. Much prefer wood. The framework, sustainable of course, is very sturdy to take the weight as I've planted, overplanted some would say, but deliberately, because I wanted something to delight the eye and the nose at all seasons. Those little yellow flowers, but...' she handed him a coffee '... you really need to go outside to fully appreciate them. They're winter jasmine, an early variety, Jasminum nudiflorum, which is very vigorous and scented.' She opened the back door. 'Take your coffee and walk slowly to breathe it in. Examine the planting and the structures and I'll join you when I've put on my coat.'

In a while. She closed the door.

Then she watched him from the window, lowering his bare head to go under the first arch, and stooping to examine something, maybe sniff the jasmine. Feigning interest. She waited till he'd disappeared from view before going to her study to fetch the incriminating document from her desk. That could go on the hall-stand till she was ready for it, when he was about to leave, when he thought she'd forgotten and would be on edge. Now where was that pile of magazines and catalogues with pergolas in them? First she'd look at a few of them with him. She picked it up from the floor and got the key to the summer house, which he should have reached by now.

Time to return to the fray.

'Lovely in summer, I'm sure,' he sort-of-laughed, banging his arms against his sides. 'Shall I take those?' He took the magazines from her and she got the key from her pocket, but relented. It was bloody cold and wouldn't be any warmer in the summer house than outside, and she might feel bad if he caught pneumonia. Might.

'Perhaps it'd be better to go back to the house?' She led the way back.

Did you read the spreadsheet? That was what he wanted to know. The words seemed to hang in the air with his frozen breath, but when they were back in the kitchen, he sat down and pretended to read one of the catalogues while she poured more coffee. Was he thinking of hardwood, she asked, handing him a cup, or softwood or tubular steel? Did he like arches or something more angled? Would he like roses or clematis or hydrangea petiolaris, annuals or perennials?

'Viv, you're the expert,' he interrupted. 'I'll be guided by you and there's no hurry.'

I want my spreadsheet back. That was what he wanted to say. He finished his coffee. She finished hers and glanced at her watch. Half past nine, she really did have an appointment at ten, and he had perhaps suffered enough? She got up. 'Sorry, I've got to go, but take those with you.' She nodded at the pile of catalogues and brochures. Then she led the way back down the hall, handed him his hat and opened the front door. The nerve in his cheek was doing hop, skip and jump as he put on his hat.

'Oh, and I think this is what you came for.' She handed the document to him, looking him straight in the eye.

26

ZELDA

Morag was watching Zelda pull on a pair of black opaques. It was a day for opaques and boots and a high-necked sweater. She should perhaps tell Viv where she was going, but she couldn't because she'd let her think she'd never see History Man again. The little dog looked severe. *Pick up the phone.* That was what the look said. But there was no need. This wasn't a date. It was a walk, an official walk, maybe with other students. Somehow, she'd agreed to go on it, sort of.

'There's a Bunyan walk I do round the town following in the great man's footsteps. Would you like that?' It was just before she'd been hauled away by Viv and she must have nodded, or even said yes, because he'd texted soon after she'd got home to 'firm up arrangements' and tell her his name was Felix, Felix Freeman. He said it was only fair as he'd heard her friend call her Zelda, which was decent of him. He said he hoped he'd got the right spelling. She *didn't* tell him her surname and was pleased to get his name because it was useful. She'd looked him up on the Retirement Centre website.

Felix Freeman is a lecturer and teacher of History and Politics. He read these subjects at Bristol University and was a history teacher at various public schools before retirement from full-time teaching in 2001, when he started work here.

Clearly, he was well educated, and old – older than he'd claimed. She'd worked it out; he must be at least ten years older than the sixty-three he'd said. No points for honesty, then, but she liked the sound of Beginners Family History on Wednesday mornings and his historical walks. She made a note of the fees. Though short of cash, she'd feel more comfortable paying. Unfortunately, there was no mention on the site of an official walk today.

Sophisticuts was in Mill Street, where they'd agreed to meet, in front of the Bunyan Museum, though it was closed for winter. She would be mortified if Carol or any of the stylists saw her with him. On the other hand, she was looking forward to another discussion. When she'd got home after meeting him she'd found her *The Pilgrim's Progress*, a Sunday school prize, and read it from cover to cover.

'Out of the way, I'm going.' Decision made, she had to step over both the Westies lying in the bedroom doorway. They followed her downstairs and sat by the front door, watching her as she checked the angle of her silver-fox hat, faux of course.

'Don't worry. I'll make it very clear this isn't a date and tell him I'm signing up for one of his classes, maybe two.' It would soften the blow. And at least Felix Freeman wanted to see her.

* * *

She parked in the high-rise and tried not to think about the young man who'd thrown himself over the side from floor three. She'd read about it in the local paper. Poor man, whatever made him do a thing like that? If only you could tell the young that things that seem unbearable at the time are bearable and that happy times would come again. They would. They would.

She found the museum easily enough, set back from the road, which was why she hadn't noticed it before. But where was he? There were other people in the porch, sheltering from the snow, an oldish man and a younger couple. Or maybe they were waiting to go in? Should she tell them it was closed till March? Gosh, it was cold. She turned up her collar. Snow turning to sleet was forecast, and it was here. She'd give Felix Freeman five minutes max.

'Zelda?' The oldish man stepped forward.

'Ye-es? Oh. *Oh!* Yes!' She laughed. 'Sorry. I didn't recognise you.' He'd had a haircut and a shave – he was still bearded, but tidier.

'Had my annual shearing. Rather wish I hadn't.' He stuck out his hand and she shook it. Formally. Like pupil and teacher. Good. But just him and her. Not so good. The other couple walked away, and when they set off down Mill Street in the direction of High Street, he took hold of her upper arm. She tried to shrug him off but couldn't. Nor could she speed up because his grip was firm and as they approached Sophisticuts he started puffing.

Hoping none of the staff were looking out, she kept her head down, and heard him say, 'Took the liberty of booking a table at The Swan, by the way.'

'I came to see the Bunyan sites, Felix.' Could she mention payment now?

'There's one over there, where the gaol was.' They'd reached the corner with the high street and he let go of her arm to point in the direction of a metal sculpture of two giant heads dominating the corner with Silver Street. 'There's a plaque in the pavement in front of those monstrosities, shows where he wrote *The Pilgrim's Progress*. Want to see it?'

Free of his grip, she said she could give it a miss. It was snowing heavily now, and a cup of coffee at The Swan had started to seem attractive. Switching her bag to the other side so it was between them, she set off with him in the direction of the hotel, slowing her pace to match his. He was out of breath again by the time they reached it.

'Want to see where he was baptised?'

She said that she did and they crossed the road to the stone bridge crossing the Ouse and he pointed again as they peered into the murky waters below. 'Up there, about two hundred yards, that's where all his sins were washed away, by full immersion of course.'

She shuddered. 'Not on a day like this, I hope,' and didn't need persuading when he suggested coffee. 'Coffee, not lunch, Felix.' But they soon got into another interesting discussion, and coffee somehow segued into lunch, in the formal dining room.

'You look wonderful in that hat,' he said as she took it off, and disconcertingly he started humming 'Lara's Theme'.

'Julie Christie, I am not, Felix.' She put her hat under the table.

'I'm glad you're not, my dear.' He looked a bit too admiring.

'Felix, I've been thinking—' of signing up for your class, she was about to say.

But he jumped in. 'That's what I like about you, my dear. You're a very bright girl.'

'Woman, Felix.'

'I don't doubt it.' He sighed 'But I was thinking girl as in grammar-school girl, yes? See, I've done my homework.'

'And I've done mine, Felix.' She took control at last. 'We haven't got much in common.'

'But opposites attract, don't you think?'

'Not always, Felix. I'm honest. You're a liar.'

'What makes you say that?' He looked astonished.

'Sixty-three, Felix?'

'Oh, everyone does that.' He shrugged.

'I didn't. And your profile photo was taken years ago, but you call yourself "a sincere sort of guy"?'

'At least I posted a photo. You didn't.'

'Didn't I?' She thought she had. He insisted she hadn't.

'And you should if you want to *pull*, which is, I believe, the term. But please don't, my dear, not now. I'd really rather not have the competition.'

She paused to think while they ate. She finished her delicious halibut and hollandaise sauce, but he was only halfway through his posh burger when he said, 'Where did you say you were born?' His question took her by surprise.

'I didn't.' And she wasn't sure she wanted to go into that, but she did want his help tracing her family history so she told him it was Hitchin, just after World War II. 'My father was an African American GI who went back to the States not knowing he'd left me behind. How about you, Felix? What's your family background?'

'Not half as interesting as yours, my dear.'

'Flannel. Other people's stories are always interesting. Where do you come from?'

'Salisbury.'

'What sort of school did you go to?'

'Minor public, you know.' He went back to his burger.

'No, I don't know. Haven't a clue. We're from different worlds, Felix, so tell me about yours.'

'Sent away at seven—' chew '—so parents had more time to play tennis—' chew '—crammed, bullied, survived—' chew. 'The usual story.'

'Poor you.' She meant it. 'But then university and a good job?'

'If you think teaching is a good job.'

'I certainly do.'

He ate slowly, *very* slowly. Her plate was empty, so all she needed to say now was, 'Thank you, Felix, that was pleasant, but this is the last time we meet socially. From now on I'll see you in your Wednesday morning class.' He pushed his plate aside.

'Burger tough?'

'Not a big eater.' He wiped his mouth on the linen napkin and as he did she heard Janet in her head. *Do you want to get lumbered with a toothless old man, Zelda?*

'Would you like to do that?' The words came from the side of his mouth, which hardly moved because he was trying to hide that he was *a toothless old man*.

'What? Like to do what?' She'd missed something.

'See where Bunyan played tip-cat on Elstow village green before he gave up the pleasures of the flesh?'

Before she could say no, thank you – not with him – the waiter came to clear their dishes and offer dessert and coffee, which she declined. She picked up her bag from the floor and found enough cash for the meal in her purse. As she did she heard Felix asking for the bill. Quick. She got to her feet and reached for her coat on the back of the chair, but suddenly sprightly, amazingly sprightly, he got there first.

'No, no.' He declined her cash with a shake of his head as he held out her coat. 'My pleasure, dear. Don't forget your hat.'

'My turn next, then.' It came out automatically, as she got her hat from under the table, as it did with women friends to avoid the split-the-bill tussle.

He smiled, briefly, as she stood up, just a twitch of the lips, but enough to give her a glimpse of the little brown stubs in the near-empty gums. Felix was old and autocratic. If that was ageist, ageist she was. She didn't want to see him again, except from the back of a classroom.

'I think you should see a dentist, Felix. You would enjoy your food more.' She left as the waiter arrived with the bill, deciding to text later to say she'd changed her mind about meeting again. When she got home she'd ring Janet, if it wasn't too late, and thank her for her warning.

27

JANET

Janet would have welcomed a call from Zelda, or anyone. She wasn't asleep though it was late at night and way past her bedtime. How could she sleep with *that* going on in the room next door? A loud ringing tone might have reminded Grant and Belynda that she was there. Didn't they know she could hear them? Didn't they care? Were they trying to make her feel uncomfortable? She left early next morning for a solo break and arrived at The Chequers late in the afternoon, looking forward to an uninterrupted night's sleep.

At last! It was the first building she'd seen for miles, a white hacienda-style house, with a red-tiled roof, that reminded her of holidays in Spain. Her head was pounding. The sooner she took a couple of paracetamols, the better. There was only one other car in the car park behind the house, so plenty of room for the Mitsubishi Outlander she had at last got the hang of. There were a couple of vehicles in front of the buildings at the far end, a tractor and a fork-lift truck piled high with crates, silent though, so work must have finished for the day.

This was a working vineyard, she reminded herself as she eased herself out of the car and straightened up slowly, so she must expect some noise while she was here, probably starting early in the morning. Tony and Maria Morello were prize-winning wine makers who offered B & B, or homestay as they called it here, in the very beautiful Marlborough region, where the very best Sauvignon Blanc came from. Well, that was what it said on their website. They were famed for their friendliness and informal conviviality. Guests ate with the family. But not tonight, she hoped, noting that the other car was in fact a yellow van with the Chequers logo on the side, so it looked as if she was the only guest. Excellent. She would ask for a meal on a tray.

* * *

'Come on in, Jan. We're expecting you.'

Tony Morello looked like that actor, 'Catch a Falling Star' – Perry Como! – when he was playing a priest in a film she couldn't remember the name of. It was the white polo-necked shirt that looked like a dog collar that did it, under the black sweater, along with the dark hair and greying temples and blue, very blue, eyes. He looked Italian but sounded pure Kiwi as he took her bag. 'Coffee or tea or a glass of Sav before you go to your room, Jan?' He hesitated at the foot of a wide wooden staircase.

'No, no, thank you.' She shook her head and grabbed the newel post as the tiled floor rose to meet her. She really must get her head down.

'Steady on.' He touched her arm and held it there for a moment. 'Expect you need a kip. Long drive. Okay now? Then follow me.'

She had to accept his arm to help her up the stairs, which made her feel like an old woman. There was no need for him to stay when they reached her room. All she wanted to do was lie down on the double bed with its crisp blue and white gingham cover and sleep. The room looked well appointed, but everything was very obvious, so he didn't need to point out the fridge with milk and water, the tea- and coffee-making facilities in the bedside cupboard, the en suite to the left and the fire escape to the right, et cetera, et cetera, but he did, along with the extra pillows in the wardrobe and the small balcony where she could have her breakfast in the morning, and the view, the wonderful view, all the way to Golden Bay, which was...

'Thank you.' She needed to take some paracetamol.

'I'll leave you to settle in, then, Jan, if there isn't anything else?' He was at the door.

'Dinner?' It might be hunger causing her headache.

He looked at his watch. 'Best New Zealand lamb do you, with home-grown veg?'

'Perfect.' It was a long time since the delicious packed lunch that Grant had made her, while Belynda had read a book at the breakfast table.

'See you around seven, then?' He closed the door quietly behind him and she collapsed onto the blissfully comfortable bed.

The house was still pleasantly silent when she woke two hours later, headache gone thank goodness, and when she got downstairs to the hallway, after a refreshing shower, only the odd clatter from behind what she supposed was the kitchen door indicated there was anyone about. A whiff of garlic and rosemary suggested the meal was well on its way, and through a half-open door she could see the dining room, tables covered by red-and-white-check cloths.

'Hello, there. Sit yourself down, Jan.'

Oh! She jumped as the proprietor's head appeared from a serving hatch, bringing Punch and Judy to mind.

'Sorry.' Tony laughed. 'Here. Have a taste of this. It'll calm your nerves.' He held out a glass of the famous Sav, which was delicious, by far the best she'd ever tasted and he looked pleased when she said so. 'Cheers. Scallops for starters do you?'

'Fine.' Scallops, fine, and maybe she was up to eating with other people if there weren't too many. She looked around the room to see which table was laid. Not the family-sized refectory-type near the hatch, and there was still no sign of any other guests, so just Tony and Maria and herself perhaps? Fine.

'I've laid the table in the window. Take the chair looking out so you can see the view and the sunset later on. It'll be great. Must get on.' He went back into the kitchen.

But the table was set for two.

Calm down. You are a mature and confident solo traveller. There is probably another guest, another solo lady-traveller upstairs, getting ready to come down.

The view was stupendous, peaked mountains silhouetted against a sky already the colour of strawberries she'd eaten an age ago, but she sat herself in the chair facing the serving hatch where she could see when Punch popped up again. Where was Maria? Was she in the kitchen too? Was that her in the photograph above the sideboard? Janet got up to have a closer look. There were more photographs standing on the sideboard among a lot of silverware, cups and bowls and framed certificates, mostly of Tony and a petite dark-haired woman, who looked younger than him. He, she guessed, was in his early sixties, Maria in her fifties.

'Top up?' Punch was on stage again, eying her empty glass.

'No, no, thank you.' Gosh. She must slow down.

He laughed. 'I'll be with you shortly.'

Calm down. You can handle this. This is New Zealand where people are friendly and informal. Having a meal with the proprietor of a bed and breakfast establishment is no big deal. If only it weren't so quiet. If only there were more customers, or one more at least, or more staff. Now she remembered the long drive here, that last stretch without seeing another vehicle or even a building or a person. The Chequers was miles from anywhere.

'You're our first guest of the season, Jan. Sorry.' Tony was back again, by her side refilling her glass, and she'd jumped again. All this now you see him, now you don't, wasn't helping her nerves. He vanished again. *Our* first guest of the season. She clutched at a straw. Now straining to hear, she heard the scrape of a spoon against a pan on the other side of the hatch and a bit of sizzling. But no other voices. None at all. She took a gulp of the prize-winning Sav and crossed to the other side of the room, near the door, to read yet more certificates. Gold Medal 2007. Silver Medal 2008.

'Oh, there you are, checking my credentials.' He'd kicked the door open, and was holding two dishes, in oven-gloved hands. 'Quick, Jan. Sit yourself down. These are hot. No, you sit there, facing the view.' He put a sizzling dish in front of her and another in the place facing her, where he put himself. 'Have you ever seen a sky like that?'

It was as red as her face. Burning. On fire.

Make light conversation. Comment on sunset. Or wife.

She turned towards the photographs. 'You're obviously part of a very successful team, Tony.'

He studied his plate for what seemed like a long time, then stood up, wiping his hands on a napkin '*Were*, Jan. It's a long story. I'll get more Sav and check on the lamb.'

Oh dear. Had she blundered again? Was he a widower?

* * *

No, Maria had left him, walked out, but, poor man, this was maybe worse. His wife had chosen to leave. He spoke in a deadpan voice but there was pain, *anguish*, in his eyes. Maria had left him just before their twenty-fifth anniversary, saying their marriage was a sham, a business partnership only, and he had to be fair, something had gone wrong. They'd let things slide, the romantic side. *He'd* let things slide. It was all his fault. He'd neglected her. He'd been too busy nurturing the business to nurture their marriage. He hadn't noticed that Maria was unhappy, that she wanted different things from him. She was younger and wanted more bright lights, more fun. He wanted to work on it, but it was too late, she said, she'd already found someone else, one of their customers, a restaurant owner, who they'd met, he thought, *he'd* met, only once or twice a year.

'I was devastated, Jan, broken. It was a double blow. My marriage and my business. The guy had a thousand bottles a year from us, so I lost a good customer too. But worst of all I lost my lovely... Maria.' There was a catch in his voice.

She sympathised. 'Was it long ago?'

'Three years, I've been on my own for three long years, Jan, and I still feel raw. How about you?'

She said it was getting on for three years for her too, since Malcolm, her husband of forty years, had died.

'Sorry for your loss, Jan, but good on yer, forty years together, you must have made it work.'

'Not really.' In vino veritas. 'Malcolm wasn't what he seemed either.'

He topped up her glass, apologising for the delay with the lamb. 'Sorry, Jan. Didn't realise when I put it in how long this recipe took. Guess I'm still on a bit of a learning curve, but no worries, we're not in a hurry, are we?' His hand covered hers.

She forgave him learning curve. She forgave him calling her Jan too, she quite liked Jan, in fact. Jan was a nice sympathetic person, more open, more relaxed, more honest than Janet.

'We rubbed along like I thought most couples did,' she said, taking another mouthful of the delicious Sav, 'but now I think we rubbed each other out.'

'I know what you mean, Jan.'

'We didn't...' She remembered her broken night, 'have much of a...'

'Sex life? Can't believe it was your fault, Jan, a sensuous woman like you.'

'But it wa-a-as!' she wailed. 'Headaches, I always had headaches.' She had one now.

'Maria says sex is the best cure for a headache she knows.' His hand was warm and firm on hers, the hairs on his wrist dark and fine, his fingers long and tapering. 'Don't blame yourself. Men have responsibilities too.' He turned her palm upwards and pressed his lips into its centre, sending shivers through her.

'How was the lamb?' He had a glass of red in his hand.

Lamb. When did that appear? Where had it gone? Her plate was empty.

'Delishus.' Something fell off her fork.

'No, leave it, Jan.' Now he was standing by her side, taking the fork from her hand. 'Time to call it a day, I think. Come on. I'll show you to your room.'

Such a nice man. Such an understanding man.

'Shorry.' The room was swaying.

'Nothing to be sorry about, Jan. I shouldn't have opened the red. Lean on me.' He led her out of the room and up the stairs, into her room, where he helped her walk to the bed, one unsteady step at a time. He helped her sit on the bed, pushing her gently against the pillows, then lifting her legs, one then the other. Eyes closed, she felt his hand grasping one of her heels, removing a FitFlop, and then the other. She heard them flop on the floor.

'Thank you.' She heard the door close. Sigh. Alone at last. Now she could sleep. She wriggled down the bed.

'You're very tense, Jan.' Not alone! He was still there. She tried to open her eyes.

'Relax, Jan, it's only me, Tony.' His voice came from the end of the bed. 'Would a foot massage help, a bit of reflexology?'

Reflexology, she liked reflexology. 'Yesh, I mean...'

'It's okay, Jan. You just lie back and forget all your worries. Trust me.' He took her feet in his strong hands and she gave herself up to the feel of his fingers separating her toes one by one, pulling them apart, probing the spaces between them, sending tremors through her foot, then a firmer touch with his thumbs pressing into her insteps, stroking, spreading pleasure through her ankle, through her calves, through her knees, through her thighs and places beyond.

'Nice, Jan?'

'Love-ly,'she gasped.

Darts of exquisite piercing deliciousness were tingling through her but oh, oh, oh, what was happening now? The bed was shaking. The room was shaking. She was shaking. Oh, God! It was an earth-quake! As her body shook, the tumultuous waves gathering force, she waited for the walls to collapse and crush her to death, and strangely she didn't care.

28

JANET

Waking up next morning, Janet wondered where she was.

Light was streaming through the gaps in the blinds onto the wall opposite. Star-fished across the bed, floppy-limbed after the best night's sleep she'd ever had in her life, she felt great. There were her clothes piled on the chair beside her bed, but where on earth was she? It was a few minutes before remembered she was staying at The Chequers and then the earthquake of the night before. How amazing it was that she was *alive* and yes – she lifted the duvet – *unharmed*. What a miracle! Not a scratch or bruise on her skin and – she looked all around – no signs of damage in the room. Not a crack in the walls or ceiling, not a picture askew.

'Jan.' Someone was knocking on the door. 'How are you this morning?' It was Tony the proprietor's voice. How kind that he was checking in with her.

'Fine, absolutely fine, Tony. Amazingly fine. But how are you? Come in and let me see you.'

Was that appropriate? She sat up, hurriedly pulling the duvet up to her chin.

Tony looked fine too, as if he'd just had a shower. Hair still damp, he was wearing denims and a fresh white shirt open at the neck. 'Well, Jan, that was er... quite a night.'

'An understatement if I may say so, Tony. We've been very lucky. Is there a lot of damage?'

He looked puzzled.

She scanned the room again. 'Honestly, I can't believe I'm still here, that *we're* still here, no harm done, that there's not so much as a crack in the walls. How's the rest of the house?'

He ran his fingers through his hair. 'Sorry, Jan, you've lost me. What *are* you talking about?'

'The earthquake.'

He came in and sat on the bed looking at her as if she were crazy.

'Earthquake, you think we had an earthquake?' He shook his head slowly from side to side, then took her hand, smiling. 'How do I put this, Jan? That was no earthquake, though the earth clearly moved for you. You *came*, Jan. You came. I've never seen anything quite like it.'

Came. It took time for the word to sink in. Did he mean what she thought he might mean?

'Don't think they're all like that.' Tony stood up. 'I'd say ten on the Richter scale. I'll go and make coffee.'

I came. I had an org... She couldn't quite form the word even in her thoughts.

She sank back against the pillows to absorb this life-changing information. For years she'd been of the opinion that writers who went into graphic detail about this aspect of sex and several others were making it up, fantasising and sensationalising, and she'd said so once, possibly more than once, in her book group. Certainly when they'd discussed *For Whom the Bell Tolls* she'd dismissed 'the earth moved' as a hyperbolic male fantasy. A couple of women had agreed with her – most had looked at their hands, she now remem-

bered – but the woman who ran the art gallery in town had snig-
gered and so had the woman sitting next to her, and maybe one or
two others, and now she knew that the sniggerers were right. Tony,
wonderful Tony, had proved them right with his skilful fingers.
Luxuriously, she stretched her toes beneath the duvet. Tony had
jolted her – that *was* the word – out of her ignorance. He had
opened her closed little mind. Now she knew that she'd spent her
whole life being stuffy and disapproving, uptight and censorious,
priggish and puritanical. Oh, Tony was back with the coffee.

'Tony, about last night...'

'First things first, Jan, would you like your breakfast downstairs
or here on the balcony?' He opened the blinds, flooding the room
with sunlight.

'Oh, the balcony would be lovely, and—' she saw a new life
beginning '—would you join me?'

When he'd gone she sprang – well, sort of! – out of bed and into the
en suite. OMG. What did she look like? How could he fancy that?
She quickly cleaned her teeth, jumped into the shower, washed
hair, washed everything, towel-dried, pulled on a cotton wrap,
applied lipstick and she was done! Just in time, as Tony reappeared
with a laden tray.

'Fruit, Greek yogurt and Danish pastries suit you, madam?'

'Perfect. Except maybe for...' There was a man in the yard below
moving pallets with a forklift truck.

'No worries, Jan. He can't hear or see us.' He put the tray on the
balcony table.

I want to stay here for ever.

She laughed at herself, happy if he could read her thoughts, for
how could she say what she wanted to say? She sat down opposite

him, her breasts tingling beneath the thin wrap, and he covered her hand with his, sending more shivers to places she'd only recently discovered.

'Holy shite!'

Following Tony's startled gaze to the yard below, Janet saw a yellow van with a Chequers logo on the side, spraying gravel as it came to a sudden halt. Then he was on his feet, heading for the door, knocking coffee off the table in the rush.

'What, Tony? What's the matter?'

But he had gone. She heard him clattering down the stairs, then banging doors, and minutes later she saw him kissing the lips of the woman who had opened the rear doors of the yellow van. Maria, it had to be her, or her twin sister. Older and plumper than the woman in the photographs, she was smartly dressed in navy cropped pants and a white shirt with a red scarf knotted at the neck. And the kiss she was giving him didn't look like the kiss of a shame-faced runaway returning after an absence of three years. It looked like the kiss of a woman who had returned earlier than expected to see what her husband was up to.

29

ZELDA

Zelda deflected Felix's kiss.

They were in the car park of The Red Lion, she not quite believing she was meeting him again.

'You look lovely, my dear.' He sounded as posh as ever and looked smarter, she thought, but didn't say. She was determined not to say anything that would give him the slightest encouragement. He was wearing a suit with a white shirt and black tie, as if he'd been to a funeral. Was that why he was late? She'd dressed down, in jeans and a cagoule, as if for a walk with The Ramblers. He did look different though. Younger. Dorian Grey came to mind. It was probably just the clothes and the haircut. But no mistakes this time. She would make it clear this would definitely be the last outing.

Teeth!

She was halfway through her fish and chips when she noticed. He was saying something she couldn't hear – 'Jingle Bells' was blasting out of the tannoy – and he suddenly smiled, a deliberate, lingering Cheshire Cat smile, baring his teeth, before going back to his sizzle steak, which he was disposing of quite efficiently. *Yes, teeth.* Felix had taken her advice. Since they'd last met, he had undergone some extensive and doubtless expensive dentistry. Whitish incisors had replaced the brown stubs. Whitish, that was all you got these days when you replaced old gnashers with new. She'd had a new crown recently and had been taken aback by the dingy range of greys and yellows the dentist had offered as a match for her own. Felix was making an effort, but that mustn't weaken her resolve.

'I'm looking forward to seeing the Bunyan sites, Felix, but—' she raised her voice '—this is the last time we meet socially.'

He paused, fork in air, and pointed to a holly-green paper bag beside her plate. 'Just a little something I thought you'd find useful. Not really a Christmas present.'

'I'll pay you for it, Felix.'

'No, I didn't mean...'

'But I do.'

It was a book called *Research Your Ancestors* and he said he'd written a chapter himself. She said she'd look forward to reading it, and told him she'd signed up for his Introduction to Family History course and might sign up for the Bunyan course too.

'My dear...' he bared his teeth again '... if you can't afford—'

'Felix! Listen.' She put down her knife and fork. 'I don't want you to pay for me. I don't want to go out with you. Sorry. But.' Was that clear enough?

He got a handkerchief from his pocket and dabbed his eyes.

'Not your fault, dear.' He blew his nose. 'Excuse me if I seem a little preoccupied. I shouldn't have come, not today of all days. I nearly cancelled but when I rang my therapist for advice she said she thought I should. After putting flowers on Irene's grave, perhaps, which is what I did before I came here. Lilies, her favourite.'

It was, she caught on, his late wife's birthday.

So it wasn't her announcement he was taking badly. Good.

'You must have loved her very much, Felix.' She touched his hand lightly.

He nodded. Irene had been his wife, his best friend, his everything.

'I don't think that happens more than once in a lifetime, Felix.'

Point made, she hoped.

'Soulmates.' He took a photograph from his wallet.

'That's wonderful, Felix, about being best friends, I mean.'

She could only say that about Harry, though she had been Gary's friend when they were apprentices together. It had all gone wrong when she'd let it go further and got pregnant. He'd scarpered after the miscarriage to work on the oil rigs. Igor? No, they'd never been what you'd call best friends or any other kind. The hours he worked as a chef didn't give much time for friendship to develop. He didn't speak much English and it was bed or nothing with him. Great while it lasted but that wasn't very long.

'I'm just going to powder my nose, Felix.'

She left him looking at the photograph of his wife and stopped at the bar to settle the bill. It was when she entered the ladies that she got a whiff of a scent she recognised and thought, *Oh no, Viv's here!* because she was sure it was the one Viv always wore. Then she laughed at herself for thinking Viv was the only person who wore Eau Dynamique.

Viv

But it was Viv, now sitting on the loo in a state of shock. She had rushed into the ladies when she saw Zelda with the hairy guy,

History Man, who she'd said she'd ditched. But was that Zelda who'd just come into the cubicle next door? She nearly called out to ask, then thought better of it. It might be someone else, who would think she was crazy. Now she wished she'd gone over and said hello when she'd first walked into the pub and seen the two of them there together. But how could she have done? It had obviously been an intimate moment. Their heads had been close together, Zelda's hand on his. It was the same guy, she'd stayed long enough to be sure of it, though he seemed to have spruced himself up a bit. But why had Zelda kept it secret? It was embarrassing catching her out like this. And upsetting.

The Muscateers are finished.

Whoever it was next door was flushing the loo. Viv bent double. There was a gap under the partition between the cubicles and she could see feet on the other side. Black leather ankle boots with wedge heels. Russell & Bromley. Hadn't Zelda bought a pair like that in the sale? And those herringbone tweed trousers, straight cut from M&S, didn't she have a pair of those?

What are you doing?

FFS. She sat up straight. What *was* she doing nearly standing on her head in a public toilet? She could get arrested. What should she do now? She flushed to make a noise, then opened the door an inch to peer out, carefully so as not to be reflected in the mirrors behind the basins. Yes. It *was* Zelda, now anxiously inspecting her face and re-applying her lipstick. To make herself look her best for Hairy Man waiting back at the table? Was she so desperate?

Why couldn't she tell me?

Leaving the pub by the back door felt furtive, but it wasn't her fault. She hadn't planned to spy. She'd only called in because she'd needed the loo rather desperately, because she'd stayed to have a second coffee with George Beaumont. She'd gone to Beaumont's for a hard-to-please customer, who wanted one of George's new hybrids and to get her mower serviced, but had lingered too long because George made her feel good. Was *she* so pathetic? They'd sorted the order quite quickly but then he'd commented on the scent she was wearing and wondered what might be in it. George had a good nose. That was part of his success. Did he detect citrus? She'd thought not but wasn't sure, so they'd gone online and ended up laughing when they'd found that one of the ingredients of Clarin's Eau Dynamique was the dreaded weed, mare's tail. 'Equisetum arvense,' she'd read out. 'Perhaps we should cultivate it and create our own brand?'

'A partnership. I'd like that, Ms Halliday. What would we call it?'

'Halliday and Beaumont? HB?'

'Sounds like a pencil.' He'd shaken his head.

'Arvense?'

He'd pulled a face.

'Equus? We could sell it to horses.'

He'd laughed, and she'd accepted another coffee. Mistake.

'Maybe you should get a lover, Mum.' Em was opening the bottle of red Viv had brought in case of drought.

'Is this my daughter speaking?' This was outré even for Em.

'If you can't beat em?'

They were in Em's kitchen, which was all warm pine and scented candles, and Viv had just told her youngest daughter how hurt and surprised she'd been by Janet and Zelda's secret liaisons, how left out she felt. But time to put the record straight about her own completely acceptable single status. 'FYI, Em, I haven't felt a twinge of desire for anyone since your father died. No one has excited a frisson. And I'm dead below the waist even for DIY.' Two could play at outré.

'Poor Mum.'

'Don't _poor Mum_ me. I had forty great years with your dad and now I'm a very happy career woman. Give me that drink.'

'Here.' Even teetotal Em understood the need for alcohol once she'd heard about her horrendous journey, three hours on the A1 and another hour through snowy Yorkshire lanes while feeling abandoned by the Muscateers. 'Muscateers?' Em pulled a face as she filled her mum's glass. 'Sounds more like the Widows' Wine Club to me.'

'Well, there hasn't been a lot of *all for one* lately.'

'They must have thought you'd disapprove.'

'Am I disapproving?'

Em didn't answer. What did that mean?

'Isn't Janet the prim and proper strait-laced one?' Em had heard about Janet and Zelda but hadn't met them.

'Less strait-laced these days, I suspect.'

'And didn't you say Zelda said she was through with sex?'

'She thinks she can find a man who'll settle for companionship.'

'And a pig who can fly?' Em raised a glass of murky green liquid. 'Cheers, Mum. I hope that red goes with my aubergine bake.'

'Cheers, daughter. The red's fine.'

'And you, are you really fine, Mum?' Emma was giving her a searching look.

'Very fine, thanks, and will be even better when you've helped me with a couple of my projects.' *And what about your love life, dearest daughter?* Dared she ask? There was a man, she thought, someone at the posh school Em taught at. Married probably or why not say? But the sudden whirr of a blender pre-empted any more questions.

'Go and sit down, Mum. Put your feet up. I'll call you when it's ready.'

Stretched out on the sofa, she could see Em through the doorway. How unlike her sisters Em was. Sally and Beth were tall like Jack with Jack's fair colouring, but Em was five feet two, like her granny, Viv's mum, who she got on surprisingly well with. Em's hair was short and spiky and dark. She was much, *much* more stylish than her mum. Today she was wearing black opaque tights and a black tunic top appliquéd with a funky abstract design in shades of jade and emerald-green. She made a lot of her own clothes or bought basics, often from charity shops, and customised them, a practice much admired by her nieces. A fun auntie when she turned up for family events, she'd so far showed no signs of wanting children herself, which was probably as well as she was thirty-eight next birthday.

'Smells good, Em.' She stepped into the kitchen for a refill. 'How long will this bake be? Have we got time to look at your studio before it's ready?'

'If you can stagger up the stairs.'

'Cheeky. I'm keen to start picking your brains.'

'Okay, but the stairs are steep.' Em picked up her overnight bag. 'And mind my new carpet if you're bringing that red wine.'

Suppressing a retort – cream carpet! – and parking her wine on the kitchen table, Viv followed Em upstairs to the tiny landing, noting in passing that a double bed nearly filled her daughter's room, but hers, in the room next door, was a virginal single with a white coverlet.

'Where would I put my lover, Em?'

Em laughed and pointed out of the window, 'Terrific view in the morning, Mum, over the reservoir. Just hope the birds don't wake you.'

Skilful change of subject.

They moved into Em's studio, a converted third bedroom. She started to talk about light and glare and orientation and the possibility of a Velux window in the room Viv was going to use. 'Dad rated your painting, Mum, he'd be chuffed with what you're doing.' Lovely daughter! 'And I've started thinking about your Art of Gardening course. You're right about artists in the past not depicting fruit and veg, well, not humble home-grown ones. They weren't celebrating the ordinary, that's why, but the wealth of their rich patrons. They wanted pictures that showed that they could import food from abroad or grow it in their hothouses, or how much land they had for hunting. That's why you get a lot of dead deer.'

* * *

Downstairs, there was a pile of postcards by her plate.

'Have a look at those.' Em bubbled with enthusiasm as she dished up. 'Most are reproductions of twentieth-century paintings but the one on top's an honourable exception from the seventeenth century, *Still Life with Apples, Cabbage, Parsnip and Lettuce* by Giovanni Battista Recco. And underneath there's a surrealist-before-his time, Arcimboldo, who painted amazing headdresses made of veg, but you have to wait till the twentieth century for a proper appreciation of the ordinary. Van Gogh is spot on as always.' She hardly paused to eat. 'What did he say?' She googled. '"To learn to see things with fresh eyes is an enlargement of spirit which makes for... er better and happier human beings?" Yes?'

'Yes! *Yes!*' They were on the same wavelength!

'Look at his potatoes, Mum, so solid, so earthy, in the original anyway.' She'd seen it in Arles.

'Em, hold on, I'm still writing that quote down.'

Em paused but only for a few seconds. 'And there's the very rude Sarah Lucas... and you could show them Derek Jarman's film *The Garden*? That would fill a session.' Em was keen to help with her course, but even keener on getting her mum to be creative. 'You must paint while you're here. Having a go yourself is the best way of appreciating other artists.'

'I so agree, Em. That's exactly what the Pitmen Painters discovered, that they had to draw and paint and sculpt themselves, to find out what art was. Studying the old masters didn't do it for them.'

'I'll set up a still life for you tonight, Mum. You'll have three whole days to yourself while I'm at school.'

* * *

So that was exactly what Viv found next morning, when, still in her pyjamas, she went into Em's studio. On a table beside an easel with a stretched canvas was a crinkly savoy cabbage, three shiny, red-skinned onions, a bunch of smooth, sleek leeks and a cauliflower with curds like clotted cream.

> *Dear Mum,*
>
> *Start NOW. Use anything of mine you like. Acrylics, oils what-ever. Go for it! There's charcoal too. Be bold. DON'T cook. Snacks in fridge. We'll eat out tonight. Love Em X*
>
> *PS No excuses!*

None, except the daunting blankness of the canvas. But inspired by Em, or fearing her scorn, Viv took a piece of the velvety charcoal between her thumb and finger and made a mark, then another... She noted where the light fell and where colour drained into dark-ness, and tried to capture something of what was in front of her... Only a coffee craving made her pause. What time was it? Retrieving her mobile from the bedroom where she'd left it charging, she found it hard to believe more than an hour had passed, and she noticed she'd missed a text pinging in.

Mum asking for you. Larry.

'Shit!' wasn't the correct response. Guilt followed. But the phone rang before she had time to check what time the text had come in. It was her brother again.

'Sorry, Viv, but she's taken to her bed and she's asking for you.'

'Coming. Now.' She stepped out of her pyjamas and put the

phone on speaker. 'Have you phoned the doctor?' She pulled on her pants with one hand, and found her denims with the other.

'Of course...'

'Larry, I'm halfway there, luckily, at Em's, so it won't take me long. I'll be there in...' But she was talking to herself. They'd lost contact. She tried ringing back but there was no connection. Mum taken to her bed. Mum asking for her. Was this the end? Was this It?

She dressed hurriedly and drove like the proverbial.

* * *

Your mother's death was the Big One, someone said. Bigger than that of your husband of forty years, or your dad's when you were sixteen? Really? Your mum was your one truly life-long love, that same someone had said. You've loved your mum since the moment you were born, and even before, so it's your strongest bond. When she goes it's huge. Worse if you didn't get on.

Shit. When did she last see her? When did they last speak? Sunday as usual, only a few days ago, but – shit again – they'd had a row. About Jack. Mum had never approved of Jack. 'I didn't send you to college to marry a bricklayer, Vivien.' Mum had accused her of worshipping him and not for the first time, but it was the first time she'd replied.

'No, Mum, I didn't worship Jack, I just fucking loved him.'

End of conversation. Mum hadn't answered her calls since. Foot down. Foot down. Sod the fucking rain. Was this love that was surging through her, pressing the accelerator to the floor? Was this love that was urging her to get there in time to hold her mum's hand and say kind things before she went? Or was it life-long guilt?

31

VIV

Viv braced herself before opening the bedroom door.

But there was Mum, alive and well, resplendent in an ivory satin nightdress, reclining against the pillows. Mum hadn't got her hearing aid in, so she hadn't heard Viv open the front door, let herself in and climb the stairs. Mum was turning the pages of a glossy hardback, *The Golden Girls of MGM*, and from the rapt expression on her face she was one of them, dancing with Fred Astaire or gazing into the eyes of Clark Gable. Mum didn't hear Viv creeping back down the stairs to try and recover from her adrenaline-fuelled drive before she went back to say hello.

I've been had.

Mum didn't see love, if it was love, or guilt, if it was guilt, turn to anger. What was Larry up to scaring her like that? Viv made a coffee and rang him from the phone in the kitchen, but Larry wasn't there. His answerphone said he was sorry, but he appreciated her call and would get back to her as soon as he could if she left a brief message saying who she was.

'It's me, Viv. I'm at Mum's. It's one o'clock. She's fine.'

She waited. Larry was one of those people who triaged his calls.

Usually he rang her straight back. But not today. She checked her mobile for messages. Damn. Blank screen. The battery was flat and she'd left her charger at Em's in the rush to get out of the house. She hadn't had breakfast either. Looking for something to put in a sandwich, she noted Mum's well-stocked fridge. Cold meats, Cheddar cheese – Mum ate no other variety – eggs, tomatoes, a quarter of a cucumber, a four-pack of yogurts, a jelly in a dish, half a lemon meringue pie, a carton of cream, half a lasagne, a pork chop, sausages, bacon, orange juice and milk and two bottles of Liebfraumilch, one opened, all proved Mum was very well cared for – and eating well.

'Hello, Vivien.' She presented a rouged and powdered cheek when Viv finally made it upstairs. 'Fancy you coming to see me.'

* * *

Larry came in the evening, her big brother, taller but almost her twin in looks. Less hair than her, quite a dome now, but the same reddish-brown colour now sprinkled with grey. They laughed about that and a lot more as they sat at the kitchen table. He as unlike his namesake, Laurence Olivier, as she was unlike hers, Vivien Leigh. They even laughed about Mother. It was hugs and soddits and apologies all round. If only Viv had hung on a bit longer he'd have explained, Larry said. He'd started texting to say Mother had taken to her bed, then decided to ring to explain as writing wasn't really his thing. He would have told her that Mother was acting, playing up. Faking. If they hadn't lost connection she'd have heard him say he had seen the performance several times.

'But when you said she'd taken to her bed...'

'I'd have explained that when Heather and I are here she refuses to get up. She says she can't, that her legs have gone, but she's still using the bathroom when we're not here. There's evidence. I gather the waterworks are only as good as can be expected in a woman of her age, but she takes appropriate action, and is by no means helpless – when we're not here.'

'Oh dear, is it because she's lonely?' Guilt stabbed at her again.

'Lonely?' Larry pointed to the calendar on the wall. 'Lunch club Monday, whist Tuesday, choir Wednesday, Knit and Natter Thursday, Local History Friday, not every Friday, it's true, but probably once a month. Other friends and relatives call in, including Dad's relatives, and Mr Charlton takes her to chapel on Sunday and to other chapel events in the week. You forget how popular our mother is. And Heather or I are here several times a week.'

'So why's she doing this?'

'Maybe she's peeved because Heather's mother has had a stroke and she's getting slightly less attention? Heather's mum and dad need more of her time now, but I'm still managing to see Mum a couple of times a week.'

'You're a saint. You're both saints.'

What does that make you?

Not a saint, but for forty-eight hours she tried her best to be. For two whole days she waited on her mother hand and foot, trying to anticipate her needs and obeying her instructions when she didn't. Fetch this, Vivien, fetch that. Not that one, Vivien, the other one.

* * *

Now she was driving away. Not home. Not yet. But if she remained in her mother's company one minute more she might say something she would regret. For two long days she had tried to make her mother happy and failed. For a lifetime she'd tried to make her mother happy and failed...

Why are you so cross?

Because she's a hypocrite.

You'd rather she was really ill?

I'd rather she was honest! I'd rather she was as charming to Larry and me as she is to other people. Instead of playing the helpless invalid like an aging movie star, using her theatrical talents, unrealised by her disappointing children, to deceive and manipulate us.

But Mrs Satnav broke into her thoughts. 'In half a mile, at the roundabout, take the third exit to the right towards Woodhorn Colliery.'

The Pitmen Painters at last, if she could do it. She didn't have to. If she carried on driving she would come to the stunningly beautiful Northumberland coast where a bracing walk by the sea might do her more good. But she had to do this, she chose to do this for Jack.

32

VIV

Viv thought for a moment that it was closed as the car park was empty. The drab buildings on three sides, locked-up sheds, a lift shaft and a tall chimney brought several of the miners' paintings to mind. But today there were no hunched figures with blackened faces blinking as they stepped out of the darkness into the light. No pit ponies emerging from underground to enjoy the feel of fresh air on their backs, no smoke spiralling from the chimney, no movement at all. A conveyor belt conveyed nothing and the pit wheel was still.

There was a coach in the far corner, she now noticed, so there were other people here. Would this have been a car park in the thirties? she wondered. Surely the miners would have walked or cycled the two miles from Ashington? She wondered if they would have gone home at the end of the shift to wash and eat and change their clothes before walking or cycling back. They always looked clean and in their Sunday best in the few photographs she'd seen. Keen to learn what great art was and 'better themselves', they had commissioned classes from a lecturer at Newcastle University. They had met once a week in a hut like one of the ones she could see, though sadly the actual one had been demolished years ago. But that wasn't all, they had also worked between classes on the kitchen table at home, or in their garden sheds, because, one of them had said, he couldn't stop. Painting made him feel 'real'. All week he worked for the bosses but this he did 'for his own soul'.

Welcome warm air met her as she pushed open a glass door and stepped inside. Arrows pointed to workshops, archive rooms, a study centre, cloakrooms, the café and finally the art galleries – to the right. She set off down a sloping corridor beneath colourful trade union banners extolling the virtues of work and comradeship and solidarity. Close the Door on Past Dreariness, urged one, The Way to Prosperity Is Work, said another. Then, after a left turn and a right, she was there, in front of dark green doors and a sign saying Pitmen Painters.

It felt like stepping into a church. The paintings, lit from below, glowed like stained-glass windows in the semi-darkness. Had the men ever seen their work displayed like this? Probably not, but if they had they would surely have felt honoured and proud, for the setting enhanced their success. They had aimed to capture reality, *their* reality, the extraordinariness of ordinary things, and they had succeeded. The men hadn't wanted to romanticise or prettify or falsify their lives. They'd told the truth, *their* truth, and made it holy. Holy was the word that came to her lips as she moved from one picture to another, some showing mastery of technique, some not, but all truthful. She saw what their lives were like, not just underground at the coalface, but in their homes and on their allotments and in the YMCA hut where, another of them said, he was '*more himself* than at any point in his working day'. There was home decorating and rug progging and shot-hole drilling and leek growing and whippet racing, all human life was here – and death. She was in the corner of the gallery looking at *Pit Incident*, a sombre depiction of pitmen carrying a body home on a stretcher, when someone else walked in.

She hoped it wasn't the coach party, but whoever it was wasn't followed by more and she heard footsteps going to the other side of the room.

The man on the stretcher was bundled up in a brown blanket, his face covered. As the stretcher bearers made their way past a school some bystanders had turned away, but most, including children, looked on, their faces curious. She'd heard about this, that when children saw a stretcher going past they ran out of the school-yard to see whose daddy it was. How would they know? Did they lift the blanket to take a look? It wasn't like that for her. When the school secretary interrupted an English lesson to take her to the headmistress's study – 'It's about your father, dear,' – she'd wanted to run away but couldn't because the secretary had her arm in a grip.

She sidestepped to the next picture, more cheerful, she hoped, but her breath stopped when she saw the man who'd just come in.

You've come. Of course. I knew you would.

He was looking at a picture, his back to her, but she was certain; there was no doubt in her mind. She knew the back of that head better than she knew anyone's. She knew the shape and shine of the scalp, too much of it to be called a bare patch, whatever he said when the girls teased him. She knew the broad back beneath that jacket, the feel of the warm skin, the salt smell, because for forty years she'd slept with her nose close to it.

Turn around, please.

Joy flooded through her. A stupid smile was pulling her lips up to her ears and tears were streaming down her cheeks as she yearned to see his face. It was and wasn't him. She knew that too. She wasn't mad. She'd heard about this happening and had longed for it to happen to her. Ever since a friend had told her that her husband had returned the day after he died, and stayed for several minutes to tell her that she would be fine and that he was fine before fading away, leaving her friend feeling comforted and at peace. He was a ghost, a loving, comforting ghost, and she'd settle for that.

'Stay a bit longer, Jack.'

'Are you okay?' He half turned to look at her.

Not Jack.

Had he heard her speak?

Not Jack. Nothing like Jack really.

'Sorry. I thought...' She fled.

Out of the door, onto a landing, into the light. Down a slope, up a slope. Where was the bloody exit? She had to get out of here. Was this the most badly signed building she'd ever stepped foot in? Now it was pitch dark. Where the hell was she? Clanking, hissing, drilling, drumming sounds bombarded her ears, the darkness getting darker, as she was carried down by some sort of conveyor belt. Then a voice-over said she was on her way to the coalface with – she didn't catch the name – a fourteen-year-old lad on his first day in the pit. Hell was the word, a living hell. The lad must have endured this for eight long hours or more, but mercifully she didn't have to. A door opened and she stepped out into dazzling brightness. The gift shop. Where there was a gift shop there was always an exit, though you had to go past all the merchandise first. She had to weave past pyramids of mugs and piles of tea towels keeping her elbows tucked in. Past carousels of postcards and tins of biscuits and jigsaw puzzles and books and hideous objects made of coal or something that looked like it. Finally she reached the door. But it wasn't the exit. She'd come into the cafe.

'You all right, pet?' A tea lady, grey-haired and motherly, stopped wiping the pine table she was clearing. 'Come on in and have a cup of tea, love. Takes some folk like that, it does.'

Too stunned to argue, Viv followed the woman to the counter.

'Nice and quiet today.' She picked up a cup and filled it. 'Weather keeping folk away, though I was expecting a school party – oh, speak of the little devils. Knew it couldn't last.' She handed the cup over.

From outside came the unmistakeable sound of children on the loose. Then a door in a glass wall opened and a red-headed boy bombed in and bagsied one of the wooden tables, followed by thirty or more boys and girls who quickly filled up the tables, teachers at the rear. Viv, tea in hand, wondered where she could sit.

'You,' a teacher called out to a couple of girls about to sit at a table in the corner. 'Let the lady sit down.'

Viv was sitting there when he came in. Aware the only free chair was the one opposite her own, she kept her head down, not-reading the book she'd brought with her.

Don't come here. Don't come anywhere near me.

But the tea lady was pointing out the empty seat.

I don't want to share.

'May I?' He stood about a foot away, tray in hand.

Pretend you haven't heard.

But she made room pulling the book towards her.

Not at all like Jack.

'You mistook me for someone else?' He put the tray by the chair and sat down.

She nodded and went back to her book.

'I'm sorry I wasn't who you wanted me to be. Is it worth buying? Saw it in the shop.' He nodded at the book.

'Oh, P-pitmen Painters. Yes. Very good. The author was art critic on *The Observer*.'

He raised an interested eyebrow, taking a sip.

'It's part history of the group, part philosophy of art. The men discussed the nature of art and whether anyone can be an artist, as well as doing their own work.'

'And what do you think?' He put the cup down.

'Th-that it's human to be creative. That we all have creative impulses, but in most people they're unrealised.'

'And why do you think that is?'

What was this, a tutorial? She felt a bit like a student in front of an attractive tutor.

Act your age, then. Mugwort was on her shoulder. She took a deep breath. 'E-education or the lack of, or the type of, that's the main reason. Art, the arts, I can't believe how they're degrading them in the school curriculum and in universities...'

She stopped, her voice too loud in the silent room. Where had everyone gone? Did he just glance at her ringless hands?

You're kidding yourself. Mugwort sneered.

The school party had gone but the tea lady was still there, her back to them, chinking cups and saucers behind the counter, but looking as if she was trying not to. Viv glanced at his ringless ring finger, not that you could always tell.

'Anyway...' she gulped cold tea '... your turn now. What made you come here today?'

'The play.'

'Me too!'

He drained his cup. 'I'd never heard of the Pitmen Painters but my son got tickets, and when I saw it... well, I was blown away. It said everything I believe.'

'Me too, me and my husband, my l-late husband.'

He didn't comment, just said he'd been intending to come and see the paintings ever since, but had only just got round to it, combining work in this area with a bit of leave.

'From what?'

'I'm an architect, based in Liverpool.'

He had a slight Scouse accent. He liked converting old industrial buildings, he said. He'd done quite a bit of work on Albert Dock, and he loved what they'd done here in Newcastle, at the Baltic Centre. *Relax.* All she had to do was listen and calm down, but he came up with another question.

'Have you seen Gormley's iron men on Crosby beach?'

'No. Love his Angel of the North but...'

'But?'

'I went off him a bit when I found out that he wasn't Joe Gormley's son.'

'Sorry, you've lost me.' He shook his head.

'I had it in my head that he was working class, and son of the seventies miners' leader.'

He doesn't know what you're talking about, old lady. He's younger than you. Leave now.

Mugwort was right, she'd better leave before she made a fool of herself. He was an attractive man and she was attracted if her heart rate was anything to go by. And it was closing time. The tea lady was lifting chairs onto tables and Not Jack – she didn't even know his name – was getting to his feet, easily, smoothly, energetically. It was a mistake she was always making these days, assuming people ten or even twenty years younger than her were the same age as she was. Who was she kidding? Flashback, to a school reunion a few months ago, when she'd walked into the room and then out again thinking she must have come to the wrong place. Those old women with wrinkled faces could not possibly be her contemporaries, could they?

But they were.

He wasn't. She watched him carrying the tray to the counter, weaving deftly between the tables. He was most likely in his fifties, late fifties, but she probably seemed ancient to him as well as mad.

Stuffing her book into her bag, she headed for the door. If he looked her way she'd nod a goodbye, wave perhaps, and if he didn't, well, no harm done...

But he reached the door first and held it open.

'Gormley went to Ampleforth, the public school. His parents were well-heeled, but Hockney would qualify as one of your working-class artists.'

'I don't *need* artists to be working class.'

'But you prefer when they are?'

'I'm glad when they are.'

They got onto Richard Hoggart and *The Uses of Literacy* as they headed for the car park and by the time they reached their cars, the only two, parked side by side, they were back onto creativity. Could it be taught and was art anything you wanted it to be?

'Andy Warhol, do you agree with him?' He hesitated by the door of his Range Rover, a later model than hers.

'No!'

He laughed. 'We can't leave it there, can we? Don't suppose you're free for dinner tonight?'

33

VIV

She had a date, a *date*!

Viv turned off Classic FM. She didn't need surging violins.

You don't think he fancies you, do you?

Go away.

You can't go.

I know that.

So why didn't you say so?

She braked. Suddenly. Did that sign say 5 mph? She was still on the colliery site.

You're too old.

I pulled.

He felt sorry for you.

Shut up.

You reminded him of a teacher he liked.

His card was on the passenger seat. Patrick O'Malley RIBA. It gave his Liverpool address and phone numbers. He'd handed it to her when she'd said, 'Not sure.' He was staying at the Malmaison in Newcastle, he said, by the river. That was only a twenty-minute drive from Mother's.

'I'll book a table for eight o'clock and hope for the best,' he'd said.

* * *

Could she, should she? Still undecided at six o'clock, she put half an M&S meal for two in the fridge and carried the other half upstairs. How convenient that she hadn't managed to persuade her mother to get out of bed and come downstairs! How opportune that Mother wanted to be waited on hand and foot and eat in her room. She who'd spent a lifetime railing against slatterns who brought milk bottles to the table – a jug, please, Vivien! – now ate from a tray in her bed.

'I think perhaps I have been doing too much, Vivien,' she opined, sunk against the pillows.

'Too much what, Mum?' Eating perhaps? A five-ounce steak in a port and red wine jus, with pommes de terre boulangère and finely cut green beans in garlic butter, had disappeared quite rapidly. And then a dish of crème caramel with raspberries and cream, all washed down with Liebfraumilch.

It was six-fifteen by Mother's beside clock.

'What would you like to do this evening, Mum – watch a film, play cards?'

'I no longer *do*, Vivien.' Mother closed blue-shadowed eyes.

Her eyes were still closed at six-thirty when Viv looked in to see if her mother wanted cheese and biscuits. They were still closed at six forty-five when she looked in again, and at five to seven when she double-checked. Now in a silk shirt and her best-fitting denims, she thought she might go out. Thought. Who was she kidding? Luckily, she'd packed something smart in case she went out with Em. A charity-shop velvet jacket hung on the newel post downstairs.

'I'm thinking of popping out, Mum.'

Pop. Such a useful word. Pop out. Pop in. Pop up. Pop back in a minute. You won't notice I've gone. Said very quietly you might not even hear.

'Pop where?' Mother's blue eyelids went up like shutters.

'Jenny called.' Mother liked Jenny, an old school friend.

'Couldn't she come here?'

'No.' She could not. She definitely could not. Her grandchildren were staying and one of them had chicken pox and the other had measles... Why was she lying to her mother, making up stories like a naughty teenager?

Because she had a date and Mother would not approve. She was late but before she could leave Mother needed the loo. And to be helped back into bed. And the second crème caramel. Not to mention the cheese and biscuits and another glass of Liebfraumilch. And the DVD player set up, so she could watch *Gone With the Wind* again. But finally she was at the Metro station, only three minutes from Mother's. Lucky she'd remembered it. Built in the eighties, it hadn't been here when she was a girl. But it was quick, much quicker than driving, only ten minutes to the town centre according to the website. And then, what, ten more to the quayside if she walked fast? The Malmaison was by the river. She'd checked.

Let me know by seven.

Not a chance, it was twenty-five to eight already. She'd text in a minute when she was on the train. The train was due. People were waiting, young people joshing each other. They looked like students going out for a night on the town. *Me too! Me too!* But first there was a bloody ticket machine to grapple with.

'Choose station. Choose zone.' *Why am I reading aloud?*

'Here.' Helpful girl behind her in the queue, impatient, presses green button.

Helpful girl thinks you're geriatric.

Helpful girl points to coin slot but coins fall out as train comes in! Helpful girl says, 'Get on train. I'll do it.'

'Thank you!'

On the train at last, she looked for Patrick's card so she could text him. But the card wasn't in her bag. Or her pocket. Or her other pocket.

It was, she realised, in... the... bloody... car... on... the... bloody passenger seat.

* * *

It was five to eight when she reached the Quayside, puffed out from running. She stopped to get her breath and enjoy the view. What a view! How things had changed! Nothing like the murky dockside of her youth. Bridges like rainbows criss-crossed the river, luminous in the dark, their reflections forming dazzling circles on the water. A cubist fantasy of blocks and cylinders in psychedelic colours had replaced the mills and belching chimneys.

As church clocks all over the town struck the hour she arrived at the Malmaison. Eight and no doubt too late, but there was no harm in looking. To think this was once the Co-op warehouse. A flight of steps led to a doorway flanked by spirals of neatly clipped box, wrought-iron sculptures echoing their shape in a not bad attempt at turn-of-the-century art nouveau, but the dark interior on the other side of the revolving glass doors looked more like a seventies nightclub.

'Go if you're going, love.' Somebody behind her nudged her forward into the moving door and out onto a carpet covered with swirling shades of purple. 'Oh!' Someone else in a hurry nudged her arm. 'Oh! Oh!' It was *him, but not* nudging, holding.

'Got you. Sorry. Didn't mean to scare you. Don't want to lose you in the gloom.' He released her arm and took her hand. 'It's stupidly dark in here, isn't it? Brasserie okay, downstairs, rather than the formal dining room? I didn't book when I didn't hear from you. Just hoped.'

McDonald's okay. Greggs okay. Grass fine.

But how would she eat with her heart in her mouth?

Candlelight cast flickering shadows on Patrick's strong features. Tanned, from working on building sites or foreign assignments in warm climates perhaps, with pale lines where his eyes crinkled, grey eyes. Somehow she managed to order a starter and fish for main and a glass of Sancerre as an aperitif.

Thank God for the view – silence wasn't out of place. He was looking at it too. Their table by the window overlooked the Millennium Bridge, a shimmering rainbow of colours, pink, turquoise, neon yellow, pink, turquoise again... It was mesmerising.

'Wish I'd designed it.'

'Who did?'

'Eyre and Wilkinson?' He turned to look at her. 'If I remember correctly, there was a competition with certain criteria...'

You meet all of mine.

'It had to be tall enough for ships to sail under it, but not so tall that it overshadowed Stephenson's bridge. They asked local people to vote on the designs, over a hundred entries, I think. Did you vote?'

'When would that have been?'

'Late 1990s?'

She did calculations. 'We'd have moved south by then, my
husband and I...' She did her queen voice because she couldn't not,
and he smiled. It was a great smile. Good teeth. She explained
about Jack setting up on his own and moving south to take advantage of the building boom in Milton Keynes. And the art deco
house they'd both fallen in love with and restored together.

'Sounds as if you had a happy marriage.'

'Yes.' She remembered her sea bass.

'And what do you think of this happy couple?' He pointed to
pictures on the wall either side of the window, well-known portraits
of Napoleon and Josephine, but blown up to more than a metre
high and pop-arted.

'Not improved by the blobs.' They were all over them in Smar-
ties colours. 'Didn't one of the Pitmen Painters say something about
blobs in the play?'

'If you were the first person to see blobs in everything that was
originality, but...'

'... if you just copied the first man who did the blobs...' she
carried on.

'... that was imitation?' he finished.

'Something like that but...' she looked at the portraits again '...
why Napoleon and Josephine, here? Oh—' she remembered even as
she asked '—got it! Malmaison was where Josephine lived, near
Paris. There's a rose named after it.'

'Seems she was a keen gardener.' He paused while a waiter
cleared their empty plates, but she couldn't remember eating.

Time was racing and she had to get back.

'Well, that's what it says in a leaflet in my room. I'm no expert.
She bought the house while he was away in Egypt, confident he'd
pay for it with the spoils of war, but, alas, he was none too pleased
when he got back.'

But she was older than him and hot in bed so she probably won him over. Thank God he couldn't read her thoughts.

'Well, are you up for it?' OMG he could! But, just in time, she saw the dessert menu in front of her.

'Madam?' The waiter was hovering.

'No, thanks.'

He declined too.

'Coffee, madam?'

She nodded, needing to sober up. He nodded too.

'Here or in your room, sir?'

Patrick's eyes met hers enquiringly. It was noisy in the dining room, but he could probably hear the blood rushing through her veins. She said she thought they'd hear each other better in his room and he signed the bill. Did he know she'd stopped breathing? She glanced at her watch. Gone nine already. What *was* she thinking? He was standing beside her now, hand reaching out.

If I take it I'm done for.

Done for. The mirror walls in the lift multiplied her ruin. A dozen or more Vivs and Patricks looked into each other's eyes and held hands hungry for each other. When the lift doors opened they became two again and walked hand in hand down the long, carpeted corridor. Somehow her legs didn't give way, somehow, she stayed upright as he unlocked the door to his room and pushed it open to reveal a bed three pillows wide, the top sheet folded back in a neat triangle.

'It's been a long time...' The door clicked behind them as her velvet jacket fell to the floor.

'We'll be fine.' He eased the silk shirt from her shoulder and his lips found the little dip above her collarbone that made her gasp... and the phone in her bag on the floor started ringing.

'Viv cannot take your call right now.'

She cannot. She cannot.

'Viv will get back to you later if you leave a short message after the pips.'

Viv's hand loosened the knot of her lover's tie as his hand unhooked her lace bra.

Then – *why?* - Viv stopped to listen to her phone.

'Vivien, come home. Now, Vivien. *Now.*'

Viv's hand fell to her side at the sound of the all too familiar insistent voice.

'Vivien, I've had an accident. Tell Jenny you've got to come home. Now. *Now*, Vivien! Now!'

35

VIV

Viv got home in record time in a taxi the lovely man phoned for.

Viv found her mum alive and well, again.

You are a manipulative, domineering old woman! She didn't say that. 'I thought you were hurt. That you'd broken your leg, or a hip, or your spine.'

'I'm sorry, Vivien.'

But what exactly was Mother sorry for? As she watched the ambulance pulling away from the kerb, driving away to a genuine emergency, her mother sat in bed behind her, clean and dry and upright, dabbing her eyes with a lace-edged handkerchief.

'I didn't ring 999, Vivien. You did. If you'd been here...' Mother was playing Hurt Old Lady big time and Mother was right about Viv ringing the ambulance if nothing else. Viv had rung 999 from the taxi as soon as Patrick had helped her into it. She'd reached her mother's house before the ambulance, to find her sitting on the loo, alive and well, wet pants as far away from her as she could kick them. It was ten minutes before the paramedics arrived and checked Mother over very thoroughly, doing all sorts of tests including an ECG. Needing to pee suddenly can be a symptom of an imminent heart attack, they said. They must check her over, and they had, but then pronounced Mother's heart very strong for a woman of her age, and her blood pressure remarkable. In short, they couldn't find anything wrong with her.

'I thought I'd find you on the floor, Mum.'

Mother's 'accident' was failing to get to the lav in time. She had left it too late to get to the bathroom so she'd peed herself on the landing. Then she'd called Viv to come home and sort her out, and Viv had come home and sorted her out, trying not to show her fury, trying not to think about what she'd left behind as she'd rushed from that hotel room.

'You lied to me, Vivien.' Mother dabbed her eyes again. 'You don't need a taxi to get from Jenny's.' Her mum must have got off the lav to go to the window to see the taxi arrive, so she could move when she wanted to. 'Where were you going anyway, dressed up like a dog's dinner?' Had she suspected all along? Had she called her deliberately to spoil her evening? Mother's magenta mouth crimped. 'You always were boy-mad.'

Viv left next morning. Early. Despite Mother's protests. 'You've only just arrived!'

Patrick hadn't answered her texts or calls. She'd texted him to thank him for his help and to say:

Let's meet again soon.

But the text had returned undelivered. 'Let me know how it goes,' he'd said as he'd helped her into the back of the cab. And so she had let him know, or tried to, but the texts had kept coming back undelivered. Phoning hadn't worked either. In the morning she'd tried again and failed again and had then rung the hotel on the landline in case the cause was poor mobile reception. It was always dodgy at Mother's. But the man on Reception had said Mr

O'Malley had checked out early that morning. Where had he said he was going? What had he said he was going to do next day? She wracked her brains trying to remember. Did he say he was going abroad? On a business trip? With an early morning plane to catch? Why, why hadn't she listened? *Because you only had one thing on your mind, tart.*

She had to concentrate on driving, even though she was only crawling now, in a line of bumper-to-bumper traffic. She hadn't reached the A1 yet, was still on the approach road and there were lorries ahead for as far as she could see. And was this snow? Yes. Bloody great flakes of it. The windscreen wipers were going crazy. It would have made sense to wait till the rush hour was over, but if she had she might have murdered her mother.

36

JANET

Janet left The Chequers as quickly as she could throw her things into her bag. She settled the bill with the smirking Maria, got in the car and put her foot down. At this rate she'd be back in Banks Peninsula by late afternoon, if she didn't skid off the winding road first. Grant and Belynda would not want to see her three days early. She did not want to see them sooner than she had to. She reduced speed and pulled into a layby. According to the satnav it was two hundred and fifty-three miles direct or three hundred by the scenic route. Either would get her back much too soon.

Two days in a luxurious hotel on the Kaikoura Coast restored her spirits, but whose spirits would not be restored by the sight of a turquoise sea against a backdrop of snow-capped mountains, and seals basking on the shore in brilliant sunshine? Whose appetite for life would not be revived by crayfish as delicious as the guidebook claimed, and copious amounts of a very palatable Pinot Gris. Sav would never pass her lips again. But as she sat on the sand, hugging her knees, waves crashing towards her as she kept a lookout for the fin or waterspout of a whale, she reconsidered that decision. Sav had been part of the most amazing experience she'd ever had in her life. Sav was delicious.

No regrets. *Je ne regrette rien.*

As the sea lapped her toes her thoughts turned to Alan Loveday. Could the clever fingers that had so deftly removed and replaced a door seal be equally deft at a foot massage? She would write and say she was looking forward to seeing him. But first the new enlightened Janet must go back to Banks Peninsula and be the perfect guest for one more night. She would book herself another short holiday to fill the last few days and leave them to their love-making. She would not mention the funeral. What was the point? Let bygones be bygones. She was moving on. Moving forward. Moving up. It was wonderful that her son had a happy marriage and a happy family life. Grant and Belynda could make love as loudly as they liked for as long as they liked.

Back in the hotel, she went online and booked a short package holiday in the temperate rainforest in the south of the island. She then texted Grant to tell him she was coming back one day early, but only for one night. That would be acceptable, surely?

* * *

But Belynda, alone in the back garden, on a hammock strung between two cabbage palms, looked none too pleased to see her. 'I thought you weren't coming back till tomorrow!' She struggled into a sitting position.

'A change of plan. I did tell Grant.'

'The Chequers not up to your high standards?' Belynda manoeuvred herself into a bikini top, her long braid swinging over her breasts.

'It was...' Janet aimed for harmony '... rather quiet.'

'Too quiet for *you*?' Belynda was in the kitchen before she resumed her assault. She was cross. Understandably. Her peace had been disturbed. But the new Janet was keeping her cool.

'There was,' she said carefully, 'just me and the proprietor.' No need for the full story.

'Oh. *Oh*. Got it.' Belynda smiled as she filled the kettle. 'You feared for your honour.'

Deep breath. Count to ten. 'I'm sorry I disturbed your solitude.'

'No worries. They'll all be back soon anyway. Coffee?' Belynda reached for mugs. 'But that explains a lot, it really does.'

'Sorry. What explains what?' She had lost the thread. 'No coffee for me, thank you.'

Belynda carried on spooning instant into two mugs. 'Why you're so cold and put men down.'

'Excuse me?' This was almost funny.

'All your life, according to Grant—' Belynda put the two mugs on the table '—you were Queen Bee and they had to beware your sting.'

This was a travesty of the truth and she couldn't let it go.

'Belynda—' she sat down opposite the assured young woman '—I do not want to fall out with you. I am glad of this opportunity to tell you how much I admire you. I am grateful for the grandchildren you have given me, and the way you bring them up and most of all for the way that you have transformed my son into someone I hardly recognise. But—' she took a gulp of the hot liquid '—I must tell you that I spent my marriage in a state of subjugation. I was oppressed by my husband, and then by my husband *and my son*, who conspired against me To The Very End.' She took another gulp as Grant came through the door. 'Ask him to tell you what he did at his father's funeral.' Head pounding, she took herself to her room, prepared to leave it there.

It was they who returned to the fray.

37

VIV

Viv got home to a flood.

It was in Jack's study, her going-to-be studio, now empty of his stuff, which was a small consolation. Water was pouring through the roof and carrying on unimpeded, via the light switch, into the sitting room below where paper was peeling off the walls and rugs were near-floating. Why hadn't the neighbour's girl noticed when she came in to feed Claudia? Because, she said tearfully, she'd come into the kitchen by the back door, and hadn't seen it. The back of the house was dry.

By evening a tarpaulin covered the hole in the roof. Driers and dehumidifiers were promised for Monday and the electricity was back on in some of the house. Thankfully, she was insured – phew! But then came another blow. 'Sorry, Mrs Halliday,' said Jade on the end of the phone, 'your policy doesn't cover the cost of getting the hole fixed.' *What?* 'It covers the damage but not the cause of the damage.'

It took several minutes for this to sink in, that the insurance company would pay for the replacement or repair of damaged

furniture and furnishings, but they would *not* pay for the repair of
the hole in the roof and they certainly wouldn't pay for a new roof.
But Lee and Sons, who'd fixed the leak temporarily, said Viv *had* to
have a new roof, asap, or water would start coming in all over the
house. 'But that will cost thousands!'

The only consolation was that she had no time to think about
Patrick O'Malley.

He's dumped you.

Not a word for over a week now. Nor from Zelda, though she'd
texted about the flood and suggested lunch. What had happened to
all for one and one for all? The old Zelda would have been round
here with buckets and a pair of Marigolds and invited *her* for lunch.

Janet's email had been a surprise on Sunday morning.

29th November.
Peninsula Hotel.
Dear Both
Returning early, on Sunday 5 December, but will still miss meeting on
3rd. Can we reschedule to Friday 10th? Trying to be positive but have
losses to report. My fault. Everything is my fault. Of course.
Janet x

Oh dear. Perhaps now was not the time to tell her about Cynical
Bastard. What had turned her idyllic holiday into a disaster? Viv
replied to the joint email.

Hi Both, I can meet Friday 10th or even before? Will also report losses.
Viv x

She also sent another to Zelda repeating her offer of Sunday
lunch but didn't go into detail about the roof disaster. That could
wait. There were only two things to do when you were down: have a

drink, or keep busy. As it was only eleven in the morning she decided to tackle a job she'd been meaning to do for months.

An hour later she stood back from the cupboard in the utility room with some satisfaction. There was room for the vacuum cleaner now and the door didn't spring open when she tried to shut it. Beside her were two charity bags filled with padded envelopes she'd never reuse, umpteen rolls of wallpaper she'd never patch up with, and assorted toys the grandkids would never play with again, including a ride-on Thomas the Tank Engine. Job done, mission accomplished and all without a drop of wine passing her lips. But what time was it? Midday – too early for an aperitif?

It would help me tackle those.

She eyed the condolence cards warily, a carrier bagful, which she'd found at the back of the cupboard, where you put things whose fate was still to be decided. To keep or not to keep, that was the question. Were they to be given everlasting life in the book she'd once bought to stick them in or death by shredder? She still hadn't decided an hour later. Sorted into bundles some time ago, they were in front of her on the desk. The larger bundle was of cards with a standard message like 'Thinking of You' or 'With Deepest Sympathy' and just a few words or a signature underneath – she'd sent a few like that in her time – the smaller was of ones she treasured because they were more personal and included letters.

'Jack always struck us as a man who had everything and couldn't believe his luck,' wrote George Beaumont.

'Jack was one of the best, Viv, but you'll be okay. You're stronger than you think you are,' said Angie, who she hadn't heard from for ages.

'Jack was a decent bloke, an honest straight-dealing businessman, rare in our time,' said someone called Phil. There were several in that vein and these she would always keep, to read in her dotage to remind herself of the lovely man she'd married, and to share with grandchildren and great-grandchildren, so they would know the excellent stock they came from.

Did I answer them? She hoped so but had a feeling she hadn't, because she'd been so focussed on moving forward and forging a new life. In an even smaller bundle were a few she couldn't have replied to because she'd never found out who they were from. Who were Martin, Tom and Vi? Tom, she thought they'd eventually identified, a contractor of some kind – he'd turned up one day – but Martin had remained a mystery and so had Vi. Was there a clue in the view of Blencathra on Martin's card or the glossy photograph of a bowl of pansies on Vi's? Martin's message was short and simple, 'HAPPY MEMORIES' in manly capitals. Had he and Jack walked in the Lake District as teenagers or in their early twenties? Jack hadn't talked much about the years before he met her. Vi's note was longer, written in cramped letters beneath the standard 'With Deepest Sympathy'.

> *I knew Jack when he was a shy young man, a long-haired Viking and real charmer. Never forget how lucky you were to have him all those years.*
>
> *Sorry for your loss,*
> *Vi*

It was in an elderly hand, she'd thought then and still did, possibly arthritic. Jack's parents weren't alive by the time he died so she'd asked his sisters if there was an aunt or a godparent called Vi, but they'd said they didn't know anyone of that name. An old flame perhaps. Jack must have had girlfriends before he met her in his late twenties. But what sort of old flame would keep track of him for a lifetime? Ping! A text. Patrick?

Her stupid heart leaped.

38

ZELDA

Viv's text was from Zelda declining lunch.

You should have accepted. The Westies were on the floor, beneath the breakfast bar, hoovering up croissant flakes.

'I know but it would have been awkward. I don't know what to say to her any more.'

Because you're hiding things.

It was true, but she couldn't talk freely to Viv till she was sure she'd ditched Felix. If she let something slip now, Viv would know she'd been deceiving her for weeks. She would be hurt and cross and disapproving. Viv would think she was desperate or weak-willed or both. Oddly, she felt more in common with Janet than Viv nowadays. Viv was completely happy on her own. She didn't want another man in her life, and Zelda and Janet did. It was as simple as that.

She reread both of Viv's messages. 'More losses than gains to report.' What was that about? Had she missed a text while her phone was out of order? Another email from Encounters pinged into her iPad. The requests were coming in steadily from this new site.

Hi Vintage Champagne,
Hurray! Aging Rioja has added you to his Favourites. To find out more about him log in to your 'Fans' area, or if you can't wait click View My Fan.

Aging Rioja was a witty name in the circumstances, so she clicked. Oh, but he looked more of an Aging Rocker. Bald head with ponytail wasn't a good look in her opinion, but he did seem to have teeth and he'd sent her a personal message.

Hi Vintage Champagne,
You sound just my cup of tea! Mixing drinks can be risky but less so with food. How about meeting for a bite to eat?

Where did he live? She needed to look at his Short Profile to find out. Oh, here it was. She was getting better at this. Liverpool. He was a retired car worker with an interest in music of all kinds, and a passion for industrial archaeology. It would be interesting to know where her Liverpool ancestors had worked, a bit far though, unless...

Hi Aging Rioja, Take your point about mixing drinks, but perhaps we could risk it once? I may be coming to Liverpool before Christmas to see family, but won't have time for a meal. How about a coffee? Pleased to hear of your interest in industrial archaeology. Have ancestors who lived in Liverpool in the late nineteenth century. I'd like to know their occupations.

That was enough. No need to write a novel. She'd found the Costellos in the 1890 census. A great-grandmother on her mother's side. Would Gina object if she went out to meet someone for a drink when she was staying with her? Not that she was sure she was

going to see her sisters yet. Neither had replied to her suggestion
that she go up in three weeks' time. They were probably still huffy
that she'd turned down their invitation to go for Christmas, but she
didn't want another festive season with her brothers-in-law snoring
and farting all afternoon, not to mention their dubious jokes. She
hadn't said that of course, or that a hotel in Scotland with Tracey
was much more appealing and already booked.

Hi again Vintage Champagne,
Happy to buy you a drink if that's all you have time for. Let me know
if/when you have dates for trip to Liverpool. Suggest we meet in the bar
at the Phil. Trust you know that great pub? Names and addresses of
your ancestors would be useful beforehand if you want me to find out
possible workplaces.

He sounded interesting, kind and helpful, and a drink in the
wonderful bar of The Philharmonic would be very acceptable. She
replied saying she was hoping to come up the weekend before
Christmas and suggested they meet on the Saturday afternoon if
she did. He replied that he'd pencilled it in. She would tell her
sisters she was nipping out to do some last-minute Christmas
shopping.

Hi Vintage Champagne,
Hurray! Cheerful Charlie has added you to his Favourites. To find out
more...

And another:

Hi Vintage Champagne,
Hurray! Bald and Bookish has added you to his Favourites. To find out
more...

There were lots of people out there looking for companionship. All she had to do was make sure History Man knew he was history and start investigating.

39

VIV

Viv was raking wet leaves off Scheming Bastard's front lawn. He wasn't at home today. Surprise, surprise. She'd probably find her cheque in the greenhouse, not that sixty quid would solve her problems. A new roof! Where the hell was she going to get the money to pay for that? She was going to have to remortgage, if she could, but two lenders had turned her down already and she hadn't found a roofer to take the job on. Swallowing her pride, she'd texted Patrick asking him if he knew anyone with experience of art deco roofing, hoping a professional question might elicit an answer, but zilch.

He doesn't want anything to do with you. How much proof do you need?

It was two weeks now since she'd got back from Newcastle.

'Excuse me, erm... Mrs Loveday?' A curly-haired blonde woman stood in the drive with a piece of paper in her hand.

'No, darling.' Her partner tried a restraining hand, but the woman brushed it aside, smiling at Viv, head on one side.

'I know we shouldn't but... could we possibly?'

'May I?' Viv took the paper from the woman's hand. Yes, it was what she thought it was. 'The Poplars, a desirable family residence in a third of an acre' was up for sale, though – she glanced round – there was no For Sale sign in the garden. So, Bastard was doing it secretly, selling up and moving in with Janet to live off her. 'Sorry.' She handed back the estate agent's flier. 'I'm only the gardener, but here's the owner now.'

Alan was smoothing into the drive in his new Jag.

* * *

'I know you think I'm a total shit.'

'I can't deny it.' She sipped her coffee.

'I like spreadsheets.'

'Obviously.'

He'd insisted they talk, once he'd sent the couple on their way, saying they must make an appointment through the estate agent. He'd been doing the school run et cetera blah. That was why he hadn't been here earlier. He wasn't avoiding her, he was looking forward to a discussion actually. Now they were sitting in his pristine kitchen, the spaniel surprisingly quiet and still at his feet, the incriminating document on the table between them.

'So I'd like to explain...'

Well, he could try.

'I think I love Janet.'

'Think?' She raised an eyebrow.

'Yes—' he nodded '—think, but if you've got something to detect the real thing, some sort of litmus test for love, Ms Halliday, please let me have it. All I know is what I feel right now. That I'm longing to see Janet again, that I enjoy her company when I'm with her, that she makes me happy and I think I make her happy. But will these feelings last? Is this love the lasting kind? I was happily married for nearly forty years. Somehow against all the odds Penny and I made each other happy most of the time. So, I've been trying to work out how we did that, why it worked. This survey you despise was an attempt to be rational about it, misguided maybe, but as I see it marriages can fall apart over little things like who pays for what, who cooks and who stacks the dishwasher. They cause rows or festering grievances.' He turned the spreadsheet towards her. 'WPFW. Who pays for what? WC. Who cooks? WSD. Who stacks the dishwasher? I didn't include who cleans the lav?' He laughed. 'But maybe I should. That was one of the first things Penny taught me.'

She didn't answer.

'The thing is...' he sighed '... I was trying to maximise my chances of making it work with someone else, with Janet, I decided quite early on. I had Penny's blessing...'

She held up her hand. 'Please...' He didn't need to say any more, but of course he did.

'Viv, I can't wait to see Janet again. It's been a long month and I feel a bond between us. I've missed her and I hope she's missed me, but of course hope she's had a great holiday too. Couples should be happy when they're together but also when they're apart. They don't have to live in each other's pockets. The question is, have we, Janet and I, got what it takes to be happy together long term – with Kenny of course?' The dog sat up and he fondled its ears. 'You know Janet well. What do you think?'

She didn't know what she thought. The wind had left her sails, her legs had been knocked from under her because she had the uncomfortable feeling that she agreed with every word he'd said.

40

JANET

Janet saw him before he saw her.

Thud. Her heart really went thud.

She was pushing her trolley, after just coming through Nothing to Declare. He was behind a barrier scanning the crowd coming towards him holding a placard saying 'Mrs Carmichael's Car'. He waved when he saw her. She couldn't wave back because she needed two hands to push and steady her trolley, and if she stopped she'd cause a traffic jam. So their eyes met first, across a crowded arrival lounge. What a cliché! What a stupendous cliché! What a wonderfully accurate cliché! He beamed and made her feel warm inside. She beamed and hoped it did the same for him. His face lit up as they made contact. Hers burned beneath her suntan.

'Good to see you.' He held out his arms as she stepped beyond the barrier and she let him wrap them round her, resting her cheek against his chest. Thud. Thud. Thud. Was that her heart or his? Could you feel a heartbeat through a Barbour? Disengaging, she saw blurry lights on the other side of plate-glass doors, taxis stopping and starting. It was dark outside and cold and rainy, or she might have shed a few tears. It must be eleven o'clock or later by now. How lovely to have a personal chauffeur. How lovely to not have to find her way to the Heathrow Express.

'Come on.' He took charge of the trolley and steered it through the crowds. At last she could stop counting her bags and thinking about how to get from A to B. As they crossed the road to the high-rise car park, she felt the tension in her shoulders easing. As he fed the colossal fee into the pay machine, she could only admire how easily he found the lift, and located his car.

'New car?'

'Yes, the new Jaguar XJ. I treated myself.' He opened the passenger-side door and helped her in, and when a few seconds later she hadn't managed to do up the seat belt he leaned over from the driver's side to help her do it up.

Kiss him. But she couldn't, though her lips were close to his cheek.

'Heated seats will come on in a minute. You'll be asleep in no time.' He straightened up and started the engine.

But she didn't think she would because her body clock said it was midday, she'd slept on the flight home and the warmth under her bottom made her feel not-sleepy-at-all. 'I feel quite er... lively actually.' Too forward? Or not forward enough?

'I've missed you, Janet.' He got to the queue for the barrier.

'I've missed you, Alan.'

'I've tried to keep busy. Watered your plants. Walked Kenny more than usual.'

'Thank you. How is Kenny?'

'Fine. Did all the jobs Viv told me to do.' He reached the front of the queue.

'How is Viv?'

'Fine.' The barrier was up and he needed to concentrate. The road ahead was busy and the traffic was throwing up a lot of muddy spray. Good. She could rehearse her lines, though they had been much rehearsed on the flight home. *No need to drive back to yours when we get to Elmsley, Alan. You look tired, why not stay over? Fancy a nightcap when we get home?* Casually, as if she always offered him a late-night drink.

But by the time they reached the village at one o'clock in the morning she hadn't said a word of it. Because back in England she was the same old uptight Janet. And he was the same helpful, competent, just-a-good-friend Alan. Once her front door was open he went straight upstairs, to check the bedroom radiators, he said, taking her overnight bag with him.

Follow him. But she stayed at the bottom of the stairs. *Ask him if he'd like a drink.* But when he came downstairs to adjust the thermostat in the hall she scurried into the downstairs loo. When she came out, determined to say something, he wasn't there.

'Aren't you coming up?' He was leaning over the upstairs banisters. 'Your bed awaits you.'

Coming! But she couldn't. She started flicking through the pile of post on the hall table and he came downstairs. 'All the radiators are working fine. Bled them yesterday and reset the thermostat. They'll go off in half an hour but come on again in the morning at six-thirty.'

She nodded.

'Anything else I can do for you, Janet, before I go home? Would you like a drink or a bite to eat? There are snacks in the fridge and a bottle of white.' He looked tired and didn't need another ten-mile drive.

Yes, let's have a nightcap and then go to bed. But she couldn't say it.

She let him go into the dark night but not before he'd shared the news that her neighbour, the one over the road, had died while she was away. 'Barbara? Barbara Thornton?' *How? When?* She wanted to know, but he'd gone. She watched him driving away, feeling quite shaky. Death was always a shock even when expected and this wasn't. *Poor Barbara.* Yes, *poor* Barbara, despite everything. She'd let resentment and envy and grief – she must have loved Malcolm – eat away at her and ruin her life.

I won't do that.

As Janet sat on the sofa sipping a glass of white wine her last encounter with the poor woman came vividly back. It was the day she was leaving for New Zealand later that night. Belatedly, Barbara had accepted her invitation to come round for a cup of tea, and though it wasn't the most convenient time, Janet had thought it would be good to get it over with, ready for a fresh start when she got back. But it hadn't gone quite as planned.

Barbara, garbed in her usual charcoal suit and white shirt, had sat on the edge of her seat in the conservatory. She'd accepted tea and a piece of cake, which she'd nearly dropped when Janet had mentioned the letters. 'Let*ters*?' she'd hissed. 'Did you say let*ters*? I wrote only the one when I wasn't quite myself.'

Janet had pointed to the pile on the coffee table in front of her, filed in chronological order over the years, the first to arrive all those years ago on top. Barbara had dismissed it with a flick of her hand. 'I wouldn't say "He *don't* love you." I'm an educated woman.'

So Barbara wasn't the only one. As this realisation had hit Janet, she'd seen it hit Barbara too, perhaps harder. Her lip had trembled. 'I know how you feel,' Janet had said gently, hoping it might draw them together. 'Malcolm treated us badly, and others, obviously.'

But Barbara, suddenly aware she wasn't the sole love of Malcolm's life, had been struggling to her feet. She'd headed for the door and the last Janet had seen of her was her bowed back scuttling down the drive to her own front door.

Was it too late to ring Maggie and ask how and when Barbara died? But yes, it was much too late, half past one by the clock on the hall table, the carriage clock that Malcolm received for twenty-five years at the bank. She was even more wide awake now, so she started to sort the heap of mail half covering the table, into two piles, junk and everything else, until a picture postcard from New Zealand caught her eye.

Hi Jan, sorry we were interrupted. Will look you up when next in UK. Tony.

'No!' She tore it up. Were all men the same? She climbed the stairs. No. A good man had switched on the bedside lamps in her beautiful bedroom and turned back the duvet in her lovely bed. A kind and decent man – oh bliss – had put a hot-water bottle in the exact spot where her feet reached. That man must be called back. She lifted the phone but put it down again. He was tired. What if he came off the road answering her call? She looked at the empty pillow beside hers. She *had* changed, she had, she had.

But not enough. Yet.

41

ZELDA

'So, how do I get him into bed?'

Zelda leaned forward to hear better. Had Janet really just said that? She must get her hearing checked. 'Jingle Bells' wasn't helping and neither was sitting in this booth in the corner under the speaker, but Viv who'd booked, said she hadn't had a choice. With Christmas only two weeks away, The Wagon and Horses was packed with noisy partygoers.

'Ask him?' Viv didn't see a problem. 'Say "I'd like to go to bed with you"?'

Janet's face twisted in anguish. 'I've tried, but it won't come out.'

Viv raised an eyebrow.

'Ouch! That was me, Janet.' Zelda rubbed her leg. Drinking fizzy water, she felt like an outsider. It was all right for those two in their local, they could totter home on foot. But so far so good. Perhaps she could relax? Viv wasn't asking her any awkward questions and, interestingly, she seemed to have forgotten Alan Loveday was Calculating Scheming Bastard. Or why was she encouraging Janet to go to bed with him?

'Sorry, Zelda.' Janet took a gulp of Prosecco. 'I meant to kick Viv.

And, sorry again for saying sorry, but there's another thing I need your help with before you two have your turn.' She looked only slightly less anguished than before. 'I've got this *turkey*.'

Running wild in her kitchen? Gobbling in her garden? No, it was in her freezer, though there was hardly room for it. It was a giant turkey. Oven-ready, it had arrived that morning from Fortnum & Mason. A client of Grant's had wanted to send it to him not realising he lived in New Zealand and he had asked the client to send it to Janet.

'And the problem?' Zelda wondered if she'd missed something.

'What do I *do* with it?' It was a Janet-wail.

'Roast it?'

'Thank you, Zelda. I'd got that far myself. My problem is *when* to roast it and for *whom*? It weighs ten kilos and is not a meal for one.' She looked from one to the other. 'I don't suppose either of you are free on Christmas Day, are you? No, no—' she shook her head, answering her own question '—you won't be, of course not, but perhaps a few days before?'

Zelda felt torn in two. Poor Janet! Was she going to be by herself, *alone* on Christmas Day? She opened and closed her mouth, wanting to invite her to come to Scotland with her and Tracey. But she couldn't do that without asking Tracey. Fortunately while she was agonising, wishing she could photocopy herself, Viv, more quick-thinking, was having a light-bulb moment.

'Alan! Invite him. Two birds with one stone? Romantic meal for two?'

Zelda nearly clapped.

But Janet was shaking her head. 'He'll be with his family. It's their first without Penny. You know she died on Christmas Day?'

How cruel Fate could be! Harry had died on her birthday. 'Could you,' she said tentatively, 'give it to a food bank, or to the old people's home in the village where you help out, or invite people who haven't got family, from your church perhaps?' That would solve the lonely Christmas Day problem.

'Actually...' Janet looked thoughtful '... that's not a bad idea, Zelda. Last Sunday I heard one of the very old ladies at church saying she never wanted to cook another Christmas dinner ever again – her husband's got Parkinson's – and I thought then that if I were a really nice person I'd say, "Well, don't, come to mine." And that was pre-turkey.'

'Sorted, then,' said Viv. 'You *are* a really nice person and I bet there are several who'd love an invite. Now, Zelda, your turn. Gains and losses since last time. What's the latest on History Man?'

Why bring him up?

'Viv, he was aeons ago.' Janet topped up their glasses.

I wish. But Viv was giving her a funny look. Fortunately, Janet suddenly remembered that her neighbour had died while she was away, *their* neighbour, Barbara, the one who used to send the nasty notes. 'Maggie says there's going to be a post-mortem and they haven't ruled out suicide.' What had Viv heard? The two of them talked about that for a bit, and Janet said she felt a bit guilty. The woman, the 'poor woman' now, had died about three weeks ago. Should she have tried harder to be neighbourly?

'Don't beat yourself up.' Viv emptied her glass. 'You were amazingly forgiving, considering what she did to you. Didn't you write her a note inviting her to coffee?'

Janet nodded. 'And she came, well, for tea, the day I flew to New Zealand.'

Zelda hoped for more detail but Viv was giving her that look again. 'Your turn, Zelda. What do you want to tell us?'

It felt a bit *pointed.*

'Well, if I go to Liverpool next week to see my sisters I might meet up with this chap I met online who calls himself Aging Rioja.'

'Sounds fun. Is that all? Sure? Okay, my turn.' Viv took a very deep breath. 'I need to confess, offload, call it what you will, that when I went up north to see my mother last month I met a man, an attractive man, and made an absolute bloody fool of myself.'

For the next few minutes she described what amounted to a *one-night stand* with a man she'd met one afternoon in an art gallery and hadn't heard from since. Zelda stopped her jaw dropping to the floor, but was utterly flabbergasted. Was this if-you've-had-the-best-you-can-keep-the-rest Viv? Amazingly, Janet was nodding away, totally sympathetic, empathetic even. 'How *frustrating*, Viv! I know how you feel. But all is not lost, if he was going away on business next day. In some places they don't have Wi-Fi. Have you not got his postal address?'

Viv hesitated, then took a business card from her wallet.

Zelda felt like the grown-up in the room as Janet drooled. 'Oh, stylish card. You must write him a proper letter on your headed notepaper.'

'Janet...' Zelda wanted to inject some realism, but – phew – Viv seemed to be coming to her senses on her own.

'It's been three weeks now. I think the message is clear. He could have, *would* have got in touch if he wanted to. I have my pride.' She put the wallet back in her pocket.

'But, Viv,' Janet persisted, 'you've been urging me to be proactive.' Janet still had the business card in her hand, Zelda couldn't help noticing.

'Because it's totally different, Janet. You've known Alan for years and have evidence that he's a decent person.'

What made Viv change her mind?

'I-I got carried away,' Viv went on. 'Pheromones I suppose. He seemed lovely and was very good-looking. We clicked. He seemed to feel the same way. And you needn't look so superior, Zelda. I saw you in The Red Lion with History Man, holding hands.'

'Oh no!' She spluttered water all over the table as Viv and Janet skewered her with accusing looks.

But it was eventually a relief to confess and explain and consult about her difficulties with History Man aka Felix. Not least because he'd invited her to a 'festive gathering' at his house to meet his other students, which she'd like to do. Well, she'd like to meet the other students. But should she go? Was it wise to go to his house? They thought that would be okay as long as one of them was on standby. All for one! By the end of the meal The Muscateers were back on course, their bonds even stronger. Janet insisted on paying the bill as her Christmas treat to them both, and when she got back from the bar she gave Viv the business card she said she'd *inadvertently* put in her pocket. Inadvertent Janet? That was almost as unlikely as 'how do I get him into bed?' Janet or Viv's nearly-a-one-night-stand.

42

VIV

Viv, just home from work on Monday, hadn't yet opened the door. As snowflakes fluttered round her head, she was extracting the post from her overflowing letter box when a Liverpool postmark caught her eye. On a buff envelope with a typed address, it stood out from the rest which looked like Christmas cards. *Calm down, it's probably a bill.* But *his* address was on the back! She tore it open.

Dear Ms Halliday
    Thank you for getting in touch. I have read your brochure

How did he get my brochure?

and visited your website as suggested. The services you offer are interesting and your references impressive, but I need more detail. In the light – or even dark! – of our previous meeting I feel sure we could work creatively together. I would like to discuss the possibility of future projects and will be down your way later this week, staying at The Cedars in Northamptonshire. (www.thecedarsnorthants.co.uk.) Could you possibly join me for

a working lunch on Wednesday or Thursday? FYI my mobile is
working now that I am back in UK.
    Yours truly,
    Patrick O'Malley

She held his name to her lips.

He'd got in touch. He was back from wherever he'd been. He
wanted to see her again. With shaking hands she opened the front
door, dumped everything on the floor, grabbed her phone and
texted frantically, cursing her cold, fumbling fingers.

Dear Mr O'Malley, Thank you for your very welcome letter. I would be
delighted to see you again to discuss a future relationship and could join
you at The Cedars for lunch on Wednesday.

Delete Wednesday. Change to Thursday. Delete relationship,
replace with work. Just in case she'd read more into it than he
intended. Reread.

Dear Mr O'Malley, Thank you for your very welcome letter. I would be
delighted to see you again to discuss future work and could join you at
The Cedars for lunch on Thursday. Yours truly, Viv

Send.

Her phone rang.

'Hi.' His voice! *His* voice! His deep, slightly scratchy, slightly
Scouse voice. 'Sorry about the breakdown in communications. I
thought I told you I was going to Cuba where Wi-Fi is almost non-
existent.'

Pit pat boom! *Calm down, heart.* She sat on the floor before her
legs gave way.

'I did try to get in touch.' He was still speaking.

Boom! Boom! Boom! Boom! Boom! Was she having a heart attack? Should she call 999?

'Are you there, Viv? Viv?'

She nodded pointlessly till her voice came back. 'Yes, yes, I am.'

'See you Thursday, then.'

'Yes.'

If she lived till then.

43

JANET

Janet was refilling Alan's coffee cup. 'How many would that be if they all said yes?'

'Eight.' He was counting the names on their list.

'I thought seven.'

He'd rung earlier to say he needed advice on presents for his daughters. She'd said, 'Come round for coffee and help me draw up a list of people from church who might welcome an invitation to Christmas lunch.' They were sitting side by side so they could both see the list. At the top were Mr and Mrs Jefferson – Alan also remembered her saying she never ever wanted to cook another Christmas dinner in her life again. Then came another couple, Mr and Mrs Hughes and then Marcus, the quiet, rather odd young man who printed their leaflets. He didn't seem to have any other friends and nor did Miss Taylor, the organist.

'Still seven.' She was sure. 'With me.'

'Oh,' he said, turning to face her. 'Don't I get an invite?'

'But...' She was a bit flustered, as she'd assumed he'd be spending the day with his daughters. He, unflustered, said both of them had invited him, but to their respective in-laws' houses, not their own, and frankly he wasn't too keen. He had invited both girls and their families to his house – he'd offered to cook – but they had both declined. They thought doing what they usually did, all of them round the table at The Poplars, would be too painful and not fair to the children. 'So, I told them to do their own thing and I would do mine. They protested a bit, but I think they were relieved. Of course, if you don't you want me...' He looked a bit Eeyore.

'Of course, I want you!'

What had she said? The words hung in the air mixed with his spicy aftershave.

'I mean, I would *like* you to come, to lunch. To help with getting people here, and serving up, and... eight's rather a lot, isn't it...?' She tailed off, aware of his hand covering hers.

'Janet, I can help with all of that. I'll be sous chef, chauffeur, washer-upper, whatever you want.'

Lover? Why couldn't she say it? *I want to go to bed with you.*

Hurriedly she picked up the empty cups and headed for the kitchen where a red light was flashing on the dishwasher. A warning? But what about? Rinse agent. As she bent down to look closer she felt a bit dizzy and wobbled.

'Janet...' he was behind her '... leave that for a minute. You need a hug.'

He held her for a moment but then pulled away. 'Sorry.' He looked at his watch. 'I'd love to stay but told Brighton daughter I'd be there for lunch.'

'But we haven't discussed presents for your daughters and granddaughters.' She still felt a bit swimmy.

'That's okay. I'll give them cash. They love cash.'

'I'd like to go to bed with you. I'd really like to go to bed with you. Let's go to bed. Now.'

It was easy to say out loud when he was reversing down the drive.

44

ZELDA

Was this her Pemberley moment?

Zelda hadn't read *Pride and Prejudice* since sitting English Literature O level at school, but as she stood in the porch of Felix's house she recalled the moment when Lizzie Bennet saw Darcy's pile and wondered if she'd been blind to his attractions. The Edwardian semi was elegant, and would look even more so if he tidied up the overgrown garden. There wasn't much of it, for heaven's sake.

She rang the bell again. When she was a girl she used to walk past houses like these on her way to the grammar school and wonder what sort of people lived behind the smart front doors with their stained-glass windows and brass door knockers. Sometimes she'd stop, pretending to tie a shoelace, so she could peer inside at the pictures on the walls and the ornate fireplaces. One summer's day she'd heard a girl playing a cello in a book-lined room; the notes had been so deliciously sad and shivery that she'd lingered for a while. Was that where her love of classical music began?

Come on, Felix. It was starting to snow again.

Next door's front porch was boxed in with ugly ridged plastic sheeting and it looked as if it was divided into flats – a lot of houses in the street were – but Felix's porch still showed signs of former splendour. The front door, dark green, like the bas relief tiles on the wall, had a stained-glass fleur-de-lys in the centre, in cobalt blue. It glowed, or would have done if someone had washed it or maybe put on a light inside. The yellowy light from the street lamp didn't reach.

Was Felix in? Had she got the wrong night? The house seemed to be in total darkness, no sign of an inhabitant let alone a party. She pressed the bell again but couldn't hear it ringing inside, so rapped on the door with the brass knocker, another fleur-de-lys needing some Brasso and elbow grease to make it shine. Now if she lived here...

'Were you admiring my abode, my dear? Well, do come in.'

The door had opened silently and a light had come on, revealing Felix in mine host mode, wearing a blue-and-white-striped butcher's apron topped by a red silk cravat. Had he been standing behind the door watching her? And had he had a cook's glass or two beforehand? His face was flushed, his arms open wide. 'Let me take your coat.'

'I'll keep it on for a bit, thank you, Felix.' She'd sidestepped into the hall avoiding his open arms, and it was quite chilly. 'Am I the first?' The place was eerily quiet, with no sign of any of the other guests, no other coats on the hall stand, only his coat and scarf. She couldn't hear any voices or music from behind the closed doors which ran down the left-hand side of the hall.

He was wearing slippers and the soles of her boots seemed loud on the black and white tiles as she followed him down the long hall, past a wall covered with dusty family photographs, a lot of Irene, or so she assumed. In a large one taken at the seaside she wore slacks and an open-necked shirt and held the hands of two small boys. In a studio photograph, she was in classic twinset and pearls. And here was their wedding with several of Felix in morning dress.

'First door on the left at the top if you need the lavatory.' Felix was pointing upstairs, where there were more photographs beside the curving staircase.

'Right at the top?' It was three storeys high.

'No, first floor.'

Good, but you still wouldn't need to be in a hurry, especially with all that washing girding the banisters.

'We're in the kitchen, by the way.' Felix had moved on to the end of the hall where he stood with his back to an open door.

'In here?' The room was huge – the ground floor of her own house would have fitted inside – but it looked grubby and smelt stale, despite the whiff of cinnamon emanating from the stove. A single step confirmed her first impression. The sole of her boot zipped like Velcro on the sticky floor, which couldn't have been washed for weeks.

He registered her dismay. 'It does lack a woman's touch, I fear.'

'Can't men clean?'

It could have been lovely, and probably was when Irene, or more likely her cleaning lady, washed the tiles and polished the furniture; when the blue and white china on the pine dresser nearly filling one wall gleamed, when clean curtains adorned the French windows at the far end, when the sink... but best not to look at the sink.

She should have gone then.

But Mr Darcy wouldn't have been handy with a squeezy mop, she told herself, giving him the benefit of the doubt when he said the others would be here soon. She accepted a glass of punch, after he'd washed, at her insistence, a pretty engraved glass with a handle, which he said was a family heirloom. The alcohol would have boiled away, she calculated, along with any lurking bacteria.

The pan of punch smelling of cinnamon was on the stove but there was no sign of food, which was a relief as she wouldn't have fancied it. As she checked the time, half past eight, a text pinged in from Tracey about travel arrangements to Scotland, and she asked him where the other guests were. But this time he didn't seem to hear and urged her to take her coat off – 'To feel the benefit later' – but she said she was chilly and sent a quick text to Viv reminding her where she was. She was starting to feel uneasy.

'I asked where the other guests were, Felix.'

'Oh, they'll be here shortly.'

But they weren't. Twenty minutes later, she was alone with Felix sitting at the end of the long pine table, a patch of which she'd cleaned with some make-up wipes. She'd already heard all she wanted to hear about his courses, popular, his sons, talented, and his views on the National Health Service, unsustainable. And he'd started talking about a man called Crouton who had written a book about sexual desire, called *A Philosophy of the Erotic,* something like that. Crouton believed that women liked men to be masterful. Time to leave. Others might have been invited but she doubted it. If they had they'd obviously declined. Wisely.

'Well, Felix, I believe that women should do exactly what they want.' She stood up. 'I'm sure an educated man like you knows the story of Sir Gawain and the Loathly Lady.' She made for the door, leaving him getting to his feet. But he caught her up halfway down the hall, where she'd stupidly hesitated at the bottom of the stairs wondering if she needed the loo before she left.

He grabbed her arm.

'Let go, Felix.'

'I... I...' He was stuttering.

'What is it, Felix? What's the matter?'

For a moment she thought he was having a heart attack because his face was twisted as if in pain, like Harry's had been. She reached in her pocket for her mobile to ring 999 as he jerked his head upwards towards the landing.

'Yes, Felix?' Did he want her to fetch some medication, for angina perhaps?

'Would you...?' He still had hold of her arm.

'Of course.' She wasn't a monster. 'What? What do you want me to do?'

'Help me change my duvet cover?'

So that was what was festooning the banisters.

'No, Felix, I won't.' Not sure whether to laugh or cry, she managed to shake herself free and head for the door. But he, suddenly sprightly, was close behind, and then ahead of her, and then with his back against the door.

'You're n-not going anywhere, my dear.' Mr Masterful barred her way as the doorbell rang.

'A takeaway you've ordered?' Sounding calmer than she felt, she tried to see through the stained glass.

The bell rang again. 'Your Amazon delivery, sir.'

With relief Zelda recognised the voice.

'Keep quiet.' Mr Masterful was at it again.

She watched him reach for the security chain but before he could she shoved him sideways against the hall stand. As he staggered to the floor and his coat and scarf fell on top of him she opened the door, letting Viv and Janet burst inside.

'You okay?'

'Now you're here!'

She would never forget the look on his face as the three of them looked down at his spreadeagled form before making their triumphant exit, slamming the door behind them. The get-away vehicle was parked outside, a snazzy white Fiat with a red and green stripe.

All for one and one for all.

45

VIV

Viv, parked on the road outside the entrance to The Cedars, felt like a diver poised to plunge into the deep end. She was though looking down a long tree-lined drive at a hotel just visible beyond ancient oaks and beeches whose bare branches formed an arch. Grassy parkland rolled away on either side, on the right a lake with swans gliding by, on the left a herd of deer beneath a cedar tree in all its winter glory.

Leave now before you make a fool of yourself, again.

She was early, it was not yet twelve o'clock. That was why she'd parked outside on the road, but it was a mistake stopping, giving Mugwort time to jump on her shoulder. She'd thought this out. Carefully. She didn't need to think any more. She'd done her research, made her decision and prepared. 'Country House and Business Centre' a board proclaimed. 'Outstanding Business Services', she'd read online, meetings small and large catered for. She got his letter out of her bag and read it again. Checked the date. Yes, it was now Thursday 16 December. But had she read too much between the lines, seen wit and irony and love where there was simply business acumen? Possibly, but their phone conversations since had suggested otherwise. Business and pleasure, she'd come prepared for both, dressed for both, in needlecords, soft cotton shirt in sensible checks and her Barbour.

And lace knickers. Tart.

She started the car again and as the former Georgian vicarage came into view she admired the honey-coloured stone that glowed in the low winter sunshine. Long windows either side of the door caught the sun too and gleamed. Lucky old Georgian vicar to live here! Would it be business first? Last night he'd said he'd just got a very interesting new assignment and had a proposition for her. To landscape a building perhaps or design a planting scheme for a new development? She stopped the car again to check her brief-case. Yes, she had her portfolio with her. Yes, she had photographs of previous projects. Yes, she was equipped to talk business. She parked, got out and stretched her aching back, checking to see if she could spot his car.

Perhaps he's changed his mind.

But he hadn't.

Here he was coming towards her with his easy stride until he was right in front of her, stooping to pick something off the floor. Her car keys. When did she drop them? Then his arms were round her, and her nose was squashed against his chest, her heart or his was beating fast, and she thought she would die of happiness. Man hugs, how had she lived without them?

'Well, are you hungry?' he said eventually.

'Yes! Very!'

His smile was like the sun coming out.

* * *

She ordered from the menu somehow. She ordered a drink somehow. She drank a glass of Chablis much too quickly while they waited for their food. That was the same as last time, but everything else was different. They could see each other in this lovely dining room, illuminated by long shafts of winter sunlight coming in through the sash windows. A log fire smouldered in the Adam fireplace, and, in the entrance hall outside the room, a Norwegian spruce as high as the ceiling sparkled with fairy lights and silvery orbs, like a photo shot for *Country Life*. Was there a four-poster bed upstairs?

'You said on the phone that you didn't send me your brochure. Have you found out who did?' It had come in the post. That was how he'd got her address.

'I have my suspicions. Did you bring the envelope it came in?'

He handed it over and she spied Janet's neat handwriting. *Thank you, Janet.* She told him briefly about the Muscateers and they raised a toast to her friends.

'And take a look at this.' He handed her a photograph of an old white building bathed in sunshine, against a background of cypress trees like dark green flames and an indigo sea.

'Where is this?'

'Greece. The Peloponnese. The building's a small monastery and I've been asked to convert it into a house. The clients want to restore the gardens too, which is where you come in, I hope. They were physical gardens, in the sense of plants for physic. The monks had an infirmary. Interested?'

Interested!

'Of course, we'll do a reccy before you decide.'

A whole new life opened up before her as the waiter came to clear their dishes, and she reached for her iPad to copy the photograph, but as she did his hand touched the back of hers. 'Can't work wait, for an afternoon? Coffee in my room? Isn't that where we got to?' Shivers ran through her.

Ask him, tart!

She pulled back her hand. 'Are you married? Because if you are...' If he said yes, she'd drive home. She would. She would. She would leave now.

'Viv, listen to me.' He reached to touch her fingertips. 'I have just said I am not married, and as we say in contracts, for the avoidance of doubt, I am not in a partnership either, haven't been for some time, well, only a business one.'

Let's go to bed, then.

Did she say it? Did she need to when her body was shouting it out? Why was he still blathering on?

'I was married once, in my early twenties. Stella was the girl next door, well, round the corner, childhood sweethearts you could say, but it didn't work out. When I left to go to university down south, she didn't want to come with me, didn't want to move away from her mum and dad and sisters.'

'Did you have children?' She made herself show interest.

'One. He was the reason we got married and I'm not sorry about that. Guy's great.'

'Grandchildren?'

'Guy's gay. He has a partner of some years, and I'm not ruling it out, but, so far, they haven't mentioned wanting kids. Not to me anyway. Guy did Art History at the Courtauld Institute and works for Sotheby's.'

'Em, my daughter, did Fine Art at Leeds.'

They talked a bit more and he topped up her glass, after checking that she wanted more, and really didn't want to drive home. 'Is there anything else you need to know?' Her emotional antennae were on high alert, fine-tuned to detect sarcasm or impatience or tetchiness, but she heard only a straight question, which deserved a straight answer.

'Where's your room?'

He laughed. 'Let's turn our phones off now.'

Skin on skin, lips on lips, firm hands finding delicious places, as bodies mingled on a four-poster bed. As the fire flickered in the hearth, warming the soles of her feet, Viv felt her body tingling, singing, coming back to life.

46

ZELDA

Zelda was early for her date because the train from Crosby hadn't taken as long as she'd thought. She'd arranged to meet Aging Rioja inside The Phil at the horseshoe-shaped bar, the overhead lights of which she could just about see, but the crowd round the door was making getting inside difficult. It wasn't just smokers but overflow from inside. 'Excuse me. Excuse me.' Could anyone hear her above the sound of 'Do They Know It's Christmas?'? She was a bit nervous – or maybe just hungry. Could she order something to eat and eat it before he got here? If she ever got inside. 'Excuse me. Excuse me.' The walk on the beach with Gina – they'd gone to see the famous iron men – had given her an appetite. Not that they'd seen the sculptures because the tide was in, completely covering them, which was probably as well as Gina would have been upset if she'd liked them, as she thought they were a waste of money. Zelda spotted a couple getting up from that corner-seat by the fireplace and raced over to occupy it. It was a good seat with a view of the bar, and if she stood up from time to time he'd see her, with luck.

'Remember Rory Storm and the Hurricanes?' Two men at the next table were discussing the sixties pop scene. 'Yeah, Ringo played for them.' She checked neither of them was Aging Rioja but neither was bald with a ponytail. 'Remember The Scruffs?'

I do. She nearly joined in.

'Gerry and the Pacemakers?'

Bet he's got a different sort of pacemaker now. She spared them her wit but it was fun remembering. Having Liverpudlian cousins to go and stay with when she was a teenager had boosted her street cred no end back at school. She could say truthfully that she'd been to the Cavern and heard most of the groups. That was with her older cousin Thelma, who'd given her the golden rule: 'Always wear your panty girdle over your panties.'

'Vintage Champagne?'

'Aging Rioja?' She stuck out her hand.

He didn't look at all bad, better than his mugshot at least. The black polo-necked sweater looked smart and the tied-back hair freshly washed. He said sorry but he was starving and would really like to eat. Did she mind? She said she was starving too, and after consulting the chalkboard on the wall and agreeing on pork chops with bubble and squeak, he went off to order. A good start.

When he came back with a beer for himself and a glass of Prosecco for her, apologising that it wasn't champagne, she assured him that was fine. He sat down beside her a tad too close but that wasn't his fault. The men discussing the sixties pop scene had budged up a bit but there wasn't a lot of room. Unfortunately, he then joined in with their conversation, correcting something one of them had said. 'Ringo was already Ringo when he joined the Hurricanes, right? He always wore a lot of rings, see, and the red suit and tie the Beatles became famous for.'

'Thanks, Grandad.' The man might have been younger, but not much.

'Cheeky bugger.' He turned back to her. 'Sorry, but been there, done... oh.' He looked up warily as someone tapped him on the shoulder, a man, a six-footer. For a moment she thought Aging Rioja had taken offence, because he got to his feet, but far from it. 'Kiddo!' He mock-punched the other man's arm. 'How're ya doing, mate?'

Kiddo? The man looked as if he was in his fifties! 'All right. How are you?' The six-footer had a beer in his hand too.

Should she go now? They'd started to catch up, they had been neighbours, it seemed, growing up on the Scottie Road. Her mother's family, the Costellos, had lived in a road nearby, she thought. She picked up that the new arrival was the younger brother of his childhood mate, hence the nickname. She stayed tuned in, thinking she might pick up more useful info. Aging Rioja was saying he hadn't reached such giddy heights career-wise as Kiddo, he'd only made it to foreman at British Leyland, but he'd bettered himself since retirement, got back into education and was into industrial archaeology.

She looked at her watch. Would they have time to talk about her relatives? Now Kiddo was saying his firm had done some work on the Albert Dock. They both seemed to have forgotten she was there, but Kiddo had just called her date Brian. Did either of them know any Costellos? she wanted to ask, but couldn't get a word in edgeways. And now they were onto sad stuff. Kev, Kiddo's older brother, had passed away a few years ago and so had his mum and dad, his dad twenty years back, his mum only last year at the grand old age of ninety-seven. Brian, aka Aging Rioja, offered his condolences. 'Let's hope you've got your mum's genes, mate, and not your dad's or Kev's.'

'Not sure my dad's genes are that relevant, Brian.' Kiddo paused to drain his glass and perhaps consider what to say next. 'Seems my dad may not have been my dad.'

Brian's eyebrows shot up, but he said top-ups were needed first, and Kiddo said he'd get them in, and Brian finally remembered she was there!

'Kiddo, meet... oh...'

'Zelda.' There seemed no point in lying now she knew his name. She got to her feet and introductions were made.

Kiddo stayed Kiddo, unless she'd missed something. When he came back from the bar, he'd obviously thought a bit and caught onto the situation. 'You two... I barged in, didn't I? Apologies.' He put their drinks on the table and said he'd go, but Brian wasn't having it.

'Not before you've told us about your old man, you don't. Our Mary would never forgive me if I didn't get the detail.' Seemed 'our Mary' was his eldest sister, who he now lived with.

'There's nothing else to say, Brian. Mum said, just before she died, when she wasn't making a lot of sense, that she'd had a fling in her forties and I was the result. I didn't ask who with and she didn't tell me.'

'I'll ask our Mary.' Brian was determined to help. 'She'll know. The women lived in each other's houses.'

'Don't bother, mate. As far as I'm concerned my dad's my dad, the one who brought me up, not the one who did a runner.'

'But don't you feel half of you is missing?' It was only as the words came out of her mouth that Zelda knew that that was how *she* felt, how she'd always felt. As if she'd spent her life looking in a wonky mirror that showed only one side of her. But now she wanted to see the other side, her dad's side. In vino veritas? Perhaps, but the words coming out of her mouth had never felt more true. 'My dad did a runner too,' she carried on because she couldn't stop. 'He left before I was born, so I don't know anything about him except that he was a black, Afro-American GI. I don't know if he was an irresponsible fly-by-night or a decent man caught up in events he had no control over. There was a war on, and he may have died in it. I don't know, but I want to find out. I came here today to find out more about my mum's side, but I've just realised I need to know more about my dad. Sorry.' She'd made a speech.

'No need to apologise, Zelda, seems natural to me, to wanna know who your old man is.' Brian wiped beer froth from his mouth.

Kiddo, clearly uncomfortable, took his leave. 'You two must have a lot to talk about. I'm sorry I crashed in.'

Now Brian gave her his full attention. 'Zelda. What a lovely name, and how lovely you are.' His look was appraising, to put it politely. 'Now, what did you say the Liverpool branch of your mum's family were called? Costello? That's Irish. We may be related but I hope not.'

But the Costellos didn't seem so important now. There were things she needed to know more urgently. Her dad was most likely dead, but it wasn't impossible he could still be alive, very old, in his eighties or nineties, but *alive*. If she wanted to meet him and get to know him she had to act fast.

'Brian—' she finished her glass '—I'll be straight with you. I've enjoyed this meeting, which has been more useful than I can explain. Something your friend said has changed my focus. I might even call it an epiphany. So on reflection I'm putting dating on hold, while I get on with more important things.'

Brian said he understood but didn't.

'Fine, Zelda, that suits me. I'm not in a rush. Got principles, I have. Three dates before I mate, that's the sort of guy I am.'

She should have said, 'And I'm a one-and-I'm-done sort of girl' but spared his feelings.

'Miss you,' Viv was whispering.

'Miss you.' His voice was husky.

'Wish you were here.'

'Wish you were here.'

They were both cooking for their families, he for his son and partner in Liverpool, she for not-sure-how-many-yet at hers. Christmas Eve carols from King's College played in the background in both kitchens. Were they doing synchronised gravy stirring?

'What are you doing midweek? I'll be free after Boxing Day. How about The Cedars if I can get a room?'

'Perfect.' She added red wine to her gravy. 'I'll be free by Wednesday.'

'Might not be the same room.'

'Any bed, anywhere, I will sleep anywhere. Sorry, must go.' There were ominous sounds from the rooms above. But they hung on like lovesick teenagers, though the thumps overhead got louder. At a guess it was Sally's youngest two, fighting over the top bunk. And here was Eldest Grandchild coming in the door. Female. Teenage. Tense. Tortured. Fiona!

'Bye.' She pocketed the phone. 'What can I get you, Fi?'

'Crisps?'

'Over there. Heaps.'

'Who were you talking to, Gran?'

Gawd! How much had she heard? 'Just a friend.' She wasn't ready to share her love life with the family yet. 'Would you like to lay the table, Fi?'

What time was it? Half past six and they were aiming to eat at seven. It was Rudolph pie, Nigella's Christmassy take on shepherd for the carnivores, a veggie version for the rest. Would everyone be here by seven? Were they here now? At last count it was four adults, three kids, two cats including her own not-pleased Claudia outside on the kitchen windowsill, a rabbit, a gerbil, two goldfish and a tank of stick insects. Beth had rung at two to say they were just setting off from Herne Bay.

Pause for another calming drink.

This might be her last Christmas in this house so it had to be a good one. Had Steve joined Sally and the girls? They'd arrived without him. Would he stay the night if he had to be in the same bed as Sally? It was that or a sleeping bag. Ah, that sounded like Lionel's bray, so the Herne Bayers must be here. That could have been the twins fighting over the top bunk. Sally must be in the sitting room with Mother and Em, doing sterling work keeping her topped up with sherry. Em, the star, had driven to Newcastle to fetch her. It was funny how Mum and Em got on. Oh, that sounded like Faith and Fliss thundering down the stairs. Had Em called them down to decorate the tree? She'd said she had some new ideas for decorations to keep them occupied. Ping.

Booked Cedars for new year. Patrick xxx

How will I live without him till then?

Another ping.

Are you ok there in kitchen? Can come and help if you like. Girls ok
doing tree. Em x

She texted back.

Fine thanks. Everything under control here. Mum x

Except my leaping heart.

But she got a meal on the table, hostilities didn't break out and
they all made it into the sitting room afterwards, all the adults
anyway, giving a not bad impression of being a happy family. Had
her poor injured house actually helped by being a focus for their
concern? Deemed dry only the day before by a man with a
dampometer – the log-burner had helped – the end wall was paper-
less, half the floor was carpetless, and the ceiling lathes were
awaiting new plaster. She'd had to endure 'Poor Mum' from the
girls and 'Poor Vivien' from Mother on the sofa beside her now, half
watching TV, but it was maybe a price worth paying. Fingers
crossed peace would prevail a bit longer and the children, in bed at
last, would sleep till morning.

Her grown-up daughters were chatting amicably round the tree.
With luck they'd find enough common ground to see them through
till Boxing Day and the next when they were departing. Their
husbands were chatting nearby. So far so amazing. Could she send
a sneaky text to Patrick or even ring him?

Mother was stirring, albeit in grand lady mode. 'Could you help
me to my bed, Vivien?'

'Yes, Mum, of course.' She'd put a bed in the dining room as the
spiral staircase was a no-go for Mother even before she'd knocked
back a bucketful of Nigella's festive punch.

By midnight she was in bed herself, sunk against the pillows, listening to the house settling around her. Across the fields the church clock struck twelve. Silent night, holy night. All was calm and bright for the time being. She reached for her phone.

Happy Christmas, my darling. Wish your arms were around me now, but can just about wait till new year.

Send. How long would it take him to reply? But wait, what was this?

STOP MUM!

Stop? And who was knocking on her bedroom door?

'Mum, stop... can I come in?' Em's voice.

'Of course. What's the matter?'

Em, in reindeer pyjamas, looked closer to fourteen than forty. 'Stop sexting, Mum.' Her phone was in her hand. 'Wrong number.'

Sexting? Hardly, but then it dawned on her. 'Shit. Sorry. What did I say?'

'Nothing too gross, it was all quite sweet really. I'm glad it's working out, but, Mum, you shouldn't text when you've had a few drinks.' She came into the room. 'Well, budge over and tell all. What's his name?'

Em seemed okay with the idea of her mum dating, but what about the others? She could swear Em to secrecy, but secrecy caused its own problems. Oh, soddit, they were all going to have to get used to the idea. 'Patrick, his name's Patrick, Patrick O'Malley...'

48

JANET

Round the corner, Janet, also in bed, was still practising. 'Alan, do you fancy a snooze?'

Was that too forward, not forward enough?

Eyes closed, she visualised the late-afternoon scene, just the two of them now in the sitting room, either side of the fire after he'd returned from taking the other guests home. He, legs stretched out, would have a drink in his hand at last after going without during the meal, noble man, and she... Oh! But what if he didn't return after taking the other guests home? She'd have to anticipate that.

'Alan, do come back for a drink when you've taken everyone home. Don't go back to an empty house.' Would that be enough? Possibly, if she kept his dog here, lured by turkey and forcemeat stuffing.

At eight o'clock next morning, having already been up for two hours, turkey in and pudding on, she was, she hoped, in control, though still in her dressing gown. The table was set with seven places and it looked lovely. The Doulton dinner service with the dark green border looked perfect on the white damask cloth and the red candles set it all off beautifully, even before the candles were lit. She checked she had matches. She checked she had a saucer to put the matches on. Yes, everything was under control, except perhaps herself.

A glass of claret helped.

By twelve noon she was ready in the tried and tested black velvet pants and the blue silk paisley top she'd worn the first time she'd invited him to supper. The other clothes she'd tried on were back in the wardrobe. With the pearl and lapiz lazuli earrings that had caught his eye that night, the outfit was complete. Yes, her reflection in the full-length mirror was pleasing, but the room behind her perhaps not. Too neat, too tidy, too bright, according to an article she'd read in *Good Housekeeping*. After closing the curtains, she rumpled the duvet and stopped herself straightening the bottom sheet. Light the candles on the dressing table? Not yet, but she could switch on the Tiffany lamps by the bed. Stage set, she went downstairs rehearsing her lines.

But did her guests know theirs?

'I'm sorry.' Mrs Jefferson, who never ever wanted to cook a Christmas dinner again, rang to say she was sorry but she was going to have to. Mr Jefferson didn't want to come out for his Christmas dinner and wouldn't, and no, she couldn't leave him on his own, and she wasn't being rude, really she wasn't, but she *didn't* want Janet or anyone to bring lunch around. They had a Wiltshire Farm in the freezer.

Janet removed two place settings.

Then, a few minutes later, when she'd just taken the turkey out to rest, the minister rang to say he was sorry, but ninety-seven-year-old Mr Hughes had sadly died in his sleep, so he wouldn't be coming, and he wasn't too sure about Miss Taylor, the church organist. She hadn't turned up for the morning service, so they'd had to manage with pre-recorded carols, and Mr Loveday was kindly driving his wife, the minister's wife that was, to Miss Taylor's house to see how she was, and they weren't back yet. He would let her know as soon as he knew the lie of the land.

Oh dear, poor Mr Hughes. His wife had died a week earlier. She removed another setting.

And when Alan arrived ten minutes later, minus Miss Taylor who he said had the flu, she removed another. 'Marcus not here yet? I saw him leaving church on his moped an hour ago.' Looking fraught, he dived into the downstairs loo without so much as kissing her cheek. So she texted the teenager, worried that he might have had an accident or got lost, but he hadn't replied by the time Alan appeared in the kitchen still looking tense, and maybe a bit Eeyore. She suddenly remembered what the day meant for him. Oh dear. This might be a very gloomy meal.

But he rallied.

After blowing his nose into a commendably crisp clean hand-kerchief, he found the bottle of Veuve Clicquot he'd put in the fridge the previous day, removed the cork with a satisfying sigh and carefully filled two of her best heavy crystal champagne glasses. 'Happy Christmas, Veuve Carmichael, we are not waiting for that hapless boy.'

'Happy Christmas!' They clinked glasses and she got her kiss at last, a warm firm kiss, on the lips, with just a hint of fizz.

'It's not from that shipwreck, by the way.' Stepping away, he held the glass to the light to view the bubbles. What was he talking about? 'In the news earlier this year?' He took a sip. 'You didn't see it? Champagne was found at the bottom of the Baltic. Dating back to Napoleon but still drinkable according to the man who bought several hundred bottles of it, lucky for him. A bit on the sweet side but only slightly tainted with arsenic.'

'No!' She laughed, pleased at his lightness of tone.

'Penny and I got this fizz in Rheims and the claret in St Emilion to lay down.'

'With?' Did she really say that?

He laughed, then raised his glass, serious again. 'To our absent friends.' She raised hers and their eyes met for a moment and she had to go and sit down at the table, her knees suddenly wobbly.

'Is that the boy, do you think?' He'd joined her at the table.

'S-sorry?' She wasn't sure what he said.

'Your phone. I heard it buzzing. In your trouser pocket?'

She had no idea. Any vibrations in that region were lost in a whirl of other sensations, but with fumbling fingers she managed to find the phone and, yes, there was a message from Marcus. '"Sorry, can't make it,"' she read it out.

So then there were two, just two.

'Uncouth little bugger. No wonder he's Marcus No Mates.' But Alan didn't seem upset as he removed a place setting, far from it. 'Refill, madam?' He got the delicious fizz and refilled her glass, which was amazingly empty. She knew she should slow down, but how pleasant it was, just the two of them, how relaxing. For the first time that day, for several days, she didn't feel tense.

As they sat opposite each other downing a plate of canapés intended for seven she felt her cares slipping away. But it was the turkey, a mountain in the middle of the table, that got her giggling. 'What is this thing between us, Mr Loveday?' she heard herself saying in a silly husky voice.

'You tell me, Mrs Carmichael,' he replied, amused, fork in air.

'I meant...' Oh dear. What had she meant? She shouldn't have had the claret before, no after, no, before, no, before *and* after the champagne. 'Alan, I would like...'

'Yes?' He was still looking, still fork in air.

'... to go to bed with you. I'd really like to go to bed with you! I *want* to go to bed with you.' Easy. Viv was right. It was easy.

He put down his fork. 'When exactly were you thinking of?'

'Now.'

'We'll miss the Queen's speech you know.' But he didn't seem bothered.

* * *

It was bliss throwing off her clothes and leaving them in a heap on the floor. It was bliss lying on a rumpled bed watching her chap standing on one leg, pulling off his trousers.

'Hurry, hurry. It's cold in here.' She held the covers under her chin but not because she was shy, oh no! Never before had she felt so bold.

'I'm coming, woman, as fast as I can. You don't want a lover with his socks on, do you?'

It was bliss with this man beside her, his body warming her, his hands on her breasts, sending darts of pleasure high and low. Bliss lying in a hot dark cave wrapping her legs round her man's broad back, laughing with pleasures new and delicious. Bliss, o wordless, speechless, breathless bliss!

'How was it for you, Mrs Carmichael, or need I ask?' he murmured later as she woke from drowsy post-coital slumber.

'Nice, Mr Loveday, very nice,' she murmured back, with a small stab of guilt for using such a 'lazy' word. Nice was a no-no in English lessons at school, where, it was true, she had never been asked to write a sentence describing a fuck on a Christmas afternoon. Fuck. How easily the word came to her lips now she was a fallen woman. 'It was, it was—' she sought better '—not an *earthshaking* fuck but it was, yes, a *friendly* fuck, a *fun* fuck—' she was doing better '—a friendly, fizz-fuelled leisurely fun-fuck.' She turned to the man beside her to see how he rated her linguistic prowess, but he was asleep, his mouth open, nose hair vibrating.

49

JANET

Only two weeks later, and now Janet felt like Lady Macbeth. But it wasn't blood on her hands after a grisly murder that she was trying to wash away, it was pee, after trying to fill a narrow-mouthed spice jar with a mid-stream specimen. Easier, she reasoned, than peeing in a pan at the STD clinic, where she might be too traumatised to pee at all. Cystitis, that was what she'd told Viv and Zelda she thought she had when she was making her excuses for not joining them today. That was what she still hoped she'd learn she had. If someone ever answered the phone and gave her an appointment. How much Vivaldi could one person stand while clutching one's stinging vulva? Fortunately, being Friday, Alan had gone to see Viv about his garden.

She dialled again, the clinic in the next town, not the local one or her own GP. How could she ask Dr Shah, young enough to be her daughter, to test her for an STD? A sexually transmitted disease. The words filled her with horror. There were other symptoms, had been for weeks now *since she got back from New Zealand.* Headaches mainly, which paracetamol didn't touch, and dizzy spells, the latest when she'd gone to feed Viv's cat when Viv was with her lover. Oh no, not again. She raced back to the loo for another stinging pee. Deep breaths.

Tony Morello haunted her. What exactly had happened that night? The memory was growing hazy. She remembered agreeing to a foot massage but was that all that had happened? He was obviously a promiscuous man who tried it on with all the women who stepped through the door of The Chequers. What if she'd caught an STD from him?

She washed her hands again. If she had one she would tell Alan, of course. She was a responsible woman, most of the time. And she knew the drill, had actually worked in an STD clinic once, aeons ago when she was a nurse, before she got married and had children. VD clinics they called them then. Venereal disease. GUM they called it now, she'd discovered after a lot of time-consuming googling. GUM, which sounded friendly and accessible and more to do with up here than down there. And Genito-Urinary Medicine sounded clinical and neutral. You might be there for a number of respectable reasons, so there was no need to be squeamish at the thought of a bit of poking around and a few intrusive questions. These were much more enlightened times. *She* was more enlightened.

Could Alan have had other partners? She hadn't asked. She had *rushed into* an affair like a feckless teenager. Alan wouldn't have been unfaithful to Penny, would he? But possibly after? Men had secrets. He certainly knew what he was doing in bed, but a man who'd been married for forty years would, wouldn't he? Mind you, Malcolm hadn't had a clue. Or so she'd thought. Till Barbara. Sod Barbara!

The doorbell rang and Janet looked out of the landing window. Viv's car was in the road outside. She stepped back from the window but it was too late. Viv was waving, and now the doorbell was ringing again.

'Just...' *going out* she intended to say as she opened the door, but Viv, cartons piled high under her chin, was inside before she could stop her. 'Cranberry juice. Have you managed to get an appointment?'

'Not yet.' She followed her to the kitchen, wondering how to get rid of her friend.

'I'll ring in a mo.' Viv was opening the fridge door. 'Zelda and I postponed, by the way, after having a drink, till you're better, by next week with luck.'

'Thank you, but, Viv, I prefer to ring myself.'

'Okay, ring while I put these away. Two in the fridge, the rest in your store cupboard, yes? Go on, phone now, and don't take no for an answer.'

'I'll go upstairs, b-better signal!' She fled.

Safe in her bedroom, door locked, she dialled the GUM in the next town. Again. Would someone answer this time before she needed another pee? More Vivaldi. Then a friendly voice, a real friendly female voice, took her by surprise. 'No need for an appointment, dear. Just come in. We are open from eight till eight. No, no, don't tell me your name. No need.'

When she came down, her urine sample hidden in her bag, Viv was at the bottom of the stairs. 'Got an appointment?'

She nodded.

'When?' Viv had her car keys in her hand.

'Now. Straight away.'

'Great. Get your coat.'

'Thank you, Viv, but I prefer to drive myself.' She got her coat from the cloakroom.

But Viv was still there, by the open front door. 'Really, Janet. Let me drive. I know what cystitis is like, nerves jangling, teeth on edge and look at the weather. The gritters are out—'

'No!' she snapped.

'But, Janet—'

'Are you deaf? I said *no*. Please respect my right to do things in my own way instead of acting like the Fascists you so frequently decry! I will drive myself.'

'I...' but whatever Viv had been about to say, she thought better of it.

'I mean, yes, please, Viv, I'd love you to go with me!' But it was too late to change her mind. Viv was heading down the drive. 'Viv!' she shouted, but her friend didn't look back. Janet watched her roaring away in a cloud of exhaust.

50

ZELDA

Zelda was surprised to see Viv on the doorstep, hardly an hour since they'd said goodbye. 'She shoved me out of the bloody door!' Viv seemed hurt as well as furious by Janet's rebuff.

'Tea?' Zelda put the kettle on, though not delighted by the interruption. She'd just found an online site called www.GItrace, which looked like the breakthrough she was looking for, but a friend in need came first. 'Don't take it personally, Viv. Cystitis makes you crazy. Perhaps Alan was taking her?'

'There was no sign of him but—' Viv got something from her rucksack '—I didn't just come for tea and sympathy. Here. I forgot to give you it in the pub. I've sent you a digital version too.'

It was a spreadsheet headed ZELDA'S MENu.

'MENu. Get it?' Viv was expecting thanks and approval, but was going to get another rebuff.

'Sorry, Viv, but I don't want it.' It came out more brusquely than she intended and Viv's face fell. 'Well, not now, maybe later. Sorry, I should have told you, I'm putting dating on hold.'

She told Viv about her change of heart in Liverpool when she'd realised that finding her dad was the most important thing in her life. 'I met this guy who said he didn't care who his biological father was and I suddenly realised that I did. I need to know to discover who I am. It was a sort of epiphany really, and I've found this website that looks promising.'

Viv nodded, vigorously. 'Makes sense to me. My MENu can wait. No offence taken. I wouldn't like to think I was cloned from my mother. Lead me to your website.'

'Move over, darlings.' Mack and Morag grudgingly made room for cat-owning Viv on the sofa, so she and Viv could look at her iPad together.

'Bloody hell!' Viv leaned back as Zelda logged in www.GItrace. 'Are you sure you want to go through with this?'

WARNING!

GI Father Finding Guide

If you are not totally committed to this search, do not begin. You have to be prepared for a long search that may take years and may never reach your goal. Your father could be dead or may not be the ideal person that you envisaged when you started looking for him.

'Totally,' she replied to Viv, scrolling down. 'I don't expect my father, or anyone else, to be an *ideal person*.'

The search may take a greater emotional toll than you realise.

Viv fortunately kept quiet. Zelda didn't want anyone else issuing warnings. *How do I find my dad?* That was all she wanted to know.

You must be prepared to share all the information you have about your parents regardless of how painful it might be for you or your mother.

'My mum's dead,' she said in case Viv didn't know. 'And knowing can't be more painful than not knowing.'

'Not even if he rejects you?' Viv broke her silence. 'Or if he's a nasty bit of work?'

'My father is not a nasty piece of work.'

'See. That's what they mean about having preconceptions.' Viv was the voice of reason. 'You *do* have this image in your head.'

Shut up, Viv.

Another instruction came up:

Get a piece of paper and list all the facts you have. Some of these may not seem relevant but write them all down.

Viv was first with pen and paper, a notebook from her bag. 'You talk and I write? Where did they meet for a start? Do you know that?'

'At a dance in a church hall in Hitchin. That's what my aunties say. Mum was seventeen and there with them, her older sisters, Doreen and Agnes, who were supposed to be keeping an eye on her. They got the blame when my mum got into trouble.' That was a bit they didn't tire of telling. 'Meet Trouble.'

'Well, I'm glad she had you.' Viv touched her hand.

'I'm glad she had me too, and that she kept me, which was more than most unmarried mothers did at the time if they found themselves with a baby who wasn't white.' Zelda had read a lot about this. 'Most brown babies, as they, we, were called in newspapers at the time, ended up in children's homes. I think, or like to think, it was because Mum loved my dad.'

'And that he loved her? So do you know his name?'

But that was where there was a big painful gap. No one knew or if they knew they weren't saying. Her mum hadn't told her, and her aunties said they didn't know, that or anything else. She'd been seven when her mum told her that her stepdad wasn't her real dad.

'Didn't you ask her about him then?' Viv looked puzzled.

'I don't think I did. I'm not sure why, but questions weren't exactly encouraged and when she sat me down one day, saying she had something serious to talk to me about, there was a bit of a listen-very-carefully-I-am-going-to-say-this-only-once atmosphere.' She laughed and did a funny 'French resistance' voice, but it hadn't been funny at the time. The house had been very quiet because everyone else had gone out and the wireless, always on, hadn't been. Her mum had turned off *Family Favourites*. 'It was Sunday dinnertime, and we'd just finished eating. Dad, as I thought of him then, had taken Gina and Lina to see Granny. I think he'd insisted it was time to tell me I wasn't his. I'd heard a row earlier. Anyway, she told me that my real dad, my blood dad she called him, was an American GI, a soldier, over here to help us win the war, and I remember thinking it was exciting, that he must have been a bit of a hero. I didn't mind hearing that I wasn't related to Gordon, my stepdad who had never seemed to like me, and all my info about America came from Hollywood so I imagined my dad looking like Rock Hudson or Clark Gable or Glenn Miller...'

'But...' Viv hesitated.

'Didn't I think that he might be black?' She felt stupid saying so but no, she didn't, not straight away. 'It's hard to explain, perhaps there weren't a lot of mirrors around, but I thought I looked like everyone else. My sisters were dark, haired that is, and curly, though not as curly as me. When someone at school pointed out that I wasn't white I was bewildered more than anything...' She tailed off, remembering things she must have pushed to the back of her mind. Pointed out! Who was she kidding? That wasn't the half of it, even at junior school. And she'd known her hair was different from the way her mum had muttered as she'd tugged a fine-toothed comb through it, or tried to. She winced as she remembered.

'So, what have you found out about your dad so far?' Viv held up the near-empty page of her notebook.

'That he was in the USAAF, that stands for United States Army Air Forces, in a regiment based in Hertfordshire or Bedfordshire or maybe Cambridgeshire in 1944.'

'We can find out the name of the regiments stationed locally.' Viv made a note. 'They would have records and, yes, there's a museum on the old airfield near us, the Glenn Miller Museum. There were American soldiers stationed in Elmsley or nearby. The Yanks, as they were called, hid tanks and weapons in the woods. I remember an old neighbour saying that after aircraft had taken off on raids in the morning the ground crews would wander down through the village, and some, a few, were black.' Viv recalled seeing something on TV. 'There was a documentary a few years ago about the children of black GIs stationed here. I'll never forget a woman, in her sixties at a guess, who'd put a bottle of champagne in a cupboard, ready for the day she found her dad. We'll do that, Zelda, I'll get the champagne, but we'll have to get moving. Your dad must be in his eighties or nineties.'

Viv had forgotten Janet's rebuff for the moment at least and it was great having her help.

51

JANET

Janet wore a grey knitted hat, retrieved from a charity bag ready for collection. Pulled low, it covered half her face but didn't give her the confidence she'd hoped for, even with sunglasses. By the time she reached the hospital in the neighbouring county, the promise of anonymity, initially welcome, had started to have the opposite effect. Why all the secrecy if there was nothing to be secretive about? There was nothing secretive about the whereabouts of GUM. The site map in the car park showed it clearly. Pink and purple arrows directed her to the *front* of the building, which advertised its wares.

How times had changed!

The bored youth on Reception gave her a numbered ticket as if she were at the delicatessen counter in the supermarket. A poster on the wall urged her to use a condom as she sat down to wait on a pink plastic chair. Pink! In the sixties the clinic she worked in was in a backstreet terrace far from the main hospital, and the walls were no colour she could remember. She'd worn a crisp white uniform with a black elasticated belt and black stockings. Here the walls were the ubiquitous pink and purple and it was hard to distinguish staff from patients. Nurses, she thought, wore unisex tunic tops and trousers in blue or maroon, but other staff – doctors possibly – were in casual dress, very casual some of them, only the lanyards round their necks depicting their role and rank.

I must not be a grumpy, censorious old woman.

Things were better now in several ways. They were. The tunics and trousers were much more practical than the uniform she wore in those *Carry On* days when male patients and doctors, mostly male in those days, thought nurses' bottoms were there for the pinching.

'Number 103, isn't that you?' The girl beside her pointed to the ticket in her hand, and then to a young woman with a tattoo of a crab on her arm standing in front of her. A *crab*! Was that a joke?

'Come this way, please.' Ms Crab led the way down a short corridor to a door at the end. 'Cancer, by the way,' she said, holding the door open, 'sign of, born in July.'

It was not a good start, though the nurse sounded more amused than offended as she ushered her into a room. A room, not, fortunately, a curtained cubicle, though there was one of those in the corner. 'Have a seat.' Ms Crab pointed to a low table, and they sat side by side as if they were going to have coffee and a friendly chat. 'Now, would you like to take off your...'

Not a friendly chat.

'... hat?' Ms Crab grinned. 'Sorry, but it's just that you look rather hot.'

All in all, it wasn't as bad as she'd feared. Ms Crab almost succeeded in putting her at her ease. She laughed at the spice jar, the questions weren't as intrusive as she'd anticipated and the dreaded examination didn't happen. No splaying your legs while a medic rummaged round with a cold speculum these days. 'Unless you've got a really nasty discharge?' Janet assured her she hadn't. So it was DIY. All she had to do was go into the cubicle and do her own rummaging, with what looked like a large cotton bud.

'Putting your foot up on the chair's best,' Ms Crab advised from the other side of the curtain. 'Just make sure you wiggle the swab about to make sure there's enough for us to analyse. I'll go and test your pee now.'

It didn't take long. She was pulling her pants up when she heard the nurse, the nurse *practitioner*, she'd said, come back into the room.

'Definitely a urine infection,' she called out, 'and I can prescribe for that. We'll send it away though, to test for STDs along with your swab. And you must have a blood test,' she said when Janet came out of the cubicle. 'If you're quick Phlebotomy will do it today. Now, just one more thing, sorry, but I have to do this...' She mock-grimaced as she handed over a sheaf of leaflets and – what was this? – a packet of condoms. 'Keep those handy, yes? STDs among your age group are skyrocketing. Seems you swinging sixties types just haven't stopped swinging!'

As she drove home, Janet recalled her teenage years, a time of tortured fumbling ruled by Thou Shalt Not. Swing in the sixties she had not. One boyfriend once got as far as unhooking her bra when they were sitting side by side watching TV and she actually enjoyed his hands caressing her unfettered back until he made his way to the front and touched a nipple, when she recoiled, as if from an electric shock. She rushed upstairs forbidding him to follow, but even then knew deep down, in parts she dared not mention, that she'd been pierced with desire, and when she pulled down her pants in the bathroom, she was disconcerted to find them damp. She liked Christopher, but he never asked her out again.

Nice Girls Didn't. It wasn't just the RE teacher who talked about saving yourself. All the teachers did if they broached the subject at all and not many did. What did they know about it, after all? They were *ancient*, forty at least. Speculation was rife in the sixth form common room about the sex lives of the staff, all women, most unmarried, all of whom had lived through the war, which had ended less than twenty years earlier. Had they Done It before all the men went off to war and died so tragically? How awful not to have Done It! Ever. No wonder they were so petty and bad-tempered and keen on sport, some of the more knowing girls opined. It was *repression* and *sublimation*. They had read Freud. Some claimed to have Done It. One of these disappeared 'to stay with her auntie' and didn't come back.

Seventeen-year-old Janet didn't participate in these discussions, but she listened and noted some of the books they mentioned. She read Anya Seton's *Katherine*, because she was doing History A level, and the recently published unexpurgated *Lady Chatterley's Lover* because D. H. Lawrence was English Literature, which she was also doing. Both books helped a bit with Biology and made her fidget under the bedclothes, but they didn't stop her exercising Self Control, which became a problem when she married four years later.

When Malcolm's married hands wandered to forbidden parts, she had to remind herself they weren't forbidden any more. She'd prepared herself by reading *The Sexual Responsibility of Woman* and knew she should be a joyfully receptive wife at all times, even if she had just put in an eight-hour shift on the wards, come home on the bus, cooked dinner, cleared away, washed up and put a load of washing in the twin tub while Malcolm sat with his feet up reading the papers. But she couldn't always manage it.

Pregnancy made things worse and childbirth brought an end to their infrequent couplings. Once again, she read the books. Sheila Kitzinger's book on natural childbirth said she would 'open up like a flower' if only she could relax, but after twenty-four hours' hard labour she didn't, so the cheery doctor made 'a little snip'. 'So much better than tearing, dear, if the baby's head is bigger than the opening you've made for it.' Or failed to make for it, if you hadn't relaxed enough, or pushed enough or panted enough, or pushed and panted too much. It was your fault, naturally. And when the doctor sewed her up again without any anaesthetic – 'You'll still be numb, dear' – he kindly put in an extra couple of stitches, 'So your husband won't flounder around like a rabbit in a top hat when you get going again.'

'Men, it's all about them!' She shouted.

But they never did get going again, possibly because they hadn't got going before, but also because she was sore for a long time, couldn't sit down unless on a rubber ring, and Grant was a cry-baby who seemed determined to prevent the conception of a brother or sister. Not that she was keen to give him one, but if either she or Malcolm made a move towards each other in bed – she was still aware of her wifely duties – Grant would start to bawl.

The windscreen wipers came on as she reached the village. The storm they'd been warned about was here and the battering rain suited her mood. When she got in she'd take the antibiotics and some paracetamol, go to bed and pull the covers over her head.

52

ZELDA

Zelda, cheered by Viv's support, was trawling through a BBC website called People's War. It was a site where ordinary people recorded their World War II experiences, but so far she'd only come across one black face. In a section called Love in Wartime there were six hundred and thirty stories but only one about love between a white woman and a black man. This sole black face belonged to the daddy of Margaret Johnson and showed him in his army uniform. Margaret had posted the photograph six years ago in 2005, saying she hoped it would jog someone's memory, at best her father's, if not a sibling's. She wanted to find her father, whose name she thought was William Dickensen. He'd been stationed at Burton-on-Trent in Staffordshire.

Had she had any replies? None that Zelda could see but there was no way of checking as the website was no longer active. She read the entry again. Margaret Johnson had a lot more information about William Dickensen than she had about her father. Margaret wrote that she'd been inspired to search when she'd seen a programme on BBC2 about an American lady called Rachel James who was looking for siblings 'sired while at Burton on Trent'. Was anyone on the other side of the Atlantic looking for Zelda, Griselda Mayhew as she then was? Did her dad even know her name? Did he know she'd been born? If he did had he told anyone? Did she have brothers and sisters over there?

So many questions! Her dad probably did know her mum was pregnant, she started to think when she read that official US forces policy was to send black GIs, but not white, straight home if they got a girl pregnant There was no question of them marrying the girl and taking her back to USA because mixed-race marriages were illegal in the majority of states. So the pregnant women were left to cope as best they could. Poor Mum, it must have been hard.

Two emails came in before she put her iPad away. One was from Viv with the MENu attached.

For if/when you resume search for a chap.

She'd also attached a photograph of a sparkling white ruin, complete with wispy cypress trees and an azure sky that could have graced a travel brochure.

The old Greek monastery which Patrick has been asked to convert into a house. He wants me to restore the gardens!

Wow! Lucky Viv! The other was from Brian aka Aging Rioja, with some info about where her great-grandfather Costello might have worked as a docker on Merseyside. He'd also found some Costello children on the register of the local Industrial School which was mainly for homeless children to learn a trade. Homeless. How poor they must have been! Was that why her granny, Emily Mayhew nee Costello, the successful seamstress, had moved south, to seek her fortune? He'd added:

Calling in a week Sunday after conference in Milton Keynes if ok with
you. Be great to spend evening together. Will be in van and can sleep in
the back.

Mmm. Did she want to see him again? She'd have to think
about that.

53

JANET

Janet was basking, buoyed by antibiotics and Alan's TLC. It was Sunday lunchtime and she was in the sitting room with her feet up. Alan was in the kitchen cooking lunch. He'd been there on and off since Friday night when she'd found him waiting for her, worried sick because he didn't know where she was. 'Tell me about it,' he'd said when she'd admitted she'd been to the hospital, 'but only if you want to, and remember I was married for forty years and have two daughters.'

'Cystitis,' she'd blurted out, 'and...' more quietly '... tests,' which he hadn't seemed to hear, which was fine because she hadn't wanted him to hear. Cystitis, he knew all about that, he'd said. Rest, liquids, antibiotics, a warm bath.

No mention of tests till now. Basking was over. She was rigid.

'Those tests,' he'd called from the kitchen, 'shall we talk about them while we're waiting to eat?' He came to join her with two glasses of red. 'Your antibiotics are okay with this. I've checked. Budge up.' He sat down at the end of the sofa, and lifted her legs onto his warm corduroyed thighs.

'M-malbec?' She took a gulp.

'Janet, what were those tests for? I can't wait any longer. I've been worried stiff.'

'STDs,' she whispered.

'I trust you don't mean Subscriber Trunk Dialling?' He looked amused.

She shook her head miserably.

'Sexually Transmitted Diseases?' Not so amused.

She nodded.

'From me?'

'Or...'

'Or?' His eyebrows shot up. He moved her feet off his thighs, got up and left the room, leaving her desolate. She listened to him moving about the kitchen turning things off, going into the hall, going upstairs, gathering his property, making sure he left nothing behind. How would he phrase his goodbye? Would he come back and explain that she wasn't the woman he'd thought she was, that he'd been misled, that he hadn't realised she was a tart? Or would he just go without saying anything? Why not? What was there to say? She listened for the front door opening and closing, the sound of happiness leaving her house.

'I'm putting everything on hold.' He stood in the sitting-room doorway.

Of course. She nodded to show she understood. *Don't cry.*

'Janet.' He came into the room. 'I mean I've put the dinner on hold, turned things down a bit. We can eat later.' He got their glasses from the coffee table, handed her hers and sat down. 'Now, are you going to tell me about your dissolute past first, or shall I tell you about mine?'

'Yours?' Was that good or bad?

'Yes.' He looked a bit shamefaced. 'Unless Viv has revealed all already?'

'Viv? *Viv!* You haven't...?' *That* she could not forgive.

'No, *no*, we haven't!' He shook his head vigorously. 'I'm referring to a piece of paper. A sort of survey...' He tailed off. 'She hasn't mentioned it?'

'No. She. Hasn't.' *Wait till I see you, Viv Halliday!*

There was, it seemed, quite a lot that Viv hadn't told her, but his revelations made it easier telling him about Tony, and then about Malcolm when he asked if her husband might have had other partners.

'Probably.' She told him about the condoms she'd found in the pocket of his best suit, and about Barbara, and that she'd buried Malcolm in the suit with the condoms. 'So they'd see what a hypocrite he was when he reached the pearly gates.'

He laughed at that. 'But didn't you have suspicions at the time?'

She shook her head, feeling silly. 'Though our sex life had stopped years before.'

'So, we can't blame Malcolm if you have an STD, which I very much doubt, by the way. That leaves this Tony – or me.' He said he'd had one partner since Penny, a brief encounter, with whom he'd taken precautions, and he hadn't been with anyone else since deciding that she, Janet, was The One. She didn't ask when the brief encounter was, or with whom, but did ask why he'd been so unconcerned, so *amused*, when she said she was being tested for STDs.

'Frankly, I was relieved, because I thought you were going to say something worse.'

It took her a moment or two to work out what he meant. 'Cancer – you thought I was being tested for cancer?'

He flinched at the word. The nerve in his cheek jumped. 'Sorry, but I couldn't go through all that again. It was a close thing last time. I couldn't cope. I did, but I couldn't again. But you haven't got it—' he reached for her hand and brought it to his lips '—so no more secrets, eh? We've got to be open and honest with each other from now on. We're in this together, so I'll take you to get the results. Right?'

'Wrong. There's no need. They ring. It's all very clandestine.'

He laughed. 'Did you go in heavy disguise?'

54

ZELDA

Zelda opened the door to another unexpected visitor.

'Dad said don't.' Tracey blurted it out before the door was closed.

'Harry?'

'Yes, of course.' Tracey obviously thought it was a stupid question, which it was, if you hadn't got another dad on your mind.

'Don't what, Tracey?' Zelda led the way to the kitchen past her little office under the stairs where she'd been on the GI website.

'Don't look any more.' Tracey stopped to pat Mack and Morag through the stair rails.

'Sorry, love—' Zelda had lost track '—but I'm confused. When did your dad say this?'

'This morning.' Tracey's eyes filled up. 'I've been to see Mrs O'Connor.'

Oh dear, had grief turned the girl's mind? Woman, not girl, Tracey was forty-two next birthday. She had taken her dad's death hard. Now the tears were flowing. Zelda reached for the kettle, wondering what she had to put in a sandwich for lunch. Tracey had mentioned this Mrs O'Connor before, a medium whose ability to contact the other side was vouched for by many friends and colleagues from B&Q.

'As soon as I got there she said there was a gentleman waiting to speak to me.' Tracey tore off a piece of kitchen roll and dabbed her beautiful brown eyes, so like Harry's. It was lovely that she felt she could confide in her like this, just like a real daughter, or even better than, but it was hard to know how to respond.

'Did he say anything else, love?' Not that she believed in this nonsense. Tracey nodded, so she cobbled together a ham sandwich for each of them, made a cup of tea apiece and told her to take them into the sitting room.

'Right, Tracey, I'm all ears. Off, Mack. Off, Morag.' She shooed them off the sofa. 'But you don't have to tell me, love...'

Tracey clutched her tea with both hands. 'I must, Zelda, though I'm warning you, it's a bit rude.'

'I think I can cope.'

The gas fire sputtered. Tracey studied her tea, but then looked straight ahead and let the words come out in a rush. 'Dad said he'd rather be in your knickers than on the mantelpiece. Sorry. I know it doesn't make sense.'

But it did.

'Dad wouldn't say anything like that.' Tracey shook her head.

But he would.

'Sorry Zelda, I shouldn't have gone, I know I shouldn't. Frankie says they're all charlestons.' Tracey had misinterpreted her silence and her wide-open mouth. She apologised again and said it had been a waste of money. 'Dad didn't say a thing about Frankie and me, which was the main reason I went. To ask if I should tell Frankie I was fifteen years older than him and probably can't have children because I've started the menopause.' She stood up and put her uneaten sandwich on the mantelpiece. 'Sorry again, but I'm not really hungry, I only came to tell you that, and I ought to be getting to work and mustn't be late. My boss is a Martinique.' Tracey was Mistress of the Malapropism. 'She'll dock my wages if I'm late. Feel a bit icky in fact. Are you all right, Zelda? You've gone quiet. Are you upset?'

Upset wasn't the word.

'Yes. No. I'm all right, I mean, but... oh—' She stopped mid-sentence as Tracey's waist, or what used to be her waist, levelled briefly with her own eyes. The top button on her jeans was undone. *Did Mrs O'Connor say anything about a small dark stranger, Tracey?* She suppressed the question. Now wasn't the time. She might be wrong. Tracey might just have put on weight as they all had over Christmas. She would be hurt. So, she didn't ask about missed periods or morning sickness or lunchtime sickness, or a bigger bra size – yes, her bust was bigger too – she just walked with her to the door and kissed her goodbye. 'Look after yourself, Tracey love, and maybe go and see a doctor about the menopause.'

* * *

Back in the sitting room, she sank onto the settee, and looked at the rosewood box at the end of the mantelpiece. Harry's message from the other side, as told by Tracey, hadn't changed her view of things spiritual. She'd always thought there was 'something else', up there or out there or in there or wherever the something else was situated. She just hadn't expected it to be so like down here. But Harry's words sounded just like Harry when he was alive, in the early days anyway.

I'd rather be in your knickers than on the mantelpiece.

'Would you now?' She addressed his ashes, which resided in the rosewood box. In the beginning, when they first fell in love, Harry had talked a lot about knickers, but not of course, and rightly so, in Tracey's hearing. His taste was rather unusual for a man, in her experience. He liked big knickers. High-waisted, straight-legged, standard cotton in white were what turned him on, to the extent that anything did. There was always more talk than action, which was completely fine by her. After a few months things settled down to a Saturday or Sunday morning roll-over as he called it, and when the prostate trouble started that came to an end, except for cuddles. Which was lovely, because, frankly, she preferred cuddles. She was able to reassure him very sincerely that there were lots of other things he could do, which she liked a lot more.

I'd rather be in your knickers than on the mantelpiece.

She couldn't get his words out of her head. If she needed proof that there was an afterlife, this was it. She had never ever told anyone where she kept Harry's ashes, well, not at first. They were on the mantelpiece now, but had previously been upstairs in the drawer where she kept her knickers. When she'd collected them from the crematorium, in a container the size of one of those old-fashioned sweetie jars, she'd been taken aback by how many there were. What on earth was she going to do with them all? Harry's children had said it was up to her, so she'd taken them upstairs and put them firstly at the bottom of the wardrobe and then in the chest of drawers housing her underwear, thinking she'd make up her mind later, but there they'd stayed for over a year. It hadn't been till the morale-raising shopping spree for new undies that she'd moved them out of the drawer. Most of them had gone in the back garden under the magnolia tree where she and Harry used to sit and have a cup of tea in the summer, but she'd put some in the pretty rose-wood box engraved with entwined serpents, a well-known symbol of everlasting life.

'I'm sorry, Harry, but there wasn't room in the drawer after our shopping trip, and the new undies weren't your sort.'

It was comforting in a way knowing that he was still around, still looking out for her. What else could he see from his vantage point in eternity? Could he see her own dad? *Don't look any further.* That was very open to interpretation. He could be saying don't look any further for a new partner because you don't need one, agreeing with what she'd already decided. Or he could be warning her against looking for her dad, which would tie in with all the warnings on GItrace. Could Harry see something she couldn't, something upsetting?

It was later, when she was back in her tiny office under the stairs googling and getting nowhere, that she thought about going to see Mrs O'Connor herself. But the moment was interrupted by a text from Brian.

Looking forward to seeing you Sunday.

Oh no! She'd thought she'd put him off. She'd meant to. But it was a bit late to do it now and she wouldn't mind hearing what he'd found about the Costellos. As long as she didn't have to spend the whole evening with him. What if she invited Viv or Janet for supper, or both? Would they be free on Sunday night? Might their chaps be available? It was about time Viv's Mr Wonderful was subjected to their scrutiny.

55

JANET

'You're fine!'

Janet felt weak at the knees with relief.

The cheery female voice on the end of the line assured her that she hadn't got syphilis, gonorrhoea, chlamydia or hepatitis B or any other of a range of nasties. The voice also assured her she was on the right antibiotic for the sort of cystitis she'd got and said that it should have cleared up by now.

'It has, thank you.' She turned to tell Alan, suddenly by her side.

'Just one little thing before you go...' The cheery voice sounded only slightly less cheery. 'It would be a good idea to get your blood checked again, in a week or so at your GP's, or earlier if you don't feel well. The white blood cell count was rather low.'

'I'm feeling fine, thank you.' She put down the phone, teary. What a relief! She hadn't realised how worried she'd been till she was told she needn't be. She reached for the cup of coffee in Alan's hand, but he withheld it.

'Ring first. Now.'

'Why? Give me that.'

He didn't. 'White blood cell count. The woman told you to get it tested.'

'You were eavesdropping. I'll do it later. The surgery phones will be ringing non-stop at this time in the morning.'

'If you ring now you can drink your coffee while you're on hold.'

'Alan, I'm fine. Go and sit down while I ring.'

But he wouldn't, and he was cross when the appointment she was offered was for a fortnight's time. 'That's the end of January. Ask for earlier. Ask for a cancellation.'

No, she mouthed as he tried to take the phone from her hand. 'Don't do that, Alan,' she said, possibly too sharply, but he was being very annoying. 'Yes, that's fine,' she said to the receptionist on the other end.

I couldn't go through all that again. I couldn't cope. He was frightened which was annoying because it made her feel frightened. It was a relief when he went out with his dog. She watched him from the front window, walking down the drive, shoulders bowed, head low, looking like a very old man. She tried hard to be sympathetic. The warning had revived painful memories for him, her too. A low white blood count could indicate serious trouble – it had done with Malcolm and Penny – but didn't always, didn't usually. It just meant your immune system wasn't at its best at that moment, for example when you had cystitis.

I couldn't go through all that again.

Well, he wouldn't have to. She felt fine, better than she had done for weeks. It was good to be on her own for a bit though. Was it really possible to relax completely with someone else in the house? When the someone had a dog with big muddy paws and left magazines with Jeremy Clarkson's face all over the place? How long would he be out? Had she got time to vacuum and ring Viv and tackle her about not telling her about that spreadsheet? And about telling Alan she had cystitis, so he'd gone to the surgery to look for her. That was a gross violation of privacy. She decided to ring Viv.

'Well, you contacting Patrick was a violation of mine.' Viv fought back. She'd worked out how Patrick had got her publicity brochure. 'Alan was worried and rang me to ask if I knew where you were.'

'It isn't the same at all, Viv. All I did was give Patrick your *professional* details.'

'For which I thank you wholeheartedly.' Viv sounded really happy. 'So we're quits, yes? It's all turned out for the best.'

'Yes,' Janet conceded, because she was happy, give or take a few dog hairs.

'Oh.' Viv remembered something else. 'Has he told you he's put his house on the market?'

'No, he hasn't! How do you know?'

'I saw an estate agent's brochure.'

'Thank you, Viv. Forewarned is forearmed. What else have you seen while hiding in the shrubbery, a line of women queuing up for his services?'

'Is he that good?'

End of conversation, well, that one. A timely text pinged in from Zelda.

Hi Both, sorry for short notice, but can you make Sunday for supper with or without chaps? Aging Rioja calling in. Don't want to spend whole evening alone with him. Need to dilute! Z

Viv said Patrick was coming for the weekend but would probably be gone by Sunday night, so she would most likely go alone. Janet said she'd definitely be there, with or without Alan. They weren't a gruesome twosome yet and if Zelda needed support, she would have it. All for one! They both replied:

YES!

Things were on the up, Janet thought as she went to get the vacuum out of the cupboard in the utility room. The Three Muscateers' friendship was stronger than ever. She'd been wrong about men driving them apart. There had been rifts, but they were in the past and if the three of them were open and honest with one another in the future they wouldn't have any more. It was as she was lifting the Dyson out of the cupboard that the room started going round in circles. Then it went dark. When it was light again she was on the floor with her head pounding. Opening her eyes, she wondered how long she had been there. There was blood on her fingers. She'd scratched herself on something, a hook or nail on the back of the door. She still felt wobbly and her head was throbbing but she must get up before Alan got back.

If he knew about this he'd be running for cover.

56

VIV

It was the first morning of Viv's Art of Gardening course. She should be checking her bag, not on the phone chatting to Patrick.

'You really don't mind meeting my friends on Sunday night?'

'Not if I've had you to myself since Friday.'

'I'll make sure of that.' She gazed out of the kitchen window at a pool of golden aconites, their heads just above the snow, harbingers of spring and happiness. A chiming clock galvanised her into action. 'Got to go. It's nine o'clock.'

'Bye, then. Break a leg.'

'Thanks. Talk tonight.'

But he was still there. She was still there. They laughed at themselves acting like lovesick teenagers. 'We're like Romeo and Juliet.'

'Antony and Cleopatra more like,' she corrected him. 'They were getting on a bit.'

'Speak for yourself, Ms Halliday.'

See, he knows you're older. Shut up.

'Bye!' She put down the phone as a text pinged into her mobile. He was ten years younger at the most. Probably less. She'd worked it out from clues here and there. He'd been at university in the seventies.

The text was from Janet, who had signed up for her class. They'd planned to drive in together.

Sorry, can't make class this morning. Have to go for tests re dizzy spells. DON'T tell Alan! Repeat DON'T TELL ALAN! Will explain. DO tell teacher I'll be there next week. Ha ha! See you at Zelda's Sunday night. Janet x

Dizzy spells. Getting tests. This was worrying even though she'd been telling Janet for weeks she should get her persistent headaches investigated. Viv rang her number. 'What sort of tests?'

'Bloods, the usual and, oh yes...' she made it sound like an afterthought '... a brain scan.'

'Brain scan?' Viv tried to keep the alarm from her voice, but bloody hell!

'Yes, I told you I was going crazy, all this falling in love.' Janet laughed, unconvincingly. 'A scan will prove it.'

'How many dizzy spells have you had?'

'Three, maybe four. Latest was when I was putting a piece of chicken in Alan's dog's dish, which is further evidence that I'm going soft in the head. Look, Viv, I've got to go, and so must you. Alan's picking me up to go for a walk in half an hour. If I'm not ready, he'll bring the dog into the house and I've just cleaned.'

'But isn't Alan taking you to the hospital? What time's this scan?'

'Viv,' Janet sighed dramatically, 'I've just said, I'm not telling him.'

'But you shouldn't be driving if you're having dizzy spells.'

'I'm not. I'm getting a taxi. The appointment's at twelve. Stop fussing, Viv. I've got it all worked out.'

'But why aren't you telling Alan?'

'Long story. I'm warning you, Viv. Don't go telling him. I really wouldn't forgive you this time.'

Headaches. Dizzy spells. Very worrying, but – Viv started gathering books and folders – she'd have to think about this later. Now she was running late, and hadn't left time to read through her notes. Her phone buzzed with a text from Zelda.

Good luck with your class! I'm at retirement centre this pm, in family history class.

She was going to that creep's class! She texted back:

Why?

Zelda replied:

Because I've paid my money. He has trade directories I need to confirm my maternal grandmother was SEAMSTRESS TO THE SELECT!

Zelda was obsessed with family history.

Also have questions for him about tracing my father. More on Sunday night at my soirée. Sooo looking forward to meeting Perfect Patrick.

57

VIV

Perfect Patrick was paying the cab driver.

'Come on, Zelda. Where are you?' Viv rang the bell again. It was freezing cold on the doorstep, a shock after a warmish spell. She rang again as Patrick joined her and the door rattled as the Westies threw themselves against it. 'Did you check the driver was on call to take us home?'

'Better. I booked him for ten, though he'll come earlier or later if we text.'

Perfect Patrick. They didn't want a late night as they were going to Milton Keynes next day to see if they could find the houses whose design Patrick had worked on during his gap year with an architect. The same houses Jack had built? What a coincidence that would be! But it wouldn't surprise her in the least. Serendipity! Everything was falling into place.

'Oh—' the door opened '—here's our hostess.'

Zelda, glam in a deep blue kaftan edged with gold, stood back to let them in and laughed as the Westies retreated to the stairwell. 'Sorry, Viv, it's not you really...'

'Well, it's not me.' Patrick let the dogs nuzzle his hands as they

poked their heads through the stair rails and Viv explained that
Claudia once got the better of Mack in a spat.

'Zelda, meet Patrick, Patrick, meet Zelda.'

Zelda studied Patrick's face as she took his coat. 'You remind me
of someone, but no—' she shook her head '—can't think who!' She
led them to her sitting-cum-dining room, now half filled by a table
set for eight, where she did more introductions. 'Patrick, meet Janet
and Alan. No, no, don't get up,' she said to Janet, who was sitting by
the fire with Alan standing by her side.

Janet looked pale. Had she got the results of the brain scan yet?
Viv made a note to ask later – but when Alan was out of earshot.

'Now, is everyone okay with fizz to start?' Zelda was very much
in charge and shooed Viv away when she followed her into the
kitchen. 'No, you can't help. I'm quite capable of opening a bottle
myself. Get back to that dishy man before Janet adds him to her
harem.'

'But where's your chap from Liverpool? I assume that's his van
in the drive.'

Zelda wasn't fazed. 'It is, but he isn't, my chap, that is. Brian, aka
Aging Rioja, aka Just A Friend, has gone to the off-licence to buy
more wine. I told him I'd more than enough, but he hadn't brought
any and felt like a freeloader.' He had, she said, been very helpful
doing things like putting in the table extensions and carrying chairs
downstairs since he'd arrived that afternoon. And most importantly, he'd brought interesting info about the Liverpool side of her
family. He had in fact been more help than History Man, if a tad
depressing about her chances of tracing her dad.

Was the way to Zelda's heart through her family tree? As Viv
wondered the doorbell rang, the dogs hurtled downstairs and a tall
black woman came in, followed by a shorter, younger, balding
white chap, positively strutting. More introductions followed in the
hall. 'Tracey, meet Viv. Viv, meet Tracey. Viv, meet Frankie.' And

then again, in the now crowded sitting room, 'Tracey, meet Patrick. Patrick, meet Tracey and... OMG.' Zelda laughed at herself. 'I give up!'

More laughter.

'And, everyone, meet The Bump!' Tracey patted her tum, where a bump was only just perceptible, and Grandma-in-waiting Zelda beamed and told everyone to sit down at the table. She said she was sure Brian would be here in a minute. Viv relaxed as Patrick went upstairs at Zelda's suggestion, to get a better signal on his mobile. He'd just got a text from his son, which he thought he should answer.

As everyone took their places Viv wondered if a new order was evolving. Alan and Janet sitting opposite her looked very much a pair, as did Tracey and Frankie, sitting opposite each other, and there was a place for Patrick, on her left or right, when he returned. Zelda, near the door, said the starter of little onion tarts was more than ready, bordering on crisp, and went off to get them.

How long would Patrick be? Viv was hoping not-long when the doorbell rang again. Zelda led Brian into the room, and Viv noted he did look like an aging rocker, as if he'd spent years hunched over a set of drums. But there was a shyness about him too, she thought as Zelda introduced him to the others. Why had she expected someone brasher? Because he was from Liverpool? But Patrick was from Liverpool and he wasn't brash. Far from it, he was quite reserved. Where was he? That was a very long phone call. She began to worry as Brian apologised for being late, saying he'd had to go into town to get what he wanted. He held up two bottles, one a Rioja and the other was champagne. Of course. Their online pseudonyms. That was what the seeming shyness was about. Brian was trying hard to please Zelda.

'Sit down, Brian.' Zelda took the bottles from him and directed him to the opposite end of the table. 'I'll put the bubbly in the fridge.' She headed back to the kitchen as Viv and Frankie, side by side, both stood up to let Brian squeeze past to reach his assigned place on her right. Sitting down again, she was about to introduce herself, when he looked up and, following his gaze, she saw Patrick coming back into the room. Brian's sudden bellow made her turn back to him.

'Kiddo! What the hell are you doing here?'

And Patrick's reply made her look at him. 'Why the hell are you here, mate?'

It was like being at a crazy tennis match. The two men obviously knew each other and, even more gobsmacking, Zelda, now back in the room, seemed to know them both too. 'Of course!' she was saying to Patrick. 'I knew I'd met you before. I never forget a face.'

'Would someone please explain?' This was disconcerting to say the least. But none of them answered and for several minutes she, and the other guests, felt distinctly side-lined as Patrick and Zelda at one end of the table and Brian at the other talked over their shaking heads and shrugging shoulders. Apparently the three of them had met before Christmas in Liverpool, but couldn't agree exactly where. Was it the Phil on Friday night or the Cavern on Saturday or some other pub on Sunday? As their voices ping-ponged past her she caught on that Patrick aka Kiddo and Brian aka Aging Rioja went way back, and were in fact childhood neighbours. Then Zelda suddenly held up her phone. 'Proof! It was the Phil on Saturday afternoon!'

As Zelda's mobile was passed round the table and what had happened became clearer not just to Viv but also the rest of the table, others recounted similar instances of amazing coincidences and it was generally agreed that it was a small world, and everyone was connected by – what was it? – six or seven degrees of separation?

'Six,' said Brian, suddenly authoritative, 'according to Karinthy's shrinking world theory anyway, though currently it's only a hypothesis.' For a while he held the floor talking about algorithms and Zelda looked impressed and pleased when it proved to be a good topic of conversation. Was she seeing a new side to him?

Almost everyone had a story about someone who knew someone who knew another unlikely someone. Frankie, Tracey's partner, had less to say than most, but, perhaps rehearsing for his new family role, he proved an agile helper to Zelda, fetching and carrying. Conversation flowed as starters were finished and cleared away. The drink flowed too and their laughter got louder. There was a break, quite a long break, before Frankie carried in the beef daube, followed by Zelda with an array of veg. Viv saw Patrick look at his watch and caught his eye, both thinking the same thing, would they be through by ten? It was half past nine before they got onto dessert, delicious boozy port jellies, and she was about to start hers when Brian suddenly reached over her – it was almost a lurch – to tap Patrick's right hand.

'Kiddo, just remembered something I've got to tell you.'

Patrick, who was listening to Frankie on his other side, said, 'In a minute, Brian.'

But Brian, who'd been knocking back the Rioja, was obviously very keen to say what he wanted to say, while he still remembered it. She knew the feeling – so she wasn't unsympathetic at first when he turned to her and said, 'Tell Patrick, as you call him, I've sussed out who his real dad is.'

Silence. Brian was loud and everyone had heard.

'This is not the right time, Brian.' Zelda glared at him from the other end of the table. It was of course a sensitive topic with her, and Viv felt Patrick go tense beside her as Brian carried on, addressing the whole table now. 'He was a Geordie like Viv here.'

Patrick picked up his dessert spoon. 'Not interested, Brian. I think I've already told you that.'

But Brian kept going. 'According to our Mary, that's my older sister for your information, it was a bit like that film, *Mrs Robinson*, where the older woman has it off with the young lad. These Geordie builders were doing an extension, see, three doors up from ours, and the apprentice lad lodged with the O'Malleys next door, and Mrs O'Malley, Kiddo's mum—'

'*The Graduate*,' said Janet, interrupting, 'That's what the film was called, not *Mrs Robinson*. That was the name of the older woman, and the eponymous graduate, played by Dustin Hoffman, was a young man in his twenties.'

'So it wasn't exactly child abuse,' Alan chipped in.

'Nobody said it were, mate.' Brian turned on Alan.

Time to change the subject? Viv felt Patrick's growing irritation and touched his hand to show solidarity. 'What's the latest from New Zealand, Janet?'

It was the best she could do on the spur of the moment and Janet took up the cue. Phew! Altercation avoided. Janet updated them on the post-earthquake situation, mentioning how Grant's firm was helping with the clear-up. Others joined in with their own earthquake experiences, Alan describing how he once slept through an earthquake in Madrid and woke up in the morning to find his bed on the balcony. 'I hadn't heard a thing.'

When Janet said, 'Why doesn't that surprise me?' everyone laughed.

Except Brian.

Preoccupied, he was searching his pockets, turning them inside out, and, finding a notebook in one of them, he tore out a page and pushed it in front of Viv. *JACK ROBSON*. The name in capitals jumped out. Of course! It was a shock, but only for the few seconds it took to remind herself that Robson was a very common name and

Jack even commoner. Brian looked pleased with himself. 'Give Kiddo that if he changes his mind and wants to go looking for his real dad. And there's more where that came from.' He tapped the notebook. 'It's all in here, everything our Mary came up with. I wrote it down. It's approximate like, as she wasn't sure of all the dates, but she was dead sure the lad's name was Jack Robson.'

Another silence and she felt everyone looking at her.

Janet laughed. 'Did you say Jack Robson? Sorry, Viv, but for those of you who don't know, it's funny, funny peculiar, because that happens to be the name of Viv's late husband. Yet another of life's amazing coincidences.'

Viv managed a laugh herself and turned to Patrick to explain about not taking her husband's name when she married, but the expression on his face made the words die on her lips. He was shaking his head slowly from side to side, his bottom lip slightly curled. It was an expression she knew well. It was an expression she'd seen when the girls had gone on teasing Jack a bit too long about his bald spot, or when an apprentice had asked him for time-off for a reason he'd thought trivial, or when she'd walked into Jack 's workshop that day to ask him to choose between three different-coloured cravats for Sally's wedding. It was a mixture of irritation and incredulity – why are you bothering me with this? – and it wouldn't last long. He'd apologise in a minute for a sense-of-humour failure. Yes, here it came, the wry smile as he reached for her hand.

But she pulled hers away.

It was no big deal to Patrick that Brian had just named his biological father. It was information he didn't need or want. He would ignore it.

But she couldn't.

Bells were clanging in her head. Jack Robson, builder. Jack Robson, Geordie. Jack Robson apprenticed to Geordie builder who'd done some work up on Merseyside years before she'd met him.

'Sorry.' She got to her feet. 'I need the loo.'

Frankie and Patrick got up too, pushing back their chairs so she could get by. She breathed in so as not to touch Patrick.

'Not something you ate, I hope?' Zelda looked worried as she reached the door.

She shook her head. As she climbed the stairs, sending the dogs fleeing before her, she heard Tracey saying you didn't realise how common your name was till you signed up for Facebook, that there were hundreds of Tracey Fieldings and quite a few Zeldas and there must be thousands of Jack Robsons. But there was only one who'd fathered a child called Patrick and never told her about it. Only one who'd kept it secret for over forty years. Reaching the bathroom at last, she sank to her knees and puked into the bowl.

'Let's get this right, Viv. You think I'm your husband's love-child because his cat likes me?' They were back at Viv's house, in the sitting-room. She was standing as far from him as she could, rigid with misery; he was on the sofa, legs stretched out, absurdly relaxed. Claudia was on his knee purring like a tractor as he stroked her upturned chin. *He who keeps his head while all about are losing theirs does not understand the situation.*

'But I'm trying to understand,' he said. He was collecting all the facts so he could work out exactly what the problem was. This was how he operated, logically, reasonably, rationally, *just like his father*, analysing a problem by breaking it down into its smallest parts and totally missing the point.

Viv tried again. 'It's not just Claudia, as I've explained, but it was weeks before she would sit on my lap after Jack died. And she took minutes to approve of you.' She'd gone over it several times since they'd got in, unable to explain in the cab on the way home, while the driver was listening. But stubbornly – just like Jack – Patrick was refusing to understand.

'If, *if* I'm his son, how does that change things?'

'You can't *see*?'

'No. I can't.' He shook his head. 'We, you and me, we're not related. We don't share genes. I am not your son. This isn't a Greek tragedy.'

'So why do I want to gouge my eyes out?'

'Viv!' He sighed heavily and Claudia got off his knee. He wasn't convinced by The Look argument either. That expression of irritation, the shaking head, the curled lip, was archetypal.

But you smell the same. She didn't say that, had never said that, but had noticed the first time her nose nuzzled his skin. *He's my type,* she'd thought, the pheromones turning her on, making him feel familiar and sexy and safe.

'You never felt like a stranger.'

'You never felt like a stranger to me. What does that prove? Oh, sit down, Viv.' He thumped the sofa.

'I'm sorry for what he did to you.' She sat, but at the far end.

'Come again?' He looked baffled.

'That he abandoned you.'

'For Christ's sake!' He got to his feet. 'What are you doing now, Viv, making a teenage boy being offered no-strings-sex by an older experienced woman into an absconding father? How old was he? Sixteen, seventeen, eighteen? What am I saying?' He ran his fingers through his hair. 'This is far from certain. If. If. If. And let's not forget, my mother did not tell my dad, the dad who brought me up, that she'd had an affair with this lad. And she didn't tell me till she was a very old woman. I bet she didn't tell him, the lad, my possible father, your future husband, whoever it was, that she was pregnant. She probably didn't know who by. Don't think I'm completely unmoved by all this, by the way, knowing my mother wasn't the most faithful of wives...'

'What was her name?' A jolt of memory. 'Wait a minute.' It took her seconds to find the carrier-bag in the utility-room cupboard, a few minutes to leaf through the cards to find the one with the photograph of pansies. 'Here. Recognise the writing?' She stood in front of him with the card open so he could read what was inside.

I knew Jack when he was a shy young man, a long-haired Viking and real charmer. Never forget how lucky you were to have him all those years.

Sorry for your loss,
Vi

He didn't need to speak, his face said it all. Jack was his father.

'What was she like?'

'Viv, I'm sorry.'

'I'm sorry too. But she must have loved him a lot to keep track of him all those years.' How had she done that? She let him take the card and pointed to the photo of Sally's wedding on the table behind him. 'See any family resemblances?' His half-sister and two of his nieces had the same mouth. Why hadn't she noticed that before?

'Viv, I'm sorry, I mean, I'm sorry that you've had this shock, not that we two met, not even that this has happened. Truth will out and it's perhaps best that it does. But nothing's changed.'

'Everything's changed.'

'We're the same people who met and fell in love.' He put down the card.

'No, we are not.'

'Well, I'm not giving up on us.' He reached for her hand but she stepped back. He still didn't get it. But he would when he thought about it. She suggested tea and he accepted. In the kitchen she made herself think positively as she filled the kettle. There was nothing lost, really. You could say it was a gain, a new member of the family. 'I have a stepson,' she said to the cat as she filled her dish. 'I have a stepson.'

That's right, face facts.

Thank you, Mugwort.

How was she going to live with herself knowing what she'd been doing? Or sleep tonight? Tea wasn't the answer. She needed a proper drink. There was only fizz in the fridge though, but why not fizz? To celebrate the discovery of a long-lost son? Bottle in hand, she returned to the sitting room where he was taking photos of her photos with his mobile – to show his son?

'We must have a family reunion so our kids can meet each other,' she said, holding up the bottle.

But he shook his head. 'No booze for me, thanks, but maybe that cup of tea? Let's sleep on it and talk in the morning.'

'Okay. The kettle's boiled, and yes...' she thought about it '... there's a bed made up in the spare room.' She turned to go back to the kitchen, but his arms were around her.

'Nothing's changed, Viv. Let's sleep on it, together, that's what I meant, and see how we feel in the morning.'

'Let. Me. Go.' She spoke through gritted teeth.

'We love each other, Viv.'

'It's different now.'

'No.' But he let her go. 'Promise me you'll think about this rationally when the shock has worn off.'

'I am thinking rationally.'

'Okay, but forget the tea.' He left the room and she heard him climbing the stairs, then, after a few minutes, coming down again. Still standing where he'd left her, she saw him in the doorway, his overnight bag in his hand. 'Sorry, but I can't stay on your terms. I'll drive into town and find a hotel, and, Viv, don't rush the family reunion. I need to think about things.'

She made a move to see him to the door but he'd gone. She heard the front door bang shut, then his car driving away into the dark.

59

JANET

'MRI scan detects abnormalities' leaped from the GP's letter, before she stuffed it under the pillow. Alan was coming upstairs.

'I trust this is to your liking, madam?' It was his Jeeves impression, standing aside to await further orders after placing the tray in front of her.

'Yes. I mean no.' It was everything she usually liked, yogurt, blueberries, coffee and croissants with jam and butter. 'But I thought we agreed croissants as a weekend treat.'

Today was Monday, the day after Zelda's astonishing supper party.

'Waste not want not, darling. They were a three for two. I couldn't resist.' He was untying his paisley dressing gown, preparing to get back into bed, but he must go downstairs.

'Waist? Not.' She looked pointedly at, yes, a paunch. He was touchy about his waistline and might depart offended, but he laughed unabashed and put on the radio.

'Your fault, darling. You feed me too well.'

Did he just pass wind? Standards were slipping. He wouldn't have done that a month ago.

But she had heard it, so nothing wrong with her hearing. Good. Couldn't smell it though. Bad. Try again.

'Alan, you know I don't like Radio 5. If you want to listen to it, please go downstairs.' She needed to read that letter again.

'Janet—' he turned off the radio '—what's the matter? Something upsetting in the post?'

Most of it still lay on the bed, travel brochures, estate agents' fliers and requests for charitable donations to charities she already subscribed to. Fortunately, before she could answer, the doorbell rang, and his dog went crazy in the hall.

'There will be no paint left on the door, Alan!'

He headed downstairs yelling to the dog to stop scratching, and she felt under the pillow for the letter, her hand trembling. No odour. What had things come to when she was sorry she couldn't smell a fart? She couldn't smell the coffee either so her sense of smell had gone. It was another symptom, another sign that her brain wasn't right, confirming her Google diagnosis.

CT scan inconclusive therefore appointment made for MRI scan. On Friday 11 February, nearly a month away, so not an emergency.

Magnetic Resonance Imaging produces a detailed picture of the brain and detects abnormalities. You are advised to bring a friend to drive you home.

That would have to be Viv or Zelda. She'd ring Viv in a minute, but she needed the loo first. Could she wait till Alan got back to lift the tray off her knee? No, she had to go straight away. It was like that these days. Raising the tray, she eased her legs out of bed, and got her feet to the floor, but as she went to stand up her legs gave way and the room started spinning, and the tray, suddenly too heavy, dropped from her hands as pinpoints of light danced behind her eyes.

Then darkness.

'Janet.' The voice came from a long way off.

She made herself open her eyes but had to close them again, for the room was a whirlwind of green and purple.

I'm ill.

'Janet, darling.' The voice was even further away.

He mustn't know. He mustn't know.

She waited for a bit before tentatively opening her eyes again to a room that was thankfully still, except for a coffee stain spreading over her beautiful cream carpet.

'Darling.' Alan was crouching beside her.

'I just fainted, that's all.' But it wasn't all.

'Let's get you back into bed.'

'No, I need the bathroom.' Though it was too late. She felt strange and scared and sick with embarrassment.

'Let me help you.' He went to take her arm.

'No!' she shouted.

He backed off but hovered at the door, his face too full of concern.

'Stop fussing, Alan! You're getting on my nerves!'

She got to the bathroom somehow and sorted herself out slowly, sitting down a lot. Luckily, she had clean underwear in the airing cupboard. When she got back to her bedroom, maybe half an hour later, maybe an hour, it was neat and tidy, the mess cleared up, the stains on the carpet lighter, but still visible. The bed was made with the cover folded back. There was a note on the pillow.

Darling,

Suggest you spend the morning in bed. Sorry, but I have taken the liberty of ringing your GP to ask advice. She says she

will make a home visit at some point today. Have gone to walk
Kenny. Will be back very soon.
     Alan xxxx

She crumpled the note in her hand. A home visit. She must be
at death's door, then. She read the letter from the surgery again –
had he seen it? – and it confirmed all her fears. There was something seriously wrong. She had a brain tumour most likely, in the
frontal lobe. She had it all worked out. It explained the headaches,
the dizziness, the collapse, the loss of a sense of smell. So who
would come with her to get the bad news? Not I-couldn't-cope Alan
Loveday. She needed someone strong and supportive who would
help her face the future or lack of it calmly. She reached for the
phone.

60

VIV

Viv welcomed the diversion of taking Janet to hospital though not the reason for it. Janet's troubles made her own seem trivial, and she'd tried to be upbeat when Janet rang. 'If you google brain tumour you're sure to convince yourself you've got one,' she'd said. In the old days it was the medical dictionary, now, it's NHS Direct and other even more alarming sites. As she drove Janet to the appointment, super-carefully to avoid potholes and icy patches, Viv couldn't risk a sideways glance to see if the swelling on the side of Janet's head was bigger than when she'd seen her last. *Pay attention.* The gritters had been out last night, but there had been rain since.

Janet, tense and upright beside her, was silent, staring straight ahead, but suddenly said, 'What reason did you give for not going to Alan's this morning?'

'The weather.' Lie. He'd rung weeks ago to ask if she was taking Janet to the hospital. He'd seen the letter about the MRI scan and he wasn't a fool. Probably wasn't a wimp either, though Janet seemed to think he was. She had another go at telling her so. 'Tell me again, why are you sure Alan couldn't cope if you were ill?'

'He. Said. So,' Janet hissed. 'Now, Viv, please concentrate on getting us to the hospital safely. You have a life ahead of you, even if I haven't.'

'Should I drive straight to Plunkett and Crombie?'

That was the end of the conversation until they reached the hospital car park where Janet relented, a bit. As they were about to get out of the car she gripped Viv's arm. 'I've been thinking. I will tell Alan if I have to, but I may not have to. See, I've become an optimist. And you, you have a rethink too, about Patrick. I've been googling on your account, and have ascertained your relationship isn't illegal or immoral. It isn't banned by either church or state. You could marry him if you wanted to. Leviticus of course banned it along with seventy-five other things, which I would have thought in your books was...'

'Janet—' Viv tried not to snap '—let's get *you* sorted first, shall we?'

'... a recommendation.' Janet finished her sentence defiantly.

She continued to look defiant as they walked, arms linked, down the long corridor to Radiology, after refusing to sit in the wheelchair Viv found in a bay by Reception. But she walked slowly and bowed like a very old woman. When did that begin? And why hadn't they all noticed the weight loss? The bones in Janet's arm felt like a bird's. But thankfully when they at last reached Radiology, Janet breathless, they didn't have long to wait in the crowded waiting room. A friendly, red-haired nurse approached with a clipboard almost as soon as they'd sat down. 'You're second on the list, Janet. Now...' She started to explain the process, but Janet cut her off.

'I've googled, thank you. They'll attach electrodes to my head and record my brain waves if I have any. It does not hurt though some recipients report otherwise. See, I know all about it.'

Red-haired Nurse looked as if she was going to say something, but decided against it and left. 'Right, Viv.' Janet turned her head slowly towards her. 'Divert me. Tell me why you're cutting that highly desirable man out of your life.'

'I am not, but he seems to be cutting me out of his. And for the record, he is no longer desirable. Not in that way. We have moved on. Well, I have. I now regard him as a son and have invited him to meet the rest of the family, several times, but he has not replied. He is ignoring all my missives suggesting dates for a get-together.' Viv was determined to keep the conversation going, but only to indulge Janet, who sat like a statue, afraid to move her head.

'I want to introduce him to the girls, his half-sisters, who, by the way, all reacted differently when I told them. Sally was upset, at first, possibly because it knocks her from her perch as firstborn. Beth said she won't believe it and doesn't want to meet till Patrick's had a DNA test. My guess is she doesn't like the idea of splitting my worldly wealth four ways when I pop my clogs. And Em was utterly delighted.'

But had she told Em Patrick's name on Christmas Eve when they'd had that lovely heart-to-heart? That was a bit of a worry. Would Em still be as delighted if she knew her mother's lover, *former* lover, was her half-brother? Viv hoped she could keep that bit from them. She had simply told the girls that their father's illegitimate son had 'turned up'.

'Why have you stopped?' Janet was sharp.

'I can't tell you here.' A crowded waiting room wasn't the place to talk about possible incest. 'I'll just say that Em's been complaining about her boringly conventional stable upbringing ever since she was a teenager. Parents still together, for heaven's sake! How could she hope to be a creative artist without a dreadful childhood and a dysfunctional family?'

'Grant should be a creative genius, then.' Janet gave a wry laugh as Red-haired Nurse returned. 'Mrs Carmichael, we're ready for you now. If you'll come this way.'

Viv texted Zelda and Alan.

Patient just gone for scan. Fingers crossed.

Zelda texted straight back.

Thanks. Keep me posted.

What now? A coffee and then an hour or so looking at her Art of Gardening course notes? She'd brought plenty of work with her but couldn't concentrate. Time passed slowly, and it seemed like hours before the nurse was back.

'Viv? Your friend would like you with her when she gets the feedback.' Was there a new sombre note to her voice, a shadow of concern behind the professional smile?

It didn't help that the room they were in looked just like the one where Jack received his death sentence. Perhaps all consultation rooms looked alike. The charts on the walls and the orange plastic chairs looked horribly familiar. As she sat down beside Janet, in front of a desk, where Dr Morgan – she read his lanyard – sat on a leather chair, her fears grew. In dark-rimmed glasses, the man looked like a sixth-former pretending to be a grown-up, but at least he didn't waste time with platitudes.

'Right.' He swung away from them and pointed a digital pen at a computer screen where what must be Janet's brain glowed dimly. 'That is the parietal lobe, and that is a tumour.' He circled part of it, a large part it seemed, with a heavy black line. It was near the top, he said, in the upper cerebral cortex, which was responsible for processing taste and smell and touch and spatial sense and—

'Hold on.' Viv was taking notes to share with Janet later. 'Could you speak more slowly, please?' That was what she'd come for, to be the rational, objective listener, but her stomach was swirling, her hand trembling. How could Janet take all this in when it was her brain he was talking about in his robotic deadpan voice? The black swirl seemed to enclose half her head, but, said the doctor, there was only one tumour as far as he could tell and no sign of metastasis, though they would need a PET scan to be sure that it was a primary, and hadn't spread to other parts of her body.

'So, what are we going to do?' He swung back to them.

'I think you'd better tell us.' Janet was still Janet! 'Brain surgery's not part of our skill set.'

Surgery was unlikely, said Dr Morgan, as if he'd seriously considered the option. Radiotherapy might be possible or chemotherapy or a mix – Viv struggled to get it all down – but the tumour's position between the something and the other made surgical removal very difficult.

'But not impossible?' Viv asked, hoping she was witnessing a tried and tested male technique. 'Jack was always doing that,' she said when the doctor had left the room, to consult a colleague. 'First he'd say how impossible a task was, then say how he might, just *might* be able to fix it, then he'd fix it and became a hero. It was always like that when something went wrong with my computer.'

'Brain surgery's probably not that difficult anyway.' Janet gave a dismissive shrug.

'Piece of cake.' Viv reached for her hand.

Then they laughed to stop themselves crying.

* * *

Dr Morgan came back eventually with the nurse, who looked almost cheerful. They had some good news, the doctor said. Ms

Wilkins, a brain surgeon with a world-class reputation who took on high risk patients, was willing to take a look at Mrs Carmichael. Viv recalled reading that some surgeons wouldn't take on high-risk cases these days for fear of lowering their ratings if things went wrong. But Ms Wilkins wasn't such a ratings chaser, it seemed. She would see Janet at her base at Addenbrooke's Hospital if they could get her there in time. She had a window, her only window that day, during her lunch hour. Cambridge was forty miles away.

'You want me to take her?' Had the NHS come to this? Viv stood up, but no, the nurse assured her, there was an ambulance waiting. It was about to leave with another patient but there was room for two inside it. An ambulance ready and waiting. Why didn't she find that reassuring? Because it screamed emergency. Didn't people usually have to wait hours, days, weeks, even months for appointments with consultants?

'Why don't you go home and get your friend's night things and take them to Addenbrooke's just in case they keep her in?' said Friendly Nurse.

'They will keep her in,' said the doctor, 'if not for surgery then for some other treatment. Mrs Carmichael is seriously ill.'

And now she came to look hard enough, Viv had to agree that Janet looked seriously ill, and smaller and thinner. It was as if she'd shrunk since they'd arrived, except for the side of her head, the right side, which looked bigger and bulgier. Why hadn't she seen it before? Why hadn't she seen what had been happening in front of her for weeks? Because she'd been too wrapped up in her own trivial concerns.

Janet was quiet now, and when a porter appeared with a wheelchair she let him help her into it. Meekly. Passively. Not Janet. As the porter pushed the chair out of the room and then along one corridor and then another, Viv hurried along beside it, wanting to take hold of Janet's hand in an act of solidarity, but the porter was going too fast and Janet was gripping the arms of the chair too tightly. They came to the lifts and the doors of one opened straight away but it was crowded and no one got out.

Good. Wait for the next one. I need to speak to her before she goes.

But people in the lift were shuffling backwards, making room for Janet and the porter, who was reversing the wheelchair in, leaving no room for anyone else. Janet looked out, her face pale, her mouth set as the doors began to close. Perhaps it was just as well. What would Viv have said, after all? You'll be all right? You're in good hands? Never say die? To Janet, who abhorred platitudes? Their eyes met just before the doors came together and there was no need to say anything, because they both knew that whatever you said, whatever you thought, whatever you *willed* to happen, things would happen.

'I'll tell Grant.' He was Janet's next of kin. His name would have to go on the consent forms. No? Was Janet really mouthing no?

'But...' Too late. Doors shut. Shit! Getting her sponge bag and nightie, was that all she could do? What had gone wrong in New Zealand? They never had got the full story from Janet. She'd had a row with Grant and hadn't heard from him since, except for the turkey, which she'd hoped was a peace-offering, but clearly wasn't. Janet had eventually written to thank him when phone calls and Skype attempts had failed. He hadn't replied. He seemed to have cut her out of his life. But Janet might *die*, for fuck's sake. Surely he had to be told that his mother had a tumour in her head as big as a fist?

61

VIV

'I'd have acted quicker if my potatoes had the blight.'

Today, at some point, Janet would have the operation, three whole days since Ms Wilkins had decided it was an emergency.

'What sort of emergency is that?'

Must stop talking to myself.

It was Monday morning, the fourteenth of February, Saint Valentine's Day, not that that was relevant. Viv was at Alan Loveday's doing work she hadn't done on Friday, hacking away at the overgrown buddleia in the front border, trying to keep her mind off Ms Wilkins hacking away at Janet's brain. The weather had improved, fortunately. Alan was working too, in the back garden. She'd got him pruning the apple trees and applying a wash of tar oil. When he'd finished that he could cut the autumn-fruiting raspberries to the ground and spray the peach tree in the greenhouse against leaf curl. Keep busy, that was what they'd decided at the weekend, among other things. *They* had decided, the conspirators, Alan, Zelda and herself, doing what they thought best for Janet. Risky. But it felt right.

Keep busy.

Was Janet being wheeled into the theatre right now? Was she already under the knife? They didn't know because the hospital would only communicate details to family, which meant Grant and they still hadn't heard from him. Viv had found his number on Friday when she'd gone to get Janet's night things – it was still on the kitchen whiteboard under a grey smear where Alan's number used to be – and she'd rung straight away. She'd got the answering service, but it had been the middle of the night in New Zealand, so she'd left a message telling Grant his mother was seriously ill. She'd left her own number but he hadn't called back. Alan had tried later, when they had decided a male voice might carry more weight with an arsehole like Grant, but he hadn't got an answer either.

How was Alan getting on with his pruning? She straightened up and stretched her aching back. Was that the sun up there in the misty sky? It *would* come out. Things *would* improve. She had to believe that. Spring *was* on its way. Under the hedge by the road some early daffodils were nodding their heads, Rijnveld's Early Sensation, and there was a flurry of bird activity in the hedge, sparrows looking for mates. That was what birds did on Valentine's Day, allegedly. She'd made a Valentine card for Jack once, drawing a couple of lovebirds and sticking on photos of their faces. She had to remember to count her blessings. She had been loved. She'd had forty lovely Valentine's days, most beginning with a laugh as they both rummaged in their bedside drawers for the cards they'd sent the year before and the year before. When did that begin – when they were hard up, or just fed up trying to find something not totally naff? His to her was totally naff. Violets weren't blue.

'Coffee?' Alan hailed her from the front door. 'Bugger off, Kenny!' His dog was bearing the brunt of his anguish.

'Yes please, and let's have a bonfire in the back, to burn the clippings and raise our spirits.'

His phone rang as they were drinking coffee by the fire, feeding it with twigs from time to time. He mouthed 'Grant' as he answered it. At bloody last. 'I'm a friend of your mother's,' she heard him say. Pause. Then, 'No, she didn't ask me to ring you, but I, we, her close friends, think you should know she is seriously, dangerously ill and is having an operation today. We think you should be by her side.' Another pause, then, 'Because you're her son. Because seeing you might aid her recovery. Because this might be the last chance you have to make your peace.' A very long pause. Alan looked grim. 'That may well be—' he stamped on a smouldering twig '—but her friends need to know how she is, and the only way we can find out is via you, her next of kin. So please ring the hospital and ask for information and then ring me back. As soon as possible.' He glanced at his watch. 'Before you go to bed, please. Yes, I do appreciate this is late at night for you.' He gave Grant the hospital number and put the phone back in his pocket.

'Is he coming?'

'He didn't think that was necessary. Bastard.'

'Is he going to ring the hospital?'

'Didn't say.'

But his phone rang an hour later.

'Thank you,' she heard Alan say, his voice breaking. There were tears in his eyes when he turned towards her to say that Janet, though still unconscious, had come through the operation, and was now in Intensive Care. The surgeon had removed a tumour from the right cerebral hemisphere, which would be sent for tests.

Teary herself, she texted Zelda, who rang back weeping, expressing relief and delight and hope for all of them. 'Remind Alan I'm expecting him for a meal tonight. You too, Viv.'

Viv declined as she had too much to do and she and Zelda were meeting that afternoon to make plans for looking after Janet when

she came out of hospital. One of them would move in to do the
night shift, the other would do days.

As she got into the car a text came in from Sally asking if she'd
got a date for the family reunion yet. The grandgirls wanted to meet
their new uncle. No, because she still hadn't heard from Patrick.
Before she could reply another text came in. It was from George
Beaumont inviting her to join an excursion to the Keukenhof bulb
fields and the Hortus Botanicus in Leiden. Interesting, the Hortus
Botanicus was on her wish list and she'd love to see the bulbs, but
the trip must be soon and she was committed to Janet for the next
few weeks.

By the time she got home the sun was out – good omen! – and
there was nothing in her outside post box. But then she saw
Claudia was standing on a pile of post in the hall. A temporary
post-person must have missed the box outside. She was relieved to
find there were no bills, only circulars, which could go straight into
recycling, and a *'We tried to deliver...'* card. What was that for? What
had she ordered? Curse aged memory, but at least they hadn't taken
whatever it was away. It was in her 'preferred place' round the back.
'Okay, I'll feed you first, cat.'

The box from David Austin Roses was on the table in the
summer house. Feeling sorry for the plant imprisoned inside,
hoping she'd remember who she'd ordered it for when she saw
what it was, she got her pen knife from her pocket.

'Oh.' The breath left her lungs as she saw the label on the
pruned bush.

Souvenir de la Malmaison.
    Large, soft pink flowers,
    cupped at first, but opening
    to flat and quartered. Strong fragrance.
    Named in memory of Empress

Joséphine's famous garden at Malmaison
and her love for Napoleon.

She had to sit down. This didn't help. It didn't help at all. He shouldn't have. Candlelight flickered as their fingers intertwined and she trembled at his touch. Why couldn't he understand that it wasn't like that now?

62

ZELDA

'She says she *feels* he's her stepson.' Zelda was talking to a baffled Brian, on the phone yet again. It was five o'clock and she wanted to get back to her research about her dad. She'd just found the website of the NPRC, the National Personnel Records Centre in St Louis, where details of American military personnel were kept. It had been recommended by Felix at the family history class.

'But he isn't her son. They're not related, for pity's sake.' Brian was in deep dudgeon. Everyone was against him. His sister Mary wasn't speaking to him because she'd told him about Kiddo's possible parentage in confidence. Kiddo wasn't speaking to him, not since telling him that his big mouth had ruined his life. Viv wouldn't speak to him, though he'd rung offering to mediate if he could. 'I can't see what the problem is, Zeld. I mean, so he's like her husband who she loved to bits. Now she's got a newer version of the same model.'

'That's crass, Brian.'

'They're in love, Zelda.'

'*Were*, Brian, *were*.'

'He loves her like I love you, Zelda.'

She let that go and didn't go into her own theory on the subject. That Patrick wasn't the problem. It was Jack. Honest Jack, the paragon among men, the solid oak among the weedier specimens. He had been felled, crushing Viv as he crashed to the ground.

'She's broken, Brian, and all mixed up. One minute she's trying to plan a family reunion, the next she's saying, not yet.'

'Why's she keep changing her mind?'

Because she knows if she saw him again she wouldn't be able to hide how she really felt, how she still felt. That was Zelda's opinion, but she said, 'I'm not sure. She says she's not ready, though her three daughters are all keen now, even Beth, the one who wasn't. Middle daughter's curiosity has overcome her suspicions.'

'Suspicions of what?'

'Patrick's motives. Beth thinks he's after his share of his father's assets when Viv pops her clogs.'

'But he's loaded, well not short of a bob.'

'I know, it doesn't make sense, but where did sense ever come into it? Look, Brian, I've got to go.'

'Okay. Just one more thing, Zelda, did you get my Valentine's card?'

'Yes, I did and I'm not your honey bun and I don't want lots of fun.' She hung up and got back to the NPRC website, but only to discover that most files had been destroyed by fire in 1973. Finding her dad's file, even if she had his name, regiment and serial number, was unlikely. Another dead end.

* * *

Alan arrived at Zelda's later but without an update on Janet. He was waiting to hear from Grant again. After the meal he fell asleep on the settee. Mouth open, he was not a pretty sight. Poor man. To think she'd fancied him once. Yes, she had. Best to be honest. But

now all she felt was sympathy and admiration. His devotion to Janet
was total. He must have been too worried to sleep much last night.
What would Janet say if she could see him now? And what would
she say when, *when* she recovered and learned the three of them
were in cahoots? *On her behalf*, she reminded herself. But would
Janet see it like that?

Alan had turned up on her own doorstep when Janet threw him
out because he'd rung for a doctor. He'd done the right thing, she'd
assured him, and Viv had agreed when she'd told her. They both
thought he was right to overrule Janet *on that occasion*, not as a
general rule. Had Janet come round from the op yet? That was the
question on their minds. Had the surgeon removed the tumour
without damaging her brain? This thought circled in her mind as
she tidied up in the kitchen, leaving Alan to sleep.

Then she heard his mobile ringing. She hurried to the sitting
room to find him on his feet, phone at his ear. 'That's a good sign,
Grant. Asking for you. It shows her brain's working. So, when are
you coming?'

Pause.

'But you've got to come. Her recovery may depend on it.'

Was Grant refusing? What sort of man was he?

'And if she has a relapse because you didn't?' Alan wasn't
accepting no for an answer.

Another pause.

'If it's a question of cash I'll pay for your ticket.'

Another pause.

It seemed an age before she heard Alan say, 'Well, let me know
flight details as soon as you have them, and I'll be there to meet you
at Heathrow.' He pocketed his phone.

Phew. But Alan didn't trust Grant to do what he said, so he was
surprised when he got a text saying Grant would be here in eight
days' time, on a flight arriving early in the morning. They both put

Tuesday 22 February in their diaries. 'Not hurrying, is he?' Alan was unimpressed, but Zelda said she thought the delay could help Janet. It was something for her to look forward to, a whole week to focus on recovery. And she was right. It was a great incentive. When Janet learned that Grant was coming she wanted to be home to welcome him, not in hospital.

Her progress from then on amazed the doctors. Once assured that Janet would never be alone in her house – she and/or Viv would always be there – and that a community nurse would check her over twice a day, the consultant discharged her. Or tipped her out because they needed the bed, if you took Viv's cynical view. Whatever, an ambulance brought Janet back mid-morning a week later, the day before Grant was due to arrive.

* * *

They were both there to welcome her home. Viv's overnight bag was in one of the spare bedrooms. The other was ready for Grant. Alan, still banished as far as they knew, was at his house on secret standby, mobile at the ready, prepared to do anything they asked. They didn't want to risk upsetting Janet by revealing that they had told him about her illness. In the evening Zelda, day-nurse, went to say goodnight to Janet before going home. 'Not long now,' she reassured her. 'Grant will be on his way to the airport now. Might even be there.'

The tea in Janet's hand wobbled. She still hadn't said why she'd changed her mind and now wanted to see her son.

'Please, Nurse Zelda.' Night-nurse Viv came into the room. 'Don't excite our patient. I'm trying to keep her calm.'

But then came the newsflash.

63

VIV

Ignore. Ignore. Viv was plugging in her mobile to charge, before getting into bed. There were always newsflashes. Always a disaster somewhere in the world. But what was this? Earthquake. New Zealand. Christchurch. Rigid, she read on. Force 6.3 on the Richter scale. Damage worse than last September's. Christchurch hit particularly hard. Injuries. Fatalities.

Grant! Where is Grant? It was midnight here. Midday there. This was happening *now* in New Zealand, at lunchtime, the busiest time of the day when all the workers were out and about. As the implications hit her Viv's phone went dead.

Downstairs, hunched in front of the TV, glad Janet was asleep, Viv heard a reporter say that a state of emergency had been declared. All phone and power lines were down, and airports were closed. The *main airport hadn't been struck* – oh good! – but *roads leading to it had been devastated.* Oh no! *Was Grant at the airport or on his way to it?* As pictures of collapsing buildings flashed onto the screen she fought despair. Was he maybe already on a plane flying towards them? Could he still be at home?

His mobile number was on the kitchen noticeboard top of the

list, beneath the Alan-smear. But all phone lines down, she remembered the reporter's words as she started to dial on the kitchen phone. Idiot. But she carried on dialling. The line was dead. As soon as she hung up though a call came in. Hope surged. But it was Alan. He'd just heard the news and had been checking. Grant's plane hadn't taken off, so Alan wasn't going to meet it of course. There was no point. They agreed to try and get some sleep. Viv checked on Janet before she put her head down. Still asleep. Good. Sleep on, Janet, for as long as you can.

* * *

'Tell me he's here' were Zelda's first words when she arrived next morning. She'd only just heard the news on her car radio. 'Tell me that Alan met him. Tell me he'd left before...' But the words died on her lips as she saw Viv's face.

They went into the sitting-room to watch TV with the sound turned down, mesmerised by the images of destruction in Christchurch, which had taken the main hit, office blocks reduced to rubble, roads split into chasms and craters. Grant worked in Christchurch. They did frenzied calculations about time zones trying to convince themselves that he could be safe, conferring in low voices. What would they tell Janet when she woke up? They couldn't keep her in her bedroom away from the TV, not for ever. And Janet was media savvy, never far from her iPhone. Could they creep into her room and hide it? Too late. They heard movement above in Janet's bedroom.

Then a short sharp cry.

Later that morning, the community nurse arrived saying she brought good news, the results of the biopsy. The tumour had proved to be benign, the prognosis was excellent. Ms Wilkins had removed all of the tumour without harming Janet's brain, but Janet wasn't interested. She was curled in a ball under the covers, her face, what you could see of it, was grey. Waking up excited, thinking she was going to see Grant that day, she'd picked up her phone in the hope of seeing a text from him, but got the first of repeated newsflashes about casualties in their thousands and fatalities mounting. Now, eyes closed, convinced that Grant was dead, she was silent as Nurse Cummings told her she would make a full recovery.

* * *

'Grant and the family are most likely safe.' Viv repeated what she'd said many times during the week.

'So why haven't we heard from them, Pollyanna?' Janet's untouched supper was on a plate beside the armchair. 'Why haven't we had replies to all our texts, phone calls and emails?' Good question. Power had been restored in places and phone-lines re-established, but the bad news kept coming in. The death toll now stood at a hundred and eighty-five. One hundred and sixty-four people were seriously injured.

'He isn't on any fatality lists.' Viv tried to put out of her mind a recent bulletin saying some bodies were so badly mutilated they couldn't be identified. 'And Banks Peninsula was only shaken by light tremors, so if he was at home at the time, as he most likely was —' she stretched the truth a little '—he'd be safe and so would the rest of the family.'

They'd learned quite a lot from the Internet. There had been some injuries in the area where Grant lived but no fatalities. 'And, as I've said before, Alan has ascertained that Grant checked in online for the evening flight, which didn't take off, so he was alive four hours before the quake.'

Janet's face showed no reaction, to the mention of Alan or

anything else. Viv didn't say that Alan had also ascertained that the office building where Grant worked had been reduced to rubble. Or that Alan hadn't managed to ascertain if Grant was in it at the time. Or that Alan had flown to New Zealand to find out what he could on the ground. He'd gone two days previously, as soon as he was allowed, armed with as much information as she and Zelda could find in the house, including photographs of Grant, his wife and children and their home address. He'd booked a flight as soon as they'd heard that Christchurch airport was up and running. Should she tell Janet Alan was there looking? He'd left it up to Viv and Zelda to decide whether to tell her or not. Was raising her hopes wise?

'Alan...' Viv was tentative.

But Janet held up a hand.

The ten o'clock news didn't help. Why did Janet insist on watching? To punish herself by confirming her worst fears? The earthquake was still the lead story. Footage showed soldiers sifting through rubble, but only for bodies, an on-the-spot reporter said, as finding anyone alive after a week was unlikely. 'Nevertheless,' he added, 'a cheerful never-say-die spirit prevails.'

'Please turn it off before he references the Blitz.' Janet sank back in the chair then asked Viv to help her get ready for bed.

Before Viv got herself to bed she checked her texts. Nothing new from Alan, nothing new from anyone, just a short one from Zelda.

Hope you're keeping our patient's spirits up.

She replied.

Sorry, no.

64

JANET

Still awake.

How could she sleep in her crisp clean bed picturing Grant, crushed under one of those heaps of rubble?

I wish I'd never met your father!

So you wish I'd never been born, do you?

Yes! I wish I'd had a life. It had burst from her after he'd been singing Malcolm's praises yet again, at supper that night. Ever since she'd arrived the my-dad-this and my-dad-that had been irritating but she'd bitten her tongue as he'd regaled Rocky and Woody with anecdotes about this warm and loving and generous father, who'd taught him chess and attended every rugby match and paid for any school trip he'd wanted to go on. She'd let it go in the interest of family harmony. But when that night he said that this wonderful grandad would have been to-ing and fro-ing to New Zealand to see his grandchildren as often as he could, she couldn't help herself.

Then why didn't he come even once?

Silence.

Because he couldn't prise open his wallet?

Point made, she hoped, she changed the subject and told the

children about the dolphins she'd seen on the coast, showing them the photographs on her mobile. It was Belynda who returned to the fray when the children were in bed.

'Janet, you shouldn't have put Grant down in front of the kids. He's very hurt.'

Hurt? He looked smirky and shifty, like at the funeral. Yes, it was the same shifty self-satisfied look.

'Belynda, did he tell you what he did at Malcolm's funeral?'

A look passed between them. He hadn't. So she did. She told Belynda how her loving, liberal, model-modern husband had gone behind his mother's back and overridden her wishes. She told Belynda what she'd found in Grant's adored father's back pocket, and a few more things besides.

She left that night. Belynda told her to. Grant was in a state of shock. His father wasn't an adulterer. He didn't have an affair with Barbara or anyone. He wouldn't. He *wouldn't*! But if he did, it was all her fault. If his dad had *strayed* it was because she was cold. And if *he* was underhand about the funeral, well, that was the way they were in their house. They didn't do open and they didn't do warm. He'd needed a lot of help to get over that. He'd put his arm round his Lyndy-Lou.

Never let the sun go down on your anger.

How many suns had gone down on hers?

She should have been bigger. She should have been forgiving. She should have said sorry and told the truth. They *did* want him. They had loved each other or thought they did when they got married. Well, she'd loved Malcolm, she couldn't speak for him of course, and he'd never said. *We started off with high hopes but it all went wrong. And we were both to blame. But I did my best.*

That was what she'd wanted to say to him. Not *I wish you'd never been born.*

But she'd left it too late.

* * *

Viv

Viv in the room next door, sleeping lightly, woke up when her phone pinged. Ignore. Ignore. She must get some sleep. It could wait till morning. But ping again. Ping ping ping. It might be Alan with news. She reached under the bed where it was plugged in, charging. It *was* Alan with news.

Landed. Mission accomplished. Grant with me. See you in two hours. A

Two hours. When did he send it? What time was it now? Half past three. It was still dark outside. He'd sent it just now. With trembling fingers she replied.

Great news. Will have coffee ready. Well done! V

Joy flooded through her. How wonderful! Should she wake Janet now and tell her? Perhaps better to let her sleep and wake up to a wonderful surprise. Could she get a couple of hours herself before they got here? It seemed unlikely, but just in case she dropped off, she set her alarm for five.

* * *

Janet

Janet woke around five too, roused by noises downstairs. What was it? She lay rigid for minutes. Burglars? Then her brain, her lovely, mended brain, engaged and she put on the light. Viv, it must be, going to the loo. She remembered she was staying and her hand reached for her head where her stubble hair was still a novelty. But why was Viv downstairs? And who was she talking to? 'Shush,' someone was saying, 'Don't disturb her' and 'Wait till she wakes up.' She heard that very clearly. Her hearing must have improved!

Then she heard Viv say, 'I'll go and see,' and footsteps were coming upstairs. The landing light went on and there was Viv silhouetted in the doorway. 'Janet?'

'I'm awake.'

'I can see that.' Viv came to the side of the bed and took hold of her hand. Were those tears in her eyes? 'Th-there's someone downstairs, someone you're longing to see. Oh, here he is. He's come up.'

She turned to look at the doorway where a man stood. A man she'd thought she'd never see again. Grant. Was it really him? Was this her son coming into the room now, sinking to his knees and *taking hold of her hand*? It must be a dream.

'Mum, how are you?'

How am I? How could she describe this feeling?

'I'm sorry you've been worried, Mum.'

Worried! As if he were twelve years old and late home from school.

'Why? What...?' But she couldn't form a sentence.

'Explanations later, Mum. It's a bit er... convoluted.' He looked like a boy caught with his hand in the cake tin. 'I've been a bit unfair perhaps, sorry, but I just want to say that I'm really happy you're feeling a bit better.'

Words still wouldn't come out, which was perhaps just as well. He pecked her cheek. Crikey. He was trying hard. 'Go back to sleep, Mum. We'll sort it out later. We'll sort everything out. Don't you worry.'

'No, Grant. Wait. I'm sorry too.' She hung on to his hand. 'I shouldn't have said those things about your dad. And our marriage, it wasn't all your dad's fault, it was mine too. I've had a lot of time to think. We were young and ignorant. But, *but*—' she must get this out '—you *were* wanted, *are* wanted and *loved*, so much we competed for you perhaps, and I'm so glad you're alive.' Glad was nowhere near it. She was *flooded* with joy, tears dripping down her face.

Grant didn't reply but she felt better for saying it. And maybe he felt better for hearing it? At least he was still there. Finally he spoke. 'Thanks, Mum. I'm glad I came. Alan was right.'

Janet's newly mended brain whirred slowly. She thought he'd said Alan.

'Great bloke. Talked to me like a Dutch uncle.'

'Who did?'

'Alan. Alan Loveday. I just said.' He looked worried now as if he suspected brain damage. 'Your *friend*, Mum.'

Her newly mended brain still couldn't make sense of what he was saying.

'Must have cost him a fortune to come and get me.'

'Who came to get you?'

'Alan. Alan Loveday.'

'He went to New Zealand?'

'Yes, Mum, that's what I said.' He patted her hand. 'You didn't know?'

'No, no, I didn't.' Because certain people had been withholding things from her. 'So where is he now?'

'Downstairs, if he hasn't gone home.'

She heard the front door opening. Was that Viv saying, 'Goodbye, Alan.'?

'Grant.' She pulled her hand free. 'Stop him. Get him upstairs. Now. Quickly. Hurry.'

65

VIV

Viv, released from duties, was on her way to The Poplars to meet the purchasers. The Arrowsmiths, Alan said, were keen to meet her, with a view to keeping her on as gardener. The cash would be useful, though not enough to buy her a new roof, still covered by a tarpaulin. What a contrast with The Poplars!

Walking up the drive, after parking in the road, Viv awarded herself more accolades to boost morale. She should be feeling demob happy. Janet was on the mend, reconciled with prodigal son and lover. She could give herself a pat on the back for a job well done, but she was still having a downer. The raised border by the drive, aglow with daffodils, didn't lift her spirits. Nor did the blue pots by the front door, looking as stylish as she'd hoped they would, green shoots already thrusting through the variegated ivy. They would look even better when the green-streaked white tulips came out.

Spring was nearly here. Just. It was the first week of March, and cold, too bloody cold to hang around, so she removed the local freesheet from the letter box and went back to the car with it. Last week's, she noted, so lover boy hadn't been home for some time.

There was not a lot of local news so in minutes she'd reached the horoscopes on the back page. Viv knew they were daft but there was nothing else to do.

This is a powerful time of change and transformation. The old is melting away and with it the tears, the pain and stagnation. Gather yourself and move forward. Root yourself in something new, a dream, a goal, a change, an idea.

'I am trying my best, Aurora.' Someone was tapping on the window. The Arrowsmiths? No, George Beaumont. She stuffed the paper under the seat before winding down the window.

'Does Aurora say a tall, balding stranger is going to walk into your life and sweep you off your feet?'

'No, it says I need a lot more work if I'm going to break even this financial year.' She caught sight of his truck further up the road.

George laughed. 'No worries, there's always someone looking for a young and up-and-coming designer with a flair for an eye-catching display.'

'Flattery will get you everywhere, Mr Beaumont.'

'Will it now?' He raised an eyebrow.

Whoops.

He laughed again and handed her a sheet of A4. 'Texted this to you a couple of weeks back and you didn't answer, but hope springs eternal.'

She scanned the paper, realising he must have sent it before Janet's operation. She vaguely remembered. It was about a three-day trip to the Hortus Botanicus in Leiden and the famous Keukenhof Gardens, which she had always wanted to see. Might that boost her spirits? It was soon though, only two weeks away, and how much would it cost?

'It's not a coach trip,' he said, as if that might account for her hesitation.

She scanned again. 'What's Airbnb?'

'B&B booked on the Internet along with air tickets, a newish thing. People rent out their spare rooms, which keeps costs down. And it's a private do, not a package, just six of us all in the trade. We've hired a university lecturer to give us a guided tour round the Hortus Botanicus. I'll leave it with you, Viv. Looks as if someone wants to speak to you.' A car had turned into The Poplars and a bearded man, who looked familiar, was coming towards them. 'Just one more thing. I've been meaning to ask. How's the Malmaison?'

'S-sorry?' It took a moment to gather her thoughts, most of them unwelcome. What made him ask about that? 'Dark, but the food's okay, in the Newcastle branch anyway.'

Now he scratched his head, then laughed. 'No, sorry, not the hotel, the rose.'

'The rose? The Souvenir de Malmaison?'

'I stand corrected, madam.' He gave a mock bow. 'Of course. How's she doing?'

'B-budding up nicely.' She'd looked at it only that morning. 'But...'

'Thought it would be okay coming from Austin's. Let me know when it's in flower, will you? I'd like to rate it for fragrance.'

You sent it? *You?* But he'd gone before she could get the words out.

* * *

'I can't remember telling George Beaumont about the Souvenir de Malmaison,' she said to Zelda later that afternoon.

'So?' Zelda handed her a cup of tea. 'I can't remember what I went upstairs for.'

'I may have mentioned it, of course, and I suppose he could have sent it as a perk. I am a very good customer.'

'On Valentine's Day?' Zelda raised an eyebrow.

'He probably had no idea what day it was. Jack needed reminding.'

'Oh.' Zelda was sarky. 'A commercial rose-grower who didn't know it was Valentine's Day?'

'But if I did mention it, it would have been months back and he must have made a note and...'

'And?' Zelda wanted her to follow that train of thought.

'It was just after I'd met Patrick when I was first, erm... infatuated and might have burbled a bit, about the rose, I mean.'

'Was that the day you came into The Red Lion and got the wrong end of the stick about me and Mr Mucky House?' Zelda smiled.

How things had changed, for *all* of them!

They were quiet for a bit then, sipping their tea, Zelda perusing the letter about the trip, which Viv had given her earlier, Viv trying not to remember that night at the Malmaison. She broke the silence herself. 'Well, what do you think? Should I go?'

'Bulb fields. Botanical gardens. Mud.' Zelda handed the letter back. 'Sounds like a dirty weekend to me. I think you should at least consider the possibility that George Beaumont has more than horticulture in mind.'

'Zelda Fielding, one minute you're saying older men are all past it, next you're saying they're all after one thing.'

Zelda had the grace to smile. 'Let's say I've adjusted my view in the light of recent experience. Check the sleeping arrangements.'

'FYI, George is happily married to Annie and has been for years, and they're business partners. They're rock solid. He's a bit of a flirt but would run a mile if I took him seriously. Actually—' it came to her '—Annie probably sent the bloody rose!'

'Well, check that she's going.' Fortunately, the Westies came in with their leads, pre-empting a longer lecture.

* * *

When she got home Viv looked at her diary. The trip was from Friday the eighteenth of March to Sunday the twentieth, which was the first day of spring, as good a time as any to try something new. *Gather yourself and move forward.* Aurora was still in her head when she went into her study and googled Keukenhof Gardens. Wow! As her screen filled with psychedelic displays of colour it occurred to her that the trip would be tax deductible. She would get some great ideas for her own designs if this year's displays were half as good as last's. And yes, she could be free that weekend, though it was pencilled in for a family reunion. But that wasn't going to happen as she'd hadn't heard from Patrick for weeks. Now she knew he hadn't sent the rose, it explained his reply to the note she'd sent thanking him for it. She reddened at the memory. At first she'd thought that he'd sent it to remind her of the candlelit supper at the Malmaison, which it had. But later she'd reasoned that a properly pruned rose-bush in a two-litre pot was just the sort of present a thoughtful stepson might send his stepmother to thank her for having him to stay for the weekend, and replied as a step-mother might with details of where she'd plant it. He'd texted back.

Sorry, you've got the wrong chap. P

She'd thought he meant 'I'm sorry you've got the wrong chap' and was acknowledging they couldn't continue as they were. But he obviously meant something different.
He thinks you've got another admirer, tart.
But I haven't and I don't want one.

66

ZELDA

Zelda wanted to get on. She'd just found something online about her maternal grandmother, the seamstress with her own business, but Brian was on her front step, the last person she wanted to see. He'd ruined her dinner party and Viv's life.

'Won't stop long, Zeld, I'm on the way back from a delivery.' His white van was in the drive. 'But I've got some info about the Costellos and a website that might help with your dad.'

So she let him in and gave him a sandwich as it was lunchtime.

Now they were in her little office under the stairs, with Mack and Morag watching from the stairwell. First he introduced her to the Genuki site, which threw up a whole bunch of Costellos who'd come from Ireland to Liverpool, including Declan James Costello from County Cork.

'Your great-great-grandad, Zeld.'

He seemed to be right, so Irish was part of her DNA too. 'Must be where you get the gift of the gab from.'

'That's racial stereotyping, Brian. Now, what have you got to help me with my dad search?'

But he stalled, didn't seem in a hurry to go, though he'd said he wanted to be home by dark. Had she got a stepladder? He'd noticed a flickering fluorescent light in the kitchen ceiling. That was another thing he did, odd jobs as well as deliveries. He had a toolbox in his van. Was he advertising his credentials? She wasn't interested, but the flicker had been annoying her for weeks so she let him go and get a stepladder. Being useful might have helped Alan Loveday win Janet over, but it wouldn't work for her. Which reminded her, she must ring Janet to talk about Viv and arrange the next lunch. Viv needed her spirits lifting, badly. Zelda had an idea she'd like to talk over with Janet. She glanced at the calendar. Today was 18 March. Wasn't that when Viv was going on that gardeners' outing to Holland or Belgium?

'Coming down!' Brian was pleased with himself when they ascertained that the flickering had stopped. 'Shall we have another cup of tea?'

'I'll make it while you find that website you mentioned. It's not www.GItrace is it? So far that's been useless.'

It wasn't. This one was going in the other direction. It was set up by World War II American veterans looking for children they might have fathered when they were overseas. Well, that was interesting and worth an extra hour of his company. Might her dad be looking for her? That would be wonderful.

Unfortunately, Brian couldn't remember the exact name of the site – or was he spinning things out? – and it was another half an hour before they found it. As the screen filled with the faces of young GIs, young in World War II that was, looking for their abandoned offspring, her hopes rose then fell. Most were white, with only a few black faces. Could one of these men be her father? She scanned their faces for family resemblances, though none of these seemed to have been stationed in Bedfordshire or neighbouring counties. They were in Staffordshire or Dorset.

Was her dad even alive? The young men were now old men,

very old, in their eighties and nineties. Some of them had died before finding what they were looking for, but their details were still up and their children were carrying on their search. There was another site created by the daughter of one of them looking for her half-siblings. Could a sister or brother be looking for her? She made a note. So much to do, so little time. If only she could afford to retire completely. She'd love to do research full time, and not just family history. History had been her favourite subject at school, dropped when she left, except for historical novels and visiting historical places. Could she find time to do a History degree?

'That's a good one, Zeld.' Brian's voice made her jump. He was looking at the quotation she'd pinned to the noticeboard above her desk. *'It was only when a lady became a widow that a glorious opportunity for authority and freedom suddenly flooded in upon her.'*

'Yes, and that was about women in the seventeenth century!' Authority and freedom, she loved that. It wasn't all doom and gloom for widows even then. Some prospered by inheriting their husbands' businesses. Some had created their own, like her grandmother in World War II. Widowed in the early years of the war, she'd supported her family of three daughters by working as a seamstress and she'd had some famous clients. She did a lot of work for the American Red Cross Officers' Club, based in Bedford. Seemed the officers didn't like flying in their heavy dark green uniform jackets, and they brought them into the sewing room to get them made into lighter 'battle blouses', paying one pound and ten shillings for the alterations, which was quite a lot of money at the time. Auntie Doreen said Emily had made the one that Glenn Miller wore on his last fateful flight from Twinwood airfield, but she hadn't found confirmation of that yet.

'But, Brian—' she got up '—I really mustn't keep you. It's getting on.' She fetched his toolbox from the kitchen and put it by the front door.

'Okay, Zeld, if you're sure there's nothing else I can do for you?' He glanced upstairs, or did she imagine that? No worries, there were two trusty sentinels at the top.

'Certain, but thanks for all your help this afternoon, Brian.'

He got his coat from the newel post but then put it back there. 'Hug before I go?' He opened his arms. With arms stretched out in front of her, she stepped forward, grasped his shoulders and cheek-kissed him twice. It was hardly a hug at all, and he didn't come in closer. Well, he couldn't, with her hands on his shoulders, that was the point, a technique she'd perfected, but credit where it was due, he didn't try. He still stood there though and suddenly Mack and Morag were hurtling down the stairs, a foam of snarling white fur.

'No, darlings, I'm okay.' She stepped back out of Brian's reach to show them.

But Morag wasn't convinced. Now the little dog was in front of Brian snarling. 'Stand still, Brian. Just stand still. It's best to stay calm.'

But Brian didn't stay calm. 'Bloody hell!' He kicked out at Morag, who howled, so Mack joined the fray.

'No, Mack. Drop!' She saw he had Brian's leg between his jaws as she scooped Morag up and carried her to the kitchen. Closing the door, she returned to the hall, to get hold of Mack, but Brian was still kicking out. 'Stop kicking, Brian. Stand still. Let go, Mack!' Neither obeyed, but she managed to get hold of Mack, prise open his jaws and carry him into the sitting room. When she came out Brian was escaping through the front door, limping. Oh dear.

After checking that the dogs were okay with no injuries she could see, she went outside to look at Brian's leg and tell him that he needn't worry about them. But Brian wasn't worried about the dogs. Brian was worried about Brian. She asked him to come back inside, but he wouldn't get out of his van, so she had to check him over while he was still sitting on the driving seat, turned sideways with his legs sticking out into the drive. There was no sign of blood, thank goodness. She checked very thoroughly. She rolled up the legs of his jeans and rolled down his tartan socks, so that she could examine his ankles and paper-white shins. But there were no marks at all, no broken skin, not so much as a scratch, just a bit of redness, which he allowed her to treat with witch hazel. Mack had tugged at his denims, which were slightly torn, that was all. She could mend them with iron-on tape, or someone could. Mack's bark had been worse than his bite, and the darling had been provoked. Seeing his sister brutally kicked when she was defending her beloved mistress had aroused his protective instincts. When she pointed this out Brian pulled his leg back into the van.

'It's a shame, Zeld, because you're going to have to choose.'

'What do you mean, Brian?'

'It's them or me, love.' He turned a sad face towards her. 'I know it'll be hard, like, but if we're going to go on seeing each other them little brutes will have to go.'

She closed the door for him and wished him a safe journey. 'Goodbye, Brian.' What time was it? Had she got time to look at www.siblingsearch before she took her darlings for their walk?

67

VIV

Why hadn't she taken Zelda's advice? Or turned back at the airport when it had become clear that Zelda was right to be suspicious of George's intentions? She'd noticed Annie wasn't in the check-in queue with the others as soon as she'd arrived five minutes earlier, cutting it fine.

'Did Annie go to the shop?' she said when George disappeared as the desk opened. 'Or the loo?' Maybe he'd gone to find her.

Silence. The other four shuffled and looked at their feet. Then the woman she thought was Liz asked warily, 'Don't you know, Viv? Hasn't George told you? I thought everyone knew.'

'What?'

That Annie hadn't been around for some time, six months at least, yes, it was back in September. She'd left George for their accountant. They thought *she* was George's new... But then George was back from wherever he'd been and they were moving forward in the queue, and Liz didn't finish her sentence. It wasn't hard to guess what she'd meant though. So Viv had spent the rest of the journey making it clear that she and George were not an item. But had the message got through?

* * *

Now she and George were the only two customers left in the Café Ruigenhoek, which marked the halfway point on Route Two, a fifteen-kilometre cycle tour of the bulb fields. Gerry and Myrtle, and Liz and Barry – she'd just about got their names by now – had left a few minutes ago, after downing beers, saying they were switching to Route Three, which added ten kilometres to their ride.

'Do go on with the others, George. I can find my own way back.' She was nursing a mug of hot chocolate, he was making a beer last. Her legs were aching and her bum was still sore even though she was now settled in a comfortable chair by an open fire. In different circumstances she might have enjoyed the experience, but the presence of George and the thought of getting back on the hard seat of the orange hire-bike made that difficult. To her dismay, when they'd got off the train at Leiden, they'd picked up the previously booked bikes. Ready to drop after the early flight to Amsterdam, she'd just wanted to get to the Airbnb, sort out a single room for herself and have a kip. But George had pointed out that they couldn't get into their digs till four o'clock.

She said again that she could make her own way back as the route was well signed, but George showed no inclination to follow the others. 'No worries, Viv, I was finding it hard to keep up with the youngsters.'

The other couples were not youngsters, but they were maybe ten or fifteen years younger than them. George nodded towards the window at the far end of the room. 'Sorry, not exactly the kaleidoscope of colour we were promised. Drawback to coming this early in a year when spring is a long time coming.' The window-framed acres of bulbs were not yet in flower, a sea of grey-green. 'Those godawful Rip van Winkles, like bloody dandelions, were the only things out.' He grimaced.

She'd thought the little daffs a welcome splash of yellow but didn't say. 'George.' She finished her chocolate and put down her cup. 'About the accommodation...'

'Should be ready by the time we get back.' He was still looking out of the window. 'The house is in the modern part of the town, by the way, so don't expect anything picturesque and olde worlde.' He'd picked up that she hadn't read the literature as carefully as she should have. 'It's a three-bedroom semi on a nineteen seventies housing estate.'

'Three bedrooms, so there might be another spare room?' She'd already learned that the other couples were in different houses in the same part of town. And she'd told him she wanted her own room.

'Possibly, but, Viv, as I've said, the room I've booked is a twin.' He wiped beer froth from his mouth. 'I booked, rebooked actually... last year... Annie and me... before... I hadn't realised, by the way, that you didn't know. Not till Liz told me. Sorry.' He was struggling. 'Anyway, that's the past.'

He emptied his glass and put it down on the table. Oh fuck, was he brushing a tear from his eye? George was still hurting. It *was* a bereavement, being left, maybe worse than hers. Annie had *chosen* to leave him, had stopped loving him and started loving someone else. But Viv knew she had to be careful she didn't let feeling sorry for him make her say or do things she didn't mean. Had she given him the wrong impression in the past? She had flirted a bit, when they were both, as she'd thought, happily married, when it was safe. But now here he was, a man who desperately needed his morale boosting, which she was all too inclined to do. She was one of life's builder-uppers, not a putter-downer. She didn't want to hurt his feelings but...

Soddit, why had she got into this? *George*, she was about to say, *we're friends, colleagues, but I'm not going to share a room with you.* But the waiter chose that moment to bring the bill, which George insisted on settling, though she offered her share. 'We'll sort it out later.' He stood up and rolled his shoulders. 'We'll sort everything out later, Viv. We're old friends, for heaven's sake, *old* friends, not sixteen-year-olds. There won't be a problem. Come on, let's get back on those bloody bone-shakers.' He put out a hand to help hoik her out of the armchair. It was a friendly gesture. Had she got this out of proportion? Was she getting her knickers in a needless twist?

68

VIV

The Airbnb looked like a lot of three-bedroomed semis in the UK, but also looked Dutch in a way Viv couldn't quite pinpoint. The lack of boundaries between the front gardens, all of them neat? Maybe. When George rang the bell a slim woman with short fair hair opened the pale blue front door.

'Hello, George. I am pleased to meet your new friend.' She greeted them both with cheery handshakes. Their host was in her forties at a guess, and she was as friendly and straightforward as Viv expected the Dutch to be. 'Welcome, Viv. My name is Marjolein.' It sounded like Mar-o-line. 'Now,' she said briskly, 'I expect you would like to see your room.' And before Viv could say anything she was leading the way up an open wooden staircase.

'Here we are.' Marjolein opened a door and stood back to let them see a bedroom with two single beds, separated by a small table with tea-making facilities. A set of botanical drawings, cross-sections of bulbs, hung on the wall behind the beds, which had matching duvet covers in brown and white stripes. A built-in wardrobe with white melamine doors filled another wall. 'The en suite is – but what am I saying? George knows all this, so I will leave him to show you. Unless you have more questions?'

She looked at Viv, who'd been doing rapid calculations. How much was this room costing? How much would a room to herself cost, if Marjolein had one to spare? Her leaky roof hove into view. Things were expensive here. The price of that hot chocolate had been eye-watering. She scanned the room again, a love nest, this was not. It was functional and she was ready to drop. 'No, thank you,' came out of her mouth. 'This is fine.'

And it was. She'd been worrying about nothing.

They quickly sorted who was sleeping where and which end of the wardrobe each of them would have. Then they both had a nap, laughing about their need for one. George fell asleep before she did and was still asleep when she woke up. He didn't wake till a call came in from Barry Sullivan, saying the others were meeting for supper at an Indonesian restaurant in the old part of town at seven o'clock. George relayed the message to her and asked if that was okay with her. She said yes and they took it in turns to shower and change. It was all managed with discretion and bonhomie.

It was fine, perfectly fine.

As they walked to the restaurant in the old town it was beginning to get dark, but the modern streets were well lit and George fortunately knew the way. He told her he was glad the others had chosen the Surakarta, because he'd been there before and the staff hadn't made a fuss about his nut allergy. They'd simply made clear which dishes he should avoid. She sympathised – what a pain! – and warned him to keep away from her as she loved satay and tended to splash. Her point had been made, she hoped, if it needed to be made, though she felt more relaxed now. He laughed and said the first anaphylactic shock five years ago had been a near thing, but there hadn't been a recurrence.

Walking briskly, side by side, swinging their arms, they moved on to things horticultural. He was hoping to fit in a visit to a rose-grower while he was here, she a trip to the Rijksmuseum to find more pics of fruit and veg for her course. Once they reached the old part of town, there was stunning architecture to admire. Who couldn't love the curlicued gable ends of the old buildings, the pretty church towers, the picturesque bridges, their reflections shimmering in the canals, beneath a navy-blue sky studded with stars like a Van Gogh painting? Leiden was a beautiful city.

'All shall be well, all manner of thing shall be well?' said George surprisingly as they approached the Surakarta, its long narrow windows glowing pinkly. The others were at a table near the window, the number of bottles suggesting they'd been there for some time. Barry saw them peering in and hurried to open the door and show them to their seats, one at either end of the red-topped table.

Perfect.

It was a lovely evening. By the end of the meal she'd got to know the others better. The table was small enough for them all to hear each other speak and share an array of dishes of the delicious spicy food. Brass lamps engraved with Asian gods and goddesses cast a warm glow and a lot of Belgian beer contributed to the warm and friendly atmosphere. Myrtle and Gerry, a gay couple who ran a nursery together, were very witty – they sat either side of Viv – and Liz and Barry, escapees from teaching who ran an online bookshop specialising in horticulture, were a mine of information. Soon they were all exchanging contact details for future reference, and in case of hitches the next day. They planned to meet by the gates of the Hortus Botanicus at ten in the morning.

On the way back to their Airbnbs they linked arms in various formations to negotiate the different widths of canal paths and bridges, past groups on the pavement overflowing from bars and cafes. It was all very comradely. And when George took Viv's arm after they'd said goodbye to the others on the corner of Groenesteeg and Vestestraat it felt okay. They were friends and colleagues. George was a decent man. Jack said so. Everything was fine.

They unlinked at the front door when George got the keys from his pocket – Marjolein had given them only one set – and back in their room, they again negotiated bathroom use with finesse. She let him go first and when he came out wearing his pyjamas, she went in. When she came out he was asleep in his bed by the window, his clothes in a neat pile on the chair in the corner of the room.

She was glad she'd come, it was a welcome break, and she looked forward to tomorrow.

69

VIV

When the six of them met at the gates of the Hortus Botanicus a few minutes before their guide was due to arrive, the arch of blue sky was cloudless. Other visitors were already streaming through the stone gateway into what looked like an Elizabethan knot garden. Sixty rectangular beds, according to George, laid out symmetrically in four blocks, each with its own speciality. George, stripy scarf looped round his neck student-style, had assumed the role of guide in the absence of their official guide who hadn't yet arrived. He held up a book to show them a portrait of the garden's founder, Charles d'Ecluse, aka Clusius, who looked every inch the Elizabethan gentleman, but wasn't of course, being Dutch, or Flemish or French. In a tight-fitting doublet with a white ruff, he looked a lot like Sir Francis Drake.

"'Sixty-seven when he created the garden in 1593,'" George read aloud from the book in his hand, "'but still vigorous", eh, Barry? Still vigorous.' Barry had joshed a bit last night about George's age, asking him what plans he had for retirement. There was a bit of needle between these two, she'd noticed, perhaps vying to be leader of the pack.

Liz obviously thought so. 'Now, boys.' She put a restraining hand on Barry's arm, but he went in for another dig.

'I bet Clusius was up and about planting tulips by nine o'clock in the morning, George, not driving the cows home.' Barry, Viv had picked up earlier, had rung George at about eight to verify arrangements and got no reply. It must have been while she was downstairs talking to Marjolein.

'What makes you think I was sleeping, Barry boy?' George replied, and Barry's mouth opened and closed, but she wouldn't have thought anything of it if she hadn't seen the pained expression on Gerry's face. Not only Gerry's, Liz and Myrtle were wincing, clearly uncomfortable with what George had said. Why?

She turned to look at him and caught on when she saw George lick his finger and make a mark in the air, smirking at Barry. One up to me, he was saying, implying he was, *they* were... What an arsehole! She must put that right. 'George was on the lav,' she said. She didn't say 'having a shit and being one' but thought it. Liz took her arm and walked her away.

She reached for the phone in her pocket. Thank God she'd asked Marjolein for her number at breakfast this morning, when George was still upstairs. She'd asked for her own set of keys too. She must have her own room tonight, to hell with the expense. She texted straight away, asking Marjolein if she could move into her daughter's room, which she'd noticed was unoccupied. She used George's snoring as an excuse, said she hadn't slept.

Daan Janssen, their guide, didn't turn up. George got a text a few minutes later to say Daan was sorry but his father-in-law was very ill. George passed on the news and offered to lead them round the gardens himself, saying he'd been several times before, but they all declined his offer. Barry said he'd heard there was an excellent labelling system.

Was George aware he'd given offence, that the others were

giving him the cold shoulder? If he was he showed no sign of it. When the others went off, after Viv had assured Liz she'd be fine on her own, he moved to her side. 'Come on,' he said cheerily, offering his arm, 'let's get moving.'

'No, George.' She stepped away sharply. 'I said I'm fine on my own and I meant it.'

After a moment's hesitation, he shrugged and said he'd go and see the rose-grower he was keen to meet. Had she made her point? Had she pierced that thick hide? Afterwards she wondered why she hadn't just said fuck off. It might have prevented a lot of trouble.

* * *

The day improved when he'd gone but Viv wouldn't relax completely till she'd got herself a separate room for the night. She checked her phone. Still no reply from Marjolein. She rang but got voicemail, so contacted the tourist office to ask what B & B rooms were available. None. Leiden was chock-a-block, always was at this time of year. She was offered only top-end hotels way out of her price bracket. There was no need to panic. Give Marjolein time. At worst she could go back to the house early and sort it out woman to woman. Meanwhile, she determined to enjoy the rest of the day.

The Hortus Botanicus was brilliant, the physic garden especially fascinating, and very useful if she ever got a chance to restore a monastery garden on a Greek hillside to its former glory. Sigh. She took dozens of photographs then set off for the famous Rijksmuseum. Rembrandt was born in Leiden, she'd belatedly discovered, so there were sure to be some of his still lifes there, with lots of glowing fruit and veg in the foreground.

It was only when she was inside the building, asking for directions, that she realised she'd made yet another mistake. This wasn't *the* Rijksmuseum famous for fine art – that was in Amsterdam, an official informed her. This was an older but smaller establishment, specialising in archaeology and Greek and Roman statuary. Armless torsos and headless warriors in the entrance hall made that obvious.

Leaving, she found herself in a pretty street called Rapenburg Straat where she had a choice of pavement cafes. After ordering a coffee and sandwich she consulted an online guide, which said the street was considered to be the most beautiful in Europe by someone in the eighteenth century, but didn't say how it got its ugly name. The street was still stunningly beautiful. Lovely green and cream timbered buildings were a backdrop to brilliant displays of tulips and daffodils. Tubs and window boxes were ablaze with vibrant reds and yellows. Still no reply from Marjolein, so sadly she couldn't linger to enjoy the sights. She must get back to the Airbnb and sort things out. With luck she'd have moved into another room before George got back.

* * *

'Hello, Vivien.' Marjolein opened the front door before she had time to get her key out. 'I apologise for not replying to your text but shortly after receiving it, I dropped my mobile in an unfortunate place.' She laughed. 'I am also very sorry but I cannot offer you another room. As you can see, my daughter Elise has returned home for the weekend.' The girl, looking like a teenage version of her mother, stood behind her. 'But here, no worries, as they say, here.' Marjolein handed her a small plastic container. 'I am hoping these will do the trick.'

Earplugs.

70

JANET

Janet's day began well.

She was having a delicious lie-in, Alan beside her. What a hero he was, going all that way to find Grant and bring him here! Not that Grant had been hard to find. Alan had simply knocked on his door and there he was. He *had* been in hospital himself briefly, recovering from minor injuries sustained while driving to the airport when the road ahead had suddenly collapsed, but he had been home for some time. He and his wife had obviously *chosen* not to tell her they were all safe and well. Had chosen to ignore all the messages she'd sent, or that her friends had sent. Had chosen not to enquire about her own health. Was it a joint decision? she wondered. But best not to follow that train of thought. Why waste time worrying about one's less than perfect relationship with one's son, when one's lover was beginning to stir?

'Hello, darling.' She studied his supine form, certain regions still a novelty. 'It's a bit like a lipstick, isn't it?'

'What is? Oh. You're an unusual woman, Mrs C.'

'This is still so new to me, Mr L.'

'I thought you were once a nurse.'

'But I looked as little as possible. The other nurses called me Prudence behind my back.'

'What would they say if they could see you now?'

'Jezebel?' She laughed, pulling herself up to look at her lopsided reflection in the mirror on the wall at the end of the bed. Not bad at all, considering. Her op-side hair had almost caught up with her non-op side and she was getting more colour in her cheeks. How lucky she was to be alive! And in love, head over heels, and sometimes heels over head – tai chi helped! Her hand reached for his. 'I like you, Mr L.'

'I like you, Mrs C.' He sat up. 'Cup of tea? I'll get it.'

It was great having a love life, she thought as she waited for her Earl Grey. And it was great having someone to think about mundane things like locking up at night or turning off the gas fire before you left the house. Alan didn't sit around watching TV like a lot of men his age, expecting to be waited on hand and foot, he did things. A lot of things. That was his USP. He was back already with tea on a tray.

'Hold onto this while I get back in. Carefully does it.' There were biscuits too, Hobnobs, though she'd told him to cut down on them. They were both putting on weight. And then she saw it. A small square box in the corner of the tray. A small square jeweller's box. She ignored it for as long as she could, chatting as she drank her tea, but wasn't halfway down the cup before he nudged the box towards her.

'Aren't you going to look inside?'

Why did he have to spoil things?

It was a ring. A dress ring, a beautiful dress ring, one she'd seen and admired in a jeweller's window months ago. Was this an early birthday present? Good choice! She'd have bought it for herself if the shop hadn't been closed. It went with her favourite earrings, the lapiz lazuli drops with pearls. The oval stone was the same deep

Prussian blue, the setting the same coppery gold, the pearls surrounding the stone creamy and lustrous.

'Well, does it fit?'

'Perfectly!' She held out her hand to show him and noted his furrowed brow. 'What's the matter?'

'I thought it went on the other hand, that's all.' He shrugged, but not casually.

'It's a dress ring.' She'd put it on her right hand. 'That's where it goes.'

'Oh, but don't you think...?' He was struggling but she didn't want to help him out. He started again. 'I thought... I hoped...' she still didn't come to his aid '... that you might, that you would, or could see it as, well, an unusual engagement ring?'

He *was* spoiling things.

'Darling Janet, I know you despise cliché, but I don't know how else to say what I want to say.' He reached for her hand but she plunged both of them under her armpits. 'Will you, please, make me the happiest man in the world?' He was by her side of the bed now, on his knees. 'Dearest Janet, please do me the honour of becoming my wife, wifey, spouse, better half and ball and chain. Let's get hitched, spliced, or otherwise co-joined in matrimony holy or unholy. Let me make an honest woman of you.'

'Alan, get up! Get out of the way! I am an honest woman.'

'No, you're not. You frequently lie, especially to yourself.' He was still on his knees. Fortunately, the front doorbell rang and his dog started barking. He got up and looked out of the window. 'It's the police. What have you done, Janet?'

At the time it seemed like a joke.

He went downstairs in his dressing gown to see what they wanted and returned saying they wouldn't tell him, and that he'd asked them to come back later. 'They asked if I was your husband,' he said pointedly.

71

JANET

Janet still didn't know why the police were here. They were having coffee in the sitting room, Alan and herself on the sofa, the two police persons, one male, one female, in the fireside chairs. It was quite friendly, till the woman, clearly the senior, Detective Chief Inspector Markham, suddenly said they were investigating the death of Barbara Virginia Thornton. Amazingly she went straight into the 'anything you say may be used in evidence' routine.

'But didn't she die of an overdose of sleeping tablets?' Janet was sure she'd heard that from Maggie. There had been an inquest resulting in an open verdict because no suicide note had been found.

The DCI didn't reply, but held out a piece of Janet's headed notepaper. 'Did you write this?'

'Yes, of course, you can see I signed it.' It was the kind, forgiving letter she'd written after much soul-searching, when Maggie had caught Barbara delivering one of her nasty ones.

Dear Barbara,
   There is no more need for deception. I now know what

happened in the past and what you have been doing more recently – and I understand. But these letters and vindictive actions must stop as no good will come of them. You will suffer far more than me if you continue.

Kind regards

Janet Carmichael

PS Perhaps we should talk about this? If you would like to meet for coffee give me a ring.

'Did Ms Thornton come for coffee?'

'No, I mean yes, she did come, but for tea. Once.' Janet was perplexed. What had her letter got to do with anything? And what was that young constable doing, going through the books on her coffee table?

'Only once?' the policewoman persisted.

'Yes, it was the day before I left for New Zealand. I hoped she might open up a bit, and we'd talk about my late husband who had treated us both badly.'

'Did she open up?'

'No. She said hardly anything.' She'd sat on the edge of her seat tight-lipped and tense.

'You invited her for a cup of tea the day before you left the country?' The DCI made that sound suspicious.'

'Yes, she, Barbara, Ms Thornton, had ignored my letter for weeks, and then just a few days before I was due to leave she said she'd like to accept my invitation. I thought I should act on the positive gesture before I left.'

'And she came for tea?'

Janet nodded. 'Yes, I've said.'

'With cake perhaps?'

'There may have been cake, yes.'

'May? You didn't make one specially?'

'No, I was using things up, as you do before you go away. I think it was fruitcake.'

'What did you mean by, "You will suffer far more than me if you continue."' It sounded sinister coming out of the DCI's mouth.

'That Barbara was harming herself by being so bitter and vindictive. She h-had sent me several anonymous letters, well, I thought she had.' Janet started to feel uneasy. 'I had thought of going to the police myself, but I was trying to be conciliatory and forgiving.'

'Anonymous? Then how did you know…?' The chief inspector paused as the young constable put a book in front of her.

The pause lengthened.

'Ms Thornton thought you were trying to kill her, Mrs Carmichael. And this—' the chief inspector tapped the book '— along with the diary her relatives discovered while going through Ms Thornton's effects, seems to corroborate that.'

'What is that book?' Janet wanted to know.

But Alan was on his feet calling a halt to proceedings. 'Mrs Carmichael will not say another word without a solicitor by her side. What you are suggesting is preposterous.'

72

VIV

Viv was still agonising about George as she studied the earplugs in her hand. Should she stay another night in this room with him or spend money she hadn't got on a room in a five-star hotel? She wasn't in actual danger. Last night had worked out okay and nothing had really changed since then, except that she now knew he was a prat. Tonight they were all going to eat at the Surakarta again, which would be fine. Tomorrow, Sunday, there was the walking tour in the morning, then they were catching the train to the airport for an afternoon flight home. After that, she need never see him again. There were other nurseries she could deal with, Gerry and Myrtle's for a start. Surely she could manage one night more in this room? Decision made, she lay on top of the duvet and managed to nod off before she heard the key in the lock.

'I gather I snore—' he was laughing '—but I told Marjolein you do too, and she gave me these.' He held up an identical packet of earplugs. 'How was your day? Did you find what you wanted?' He launched into an account of his meeting with the rose-grower, then said he needed a kip. It didn't take him long to fall asleep and start snoring. She tried the earplugs and they worked. Should she tackle him about what he'd said to Barry? Was there any point? It was a pathetic attempt of a man humiliated by his wife leaving, to boost his image in front of another male.

They had a pleasant enough evening, and he didn't make any more offensive remarks, not that she could hear. They sat at opposite ends of the table as they had the night before. Were Myrtle and Gerry and Liz a bit protective of her? When they were discussing medicinal plants in the Hortus Botanicus, she got a sense of female solidarity, which reminded her of Janet and Zelda, whose advice she'd stupidly ignored. George, knocking back the Pils, looked even more out of it. Had he caught on that he'd gone down in the others' estimation? Well, a bit of self-awareness wouldn't go amiss.

Back in their room, Viv got the earplugs out and reminded him of his, saying they needed a good night's sleep to be fit for the ten-kilometre walk round the town next day. Then she headed for the en suite with her pyjamas over her arm. Coming out ready for bed, she was a bit taken aback to find him blocking the way. Bare-chested, clutching a towel round his waist, he was just outside the door.

'Shower.' His voice was slurred.

'Well, let me get out first, George.'

Was he even drunker than she'd thought? He tottered a bit but stepped to one side and she moved quickly to her bed. As she got in she heard the en suite door close, then the shower running. Was he safe? Might he slip? She waited till the shower stopped running before putting in the earplugs, and turning out the light on her side, hoping she'd be asleep before he came out. She wasn't but pretended she was. The earplugs didn't blot out everything. She heard him moving clumsily about the room, crashing against her bed at one point, stubbing his toe, she guessed when he cursed. But at last the light on his side went out. Silence. Now perhaps she could sleep.

But she was still awake an hour later, her mind active, her body tense. Was he asleep? She took one plug out and heard snoring. Phew. On past form he'd sleep through till breakfast time. What *was* she worrying about? She put the earplug back in. If only she could put on the light and read till she was sleepy. One o'clock. Two. Still awake, but she must have fallen into a deep sleep soon after that, because she woke up, at home in her own bed, she thought, with Claudia patting her face. 'Go away. Use your cat-flap.'

'But I love you.'

Abruptly awake, she froze, realised what was happening and pushed hard against the body beside her, pushed against a sweaty wall of hairy skin. She pushed and pushed with no effect. Try another tack. Back away. Get out the other side. But now his leg came over hers.

'I love you, Viv.'

'No. George. You. Don't.' It was a narrow bed. One strong push and he would be on the floor, but he was heavier than her, much heavier, and he was pushing her onto her back, clambering on top of her, holding her down, his face horribly close. She tried to dig her nails into his back and claw him. 'Get off, George. Get out of my bed.' But he wasn't listening and now his hands were gripping her upper arms, sure they were two lonely people meant for each other, sure she wanted him as much as he wanted her. Never had she felt so angry, so powerless, her arms pinned uselessly by her sides.

'George! You will regret this!'

Brain not brawn was going to get her out of this if anything was, but his brain wasn't engaged. Beyond reason, he was trying to pull her pyjamas down with one hand, lifting his weight slightly, releasing one of her arms, but still she couldn't move as he began to thrust, clumsily missing the target thank God, but brute strength was winning.

'Peanuts, George. I had nuts. Nuts.' She got the words out as his head came down and his tongue forced its way between her teeth.

You got yourself into this.

And I will get myself out of it, though I may kill him in the process. Maybe she had thought about this before, subconsciously, when she hadn't cleaned her teeth. Despite wanting to retch she opened her mouth wide. If George wanted tongues he could have them, and a lot more besides. She'd had the smooth satay, but with luck not so smooth that there weren't a few bits of chopped peanut still stuck between her molars. One little bit could cause an anaphylactic shock she'd heard, but how long would it take? As his eel-tongue floundered around her mouth it seemed an age before he started to gasp, more than when he was trying to screw her, and it was even longer before she sensed his focus shift as he lifted his head, whooping now. Then the whoops weakened to a rattling rasp then a whistle as his airways narrowed and struggling to breathe, he collapsed on top of her.

Somehow, she managed to squeeze out from under him and out of bed. Where was the light switch? Groping for the lamp by the side of the bed, she knocked something off the table. Then she tried to find the switch on the wall. There was, she thought, one by the door to the en suite. It must be here somewhere. Here. As the room at last filled with bright light, she saw George on his back now raking his throat with his nails, his face red, getting redder by the second, but his lips blue.

'E. E. E...' He was trying to say something.

'E. E. E...' He could hardly get a sound out now.

And she watched, cold and detached. *Go to hell, George.*

'E. E. E...' He was getting weaker, the sound thinner. And she didn't care.

'E. E. Epi...'

Of course. His EpiPen, he was asking for it. Begging.

'Beg away.' But even as she said it she started to look. Not in his wallet on the bedside table. Not in his trousers heaped on the floor. Not in that pocket or that one or that one. How many pockets did men have, FFS?

'Where is it, George?' But the sounds gurgling from his throat didn't make sense.

Where the fuck was it? Not in the jacket he'd worn at the restaurant, now hanging on the back of the door? Not on the shelf in the en suite with his toothbrush, but perhaps in the sponge bag beside it? And then she saw it – a new one, still in its carton, still wrapped in bloody tight cellophane. Tearing open the pack with the help of her teeth, she searched for instructions. Here they were in fifty different languages in bloody tiny print. Need glasses to read. Find glasses on the floor and, finally following instructions in English, she stabbed it into his thigh.

73

VIV

Why cry now? Why sob her guts up now?

Because she'd saved the life of a shit, but couldn't save her own lovely husband? Because Shit was now in hospital getting all the help medical science could give him? Because Shit would get up and walk home. 'No,' she'd said to Marjolein's obvious disapproval, when the ambulance had arrived, 'I don't want to go to the hospital with him.' So Marjolein and her daughter went and she was left alone in the bland bedroom, remembering another hospital visit.

'How long?' she heard Jack ask bravely.

'Six months on average,' came the answer from Dr Doom swivelling round in his black leather chair to point out all the cancers in Jack's body on the computer screen behind him. Bright spots, he called them, unaware of irony. The bits that glowed were the malignancies in the lungs and the collarbone and, oh yes, the lymph system as well, in every fucking cell, it seemed.

They'd left soon afterwards saying, 'Thank you, Doctor,' their lives changed forever. Somehow they'd opened doors, walked down corridors, opened more doors, crossed roads, found the car park, found the car, paid the extortionate fee and driven home, Jack driving, looking straight ahead, gripping the steering wheel, not saying a word. Neither of them said a word.

What was he thinking? she thought when they passed the sign saying 'Road Ahead Closed' as he negotiated the new roundabout that would link to a southern bypass he wouldn't see. What was he feeling now he'd been told his own road ahead was closed? She couldn't ask because a tide of misery was rising inside her. How would she live without Jack? How would she live the rest of her life?

Inside the house, once the door was closed, her tears started to fall but, grim-faced, he gripped her by the shoulders. 'We'll fight this. We'll fight this together.'

And she said, 'Yes, of course,' but deep down she knew the game was up and just wanted to howl for the rotten, unbelievable sod-awfulness of it. How could their life together end like this? They were happy. They loved each other. 'I don't want to be a dried-up old widow,' she wailed.

'Darling, you won't be,' he said, holding her tight. Then they went to bed to get as close as they could for as long as they could.

'You can't be ill,' she said afterwards. Dying men don't make love. But they do. Cancer creeps up on you when you're not looking, that was the trouble. It hides and lies in wait and assumes disguises. It pretends it isn't there. Jack hadn't felt ill that day. He'd only gone for a scan to comply with the demands of a stupid insurance policy he'd decided he wanted. If he hadn't, they'd have lived in blissful ignorance for a bit longer.

As they climbed the stairs that afternoon he said, 'We'll most likely get a call in the morning to say it was a godawful mistake, a computer error.'

But they didn't.

Focused on 'fighting' he wouldn't consider what she should do after he'd gone, but they had discussed it years before. She'd come back from a conference, eager to tell him about a couple she'd met, a lovely old couple – well, they'd seemed old then – famous in horticultural circles. They'd told her they'd made a pact to die together if one of them became terminally ill, and they had the stuff ready to take when the time came. She'd thought it romantic and oddly practical, but Jack had given her one of his leery sideways looks. They'd been in bed drinking tea at the time. How did they know they'd got the stuff? he'd said. What exactly was it? Where had they got it from?

The Internet, she'd said and he'd looked even leerier. God, how bloody gullible could people be? He'd laughed and she'd started to see the funny side of it too, picturing the old couple giving each other a last goodnight kiss before they took the little white tablets, downing them with a glass of fizz or several, having another tender kiss, then snuggling down together for the long last sleep. Then waking up next morning.

'Sorry, darling—' Jack had wiped his eyes when he'd stopped laughing '—but if you get something I'm not going to top myself and don't you dare if I go first. Life goes on.' Jack hadn't had a problem with cliché. He'd said it again when he was near the end and couldn't deny it any longer. 'Don't waste the rest of your life. Enjoy every minute, and if you find a decent bloke to share it with, go for it. I won't know.'

Well, she had found one, too bloody like him. She howled again then, for Jack and all he was missing and for herself missing Jack, and for Patrick being completely right and completely wrong. But blow nose, wipe snot from face, throw sodden pillow onto the floor and phone a friend. Janet would be snuggled up with lover-boy, but Zelda might still be awake.

* * *

Janet

.   .   .

Janet was in bed with Alan but he was fast asleep and she was wide awake. He wasn't worried about a week on Friday when she would be interviewed again. She was. How fortunate, though, that she'd made Maggie her solicitor. Would Waldock and Co have responded so quickly or been so supportive or hard-working on her behalf?

Maggie had been very reassuring. She was sure there was no case to answer. It was very appropriate, she said, that the date would be 1 April and no, Janet shouldn't cancel lunch with Viv and Zelda. The meeting was at eleven and shouldn't take more than half an hour. But the police had gone off with the book about poisonous plants, and they'd stopped on the way out to take photographs of her front borders, with their clumps of hellebores. As she tossed and turned she couldn't help worrying. It wasn't as if there hadn't been miscarriages of justice before.

* * *

Zelda

Zelda was awake too, still downstairs in her office when the phone rang. Transfixed by the photo of a young black man emerging from the printer upside down, she let it ring for a bit. She'd been about to log off and go to bed when she'd found the photo on the sibling search website. Head on one side, the man looked thoughtful, or rueful. Sad was the word. It was his eyes. Almond-shaped. *Like hers.* Was that fanciful? It was a black and white photograph so she couldn't see their colour. He was in uniform, wearing a cap at an angle, but it didn't look like an official mugshot. He wasn't standing or sitting to attention, looking straight at camera.

The caption beneath said 'Picture of Daddy in His Uniform While Stationed in Bedfordshire England World War II'. It had been posted by Cynthia Richardsen in America, who'd been told by her father in North Carolina that he had fathered a child while he was stationed at Thurleigh, Bedfordshire during World War II. Thurleigh, why did that ring a bell? 'I am trying to trace the child of GI Samuel Eliot Richardsen of 306 Bombardment Group USAAF, based at Thurleigh Bedfordshire from 1943 to 1944. He was part of ground crew servicing B-17s known as Flying Fortresses before their bombing missions on Germany.'

Cynthia was hoping someone would recognise her father and help her find her brother or sister. Her daddy had been sent back home before the birth so he didn't know if it was a boy or girl. *Couldn't he have kept in touch by letter?* Silly. She wiped her eyes. She mustn't jump to conclusions. This was a long shot on Cynthia's part. This was most likely not *her* father. There must have been more than one child in Bedfordshire fathered by a black American GI in wartime, even if she had never come across any other mixed-heritage kids when she was growing up. But. *But*, she heard a voice in her head, Auntie Agnes's. 'Alice adored her Sambo.'

Sambo. It had been an aside, a slip on her auntie's part, which had come out of the blue when her aunt had been washing dishes at the sink on one of her visits. Zelda had assumed her aunt was being casually racist, and would have referred to any black man like that, as people did at the time, and still did, some of them, but maybe there was more to it than that? Why hadn't she asked?

She *had* asked, not then, but several times since, she'd asked both aunties if they knew her dad's name and always got the same answer. No. So she must try again. What time was it? Too late to ring them, but that was maybe as well. It would be better to take the photograph and surprise them with it, face to face, mention his name and watch their reactions. And what about Cynthia – should she ring her? Was there a number to ring? North Carolina was on the east coast so six hours behind GMT, so it was evening there and she'd be awake. Was her daddy, *Cynthia's* daddy, that was – mustn't jump to conclusions – still alive? Didn't he know the name of the woman who'd given birth to his child? Hadn't he said? So many questions.

The phone was still ringing and she picked it up with trembling hands, half expecting Cynthia. It wasn't, of course, it was Viv. And she was *crying*!

74

JANET

The Murder Squad were back.

This time they sat at the dining-room table and there was no pretence that this was a cosy chat. Detective Chief Inspector Markham and the constable sat on one side, Janet on the other, flanked by Maggie and Alan. Nervous, she was grateful for their supportive presence, especially Alan's hand just touching hers. The DCI had already been through the 'anything you say' routine, and Maggie was asking her to outline the case against her client, who, she reminded them, had been flying to New Zealand at the time of Ms Thornton's death. Ms Thornton had died on the night of Sunday 7 November or the early hours of Monday 8 November.

Barbara, they mean Barbara. Janet had to remind herself because it all seemed so unreal. As the DCI picked up Barbara's diary with a gloved hand, it was like watching a TV drama unfolding. She half expected to hear the haunting strains of *Midsomer Murders.*

'Friday 5 November. I went over the road to take tea with Janet Carmichael. She urged me to try her fruitcake, saying it was a special family recipe. I took a slice to be polite. Rather dry. I

washed it down with a cup of her odd-tasting tea, which she said was Earl Grey when I commented. I was not at ease, wondering if she would mention the note I had sent her when out of my mind with grief for my beloved Malcolm. And mention she did as soon as the niceties were over! Worse, she accused me of writing more! She produced the 'proof' typewritten notes going back twenty years, written obviously by herself. When I denied writing them she said then they must have come from another woman. Is there nothing that woman wouldn't do to hurt me? I was the love of Malcolm's life and he of mine.'

Maggie interrupted, which was as well, because Janet was dumbstruck. 'How much more of this fiction is there, Detective Chief Inspector Markham?' Barbara had lived in a world of fantasy. The DCI said there were two more entries and continued.

'Saturday 6 November. I feel very ill. Was up all night with stomach pains and diarrhoea and feel very weak. I cannot get out of bed but nor can I sleep because of violent stomach cramps. I keep remembering the odd taste of the tea at Janet Carmichael's and that dry cake. I also recall a gardening book on the coffee table, and a photograph of the Christmas rose, helleborus niger, flowering even now in her front garden. The black roots were, it seemed, used in the past to make a powder to kill rats and mice. Am I being fanciful? Is that woman not content with mental torture?

Sunday 7 November. I still feel ill and would consult the doctor if I had the strength to get downstairs to the phone...'

'Is that all?' Maggie near-laughed.

Janet wished she could, but felt sick. How Barbara must have hated her! To want her to suffer even after her own death.

DCI Markham closed the diary. 'That is all, Ms Scott, because Ms Thornton died that night.'

'From an overdose of barbiturates, if I have read the coroner's report correctly.' Maggie had done her homework. 'Sixty milligrams of phenobarbital were found in her blood, more than enough to kill her, even without the alcohol, with which she washed the tablets down. Copious amounts of alcohol were also found, but I did not see mention of any other poisons.'

'Pathology did not test for other poisons,' the chief inspector replied. 'They do not routinely test for plant-derived toxic substances.'

'They do not routinely test for barbiturates either nowadays, since their use was replaced by benzodiazepines, so why did they?'

The DCI didn't answer and Maggie continued.

'May I suggest that you found the barbiturates beside Ms Thornton's bed, an empty bottle perhaps?'

'You may suggest what you want, Ms Scott, but I can reveal that neither a bottle nor any other packaging was found by her bed.'

'Elsewhere, then? Or Barbara disposed of it beforehand as part of her pathetic plan to try and frame my client with these baseless accusations of murder. I note Monday 8 November was dustbin day in Elmsley. I suggest all the packaging was put in the bin on Sunday before Ms Thornton took the overdose. By now it will be in landfill. But there were perhaps a few dregs in the glass from which she drank, which instigated the testing for phenobarbital, Luminal perhaps?' Maggie went on to say that, had Barbara not been cremated, she would be asking for a second post-mortem to test for hellebore or any other poison to prove her client's innocence.

Janet still felt sick.

'Don't worry.' Alan squeezed her hand and murmured, 'Maggie knows her stuff. Listen.'

Now Maggie was saying that if DCI Markham persisted with

this line of enquiry she would ask for the release of Ms Thornton's medical records. They, she suspected, would prove that at some time in the past Ms Thornton had been prescribed phenobarbital, for depression perhaps, or insomnia. 'Which she may well have hung onto as she was a bit of a hoarder, by all accounts. It keeps its potency for up to forty years.'

Well done, Maggie! Janet felt slightly better as Alan stood up and looked at his watch. 'Mrs Carmichael has a lunch appointment at one, to which I am taking her, so if there's nothing else, Chief Inspector?'

'Sit down, Mr Loveday. Ms Thornton's suspicions cannot be so easily dismissed.' She held up the book they'd taken away in a plastic bag a week before. *Death in the Garden* by Vivien Halliday. Signed by the author, a friend of yours, I believe.'

75

VIV

Where were the other two?

Viv parked behind The Ship and checked the time again. They'd both texted to say they were coming but they were already ten minutes late. Was that meeting with the police still going on? Poor Janet! How sodding awful to be accused of murder, even if the accuser was a bitter and twisted fantasist. It put having to sell your house into perspective.

'Not the end of the world.' Say it enough and she might convince herself. 'Downsizing is sensible.' *So smile to release serotonin, go on, smile.*

She stuffed the letters received this morning into her bag. No from the building society manager to her request for mortgage extension. No from the bank manager to her request for a loan. But not even a no from Patrick, to whom she'd written a proper letter to say again that the girls would like to meet him.

Now it was quarter past. How much time did Maggie need to prove that Janet wasn't a criminal, FFS? Luckily, Janet had other things to celebrate. So did Zelda. She scrolled down through her texts.

Can hardly wait to tell you about recent developments! I am going places! Zelda x

What was that about? And then there was Janet's, sent from Brighton yesterday, where Alan had taken her for a few days to try and keep her mind off the stupid forthcoming police investigation.

Making exciting purchases! Lots to celebrate! Have ordered champagne!

A wedding ring? A wedding outfit? She'd said he'd proposed so marriage was surely on the cards. They were both churchgoers after all and were as good as married already. Alan was at Janet's night and day. Viv checked the car park again in case she'd missed an arrival. No, so plenty of time to go over her gains and losses. Losses. Unless she took Zelda's advice and put a positive take on the Leiden debacle. 'Stop, Viv!' she'd yelled down the phone. 'Stop blaming yourself right now! None of it is your fault. It's all his! And then you saved the guilty sod's life, for which you deserve a halo. Saved by satay, that's your story!'

Her phone pinged. The other Muscateers, surely? But no, it was the sod himself.

Dear Viv, Sorry for coming on a bit strong in Leiden.

A master of understatement!

Not sure what came over me.

Oh no?

Safely home now thanks to your prompt use of the EpiPen. Hope no hard feelings?

Bloody hell! How crass could one man's choice of words be? Delete. But doubts still nagged. Should she have gone to the police? Was he a danger to other women? Liz, Gerry and Myrtle thought so when she told them what had happened. But keen to get home, she'd turned down their offer to go to the police with her. 'I'm okay,' she'd assured them, 'no harm done.'

Here was Janet's Fiat at last, but Alan too, in the driving seat. He wasn't staying, was he? *Be generous.* She reminded herself that Janet had recently had a major operation and a horrible confrontation with the police. Alan was rightly in protective mode.

'No worries, Viv.' He spotted her coming towards them, when he'd helped Janet out of the passenger seat, followed by Maggie getting out of the back. 'No need to do your repel invaders act. Maggie and I are just coming in for a celebratory drink, then we'll leave you to your machinations.' Machinations?

Janet said, 'Don't be silly, Alan.' Then Zelda arrived in her red Audi.

* * *

The bubbly was waiting on their table near the window. The waiter hovered till Janet told him to open it immediately, and they toasted Maggie, who had by all accounts been brilliant. Janet said, 'I can't thank my lovely neighbour enough. She sent the police packing.'

'With their tails between their legs,' said Alan. 'If you ever need a solicitor we highly recommend Maggie's brilliance. And you might, Viv, as DCI Markham regards your *Death in the Garden* book as an incitement to murder.'

'What?'

'Joke,' Maggie said quickly, 'but she did try it on, implying you and Janet were working together. She was way out of order. Not a shred of evidence.'

Alan apologised for teasing. 'Don't worry, Viv, we're pretty sure Maggie convinced the chief inspector that Barbara took her own life after trying to frame Janet. Maggie pointed out that when Barbara's body was found by the police on Tuesday, they also found one of those automatic pet feeders outside the back door, with enough dog food for five meals. Proof surely that she'd planned her own death.'

'At least she thought about her dog's welfare.' Zelda looked close to tears.

Janet nodded. 'Maggie found the poor animal wandering in the close. That's what told her something was wrong. When she rang the bell and got no answer she contacted the police, who broke in and found the body.'

'Poor sick Barbara.' Viv's better-self vied with her worse. 'How unhappy she must have been to have taken her own life.'

'Vindictive to her last gasp.' Alan looked unforgiving but Janet touched his arm.

'Shouldn't we thank her for a lesson on how not to live?' Tentatively she raised her glass and looked from one to the other. 'To Barbara? May she rest in peace?'

They all raised their glasses, and Viv felt a surge of positivity as she took a gulp.

'To living life to the full!'

She must, she really must.

* * *

Shortly afterwards Alan and Maggie left the ladies to their lunch.

'Right, the weigh-in,' Janet said when they'd refilled their glasses. 'Who's going first?'

'You or you'll burst,' said Zelda.

'You look close to bursting yourself.' Janet shook her head.

'I'll burst if you don't tell us about that lovely ring.' Zelda pointed.

'Stylish, isn't it?' Janet held out her left hand. 'Lapis lazuli and pearls in a gold setting and yes, it is an engagement ring.'

'So when's the wedding?' Zelda, maybe not 100 per cent attentive, was leafing through some papers on her knee.

'Purchase Number Two first.' Janet delved into her bag. 'Ta da!' She held up a glossy estate agent's brochure, the sort you got for a very expensive property.

'A hotel? You've bought a hotel?' Zelda's mouth fell open.

Janet laughed. 'No, a flat. Ours is the tiny one in the left-hand corner.'

Ours.

Janet pointed to the top of the building, obviously thrilled. 'We have a sea view.'

We.

'Where is this?' Zelda was fortunately asking the questions.

'Brighton.'

Brighton! Janet was moving away.

'Looks like Viv's house but bigger!' Zelda sounded enthusiastic.

'*Neo* art deco.' Janet opened the brochure so they could see a double-page spread showing more photos. 'Or streamline moderne.' The building had the same flat roof and curved corners as her own but was much, much bigger. 'It's not as old as Viv's, not old at all in fact, so all the fittings are modern. We won't have such high maintenance costs as you, Viv. Hopefully, the roof won't fall in. Look, this is our sitting room with a balcony overlooking the sea. You'll love it.'

I hate it. And I hate myself for being so selfish.

But Zelda sounded keen enough for both of them. 'When's moving day, Janet?'

'That's up to Alan...' Janet flicked a fly off the brochure. 'But he's consulting me.'

How bloody magnanimous!

'Viv...' Janet tapped her hand. 'Sorry, but I saw your face. You weren't listening. You were making assumptions. I just said I wasn't moving.'

When? When did she say that? Viv appealed to Zelda, who looked amused. 'Janet's right. You weren't listening.'

Janet didn't say 'read my lips'. Of course not, but she did say that she'd say what she had to 'only once' in an atrocious approximation to a French accent. Yes, she and Alan were going to get married, but no, she wasn't moving in with him, well, not permanently. They had come to a very civilised arrangement. She was going to keep her house in Elmsley, but would sometimes stay with Alan in the Brighton flat. He was going to live in the Brighton flat and sometimes stay with her in Elmsley. Sometimes they would live together and sometimes they would live apart. 'To keep lust alive.'

It sounded perfect. If only... Viv suppressed a sigh.

But Janet was off again. 'All permutations are possible, including —' she produced a bunch of keys from her bag '—we three staying in the flat together sometimes, or one of us, or two of us, which may or may not include Significant Others. These—' she jingled the keys in front of Viv's still open mouth '—are going to add a new dimension to all our lives.' She turned to Zelda. 'Your turn now. Tell us everything. Viv, close your mouth.'

Zelda put a sheaf of paper on the table. 'New adventures for me too, with a bit of help from my friends, so please peruse. Only one copy of each, sorry, so you'll have to share.' She got to her feet. 'Shall I go to the bar and order today's special for us all while you're reading? It's a just-in-case, by the way. Nothing definite yet.' They nodded a united yes, absorbed by what was in front of them. Viv recognised an ESTA. Electronic System for Travel Authorization. The application form for a visa to enter the USA was top of the pile.

'Do you know what this is about?' Viv asked Janet.

'Her father?' Janet wasn't sure.

'She's found him?'

'Ask. Here she is.'

Zelda showed them a photograph of a young good-looking black man, whose eyes, in Viv's opinion, looked just like Zelda's. Kind, and surely the same lustrous, melting brown as hers? Her voice trembled with emotion. 'We – we're waiting for the results of DNA tests, but I want to be ready to go if this turns out to be my dad.'

Viv felt herself welling up. This was *huge* for Zelda.

'We?' Janet was brisk, hiding emotion, Viv now knew. 'You said *we're* waiting for results? Are you in touch with him?'

'With his daughter, Cynthia.' Zelda gripped the photograph. 'She's looking for a sibling or siblings in the UK.'

'And does this Cynthia know the name of the woman her dad made pregnant?'

'Lissy, he said Lissy. That's the only name he remembers.'

'What was your mum's name?' Viv found her voice at last.

'Alice. Alice Mayhew.'

'Alice. Lissy. They're not miles apart.' Viv felt even more hopeful. 'Did this chap – have you got a name for him? – mention your mother's surname?'

Zelda shook her head. 'His name is Samuel Eliot Richardsen and, according to Cynthia, he can't remember my mum's full name. He's eighty-nine now, and...' she looked sad '... when I showed the photo to my aunties, mum's older sisters, they had different reactions. Auntie Doreen, the eldest, hardly looked, just shook her head. I went to see them separately, by the way, as Auntie Doreen has a bit of a big-sister hold over Agnes. Agnes gasped. I'm sure she gasped. I think she recognised him but wouldn't commit. I think they were forbidden to say by my mum and her mum and secrecy has become ingrained, like the Bletchley Park workers.'

'How long before you get the results of the DNA test?' Janet was still probing.

'Weeks, possibly months. Cynthia and I both sent samples of our spit to a company called AncestryDNA earlier this week. The results of that will tell us if we're related.'

'Isn't there a quicker way?' Viv felt sure there was. 'CSI manage it in days.'

'Not without spending a fortune and no, before you offer, Janet, I am prepared to wait, but I am – what's the phrase? – cautiously optimistic.'

'What if I'm not prepared to wait?' Janet had that nothing-will-stop-me look. 'I can't bear the suspense.'

Viv topped up their glasses. 'Zelda, your dad is a very old man. There's no time to waste. All for one? Let Janet help.'

Zelda said she'd think about accepting a loan, but the ESTA wasn't the only application form she wanted help with. There was another underneath it.

'For the OU!' Janet found it. 'You're applying for the Open University, as I've been urging you to do for ages. Great! What are you going to read?'

'History, or maybe Arts and Humanities/History, which includes literature and the arts. It's something I'd like to discuss.'

They clinked glasses again as Viv thought how wonderful it was that dear Zelda *was* going places, in every sense, embracing singledom as she herself was doing. But where was the food? Viv looked around for the waiter, her tummy rumbling.

'Viv, did you lock your car?' Zelda suddenly changed the subject.

'I think so. I do it automatically.' Where was the bloody waiter?

'I don't think you did today though.' Zelda looked at Janet. 'Didn't she jump out of her car as soon as she saw you arrive?'

'Bounded,' said Janet. 'You both did as soon as you saw me with Alan – I noted – to make sure we hadn't become fused at the hip. I do think you ought to check your car, Viv. Don't you keep equipment in the back?'

Doubt set in. She wouldn't like to lose her mower. 'Okay, I'll go and check. I need a pee anyway, and I'll hassle the waiter for our food while I'm at it.'

What a turnaround! Things were on the up for those two, and when she got back to the table she would try to put a positive gloss on the changes in her own life. So, she was about to lose her lovely house. So, she'd lost a man who didn't want anything to do with her unless he could have things all his own way and be her lover, which wasn't possible now. So, she missed him like hell. But she'd survived worse. Much worse. As she washed her hands she remembered the day she'd seen Zelda in The Red Lion with History Man and feared their friendship was at an end. How wrong she'd been! The three of them were closer now than they had ever been, and life was really looking up, well, for two of them.

Back in the dining room, after checking the car – it was locked – she couldn't see either of her friends. Was she in the wrong room? Was she having a senior moment? No, that was definitely their table by the middle window and that was their empty bottle, and those their empty glasses. But they weren't there. Had they both nipped out to the loo? Surely she'd have crossed paths with them if they had, or seen them in there? She checked again. Had she come back by a different door? They didn't come to The Ship very often. No, there was only the one door to and from the loos and, only a few minutes ago, no more than five, she'd left them sitting at the table by the middle window overlooking the car park. But what was that leaving the car park? A red Audi? Zelda's? It was April Fool's Day, she remembered, but – she checked her watch – it was nearly half past one, so if this was a joke it was on them.

'Viv? Ms Halliday?' The waiter was by her side. 'The ladies asked me to give you this.' He handed her a card.

Dear Viv,

In the interests of keeping a roof over your head, we have arranged a meeting with a prospective business partner. After making preliminary enquiries we have reason to believe the outcome could be beneficial.

All for one!

Janet and Zelda

What meeting? What prospective business partner? What the hell was going on? She turned to the waiter, crossly. 'Where's our lunch? What about our orders?'

'There weren't any orders, madam.'

'But my friend came to the bar to order.' Damn. Someone had taken their table already. Oh. Fuck. Her mouth went dry. Her heart went boom and stopped.

'The ladies said they'd reserved the table for you and the gentleman, madam.'

The gentle man, the kind, stubborn, loyal, exciting, reliable, steadfast man.

Walk away. You know it's wrong.

She could. He hadn't seen her yet.

'Trust you to turn up.'

To stop you making a fool of yourself.

'And live a half-life?'

Now he had seen her. He was getting to his feet, a smile lighting his face, and as their eyes met a smile came to hers, a smile so big and wide she thought her face might break in two.

What will people say?

I don't care.

What will your daughters think?

They'll cope.

A woman of your age!

'Makes up her own mind.' She flicked the vicious killjoy off her shoulder 'Sorry, I was thinking aloud,' she said to the bewildered waiter. 'Please. Go. Leave me – us – for a while.'

For Patrick was walking towards her, and she wasn't sure what was going to happen next. She didn't know what she was going to say or do. Rooted to the spot, her stomach swirling, her pulses racing.

'I was wrong.' He took her hands in his. 'I'll be your friend, colleague, anything you want. You choose. I'll meet your family, *anything*... as long as I'm part of your life.'

She shook her head. 'I was wrong. I lost my way but now I've found it again.'

Frost doesn't always kill the blossom. Snow rarely breaks the branch it's weighing down. Some plants lie deep underground for years before something spurs them to seek the light and push up a few brave green shoots. Brave green shoots? As Patrick's arms folded round her and their lips touched, she had the crazy notion that shoots and leaves and the long, strong stalk of a golden sunflower the size of a cymbal were bursting through the top of her head, clanging!

ACKNOWLEDGMENTS

When I was a girl I liked entering competitions, partly to earn extra pocket money. Writing was my 'thing' even then and I often sent in poems and stories, and I had to get an adult to sign a declaration: This is all the participant's own work. I felt a bit guilty even in those days, knowing an encouraging teacher had occasionally suggested a different word, which made the final work better. I feel the same today. *THE WIDOWS' WINE CLUB* is and isn't 'all my own work'. I accept responsibility for it. I have written every word and drawn on my own experience, but also that of many others.

I'm hugely grateful to all the widows who have shared their stories with me – in no particular order, Jan Dye, Sue Pitcher, Lynne Clayton, Sally Tennant, Sue Draper, Kate Redmond, Margaret Nash and others who don't want to be named. This story has been a long time in the telling, and many people read early drafts. I'm grateful to Riseley Reading Group, especially Alison Blanchard, Sue Draycott, Jan Ferdinando, Liz Wilson and Rachel Old for their valuable feedback and encouragement. I'd also like to thank D Bailey, Fenella Lowden, Liz Wickins, Andrea Corby, Val Cumine, Sue Bell and 'Jam', Pedr James, for their insights and helpful suggestions. I wouldn't have finished my novel without the support of my faithful 'writing buddies' – Linda Newbery, who said 'Go for it' as soon as I mentioned my idea, also Cindy Jefferies, Celia Rees, Adèle Geras, Yvonne Coppard, Penny Dolan, and a new talent on the writing scene, Georgia Bowers, who came up with the title, *THE WIDOWS' WINE CLUB*.

Some of you have helped and I don't know your names. Sorry! I talk to people on trains. Please forgive me. I am thankful to Sue Pettit and Roy who shared books about the Liverpool sixties scene; to Anne Clarke for info about New Zealand; to Kath Scott and Bob and Brenda Swindells who gave me hospitality and provided locations; to Nigel and Andrew Gell who helped with local World War II history; to Michael Brown who really wrote the book, *Death in the Garden*; to Lucy Bland who wrote the book *Britain's 'Brown' Babies* and Tom Ianiri of Power Computers, Kempston, who has saved my widows from extinction on several occasions.

Closer to home, there's family, Sam, Mary and Josie, always supportive, and lifelong friends Sue and George Davies, helpful on so many fronts they are impossible to categorise. And my agent, Caroline Walsh, for getting behind my widows when I switched genres and for finding me the perfect publisher. I am so grateful to my editor, Sarah Ritherdon, and the amazing team at Boldwood for bringing *THE WIDOWS' WINE CLUB* to you. Enjoy!

MORE FROM JULIA JARMAN

We hope you enjoyed reading *The Widows' Wine Club*. If you did, please leave a review.

If you'd like to gift a copy, this book is also available as an ebook, hardback, large print, digital audio download and audiobook CD.

Sign up to Julia Jarman's mailing list for news, competitions and updates on future books:

https://bit.ly/JuliaJarmanNews

ABOUT THE AUTHOR

Julia Jarman has written over a hundred books for children, and is now turning her hand to uplifting, golden years women's fiction. Julia draws on her own experience of bereavement, female friendship and late-life dating.

Visit Julia's website: https://juliajarman.com/

Follow Julia on social media:

 facebook.com/juliajarman
twitter.com/JuliaJarman

Boldwood

Boldwood Books is an award-winning fiction publishing company seeking out the best stories from around the world.

Find out more at www.boldwoodbooks.com

Join our reader community for brilliant books, competitions and offers!

Follow us
@BoldwoodBooks
@BookandTonic

Sign up to our weekly deals newsletter

https://bit.ly/BoldwoodBNewsletter